THE ROGUE AND HIS FLOWER

PRINCETOWN HEIRS
BOOK 2

BEA PAIGE

THE ROGUE AND HIS FLOWER

BEA PAIGE

The Rogue and His Flower
Bea Paige
Copyright © 2024 Kelly Stock writing as Bea Paige
www.beapaige.co.uk
Cover Design: Everly Yours Cover Design
Cover Photography: Wander Aguiar
Cover Model: Diogo
Chapter page / title page artwork: Samaiya Art

NOTE TO READERS

This book is a work of fiction, but with everything that I write, I delve into difficult topics.

This book contains discussions of past childhood abuse, flashbacks of childhood abuse (both physical and emotional), and miscarriage (on page).

Please be mindful when reading.

BOOK PLAYLIST

As you all know I love a book playlist! I write to music always, and scenes are often inspired by the songs that I choose. A lot of thought goes into each song choice. All of the songs that inspired this story or specific scenes in this story can be found on my spotify playlist - The Rogue and His Flower.

"Love is the flower you've got to let grow."
John Lennon.

GUNN
Daisy and Dalton

PROLOGUE

The aftermath of last night's events weighs heavily on the four of us as we sit in the lavish bar of my father's five-star hotel. My friends, Sterling, Drix, and Benedict all wear troubled expressions, mirroring my own inner turmoil.

Dropping my gaze to the empty glass in my hand, the weight of my situation presses down on me more heavily than the whiskey I just swallowed. Empty glasses stand as evidence of our desperate need to numb ourselves, to escape from the tangled mess our lives have become.

We attempted to drown out our problems with alcohol, but it only brought them to the surface, each of us spilling our secrets, and none of us lighter for it.

Drix, my best friend, glances at me with a mix of pity, frustration and barely veiled anger, our friendship at risk from a decision neither of us are happy about.

"What a fucking night." Sterling's voice cuts through the quiet as he catches my gaze and swipes a hand through his glossy brown hair.

Drix shifts his attention to Ben, who is lost in his own unsettling thoughts. "I'm assuming you've had just as little sleep as the rest of us," he remarks knowingly.

Ben's silence speaks volumes as he looks up at Drix, his startling green eyes filled with turmoil.

"Yeah, that would be none then," Sterling says with a sharp exhale, his voice filled with bitterness and regret.

This morning feels like a cruel joke. We were supposed to be celebrating new beginnings after his father's extravagant wedding, but instead we've each been left with the repercussions of four women who have tangled our lives up in ways we never saw coming.

To make matters infinitely worse, lurking beyond the luxurious confines of this hotel, lies a world of outrageous headlines. The tabloids would have an absolute field day if they ever found out how the heirs of the four founding families of this town were embroiled in a web of forbidden love and deception.

On the outside, it may seem like we have everything we could ever want, but behind our polished exteriors lies a tangled web of scandal and vulnerability that threatens to undo us all.

Four sons. Four friends. Four men weighed down by our father's expectations, carrying secrets that could shatter the carefully crafted images we've maintained for years as the Princetown Heirs.

There's Sterling, an extraordinary but troubled artist who is expected to carry on the Blade family legacy, disregarding his own dreams.

Benedict, a man with genius level IQ who is set to inherit the Pike family's wealth that can buy a lot of things, but not a future with the woman he loves.

Drix Hammer, who carries the burden of a past mistake, and has been forced into a role he never wanted, sacrificing his own happiness in the process.

And then there's me, Dalton Gunn, born into a life of privilege and trained to excel in high society, who's about to enter an arranged marriage with my best friend's younger sister, to clear his debt so he can be with the woman he loves.

But where does that leave me?

Am I really willing to go through with this sham of a wedding to appease my father and secure my inheritance? Can I bring myself to marry the sweetest, most frustrating person I know, knowing I will hurt her deeply and ruin my friendship with my best friend of almost twenty years?

The truth is yes, yes I will. I am my father's son unfortunately, and love is a luxury I simply cannot afford...

CHAPTER ONE

A few days later

STARING at the thirty page contract before me, my trembling fingers grip the Montblanc fountain pen as Carl Gunn eyes me from the opposite side of his walnut desk. His silver hair is perfectly styled, his expensive suit tailored to fit his lean physique. He's an austere man, who has no qualms marrying off his son, Dalton, in an arranged marriage for the sole purpose of ensuring the continuation of the Gunn family fortune and, more importantly, their family line.

A small part of me regrets not choosing a more intimidating outfit instead of my bright blue dungarees and long-sleeved top with tiny silver stars stitched onto the fabric, but I wanted to be comfortable given I've just started my blasted period. Nothing like a heavy flow to brighten up an already shitty day. Besides, I doubt my quirky fashion choices have any impact on whether or not I am suitable for his son, who also happens to be my older brother's best friend and someone I have disliked since our first encounter as children.

Despite my late father and Carl being friends, he still managed to manipulate me into signing this contract. I had my own reasons for agreeing to this arranged marriage, of course, but deep down, we all know that Carl could have forgiven my brother's debt—a mere eight point five million pounds is nothing to a billionaire like him.

"Is there an issue, Daisy?" Carl asks, his silver brow raised expectantly as I glance up from the contract to meet his waiting gaze.

"No issues, everything looks to be in order," I reply, flicking my gaze to Dalton, who stands with his back to us both, staring out at the snow-covered manicured gardens of their magnificent High-wood Manor estate.

Truth be known, I've barely taken in a word. All I care about is releasing my brother from his debt so that he's free to be with the woman he loves, and no longer forced to act as an enforcer to the families that run this town. After everything Drix has done for me, it's the least I could do, and whilst I have my own complicated reasons for signing this contract, I'm willing to marry a man I hate so my brother's future happiness is secured.

"Good, then if you wouldn't mind," he replies, checking his gold Rolex watch for the time. "Dalton and I have business to discuss."

"I'm sure you do," I reply snarkily.

Dalton stiffens, but still remains facing away from me. The winter sunlight streams through the window and illuminates his auburn hair in rich red and mahogany hues, contrasting sharply with his deep navy suit. For once he doesn't have a sarcastic retort ready, which is probably for the best since I'm really not in the mood.

"You'd better get used to the intricate workings of this family, because as soon as you sign this contract, you will need to act accordingly," Carl threatens, his voice dripping with authority.

I bite the inside of my cheek, tasting blood as I try to suppress the resentment bubbling inside of me, and remind myself why I'm doing this. Right now, playing along is the only way to secure Drix's freedom, but if Carl thinks for one second I will kowtow to his expectations, he has another thing coming. I've agreed to marry his son and provide him with an heir, I have not agreed to a personality transplant.

"Of course," I reply just as tersely, pressing the tip of the fountain pen against the paper, knowing full well that as soon as I sign this contract there's no going back. I will become Dalton's fiancé from the moment the ink hits the paper, and in a little over six weeks we will be married.

"There," I say, placing the fountain pen back onto the table, and pushing the contract towards Carl.

He nods, a small smile pulling up his lip as he motions for Dalton's attention.

"Son, now you."

Turning on his feet, Dalton strides to my side, completely ignoring me and focussing solely on the contract where my signature has barely dried. Leaning over, he reaches for the pen, his arm brushing against mine as he signs with a quick flourish.

"It's done," he grinds out, straightening up.

"Excellent!" Carl grins, turning his attention back to me. "You will move in with us in a week's time. I'm assuming that's enough time to move your personal belongings over and to say your goodbyes?"

I gasp. "A week?"

"It's in the contract," he reminds me. "I will be hosting a party officially announcing your engagement a week after your arrival. Of course, I will be delighted to extend an invitation to your brother, his lady friend and her son, assuming she decides to stay, of course. I'm sure it can't be easy learning how he got caught up in such a debt in the first place."

"Drix, Lia and Toby *will* be there," I snap back, wishing I could wipe the smirk off his face.

"Of course they will."

"They can be happy now. No thanks to you," I add.

Carl laughs. "I think you'll find it's *all* thanks to me. This arrangement benefits everyone, no? Drix is now free of his debt. Dalton will inherit his riches. I get to ensure the Gunn lineage thrives, and you, my dear, get to live a very luxurious lifestyle whilst you remain married to my son."

"I'm not bothered about a *luxurious lifestyle*," I throw back. "I will continue to work at the hotel and earn my own money. I might have to live here, but I won't be some lady who lives off her husband's wealth."

"Her *father-in-law's* wealth, you mean," Carl corrects me. "*Dalton* will continue to manage the hotel until you produce an heir, and I think you'll find that you *will* indeed become a lady of leisure as soon as you're married. Page 21, point seven, says as much," he counters with a smirk. "Can't have my daughter-in-law slumming it as some lowly receptionist, now can I? Even if it is a receptionist at *my* hotel."

The blood drains from my face as I stare at him, my mouth opening and closing like a fish out of water. "But–"

"No buts. You signed the contract. You've agreed to the terms."

"Why didn't you say something?" I throw at Dalton, shaking my head in disbelief. Why the hell didn't I read the contract properly? I'm an idiot.

"It's all there in black and white," Dalton replies coolly.

"You *pig*," I accuse.

"Most women would jump at the chance to be taken care of in such a way. Count yourself lucky," Carl snaps, and with that, he gathers up the contract and slides it into the drawer of his desk, locking it away. "I'm assuming you drove here today?" he asks with a dismissive flick of his hand towards the door.

I move to stand, more than ready to leave, but Dalton rests his hand on my shoulder, preventing me from getting up. "I'd like a word with Daisy before she leaves," he says, his own tone uncompromising as I jerk away from the warmth of his touch.

"Then take your fiancé to look around. I have things to do," Carl says, opening up his laptop and ignoring the both of us.

Fiancé.

The word echoes in my mind as the reality of our impending marriage sinks in. I'm torn between wanting to run away, and facing the harsh reality of my new life.

"Daisy?" Dalton questions.

I push upright, ignoring his offered hand, and stride past him with a feigned air of confidence.

As we step out of the office, the heavy door shuts behind us with a resounding thud, the hallway stretching before us. Like the rest of Highwood Manor, this wing has been extravagantly decorated with expensive artwork and sparkling chandeliers, the only signs of life are our footsteps echoing off the marble floor, which has been polished to a flawless shine. This is not a place of warmth or comfort; it is simply a demonstration of wealth, every detail meticulously chosen to flaunt the Gunn's status and distinguish between those who have and those who do not.

Thanks to Hubert, who adopted me at the same time as Drix, I have lived a comfortable life. Our family home is well-lived in, and filled with love, unlike this place which lacks such warmth.

Picking up my pace in my haste to get the hell out of here, I ignore Dalton's penetrating gaze as he analyses my every move, matching me stride for stride. His scrutiny is unnerving, as though I'm under a microscope waiting to be dissected.

"What?" I bite out, throwing him a glare.

"I suppose congratulations are in order?" he replies with a heavy dose of sarcasm.

"Excuse me if I don't jump up and down for joy. This isn't exactly how I envisioned my happily ever after," I reply, the bitter taste of irony filling my mouth as my steps falter.

I've spent my whole life imagining what it would feel like to fall head over heels in love, to make a family of my own after I was so thoroughly mistreated by my birth parents, and yet here I am about to walk into a loveless marriage. At least I'll get a baby out of this, someone of my own who I can cherish and shower with love, something which was sorely missing in my early childhood.

"You agreed to this," he reminds me, pulling up sharp.

"I agreed to be your wife, to bear your child. I did *not* agree to give up my freedom."

"Your signature on that contract says otherwise," he points out.

Drawing in a steadying breath, I nod, turning to face him. "Fine. At least Drix is now free from his debt and can love the woman he deserves, and I get to be a mum. It's the only thing I've ever truly wanted anyway."

"So when do you plan on using me as a sperm bank to make a baby?" he asks, anger blazing across his face.

"As soon as possible after the wedding," I retort, ignoring his self-pity. "If I'm lucky I will fall pregnant quickly, then I'll only have to wait a year after the baby is born to be free of you."

He shakes his head, swiping a hand through his hair. "Fucking perfect," he mutters.

A sharp stab of guilt penetrates my heart, alongside the dull ache I always get when I'm on my period, but I ignore both. "This is an *arranged* marriage, Dalton, not a chance for you to indulge your sex addiction. You will *never* get to fuck me. Jerk off into a damn jar and hand over your sperm, I'll deal with the rest."

He flinches, then his expression hardens. "Are you forgetting we have to make this look believable? Otherwise the contract is null and void."

"In public I will play the role of your devoted fiancé and wife, but behind closed doors we will be what we've always been to each other."

"And what's that?" he prompts.

"No more than two people connected by the person we both care about. You're not my friend, Dalton, and you're certainly *not* going to be my lover."

A slow smile creeps up his face as he reaches for my strawberry blonde hair, tugging on the strands. "Yes, but you *will* be my wife, and I'll be damned if I let anyone suspect otherwise."

I laugh in his face. "We both know you won't be able to live without sex. I imagine you'll be relieving yourself as regularly as you do right now with the women you like to string along. Don't worry though, I'll play the obedient wife, and turn a blind eye so you can deal with your *urges*. Perhaps I'll find someone too," I add, just to rub it in.

"See, here's the thing, Daisy," he says as he pushes the boundaries between us and steps closer, his body dangerously close to mine. "If you'd read the contract fully, instead of staring at it blindly, you'd notice that marital affairs are off the menu, for the *both* of us. Can't have you implanted with another man's seed, now can we?"

"Your father is such an arsehole," I snap back.

He shrugs. "Get used to it."

"Back off," I growl. I don't like the way the heat from his body penetrates mine, or the gleam of challenge in his eyes. "I'm not a game to be won, Dalton. There will be nothing between us, not today, not tomorrow, not ever. So good luck with that."

"You really don't know me very well at all, do you, Daisy?"

"What's that supposed to mean?"

"I have a one hundred percent success rate when it comes to women."

"You're one arrogant bastard, do you know that?" I hiss, taking another step away from him, my back hitting the wall.

"Maybe," he replies.

The leisurely smile that pulls up his lips has my stomach coiling in anger as he leans his forearm against the wall, trapping my body against his. I'm vaguely aware of a member of staff moving at the end of the hallway, and I stiffen.

"I guess the show starts now," he replies, aware that we're being watched as he drops his head closer to mine.

"I'm assuming your arsehole father made them sign non-disclosure agreements?" I hiss, flicking my eyes to their maid who is dusting an ornament, trying and failing not to notice our interaction. "So this doesn't count."

He smirks. "The hell it doesn't, *fiancé.*"

"You wouldn't dare!" I warn, my breath hitching, as his mouth hovers over mine.

"Oh, I dare," he replies before smashing his lips against mine in a rough kiss.

For a second I'm so shocked that all I can do is let him kiss me. His lips are warm, his kiss urgent, desperate almost. I gasp, and he takes the opportunity to lick his tongue inside my mouth as his free hand reaches up, curling his fingers into my hair and tugging me closer. His scent wafts between us, a familiar cologne of warm cedarwood mixed with heady notes of musk and spice.

His groan surprises me given I can feel his anger in this kiss. His anger at me for agreeing to this charade, at his father for forcing us both into this position, and at my brother for getting himself stuck with this debt in the first place, even if it was out of love for me. There's a part of me, the tiniest, most miniscule part that feels sympathy for him. Then I'm reminded why *he* agreed, and that sympathy dissolves. Dalton is selfish, he wants to maintain his lifestyle. Marrying me and producing an heir is the only way he's going to ensure that happens.

My cheeks flood with heat, anger coursing through me as I push against his chest, not caring who sees. "And *I* know how to handle men like you," I seethe, kneeing him in the balls.

"Fuck!" he yells, doubling over with a groan, his hands flying to his groin as he cups himself.

Spinning on my heel, I stride along the hallway, ignoring his call for me to wait, to stop. As soon as I reach my car, I yank open the door, slamming it shut behind me just as he comes running outside.

"Daisy, just wait a damn minute!" he yells, and despite the look of agony on his face, that speaks of something deeper than a bruised dick, I don't wait.

Instead, I give him the middle finger as I drive away, hating that my first encounter with my husband-to-be was filled with so much anger and loathing. But, really, what did I expect? This is Dalton we're talking about. He's incapable of thinking about anyone other than himself. Gritting my teeth, I resign myself to the fact that this is going to be my life for the foreseeable future.

CHAPTER TWO

Pacing up and down in my bedroom suite, I rip off my suit jacket and throw it on my bed, then loosen the tie around my neck, yanking it free. Dragging in a deep breath, I try and fail to calm my racing pulse, but no matter how many times I force air into my lungs, I still feel like I'm fucking drowning.

Yesterday, Daisy and I signed our marriage contract, and like it or not, we're bound to each other. Afterwards, she'd angered me with her taunts about having an affair during our marriage and I did something I shouldn't have and kissed her, breaking my promise to Drix despite the lie I told him today. He's been staying in the flat above his gym ever since Lia found out the truth about his role for the families, giving her space. He's always been a good man, thoughtful, and in that moment faced with his anger, I said I'd do my best by Daisy, that I would find it in myself to at least try and make her happy.

But that's all just fucking words, *bravado*.

Truth be known, I don't even like myself very much, so how the fuck can I expect Daisy to like me, let alone tolerate me? Not to mention the fact she's infuriating. Always has been. How the hell am I supposed to live with her snide digs when I can't throw her over my lap and pinken her arse like I've done to multiple women I've fucked over the years? Don't get me wrong, they've always enjoyed such attention, knowing that with pain comes pleasure, but that is off the table for me and Daisy.

I can't even sleep with anyone else for the entirety of our relationship to get some fucking relief. The only silver lining is that neither can Daisy, because I'll be fucked if she thinks she can get her rocks off with some random arsehole whilst married to me. I let Daisy believe that particular stipulation in the contract was my father's idea, but in truth, it was mine. She may never truly belong to me, but I'll be damned if she'll belong to anyone else. If I have to suffer, then so can she. It's only fair.

Goddamn her. How could I let this happen? How could I agree to this fucking sham?

Because you're a selfish bastard, that's why, a voice inside my head taunts me.

"Motherfucker," I yell, striding towards my ensuite, needing a moment to wash away the guilt I feel.

It's not a feeling I'm used to. I'm Dalton Gunn, for fuck's sake. I take what I want, when I want it. I'm rich, and enjoy every damn minute of the lifestyle being wealthy provides me. I fuck for pleasure, and I sure as hell don't do feelings, least of all guilt, and yet here I am *feeling* exactly that. Guilt at signing the contract. Guilt at lying to my best friend. Guilt at kissing Daisy.

If her taunts had riled me up in that moment, then the hurt in her eyes as she pushed me away soon put it out. I'd overstepped. I was wrong. I deserved a knee to the bollocks.

Resting my hands against the sink, I look at my reflection. Dark circles ring my eyes, and my usually put together appearance is more than a little ruffled. Ordinarily, when I need to relieve the stress, I would grab my phone and call one of the many women ready and willing to spend the night. Whoever was lucky enough to be chosen would enjoy the best sex of their life, and a night filled with multiple orgasms, because whilst I might be selfish in all other aspects of my life, I'm not in the bedroom.

I get off on other people's pleasure, love it when the women I'm fucking trust me to take care of their needs. It excites me when I figure out what turns them on. It's like finding the key to Pandora's box. Some women like dirty talk, some prefer praise. Others like to be bound, degraded, whipped, tied up. More often than not, most women just want to be adored, to feel for once like they're the centre of someone's universe, not just a quick fuck. And whilst I never promise to love any of the women I sleep with, I do at least give them my full attention for the hours I'm with them.

Well, almost always. There was that one unfortunate night when I made the mistake of calling Drix whilst fucking the woman I was with. I made it up to her though.

Truth is, most men pay lip service to a woman's pleasure, only ever really seeking their own release. But me? *I pay attention.* I'm willing to uncover their deepest desires, and for the time they're with me, I give them everything they want. So what if I get something out of it too?

Both Drix and Daisy think I have an addiction to sex. Maybe I do. But, honestly, I could think of worse things. Besides, making women come is about the only fucking thing I'm good at anyway.

"Not anymore," I say to my reflection, a bitter laugh escaping my lips as I strip, kicking my clothes to the corner of the bathroom for one of the staff to clear up later.

Stepping into the shower, I switch on the tap, and as hot water rains down on me, I grab a handful of body wash then lean my forearm on the tiled wall, gripping my cock with my free hand.

"Looks like it's just you and me," I mutter to my dick, allowing my mind to wander, revelling in the prickles of pleasure gathering at the base of my spine as I corkscrew my palm up and down my length.

With every stroke of my cock, the tension within me eases a little, and I allow myself this moment of pleasure, needing it, *craving* it. If sex with women is an addiction, then self-pleasure is a comfort. I don't want to think too deeply about why that is, knowing that if I did I'd uncover some fucked-up emotions that I've been running from for a long, long time.

Instead, I pump my cock faster, a steady rhythm matching the beat of my heart. The water turns from hot to scalding, but I barely notice. All I feel is the rush of pleasure surging through me. Soon the guilt melts away, replaced by the all-consuming intensity of my need as I start to imagine the faces of all the women I've fucked, hearing their soft moans, and the look of satisfaction on their faces as they come. So many women, that soon they all merge into one.

Then right before I climax, one face appears in my mind, hers, *Daisy's*, and I come with a guttural roar, shocked by the intensity, fucking shaken by it.

"God-fucking-damn-it!" I shout, reaching for the tap and turning it off.

Leaning against the cooling tiles, I try to catch my breath as my thoughts twist and tumble. I'm angry at myself, at Daisy for daring to enter my mind, taunting me with her pale blue eyes, freckled skin and fiery spirit. She's not even my type, so fuck knows why she even entered my head, let alone made me come so damn hard.

Then it occurs to me, Daisy had said she wasn't a game to be won, that she'd never be intimate with me, but that's like waving a red rag to a bull. No one has ever spurned my advances. *No one.* Yet, she has the audacity to do exactly that.

Straightening up, I step out of the shower and grab a towel, drying myself. Maybe this marriage needn't be as hellish as I first thought, and despite all my promises, I decide at that moment that she will be mine, in *every* way possible, whether she wants to or not.

THE SHARP TRILL of my phone wakes me from my sleep, and I push upright, blinking as light filters through the gap in the curtains. Grabbing my phone, I stare at the screen, noticing two things at once. First, it's nine thirty and I'm already late for work, and secondly it's Drix who's calling.

"Listen," I begin, prepared to defend myself. I know with how close Drix and Daisy are, she would've told him what happened between us already.

"I'm at the hospital," he says quickly.

"At the *hospital*? What the fuck happened?" I ask. Our relationship may be strained right now, but that doesn't mean I won't drop everything to be by my best friend's side. Fuck work. It's not as if the hotel can't run itself anyway.

"Lia's husband turned up at my house early this morning," he bites out, the heaviness in his voice, the fear, making my own pulse beat harder. "He hurt Lia, Dalton."

"He did what?! Please tell me you killed the fucker."

Drix lets out a shuddering breath. "I wanted to. I didn't. He's in police custody right now."

"You called the police?" I ask, my own voice strained. This isn't what we do. If there's a problem we deal with it ourselves.

"I told Daisy to do so the second she ended the call with me. Then I broke every speed limit possible to get to them. I was just in time, if I'd been a minute later..."

"Where's Daisy now?" I ask, my fucking heart pounding as I get to my feet and stride to my wardrobe, yanking out a pair of jeans.

"She's with Lia and Toby. Lia is being checked over by the

doctor, and they've given Daisy something to help calm her nerves. They're both pretty shaken up."

"Did he hurt Daisy too?" I ask, my voice eerily calm as a sudden feeling of protectiveness washes over me.

It's a feeling I'm used to when it comes to Daisy. No matter how much she irritates me, fucking pushes my buttons like no one else can, she's still my best friend's little sister, and I've always tried to look out for her in my own way.

"No. She was upstairs with Toby, keeping him safe."

"Good," I reply, relief flooding through me as I breathe out. "I'm coming to the hospital. Give me fifteen minutes."

"No, don't. I called you out of respect, because I wanted you to hear the news from me first."

"Listen—"I begin, but he cuts me off.

"Daisy doesn't want you here. She's shaken up, concerned for Lia and Toby, for me. It isn't the right time."

"Fuck the right time. I'm coming."

"You come here now and we'll have an even bigger problem, Dalton," Drix warns. "You'll only upset her more. I said no. I mean it. Give her some space."

"She's my fiance, Drix. I'm coming," I bite back.

"Don't fucking remind me," he grinds out.

I ignore his remark, anger rising up my chest. "Whether you like it or not, in a matter of weeks she'll be my wife. I'm responsible for her as much as you are."

"And I'm her *brother*. She doesn't want you here."

"She said that?" I ask.

"What are you going to do, haul her into your arms and tell her you love her, that she's safe with you?" he retorts, ignoring my question.

I pause, hating the accusation in his voice, the loathing. "She needs to know I care."

"Do you though?"

"Fuck, Drix, what do you want from me? I'm trying my best here."

"What I want is for you to tear up that damn contract, Dalton. What I want is for my sister to find a man who wants to marry her because he fucking *loves* her," he hisses out.

"We've been over this. The contract is signed, it's done. There's no going back, and what's more you're free from your debt, Drix. As much as I hate the fact that the bastard hurt Lia, you're free of him now too. You can be happy."

"This conversation is over. Don't come," Drix replies, ending the call.

"Fuck!" I shout, throwing my phone across the room. It lands on the bed, bouncing a couple of times before falling still.

Swiping my fingers through my hair, I consider my options. I could go to the hospital against my best friend's wishes, but then what? Drix is right, what possible comfort would I be to Daisy, to him? Neither of them want me there, and with good reason.

Jesus fuck, last night I went to bed determined to make Daisy mine even when she's made it very clear that she hates my guts. That's the kind of man I am. One who's willing to hurt a woman who's sweet and thoughtful, loyal and trusting, just to appease his own fucking ego.

Even now, even knowing all of that, I *still* want to make her mine. This sick, twisted part of me needs to claim her despite everything, just to prove that I can. It's fucked-up. *I'm* fucked-up.

I can't change, not to save my friendship, not to stop myself from hurting Daisy, not even to prevent hurting myself, because if there's anything I know about myself, it's this: I'm my father's son. What I want, I get, and damn the consequences.

With that thought in mind, I stride across the room and pick up my phone, flicking through my contacts until I find the number I need. Pressing call, I wait impatiently for someone to pick up.

"Smithson's Jewellery, how may I assist you?" a crisp, male voice greets me.

"It's Dalton Gunn, clear the store for me. I'm coming right now to pick out a very expensive, very sizable engagement ring. No expenses spared."

CHAPTER THREE

Dragging in a deep, calming breath, I shrug off my pink woollen coat and hand it to the hostess. Her perfectly manicured nails graze the buttons of my coat as she takes it from me, her eyes narrowing in disapproval at the bold colours of the outfit I'm wearing underneath. The green and blue stripes of my palazzo trousers clash purposefully with my cerise pink shirt and heeled pumps, whilst my bright cherry lipstick adds another splash of colour.

In contrast, the hostess wears a demure black pencil skirt and starched white shirt, her hair slicked back in a low bun. She exudes elegance and sophistication, just like the private members club 'M' that I have entered. The name itself is obnoxious—it means 'ten million' in Roman numerals—and you can only join if you have *at least* ten million pounds in your bank account. The added horizontal line above the M indicates the multiple millions you *must* have.

"Mr Gunn is waiting for you in the lounge," the hostess says, hanging my coat in a closet behind her and pointing the way.

"Thank you," I reply, smiling politely, unfazed by her disapproving look as I glide past her, my heels clicking against the polished wooden floor.

The lounge itself is bathed in a soft golden light, casting a warm glow over the antique furniture and black velvet armchairs. Other members are quietly talking, enjoying the gentle melody from the pianist as he plays, their conversation interrupted by my entrance. No doubt my colourful outfit upset the muted tones of this terribly stuffy, and frankly, dull establishment. I'm not unaccustomed to this private members' club, after all my father was once a member, but I've never felt truly comfortable here. There are too many judgmental people here who think that wealth gives them the right to be rude, and happiness only comes in the form of a bank balance in the millions.

Ignoring their stares and the whispers that follow me, I make my way across the room to where Dalton is seated in a secluded corner, a glass of amber liquid in his hand. Almost immediately, his sharp eyes meet mine as I approach, a hint of surprise flashing across his face as he takes in my choice of outfit, before schooling his features. I can see the questions forming in his eyes, the judgement lurking behind his tight smile. But I'm not here to conform to his expectations or anyone else's for that matter. I'm here out of obligation, and I refuse to be anything other than my authentic self.

"Dalton," I say, greeting him with a forced smile of my own.

"Daisy," he retorts, gesturing for me to take a seat opposite him, and as I do, I catch the flicker of annoyance in his gaze. "Did you happen to pass through a rainbow on your way here?"

I arch a brow, pointedly taking in his own choice of outfit; a black suit with a dark grey shirt and tie. "Funny, I was just wondering whether you'd just stepped out of a storm cloud. There's no accounting for taste."

"I prefer sophistication over a circus," Dalton quips, his words laced with a subtle sting.

I meet his gaze head-on, refusing to back down despite the tension crackling in the air between us. "And I prefer authenticity over pretence," I shoot back, my tone firm and unwavering.

Dalton's jaw tightens imperceptibly, a muscle ticking in his jaw as he leans back in his chair, appraising me with a critical eye.

"You never quite fit in, did you?" he muses, swirling the amber liquid in his glass thoughtfully before taking a mouthful.

"If by fitting in you mean having my head stuck up my arse, then no, I guess I haven't. Besides, why conform to the mundane when you can dazzle in technicolour?" I quip back, raising an eyebrow challengingly.

Dalton chuckles, a patronising smile playing on his lips. "Always the rebel, aren't you, Daisy?"

Before I can retort, the waiter approaches the table to take our drink orders. Dalton orders another scotch on the rocks while I opt for a vibrant cocktail that matches the riot of colours that make up my outfit.

I watch Dalton closely as he engages in small talk with the waiter, his icy exterior momentarily melting into a facade of charm and ease. It's something I've grown accustomed to. Dalton has lived and breathed this world his whole life, and has been trained to act accordingly. He is a Gunn, and there are certain expectations he must fulfil, keeping up appearances being one of them.

"So, what is it that you wanted to speak about exactly?" I ask once the waiter leaves. "The sooner we're done here, the sooner I can go home."

"How are Lia and Toby doing?" Dalton counters. I must look surprised because he then adds, "Drix called me from the hospital. He filled me in on what happened."

"I see," I reply, blinking back the threat of tears at the memory of that awful morning. I haven't told anyone, but the whole experience has brought to the surface some disturbing memories of my own, and I've been battling with them ever since.

"Daisy?" he prompts, a frown appearing between his eyebrows.

"Lia is going to be okay. She's a strong woman, and Drix has been incredible with her. He loves her so much," I explain, swallowing hard. Their love is such a joy to witness, but it only highlights what I'm lacking in my own love life. Forcing that thought away, I continue. "Toby is such a resilient little boy too. They're going to be okay now that they have each other, and that pig rots in jail."

He nods, a muscle in his jaw flexing as he grits his teeth. "And you? How are *you* doing?"

"I'm fine," I reply tightly, and Dalton reaches across the table for my hand. His fingertips brush against my skin, and I pull away from him, crossing my arms.

"Daisy, don't lie to me," he says. "That was quite an ordeal you all went through."

"Like you care," I mutter, my heart clenching at his words, hating myself for feeling vulnerable in his presence. Dropping my gaze, I stare at the shiny surface of the table between us, the soft lighting reflecting off its surface.

"I care," he eventually says.

I laugh bitterly. "You don't have to pretend with me, Dalton."

"Daisy, look at me," he commands, his voice low, gruff.

Slowly I raise my gaze to meet his, schooling my features so he doesn't see how shaken I truly am. His piercing gaze seems to see right through me, and I fight the urge to break eye contact.

"I wanted to come to the hospital," he explains, running a hand through his hair.

"Then why didn't you?"

"Drix said he didn't want me there, that you didn't."

The atmosphere between us becomes even more tense as Dalton's words sink in. I feel a surge of unwavering love towards my brother for keeping Dalton away. I understand why he did it. Drix was trying to protect me, just like he always does. Besides, what difference would it have made if Dalton had come? It's not as if he truly cares about me. He just wants to secure his future, and a very substantial inheritance.

Before I can respond, the waiter returns with our drinks balanced on a tray, but as he reaches for Dalton's scotch he somehow manages to knock over my cocktail, shattering the glass on the table and spilling the contents all over my blouse.

I gasp as the cold liquid seeps into the fabric, staining it. My heart races as I look down at the mess, heat colouring my cheeks as everyone turns around to stare.

"I'm so sorry, madam," the waiter stammers, his expression panicked as Dalton stands.

"You idiot!" Dalton growls at the waiter as he rounds the table and grips my elbow gently, his long fingers pressing into my skin. "Daisy, are you okay?"

"I'm fine," I retort, shards of glass dropping to the floor as I stand. "I'll just go and clean up."

Dalton throws a glare at the waiter. "Clean this mess up, and replace our drinks," he snaps, before guiding me away from the table and towards the restrooms situated at the far side of the lounge, his palm pressing into my lower back.

"I'm quite capable of cleaning myself up," I say as he pushes open the door to the ladies room.

But Dalton doesn't listen, his jaw set with determination as he steers me inside.

The room is empty, the muted lighting casting a warm glow over the elegant decor. I head towards the sink, but before I can turn on the gold-plated faucet, Dalton's hand lands on mine, stopping me in my tracks.

"Let me help you," he says softly, his deep-set, blue eyes searching mine.

The air between us thins, or at least it feels that way as he regards me. Dalton has always been that man, you know the type, the ones who suck the oxygen from the room and steal if for themselves.

"I don't think so," I reply tightly, shrugging him off as I wet a paper towel and begin to dab at the stain on my blouse. Only I seem to be making it worse, not better. I let out a heavy sigh. "Pretty sure this is ruined."

"Maybe you should just dry it off?" Dalton suggests, eyeing the hand dryer.

"I guess," I mutter, unbuttoning and shrugging out of my ruined blouse as I lift my gaze back up to meet his.

The heated look in his eyes stills my hand, and I realise in that moment that I'm practically naked in an empty restroom with a sex addict, who also happens to be my fiancé.

"You're full of surprises, Daisy," he says, a little too gruffly for my liking as his gaze drops to my breasts encased in a pretty cerise lace bralette. I'm not sure if he's referring to my choice of bra or the fact that I've just stripped in front of him.

"Don't get any funny ideas," I retort, giving him my back as I place my soaked blouse under the hand dryer and let the warm air dry it off.

"Wouldn't dream of it," he mutters after a moment.

After a few minutes, my blouse is dry enough to wear once again. As I slip it back on, I can feel his gaze burning into my back. It's unnerving, yet strangely thrilling. Though I quickly shake that feeling off. Everyone knows Dalton has no discernment when it comes to women, as long as they have a vagina, he'll fuck them.

"Believe it or not, I wanted to come to the hospital. I wanted to see if you were okay," he suddenly admits. "*Are* you okay, Daisy?"

"Thank you for your concern," I reply quietly, my fingers stilling on the top button of my blouse as he steps closer, his presence looming behind me. "But I'm perfectly fine."

"You sure about that?" he murmurs, his breath warm against my ear, his body way too close for comfort.

My pulse flutters at his proximity, and I turn to face him, only to find his lips dangerously close to mine. The air crackles with tension, and I find myself questioning why I'm not shoving him away.

"I'm fine," I repeat.

"Something tells me you're lying," he adds, his gaze flicking to my lips then back up again to meet my eyes.

"You might want to back up, Dalton. You know what happened before when you stepped out of line," I remind him, hating that he sees something in me that I thought I'd hidden.

"We're in public," he counters. *"Fiancé."*

"We're in a restroom, *arsehole*," I snap back.

Before things can escalate further, the door behind us swings open, jolting us apart. A middle-aged woman enters, her eyes widening in surprise. Dalton cocks a brow, and I glare at him, seeing the intention in his eyes. Fortunately for us both he doesn't try to kiss me.

"We were just leaving," Dalton says, stepping back, his charming mask slipping back into place as he smiles at the woman and takes my hand in his.

When we reach our table, Dalton releases my hand and pulls out my chair with practised ease, offering me a polite smile that doesn't quite reach his eyes. Immediately reaching for my cocktail that the waiter replaced in our absence, I gulp it down in one go, thankful for the distraction.

"So why am I here exactly?" I ask, placing the empty glass back on the table between us.

Dalton chews on his lip, giving me a look I can't quite interpret before he reaches into his inside pocket and pulls out a small velvet box. My heart stills.

"Is that what I think it is?" I blurt out, dragging in a shaky breath.

"Open it," he replies, pushing the small box across the table between us.

Reaching for it, I flip open the lid. "It's..."

"An engagement ring, Daisy," he finishes for me, a small smile jerking up his lips.

I stare at the huge princess cut diamond set in platinum gold. I'm no expert on the value of such things, but given its size, and Dalton's reputation for extravagant gestures, I can only imagine the cost.

"This is absurd," I say, my voice barely above a whisper. "I can't accept this."

"Why not?" he asks, his voice tight.

"Because it isn't real."

"I can assure you that diamond is very real, and worth a substantial amount of money."

"That's not what I meant," I retort, closing the lid and pushing it back across the table towards him.

"Daisy, you're my fiance, my future wife. You *will* wear this ring," he hisses out, sliding it back towards me.

"This is not how I imagined things to go," I admit quietly, disappointment expanding in my chest. This ring isn't me. Nothing about this proposal is what I'd wanted for myself.

"Do you want me to make a grand gesture, to get down on one knee, is that it?" he asks, pushing upright as he snatches up the ring, removing it from the box before rounding the table.

"What are you doing?" I hiss, my cheeks flooding with heat as he kneels before me. "People will see!"

"Let them," Dalton declares, his eyes locked on to mine as reaches for my left hand, his fingers warm as they clasp my palm.

Around us, the conversations fade away, leaving only the sound of my heartbeat thundering in my ears. Dalton's expression is earnest, vulnerable almost, and yet I don't trust it, I can't. This is all an act, a show for the people watching. He's always been very good at that.

"Daisy Hammer, will you marry me?" Dalton asks, his voice ringing loud in the silence.

My stomach coils, and tears prick my eyes but not for the reason everyone here might think. This is all a lie, and even though I chose this, chose to marry Dalton, it still hurts knowing that. I always imagined an intimate proposal, just me and the man I loved somewhere secluded, romantic, not here in this members' lounge surrounded by judgemental strangers.

Dalton holds the ring over the end of my finger, as though I have a choice to say no, that this engagement will only become real if I agree to his proposal, but we both know that's bullshit. It became real the moment I signed the contract.

"Daisy?" Dalton questions, his voice dropping, his shoulders tense as he looks up at me. There's a tightness around his eyes, and for the briefest of moments he seems lost somehow.

"Yes, I'll marry you," I reply, my voice barely above a whisper.

His face lights up with a triumphant smile as he slips the ring onto my finger, and the surrounding guests begin to clap in stilted applause, as though they too suspect that all is not as it seems.

Sensing their doubt, I force a smile, my eyes flickering from the ring on my finger back to Dalton's expectant gaze. The weight of the ring feels heavier than anything I've ever experienced, a physical reminder of the choice I made, and the path I'm willingly walking down.

As Dalton rises to his feet and pulls me into a tight embrace, I can't help but feel a sense of unease settling in the pit of my stomach. We both know that this engagement isn't just a union of two people; it's a contract sealed with secret agreements and hidden agendas, and as much as I try to push down the rising doubts, they claw at the edges of my mind, whispering truths I'm not ready to confront.

Dalton eases back slightly, his fingers dusting across my cheek as he stares down at me. "Shall we seal this with a kiss?" he murmurs, and there isn't a hint of hesitation in his eyes.

If I didn't know any better I could be fooled into thinking that he really wants this, wants *me*, but then I remember our contract and the stipulations written within it. We have to make this look real.

"Fine," I whisper back. "Just do it."

He licks his lips, his arm circling my back as he pulls me tighter against him and presses his lips against mine in a gesture that should be filled with joy and promise, but all I feel is the cool press of uncertainty against my mouth.

Mine. His. Ours.

And as his lips part, and I tentatively swipe my tongue into his mouth, something shifts almost imperceptibly. Maybe it's the fact that I've downed a strong cocktail, or perhaps it's because I truly need to make everyone believe this is real, but I kiss him back, welcoming the firm sweep of his tongue with a soft moan. He reacts immediately, his fingers sliding into my hair, gripping me tighter as I press myself against him and drag my hands up the firm planes of his muscular back.

Now as we kiss there's an air of desperation. I don't want Dalton, but I guess I just want to blot out this shit-show of a proposal with something that makes me feel more than just a means to an end. Even if it is pretend.

So we kiss like lovers might, like two people in love, and for a while I give in to the feeling of it and allow myself to believe in the lie. I let him press his body closer to mine. I submit to his demanding kiss, explore it even.

But no matter how much I try, all I keep thinking is that this is just a carefully orchestrated scene, and it makes me feel inexorably sad. Sensing the change in me, Dalton pulls back, his gaze turbulent.

"Daisy, I..." he falters, brushing his fingers over my cheek, frowning as he looks down at me.

"Don't. It's done," I reply softly, shoring up my defences, straightening my spine as I plaster on another smile. As we break apart, I notice the interested onlookers still glued to us both. They clap and murmur, gossiping amongst themselves.

"Congratulations," one gentleman says as he passes us by, his gaze flicking from Dalton to me, an eyebrow cocked quizzically.

I know what he's thinking, what is a man like Dalton Gunn doing marrying the adopted daughter of Hubert Hammer? Most of the people in this town know my history, or at least the only part of it Hubert and I were willing to share. I'm nothing but a kid abandoned by her parents, and fortunate enough to be adopted by a wealthy man. Like Dalton pointed out earlier, I've never fit in. I don't belong here, and I sure as hell don't belong to him, not in the way that counts.

"Thank you," Dalton replies, twining his hands with mine. "We're very happy, aren't we, Daisy?"

I nod, refusing to buy into this charade any more than I have too. This is a marriage of convenience, a lie, and I won't ever forget that. But for now, under the watchful eyes of strangers and amidst the facade of happiness, I bury those secrets deep within me, locking them away behind a smile that doesn't quite reach my eyes. This may not be the proposal I dreamed of, but it's the reality I chose.

As Dalton leads me out of the lounge, his fingers woven with mine, I realise that agreeing to this marriage is only the beginning of a twisted dance, where every step brings me further away from myself, and I can't help but wonder if I'll ever find my way back.

CHAPTER FOUR

"You wanted to speak with me?" Daisy asks, stepping into my office at the hotel we both work at the following morning.

My eyes graze over her as she shuts the door, taking a seat opposite me. She's wearing a navy blue pencil skirt, sheer tights and a white fitted blouse with the hotel's name embroidered on the lapel. But as always, Daisy adds her own flair to the uniform with her unique earrings, bold lipstick and dramatic eyeliner. Today she has a pair of unicorn earrings dangling from each ear, and a deep purple lipstick which clashes vibrantly with her pink streaked, strawberry blonde hair.

"How are things?" I ask, flicking my gaze from her pouty mouth to her eyes. Pretty sure I went to sleep last night thinking about how plump her lips felt against mine. Frankly, that had surprised me more than the fact she actually kissed me back.

She squints at me, her button nose wrinkling, smooshing up the freckles splattered across the bridge. "Things?"

"Is work okay?" I ask, suddenly feeling like some tongue-tied imbecile. Well, this is fucking awkward.

"Is this my long overdue performance review? Are you going

to give me a raise?" she throws back with a scoff before adding, "Oh no, wait, in a few weeks I won't actually have a job anymore, will I?"

"That wasn't down to me," I retort, bristling at her hostility. I mean, I can't fucking blame her for being pissed off, but she knows as well as I do that becoming *a lady of leisure* wasn't my decision.

"Hmm," she replies, picking at an invisible piece of lint on her skirt.

"Listen, I wouldn't have minded you continuing to work. I'm not like my father."

At that she tips her head back and laughs, and I fold my arms across my chest, forcing myself not to react. Why is she the one person who so easily pushes my buttons? I'd love to shut her up with my cock in her mouth. That'd teach her.

"Seriously? You're his clone, Dalton."

"How so?" I ask out of morbid curiosity more than anything else.

"You really want to know?" she retorts, eying me, amusement and a glimmer of spite glinting in her eyes.

"May as well know how much you dislike me before we tie the knot," I reply.

"Okay, well you asked for it." Shifting in her seat, she rests her forearms on the table, flashing me a hint of cleavage as she leans forward. I force myself to look away. "For a start you're arrogant. Though I suspect that comes as no great surprise."

I shrug. "Arrogant. Got it. Anything else?"

"Oh, there's plenty more. You're vain," she continues, grinning at me in a way that looks like a dog about to bite. "Materialistic. Selfish. Terrible with women–"

"The women I've slept with would beg to differ," I interrupt.

She rolls her eyes, and my fingers flex, itching to spank her. "I mean *emotionally*."

"So you admit I'm good in bed?" I ask, cocking a brow.

"I wouldn't know. Don't want to either," she adds quickly.

"Go on. What else?"

"You're conceited."

"Isn't that the same as vain? Try again," I offer.

"How about *annoying*?"

"Okay, so I'm arrogant, materialistic, selfish, vain, terrible with women, *emotionally*," I add with a smirk. "Conceited, annoying..."

"Yep, all of those things," she replies with a satisfied smile, leaning back in her seat. "Oh, *and* inconsiderate. You could've warned me that you'd sent an email to the staff this morning about our engagement!"

"Would you have preferred I called a meeting instead? I thought you'd want to avoid the embarrassment, not to mention another public display of affection. So all things considered, I think I was being pretty considerate."

"You could've given me a heads up. I've been batting off questions all day long."

"Tell me who's being intrusive and I'll call them in the office for a chat," I immediately reply.

"I don't think so, your *chats* tend to lead to a person getting fired. I've handled it."

"Okay, anything else you'd like to add to the list?"

"I think that about sums you up," she replies, folding her arms across her chest.

"Really. I think you've forgotten a few," I say.

"Yeah, what?"

"Rich–"

"Not quite yet," she reminds me. "But I agree, rich people tend to be shitty."

"That's very narrow-minded of you. Not *all* rich people. Hubert wasn't," I point out.

"He was an exception to the rule," she replies.

"I'm protective," I add.

"Protective? *Interfering* you mean," she corrects.

"Still not forgiven me for firing Lewis, I see. Need I remind you that he was the arsehole shagging another woman whilst he was dating you? I did you a favour."

"You *interfered*," she reiterates. "Stuck your nose in business that had nothing to do with you. I would've handled it. Besides, he was just a fling. You assumed he meant more to me than he did."

Now it's my turn to scoff. Daisy has a bad habit of falling for men that are no good for her. Not too long ago she'd dated that little shit Lewis who used to work at this hotel as a porter until I fired his arse for fucking her over. "Don't lie. You would've listened to his piss-poor excuse, forgiven him and let him walk all over you."

She scowls. "You're mistaking me for the women you've fucked. I honestly don't know why any of them went back for more given your reputation."

"That'll be because I'm *excellent* in bed," I goad her, levelling my gaze with hers. "I may not have given the women I slept with any promises, or emotional connection, but I did give them all *multiple* orgasms. *That's* why they kept coming back."

"Good for you," she snaps, pushing up from her seat. "Are we done? I have a lot of work to do."

"Sit down, Daisy. I'm not finished with you yet," I command.

"Don't tell me what to do, Dalton Gunn. Just because you're my *fake* fiance–"

"I think you'll find this is very real, Daisy. You *are* my fiance and we *are* getting married. There's nothing fake about that," I remind her.

"On paper, yes, but not in any way that counts," she counters, anger suffusing her words as her eyes gleam with hatred, which only serves to rile me up further. "And that doesn't give you the right to demand anything from me!"

"Right now, I'm still your boss. So sit your peachy arse back on that seat before I do something we'll both regret!" I grind out. God, she's pissing me off.

"Threatening me now are we? Do I need to add *prick* to that long list of terrible attributes?"

We glare at each other for long moments before I wind my neck in and heave out a sigh. "Please, Daisy. Will you just stay a moment longer? I did have a valid reason for wanting to see you."

"You've got one minute," she agrees reluctantly, planting her arse back on the seat.

"I wanted to give you this," I say, reaching for the gift bag on the floor beside me and placing it on the table.

"I can't be bought," she says, glancing at the bag warily.

"We both know that's a lie," I reply, lifting a brow.

"Signing a contract agreeing to marry you, to release Drix from his debt, is not the same as being bought. I would call that an act of *kindness*, Dalton. Which is a concept you clearly have no idea about."

"Just open the damn gift," I snap, pushing the bag across the table towards her.

The right thing to do in this instant would be to apologise, but I've never done the right thing in my life, and I'm not about to start now just to appease a woman who clearly hates my guts.

"Fine!"

She reaches for the bag and pulls out a large white box. Across the lid in swirly gold lettering is the name of the store I bought the items from this morning. *Joli* is an upmarket boutique frequented by the wealthy women who live in Princetown.

"If you've bought me lingerie, I might just strangle you with it!" she says, glaring at me.

"Sounds positively erotic," I counter, trying and failing to keep a straight face.

"Oh, shut up."

"Did you need new lingerie? I mean, I'm more than happy to

buy you some," I add, hitching a brow and loving the way her cheeks heat.

"I do not. And for the record, I buy my own lingerie."

"You might want to reconsider because I know a thing or two about quality lingerie, Daisy. I also happen to be an expert at removing it."

"Number one, that was the first and last time you'll ever get to see me in my underwear, and number two, you'll never have the opportunity to remove my lingerie. Just so we're clear."

My lips twitch with another smile as she glares at me. "Go on, open it."

Dropping her gaze from me to the gift box, she lifts the lid, her fingers parting the lavender scented tissue paper. When she pulls out the first of three silk blouses that I bought for her to replace the one that was ruined last night, I can't help but feel a glimmer of satisfaction at the look of shock in her eyes.

"You bought me a replacement?" she questions in disbelief, frowning as she pulls out the pale blue silk blouse that I thought would match the shade of her eyes perfectly.

"Three, actually. They didn't have the same exact colour as the one you wore last night so I picked out the ones I'd thought you'd like. If they're not suitable I can have them returned," I offer with a shrug.

"No, they're... fine," she replies with a shake of her head as she folds the tissue paper back around the pale blue blouse, and rests it on the table before looking at the next two. One is a dusky pink, a colour I've noticed her wearing a lot, and the last is a deep red, my favourite.

"Good. Well, that was all, really," I say, feeling a strange mix of satisfaction and unease. I had hoped my gesture would soften her towards me but now I see she's still guarded.

"Thank you, Dalton," she finally says, tucking the blouses back into the box, and the box back into the gift bag.

"You're welcome."

"You know, some people might see this as a sign of remorse or a way to make amends," she says, pinning me with her gaze.

"And how do you see it?" I ask.

"If I didn't know you well enough, I'd assume the same thing."

"But..."

"But I do know you, Dalton, and as pretty as these are, this gift feels like you're trying to buy my affection."

"I'm not."

"Or at the very least, my obedience," she adds.

"Not that either," I retort, flinching at the accusation. "I've also booked you in for a massage this afternoon after you finish your shift, but just so you know I haven't done that to buy your affection or your obedience. You've had a rough few days, and I thought it might help."

"Lia, Drix and Toby have had a rough few days. Like I said to you last night. I'm fine."

"Either way, I've booked you in. Have the massage or don't. It's up to you."

She hesitates for a moment, her gaze locked on the gift bag before her. "I'll give you the benefit of doubt, and accept these blouses as a thoughtful gift. The massage... sounds nice. I'll consider it."

I try to read her expression, but she keeps her emotions guarded, so I respond with a simple, "That's good to hear. Enjoy the rest of your day."

"I will," she responds, standing up from her seat.

As she adjusts her skirt, the glint of her engagement ring catches my eye. I half expected her to leave the ring at home, but seeing it on her now causes a storm of possessive emotions to stir within me. *She's mine.* Unwillingly, yes, but she's mine regardless, and now that she's committed to marrying me, she's bound to me whether she wants to be or not, the good and the bad. For better or for worse.

For a while, at least.

"SAMANTHA, DID DAISY LEAVE ALREADY?" I ask, stepping up to the reception desk. It's a few minutes past four and I was hoping to catch Daisy before she left, figuring she'd pass up the opportunity for a massage to spite me.

"Actually, she went to the spa for the massage you booked for her," Samantha replies, trying to smother her smile. "Congratulations, by the way."

"Thank you, we're very happy," I reel off, a little distracted by the thought of Daisy naked and relaxed. She may not be my type, but I'm still a man, and it's been over a week since I've slept with a woman. Which, for me, feels like a fucking year.

"Seems like it," she mutters in response, slamming her mouth shut when I snap my attention back to her.

The email I sent this morning about our engagement erupted in a torrent of gossip that has only seemed to fuel Daisy's ire throughout the day when I've caught glimpses of her at work. I probably should've consulted her first, but it's done now. Nothing I can do to change it.

"Who is she booked in with?" I ask, moving the conversation on.

Samantha returns her attention to the computer screen, clicking on the mouse a couple of times before glancing back up at me. "Tomasz."

"You're fucking joking, right?" I snap, that possessiveness I felt earlier rearing its head.

"Is there a problem?" Samantha replies, almost a little too sweetly for my liking. "Daisy asked for him specifically," she adds.

"I bet she did," I mutter, grinding my teeth. "Which room is she in?"

Samantha's eyes flick back to the screen, her lips twitching as she tries to smother another smile. "Room three."

I don't bother to thank her as I push off from the counter, striding towards the spa. As I approach Room Three, my initial plan is to burst in and fire the bastard who dared to lay his hands on my fiancé's naked body. However, a different idea crosses my mind and I decide to use this as an opportunity to get back at Daisy for choosing Tomasz as her masseuse. Sure, she's made it perfectly clear that she doesn't want to have sex with me, but she hasn't mentioned anything about me *touching* her, and I intend on exploiting that. Composing myself, I reach for the door handle, taking a deep breath as I push the door open.

Inside, the room is dimly lit, with the scent of essential oils permeating the air. Daisy is lying face down on the massage table, a white towel folded across her arse, the rest of her naked and exposed as Tomasz's skilled hands glide up her calves. It takes everything in me not to punch his fucking lights out, especially when she murmurs how *good it feels*. Instead, I lift my finger to my lips, motioning for Tomasz to come outside the room.

"Excuse me, Daisy, I'm... needed. Please relax, I won't be long," he says, picking up on my vibes not to tell her it's me.

As soon as the doors shut, I glare at him, hissing out the words like a rattlesnake about to strike. "In the future, if Daisy asks for you to give her a massage you will say you're busy, understand?"

Tomasz nods. "Yes, of course. Apologies, Mr Gunn, should I get one of the female masseuses to finish her session?"

"No. Leave this with me," I retort tightly, shrugging off my suit jacket and handing it to him. "Take this to my office."

"Of course, Mr Gunn. Apologies once again," he says, before spinning on his heels and leaving.

I watch him walk away, anger bubbling in my chest as I angrily roll up my shirt sleeves. A large part of me wants to go in there and give Daisy a piece of my mind. She may not be fucking another man, but she's pushing the boundaries of our contract by allowing another man's hands on her body, and for that I'm going to make her pay.

Stepping into the room, I close the door softly behind me. Daisy stirs, her head lifting, but I place my hand on the centre of her back, hoping to fuck she doesn't sit up.

"You're back, everything okay?" she asks.

I grunt my response, not wanting to give myself away. Daisy doesn't seem bothered by my lack of words, and lets out a long sigh that has my cock twitching and my anger growing.

"I'm so relaxed, Tomasz. You have magic hands."

I'll give her magic hands.

"Please don't be offended if I fall asleep. In all honesty, I'm pretty tired. It's been a testing week."

I grunt again, gritting my jaw at the simple fact that she can be honest with Tomasz but she refuses to open up to me. Flexing my fingers, I quickly add some oil to my palms and warm up the liquid before placing my hands on her ankles, gripping her gently. I may not be a trained masseuse, but I've massaged a lot of women in my time, and I'm an expert at making them quake from my touch.

Flattening the palm of my hands against the sides of her ankles, I use my thumbs to draw circles across her skin, moving slowly upwards. The soft moan she releases is like a shot of pleasure straight to my cock, and it takes everything in me not to groan in response.

Fuck knows how Tomasz remains focussed and professional, he must have a raging hard on most of the time, or perhaps, unlike me, he's just a decent guy who doesn't have an addiction to the female form. Yeah, it must be that.

Daisy relaxes further under my touch, and I can feel her muscles loosening under my thumbs as I slowly slide my hands up her calves and towards her freckled thighs. Her creamy skin pinkens a little from my firm touch, stirring up thoughts of her stripped naked, my handprints colouring her skin.

A shiver runs through me at the thought as my palms slide higher, my fingers gliding over the smooth skin of her inner thighs. If she were truly mine, and willing, I would slip my hands higher, exploring the soft folds of her pussy, but for now, I inch my hands just below the towel that rests across her upper thighs, feeling the heat radiating from her body before sliding my palms back downwards.

Daisy lets out another soft sigh, her body liquefying under my touch, the sound is a sweet symphony of satisfaction that I alone am responsible for. Not to brag, but I've made women come touching every part of their body except their obvious erogenous zones, and I'm willing to bet Daisy would come just as hard from my touch, *if* I let her.

Working my hands slowly back down her legs, I pay special attention to the back of her knees, working small circles there. Daisy's soft breaths begin to thicken imperceptibly, and I glance upwards, grinning at the way her fingers curl around the padded bed, her arse cheeks clenching beneath the towel. A slow smile pulls up my lips. I bet she's wet. Before long she'll be dripping for me.

Or should I say *Tomasz* given that's who she thinks is massaging her now.

Fuck sake.

Gritting my jaw, I take all my anger out on my perfect teeth and lightly draw my fingertips over the back of her knees, I trace the lightest of touch across her skin. The fine hairs on her arms lift as they cover in goosebumps, another telltale sign that she's aroused. As my hands glide lower, I notice her toes curl in response to my touch, and I can't help but feel another surge of arousal. Gripping her ankle, I press my thumbs into the dip either side of her Achillies heel, before smoothing my palm over her pretty feet, paying particular attention to her arch.

Her sigh deepens, and her fingers release their tight grip on the padded bed, as she relaxes once more. But I don't want her relaxed, I want her coiled tight, desperate, *needy*.

I want her on the edge of her proverbial seat, fucking panting for release.

So I work my hands back upwards again, feeling the heat radiating from her body as I coast my palms back over her calves, the back of her knees and up her thighs. They clench together from my touch, and I can't help but smile to myself, knowing that she's completely at my mercy, that I'm about to push her to the brink of pleasure, in a state of overwhelming arousal, only to leave her there, wanting more.

It's no more than she deserves.

Slowly, I run my thumbs along the inside of her thighs, barely touching the sensitive skin, and they part imperceptibly. A huge part of me is angered by her reaction given she believes that I'm Tomasz. The other, part of me, the part addicted to the sins of the flesh, can't think beyond how soft she feels, how warm her skin is, how her chest heaves from my touch, how her sweet moans sound. She's so receptive to my touch, so responsive, and it turns me the fuck on.

Jesus fucking christ.

My cock thickens further, pressing against the zipper of my trousers, and I can feel the delicious heat between her thighs just inches from my fingertips. With a sly grin, I begin to massage her inner thigh, pushing her legs wider to gain access, moving my fingertips in slow circles. She's trembling now, and I know she's desperate for me to sink my fingers inside her pussy just as much as I am.

"Oh God," she murmurs, her voice a husky plea, as I continue to tease. "This isn't right."

This isn't right...

My hands still, something close to regret flooding my senses. Fuck, what the hell am I doing?

She thinks I'm Tomasz for fuck sake. I came here to punish her, but really all I'm doing is punishing myself. This is all kinds of fucked-up. Backing up, I leave the room, stepping outside and closing the door behind me, trying to regain control of my body as I rest against the wood.

"Fuck," I mutter, swiping a hand through my hair. "Fuck, fuck, fuck!"

I want to yell at her for being so aroused. I want to spank her arse for desiring another man's touch, for not even *trying* to put a stop to it. I want to go back into the room and fuck her until she screams.

I'm turned on. I'm livid. It's a dangerous combination.

Twisting my body around, I grip the door handle, ready to say fuck it to everything and claim her body. They say hate sex is the best kind of sex, and right now I fucking hate Daisy Hammer, but a whimper coming from inside the room stops me. I stiffen, straining to hear. Is she crying...?

No, wait...

There's another soft moan, and I press my ear against the door, my knuckles turning white around the handle as I listen.

She's not crying, she's *moaning*.

Is she...?

She's getting herself off!

Fuck. Me.

I can't seem to move. My body stiffens as I listen, and I don't know what messes me up more, the fact she's making herself come thinking of Tomasz, or the fact that it's not my hand making her feel pleasure she's never experienced before, because Tomasz's skills are nothing compared to mine, *believe me.*

My heart races as I listen to her muffled scream of release, the sound driving a new wave of desire through my veins. But I stand firm, resisting the primal urge to burst back into the room and take her right there and then.

Finally the sounds subside, and with a deep breath, I push off from the door, striding back along the corridor. Unable to take out my frustration and anger on Daisy, I decide Tomasz will do, and two words burst from my lips as I pass him by: "You're fired."

CHAPTER FIVE

"I love that dress on you, Daisy," Lia says grinning at me as I step into the kitchen the following afternoon. "You look beautiful."

"Thanks, Lia," I reply, feeling out of sorts as I smooth my palms over my red knee-length woollen dress. Ordinarily this outfit, which I've paired with red stockings and pink ankle boots, would make me feel particularly happy. Truth be known, right now I feel like a fraud, like there's a dark cloud hanging over me, just like the heavy snow clouds floating in the sky outside.

"Is Dalton picking you up?" she asks, resting her mug of tea back on the kitchen island as I approach.

"He's sending a car. I'm meeting him at the restaurant. Where are Drix and Toby?"

"At the cinema," she replies softly, happiness radiating from her. "Drix is so good with him, I'm incredibly lucky."

"But you'll be on your own," I say, placing my clutch on the counter and chewing on my lip. "Perhaps I should cancel, keep you company instead?"

"Absolutely not. I'm fine."

"But–"

She cuts me off with a shake of her head, her green eyes softening as she looks at me. "You don't need to worry about me, Daisy. Martin's in police custody. He can't hurt me anymore. Besides, Drix has triple checked the security system. I'll be okay."

"Even so..." My voice trails off as I sit on the stool and stare at the worktop, by mind wandering to what happened in the spa yesterday. How could I let that happen?

"Daisy, do you want to talk about it?" Lia asks gently, her warm hand resting on mine.

We might have only known each other for a few months, but she has become a good friend ever since she moved in with us, more like a sister really, and I appreciate her more than she knows. I'm so thankful Drix fell in love and found his happiness, despite the challenges they've both had to face.

"Talk about what?" I hedge.

"Whatever's bothering you."

"Nothing's bothering me," I reply, plastering on a smile. I seem to be getting good at doing that lately.

"Daisy, you don't need to pretend with me. What you've done for us..." Lia lets out a sigh, her hand squeezing mine. "We're so grateful, truly. But it's a huge sacrifice on your part. I know Drix hates the thought of you being unhappy. I do too."

"I've already told you both that I'm okay with my decision. Dalton and I have both signed the contract. It's done. Besides, you, Drix and Toby mean so much to me. I want you to be happy. "

"We *are* happy."

"And you'll continue to be now," I say, placing my other hand over hers.

She sighs, lifting her pretty, pale green eyes to meet mine. "So you're moving in with Dalton this weekend?"

"I am. Most of the things I want to take with me are packed and ready to be collected."

"We'll miss you being around," she says.

"I won't be far away, and you can bet your arse I'll be coming back often for your beautiful home-cooked meals because let's face it, there's no way Dalton can cook."

"Doesn't he have staff to do that for him?"

"Exactly, I bet he can't even boil an egg." I giggle at the absurd thought.

"Probably not," she agrees, with a grin.

"Besides, I'll need someone to vent to every time Dalton pisses me off, which I suspect will be often." I laugh, trying to lighten the mood, but my smile drops as I catch the expression on Lia's face.

"Oh Daisy, I wish things were different," she says, her voice catching.

"Stop that. Seriously, things are going to be okay. I may not like Dalton all that much, but I do enjoy pissing him off, and I'm going to make sure I do that on a regular basis. Silver linings and all."

"Oh boy," she giggles. "Don't ever change, Daisy. You hear me? You are perfect just the way you are."

"I have no intention of changing," I reassure her just as the doorbell rings. "Well, that's my cab. Are you sure you're okay being on your own?"

Lia glances at her watch. "Drix and Toby will be home in less than an hour. Go and..." she hesitates, pulling a face, "*Enjoy yourself?*"

"I'll do my best," I retort, giving her a quick hug.

"I TOOK the liberty of ordering for you," Dalton remarks as he greets me at the door of the traditional Japanese restaurant.

"Seems like taking liberties is something you're skilled at," I mutter under my breath, as I follow him to our screened-off dining area. Tonight he's wearing dark blue jeans, his neck tattoos just peeking up beneath the collar of his black cashmere sweater.

"What was that?" he asks, his eyes narrowing as we both take a seat at the low table, my feet pressing against the recessed floor.

"Nothing. I'm sure whatever you've chosen will be fine," I reply, casting my gaze out of the floor-to-ceiling windows that offer stunning panoramic views of the snow-covered valley below. On any other day, with anyone else besides Dalton, I might have been able to appreciate the beauty of it all.

"Only the best for my fiancé," he retorts, his gaze drilling into mine as he presses his palms against the table. "So, how was your massage?"

I stiffen, my gaze snapping to his as a rush of shame floods my veins. "It was... *fine.*"

"Just fine?" he asks, tilting his head with a mocking smirk.

My leg jitters uncontrollably beneath the table and I press my palm against my thigh, forcing it to stop. "I'm not sure what you want me to say."

"Don't you have *anything* to add?" he persists.

"It's still snowing," I offer.

"That's not what I was asking, and you know it," he replies, steel in his voice.

"Dalton, I think–"

"You can imagine my surprise when I found out who your masseuse was. Did you enjoy his hands on you, Daisy?" Dalton asks as he glares at me heatedly.

"He's very skilled at his job," I reply, refusing to rise to the bait.

Dalton smirks. "Not anymore."

"What do you mean, *not anymore?* Please don't tell me you–"

"Fired him? Of course I fucking did. He put his hands on you, Daisy. *My* fucking fiancé," he hisses.

Guilt washes over me, and I shake my head in disbelief. "You didn't!"

"I did." He cocks a brow, daring me to object.

"Because he was doing the job you *paid* him to do?" I counter, feeling my own anger rise. "What is wrong with you?"

"No, because he had the audacity to touch what's mine!" he grinds out, his clenched fist bashing against the table top.

"I am *not* yours," I hiss, glaring at him.

"That ring says otherwise," he says, pointing to my finger.

"This ring is just for show," I object.

His jaw grits, anger flaring in his eyes as he leans towards me. "Let's get one thing straight, Daisy. You are mine whether you want to be or not."

"The only person I belong to is myself," I argue. "You can go around acting like you own me, but we both know that's bullshit. So get it into your thick head, I am *not* yours, never will be."

"If you ever let another man lay his hands on you, I'll–"

"You'll do what, *fire* them?"

"No, Daisy. I'll break their fucking legs."

I blanch, my face draining of colour. "You're insane."

"No. I'm *possessive.* Another ugly attribute to add to your very long list. Get used to it."

Exhaling deeply, I lock eyes with him. I hadn't planned on telling him the truth, but now that he's fired Tomasz, I have no choice. If I could go back and change what happened in the massage suite, I would, but that's impossible, and I can't let Tomasz suffer for my mistake.

"Why are you pretending that this is all on Tomasz, Dalton?" I ask, my fingers gripping the material of my dress beneath the table, needing something to hold onto.

"Because. He. Touched. You," he bites out, pressing his finger into the table roughly with every word.

"He was very professional at all times. He just gave me a massage," I say, pinning him with my gaze. "It was *you* who touched me. It was *you* who took liberties."

"W-what?" Dalton stammers, the blood draining from his face

as he stares at me. It's the first time I've ever truly seen Dalton caught off guard.

"You can't deny it, can you?" I insist. He remains quiet, his jaw clenching, so I continue on. "At first, I thought it *was* Tomasz who returned to the room, but after a while it felt different."

"Different how?" Dalton grinds out, and for the briefest of moments I worry that I'm mistaken, that it wasn't Dalton who stepped into that room after Tomasz left. But when he leans forward in his seat, his gaze piercing mine, I know I'm right.

"A combination of things. You have calluses on the palms of your hands," I whisper, heat flooding my cheeks as I reach across the table and turn his hands over.

"From gripping the handlebars of my motorbike so tightly," he explains, his voice low, controlled, as my fingertip dusts over his warm skin.

"You know, you really should stop racing. It's dangerous," I say, pulling my hands back and cursing myself internally for touching him willingly.

"Are you concerned I might get hurt, Daisy?"

"I'm concerned you might kill someone else," I retort. "Aren't you a little old to be racing motorbikes anyway?"

"So my rough hands gave me away? Good to know," he replies, ignoring my question. "Anything else?"

"Your scent," I confess.

He raises an eyebrow. "My scent?"

"You've been wearing the same aftershave for years," I say, feeling the tension stretch taut between us. "It was unmistakable."

"That's very observant of you, one could assume you're a little obsessed with me," he says pointedly.

"Don't read too much into it, the scent is overpowering. You might want to refrain from dousing yourself in it," I reply snarkily.

"At what point, exactly, did you realise it was me, Daisy?" Dalton asks, the heat in his gaze replacing the earlier anger.

"Does it matter?"

"Of course it matters. You were turned on."

"I was not!" I protest.

"You were moaning."

"I was out of my mind, *clearly*."

"With lust?" he insists.

"With stupidity."

"So why not stop me?"

I flick my gaze away, staring out of the window at the beautiful view, hating that I didn't stop him, that I let him touch me like that, that my decision got Tomasz fired.

"Daisy, why didn't you stop me?" he persists.

"Because I'm an idiot," I offer.

"Daisy," he warns. "Answer me now or so help me—"

"Because I liked it, okay?" I hiss. "Are you happy now? I liked the feel of your hands on me."

"You liked it?" he questions, surprise lighting his eyes. "You like me?"

"That's not what I said. I don't like you like that."

"Yet you allowed me to touch you. You enjoyed it. Explain."

"It's complicated," I admit, pressing my eyes shut as tears prick the back of my eyes.

"So uncomplicate it. Tell me what you mean," he adds, a little softer now.

I force myself to look at him. "Please, Dalton. Don't make this any harder than it already is. I should have stopped you the second I realised it was you. In fact, *you* should never have touched *me*. Why did you?"

"Because I was angry."

"You touched me because you were angry with me?"

"Yes."

I nod, my heart clenching at his honesty. Why do I always end up with men who want to hurt me? Am I really that unloveable?

"And I chose Tomasz to give me a massage because I was angry with you. So I guess we're even," I sneer, shoring up my defences.

"You still haven't answered my question, Daisy. Tell me what you meant about this being complicated. If you want me to touch you, I will touch you."

"You wouldn't understand."

"So you want me to touch you again?" he persists, swiping a hand through his hair in frustration, pointedly ignoring the fact that I've made it clear that I will never have sex with him.

"Stop putting words in my mouth. I meant what I said, I will never sleep with you, Dalton. I still hate you."

"But you'll let a man you hate give you a massage?"

"It was a mistake," I whisper, hating how my stomach coils with anxiety, how tears prick my eyes once more.

It's not that I wanted Dalton's touch per-se, it's just that in the moment it *felt* good. In that moment it felt like the exact opposite to everything I ever experienced as a child from my abusive parents who loved nothing more than to punch and kick me, to be cruel. I crave human contact. It's why I've forgiven so many men for their shitty behaviour. I overlook their flaws, desperate for their affection. So rightly or wrongly, for a few minutes I foolishly let myself submit to Dalton's touch, to his firm but gentle caress, and when he left the room I was so worked up I made myself orgasm, knowing it was wrong even when it felt right.

"The only mistake was me walking out of that room and not making you come," Dalton snaps, as he pushes up from his seat and rounds the table, settling down beside me.

"What are you doing?" I whisper as he rests his hand on my thigh.

"Finishing what I started."

"You can't."

"I can."

"I don't want you too," I say, my chest heaving as his fingers drift towards the hem of my dress, slowly dragging it up my thigh.

"Then stop me," he replies, his lips brushing against my cheek, the heat of his touch burning into my thigh. "Stop me like you should've stopped me yesterday."

"Please, don't do this," I whisper, my voice cracking as I fight that part of me who craves human affection, knowing that this is just some twisted game to Dalton, a power-play on his part.

"You want this," he persists, his fingers edging higher, crackles of electricity erupting between us from his touch.

"You have no idea what I want," I whisper, my breath catching as his fingers reach the top of my stocking.

"Fuck, Daisy, are those stockings you're wearing?" he asks, the gravelly timber of his voice making me shudder.

"Get your hands off me," I insist, hating that my request sounds so feeble.

"If you don't want my hand on you, remove it then," he rasps, his fingers slipping higher.

"I don't want *this*," I whisper, all the while parting my legs.

"Tell me what you want then," he persists, the tip of his nose nudging against that sensitive spot just below my ear as his fingers draw teasing, soft circles so close to my core that I'm left panting.

My eyes drift shut at his touch, and I know, *I know* this shouldn't be happening, but I can't seem to stop him as his fingers graze higher, tantalising close to the apex of my thighs. His lips burn against my skin, lighting me up in a way I wish he wouldn't.

I don't want this. I don't want him... Do I?

"Daisy..." he laments, and the catch in his voice, the *need*, it sends me spiralling.

In this moment I know that the decision I make will determine not just our future, but my own sense of self-worth. I could do what I've always done and ignore the red flags and let him touch me or I could stand up for myself and put an end to this toxic cycle

I always seem to find myself in. With a surge of determination, I push Dalton away.

"I should've stopped you yesterday, but I won't make the same mistake twice," I declare, my heart pounding in my chest as I put much needed space between us. "I deserve better than this, and Tomasz didn't deserve to be fired. Make this right, Dalton."

His nostrils flare, and for a moment I think he's going to ignore my request, but eventually he nods and says, "I will provide him with a substantial severance pay, but I will not offer him his job back. That's the best I can do."

"Thank you." I move to stand but he rests his hand on my arm.

"Will you stay? Eat with me at least?"

"I'm suddenly not very hungry."

"Daisy..." His voice trails off as I shake my head.

"I'm going home. I'll see you Saturday, when it's time to move in."

"Daisy, wait!"

But I'm already heading towards the exit, and this time Dalton doesn't follow.

CHAPTER SIX

Drix and I stand in awkward silence on his driveway as Daisy says her goodbyes to Lia and Toby. I watch as he climbs up into Daisy's arms, and plants an affectionate kiss on her cheek. She hauls him tighter against her, smiling through her tears as she presses kisses against his face. Fuck, the love and affection they share is so alien to me, leaving me feeling confused and uneasy.

Growing up, hugs were never a part of my life. Fuck, *any* form of affection. My father has always been emotionally distant, whilst my mother simply upped and left without looking back as soon as their divorce was finalised when I was eleven years old. I haven't seen her in over twenty years. She's essentially a stranger to me except for the occasional stilted phone call here and there.

"They're going to miss her being around," Drix murmurs, watching the three of them. *"I'll* miss her."

"She's only a ten minute drive away. Nothing's changed," I reply, swiping a hand through my hair, the air fraught between us.

"Everything's changed. You are now responsible for my sister's happiness, are you certain you're up for the challenge?" Drix presses, glancing at me.

Am I? The truthful answer is a definitive, *fuck no*, but I'm not about to admit that if I want to remain conscious, so instead I answer with, "Honestly, I'm not sure." It's about as close to the truth as I can get.

He lets out a bitter laugh. "That's probably the most honest thing you've ever said to me."

"Look, Drix," I begin, eying him cautiously, "I know this isn't what you want for Daisy. It isn't what I want either, but there's nothing I can do to prevent the inevitable. We're getting married in a few weeks with or without your blessing."

"I will be there for Daisy, but I can't give you my blessing."

"I understand," I reply with a nod of my head. "Will you be coming to the engagement party next weekend?"

"I will."

"I appreciate that."

"I'm not doing it for you," he bites back.

In all the years I've been friends with Drix, I don't think we've ever had our friendship tested like this. Sure, we've had disagreements before, but I've never felt like our friendship was ever in question. Until now.

"I want you to know, despite what you think of me, that I *will* do everything in my power to take care of her," I say, knowing that too is a stretching the truth, because whilst I can shower Daisy with expensive gifts, wine and dine her at exclusive restaurants, and whisk her away on holiday to exotic locations, I can't give her what she truly needs and that's emotional support, affection, *love*. I'm just not fucking capable.

Drix shoots me a curious look. There's doubt in his gaze, lingering anger, but there's also a dash of hope, and seeing that makes me feel like a prick. Aside from Sterling and Ben, and the people I race with at the track, he's one of the only people I truly count as a friend, and I hate deceiving him.

"Are you ready to go?" I ask as Daisy steps up to us both, ending our tense conversation.

"I guess," she replies with a small smile, her gaze drifting to Drix.

"Come here," he says roughly, pulling her into his arms and crushing her against his chest.

"As much as I love you, Drix, I can't actually breathe," she laughs after a moment, and he pulls back apologising, a sheepish look on his face which soon turns serious.

Gripping her shoulders, he says, "If at any point it gets to be too much, you come home, okay? No matter the consequences. You come home."

I flinch at the intensity of the unspoken accusations in Drix's tone, but I can't fault him for it. He's protective of Daisy, always has been, and I know he'd willingly suffer the consequences if she were to break the contract.

"I love you," she retorts.

"Love you too," he replies.

With that, she unravels herself from Drix's arms and pulls open the passenger door, shutting it quietly behind her.

"Don't let me down, Dalton," Drix warns.

I can't respond with words, knowing how feeble they'd sound, so instead I give him a terse nod, then twist on my heel and climb into the car too. Moments later we're pulling out of his drive and speeding towards a chaotic future that neither of us can avoid.

Beside me, Daisy sits quietly, her fingers tapping nervously on her thigh as she stares out of the window. The silence between us is thick with uncertainties, and I can't help but steal glances at her from the corner of my eye, taking in her profile against the passing scenery. The winter sun shines through the strands of her unruly curls, illuminating them in a warm glow, and her soft lips are tipped down at the corner as though weighted with her unhappiness.

"You good?" I ask, knowing it's a stupid question as a solitary tear slides down her cheek. Of course she isn't.

She swipes at her face. "I'll be fine," she whispers.

My fingers tighten on the steering wheel, feeling ill-equipped to deal with her emotions as my brain scrambles to come up with something reassuring, but before I can open my mouth she breaks the silence between us.

"I've been thinking about this..."

"This?"

"*Us*, I mean," she corrects, blowing out a tremulous breath.

"Go on," I urge, thankful that I don't have to bluster my way through trying to reassure her that everything is going to be okay when we both know it's going to be a shitstorm.

"I know this isn't what either of us wanted," she begins, her voice steady despite the tears still lingering on her lashes, "But I believe we can at least try to make the best of this situation."

"How?"

"By putting some rules in place, setting some boundaries between us."

"This is about what happened at the spa, isn't it?"

"Partly, and at the restaurant," she adds, eyeing me.

I grit my jaw, nodding. "I overstepped."

What I don't say is that I wanted nothing more than to make her come. I wanted to watch her face flush with pleasure, I wanted to feel her pussy contract around my fingers as she came. I wanted to taste her skin, kiss her lips, fuck her mouth with my tongue. Should I want that? No, absolutely fucking not, would I have risked everything to take it regardless if she hadn't stopped me, emphatically yes.

"But also because I feel we need to make things crystal clear, for both our sakes," she continues on, oblivious to my thoughts.

"We've already signed a contract with a long list of stipulations we must follow, and you want to add even more?" I ask, a tinge of annoyance in my tone.

"This is different. This will be something we can both agree on, an addendum if you will. We've got to find a way to live together, right?"

I nod slowly, processing her words. Maybe she's right. Maybe setting some boundaries will help us to navigate this unconventional arrangement. Then again, I'm not particularly good at respecting someone's boundaries, that much is clear already. Still, I humour her.

"Okay, I'm listening," I say, stealing another glance at her. "What do you have in mind?"

"First off," she begins, her voice gaining confidence with every moment that passes, "We need to communicate, no matter how difficult or awkward it might feel. Agreed?"

"I'll try," I offer, knowing that's about as likely as me ripping up the contract and living the rest of my life as a pauper.

"Dalton…"

"Okay, we communicate. Got it. What else?" I say, fixing my gaze back on the road ahead.

"Secondly," she continues, "We respect each other's personal space. We're going to be spending a lot of time together, so it's important we give each other room to breathe."

"Understood."

"And finally," she says, her voice softening. "I also think we should try to find some common ground."

"Common ground?" I question, slamming my foot against the brakes as a reckless driver suddenly swerves in front of us.

Daisy lurches forward, and I throw my arm out instinctively even though she's buckled in. The other driver has the nerve to curse at us before speeding away in the opposite direction. I give him the middle finger as he passes.

"Seriously, can no one drive properly around here?!"

"Jesus," Daisy exclaims, eyes wide.

"What a prick," I add, scowling. "You okay?"

"You seem to be asking me that a lot lately," she retorts, cocking her head to the side as she studies me.

"Contrary to popular belief, I'm not a *complete* arsehole," I say before pulling off once more. She throws me an incredulous look. "Only ninety-nine point nine percent of the time?"

"So you were saying?" I counter, bristling.

Daisy clears her throat before continuing. "I thought we could try and figure out some activities or interests that we could both enjoy doing together. It might make this arrangement more bearable if we can share some positive experiences."

"Positive experiences? This isn't a therapeutic experiment."

"Yes, positive experiences," she persists.

"The only activities I enjoy are racing my motorbike and fucking," I comment wryly. "I know fucking's off the menu."

"We've already established that," she confirms evenly.

"And I'm pretty sure you're not interested in watching me race."

"I never said that," she argues.

"So you'll come to the track?"

"If that's what you want."

"Maybe," I reply, noncommittally. Frankly, she'll probably serve as more of a distraction than anything else. "So what do you like to do?"

She thinks for a moment, chewing on her bottom lip. "I like to draw."

"You draw? What, like landscapes or people or something?"

"Well, more like clothing," she admits. "Though I am known to decorate my own wrapping paper with silly doodles. Drix has kept every single sheet of wrapping paper I've decorated with my art since we were kids."

I raise a curious brow. "I didn't know that."

She shrugs. "Well, now you do."

"So you design outfits?" I ask.

"Don't sound so surprised. I like fashion, I thought that was obvious."

"You like *colour*..."

"Are you saying I have no fashion sense?" she asks, her tone a little defensive.

"You definitely stand out in a crowd," I comment, side-eyeing her turquoise jeans and yellow puffer jacket ensemble.

Daisy rolls her eyes. "At least I'm not boring."

"You're far from boring, Daisy," I concede, indicating right before pulling onto the private, mile long drive that leads to my home, Highwood Manor Estate. "But hey, who am I to judge? Fashion's subjective, right?"

"Yeah, it is," Daisy agrees. "I guess we can add 'respecting each other's personal style' to our list of agreements."

"I can get behind that. Are there any other secret hobbies you have that I should know about?" I ask.

"I think you're aware of my other hobby."

"Are you referring to that obscene collection of unicorn figurines?"

"Yep."

"What is it with you and Drix and your obsession with toys anyway? I can think of a million things I'd rather collect than plastic figurines."

Daisy's expression falls at my words. "I guess never having parents who could afford, or even want to buy you toys will do that to you," she says softly, her tone heavy with emotion.

"I'm sorry, I didn't think."

"It's fine," she brushes off my apology with a wave of her hand, turning to look out of the window as we drive up to the imposing manor that I call home.

Highwood Manor Estate has been owned by our family for

generations. Nestled among thirty acres of vibrant greenery, springtime is especially magical here when the gardens burst with colourful blooms and the lawns are meticulously maintained. I used to love getting lost in the maze as a child, sometimes taking hours to find my way out. The manor also boasts luxurious amenities like a swimming pool, ballroom, gym, spa, and even a private cinema room. And let's not forget the helipad and garage filled with antique cars and motorcycles. Despite living under the same roof, I rarely see my father unless it's for our regular business discussions; that's just how grand this estate is.

"So here we are," I say, putting the car into park, and turning off the engine.

"Here we are," she agrees, chewing on her lip.

"I'll show you to your suite," I say, stepping out of the car and heading towards the front door. When she doesn't step into stride next to me, I turn to find her opening the boot of the car. "What are you doing?"

"What does it look like? I'm getting my suitcase," she replies.

"We have staff for that. Leave it, come with me."

"It's fine, I've got it," she replies, the suitcase dropping to the gravel driveway with a thud.

"Here let me," I say, jogging towards her and grabbing the suitcase.

"Thanks," she mutters, smothering a smile as I grimace at the weight of it.

"What have you got in here anyway?" I ask.

"You didn't think I'd leave without my collection of unicorns, did you?" she deadpans.

"You're kidding right?"

She shakes her head, her lips quivering in a smile. "Of course I am, I can't imagine Carl letting me display them next to his priceless antiques, can you?"

"God forbid," I agree, shaking my head at the idea.

Once inside, I point out the various rooms on the way to her suite situated in the west wing of the manor. She walks silently beside me, offering smiles and soft hello's to the staff we pass by.

"Are all your staff so—"

"Polite?"

"No, *quiet*. Aren't they allowed to talk?"

"They're paid to do a job, not to pass the time with idle chatter."

Daisy raises her brows. "I see."

Eventually we reach her suite, and I prop open the door with her suitcase. "Dinner will be at eight. I'll let you settle in."

She doesn't reply right away. Instead, she steps into the room, her mouth gaping as she casts her gaze around. "This is... *beautiful.*"

"What were you expecting, a box room with a dirty mattress on the floor?"

"What did you just say?" she asks, her voice tight as she whips her head around to look at me.

"I was joking, Daisy," I reply, holding my hands up in surrender.

Something flickers behind her eyes, and despite her shoulders relaxing, I can't help but wonder why my words seemed to have triggered such a reaction. I bench that thought for later.

"Of course you were," she mumbles, stepping further into the suite as she takes in her new surroundings.

The suite itself offers luxury and refinement, with no expense spared. The walls are adorned with intricate floral patterned wallpaper, hand-painted with gold accents that catch the natural light streaming through the huge arched windows that overlook the gardens. To the left of the four poster bed, which is draped in cream silk curtains, sits a plush, dusky pink, chaise lounge. Opposite the bed is an ornate reading nook filled with leather-bound books and a mahogany writing desk, its surface polished and shiny, as well as a sitting area graced with a huge sofa that is comfortable enough to sleep on. A marble fireplace frames an open fire that's crackling in the grate, filling the room with a comforting warmth.

"There's an ensuite bathroom through there," I say, pointing towards a door on the far side of the suite. "It has a bathtub, but if you prefer to shower, then just along the hall is another bathroom."

"This is..." Daisy stammers.

"Your home now," I finish for her.

She nods. "My clothes?"

"Already hung up in your dressing room," I explain, pointing to another door situated to the left of the reading nook. "I had our staff prepare everything for you so you could just relax."

"Thank you."

"Well, I'll leave you to it. Dinner will be held in the parlour in the east wing."

"Okay," she replies with a nod.

"Would you like me to put your suitcase in the dressing room?" I ask. "I can send someone to unpack for you."

She shakes her head, pulling off her coat. "No, I can manage."

"Okay. See you later." I twist on my heel, about to leave.

"Sure... Oh, and Dalton?"

"Yes?" I question, turning to face her once again.

"Where is your room?"

"A little further down the corridor," I reply. "Why do you ask?"

She flicks her gaze away. "No reason."

As I make my way to my own suite, I can't help but feel a twinge of guilt from our earlier conversation about her and Drix's fixation with collecting toys. It only serves to remind me of my own privileged childhood, where I was given everything I wanted but lacked any emotional connection with my parents. I guess in that respect we are more alike than I'd care to admit.

CHAPTER SEVEN

"I trust that you've settled in, Daisy?" Carl asks me from the head of the table, his steely gaze resting on mine as he clicks his fingers at one of his staff, presumably to clear away his plate.

He's such an arsehole.

We've just finished eating food fine enough to be served in any Michelin star restaurant, and whilst it was delicious, I would've much rather spent the time gouging my own eyes out than be in the company of a man who clearly has zero respect for his staff, even less for me. Pretty sure he was oblivious to my presence for the duration given he barely looked at me, let alone tried to converse until now.

"I have. *Thank you*," I add, smiling up at the maid who takes my plate, because even if he can't be courteous, I can.

"Excellent," he replies, his eyes dropping to my bright green sweater with the words: *Be a unicorn in a field full of horses,* printed across the front. "You might want to reconsider your choice of outfit next time we sit down to eat dinner together."

"What's wrong with my outfit?" I ask, my overly sweet tone tinged with warning.

"It's... tasteless," he says with a sneer.

"Father, that's enough!" Dalton snaps, but I shake my head at him.

I can fight my own battles, thank you very much. Besides, it was only a few days ago that he was commenting negatively about my clothes too. Like father, like son, I guess.

"It's *comfortable*, and I happen to like this sweater. Besides, why be boring when you can stand out in the crowd?" I question, eyeing his black shirt and dark grey, tailored trousers. He might not like my taste in clothes, but he's going to have to suck it up, because I'm not changing who I am to suit him.

"Our image is important," Carl counters, taking a sip of his expensive wine. "We wouldn't want people to get the wrong impression of us now, would we?"

His condescending tone grates on me, but I refuse to let him see it. "And what impression might that be?" I ask pointedly.

"People judge you on how you present yourself, and if they're judging you, they're judging *us*," he replies, as he leans forward, his gaze locking on to mine.

I take a deep breath, before responding as calmly as I can muster in the moment. "And what does my outfit say about me? That I'm an individual and unafraid to stand out? If that's the case, then I'm good with that."

Carl's nostril's flare. "You need to understand the importance of image to this family. This," he says, waving his hand in my general direction, "Is not becoming of the future wife of one of the most eligible bachelors in the United Kingdom."

"Perhaps you should've thought about that before you offered me the *position*," I snap back, not giving two shits that there is still a member of staff in the room. Her eyes widen, and Carl notices.

"Out!" he demands before turning back to face me, a storm brewing in his eyes. Opposite, Dalton shifts uncomfortably, a muscle feathering in his jaw. "Out of respect for your father, I will give you some grace, but do not push me, Daisy," Carl continues. "I will not tolerate you mentioning this arrangement again in front of our staff. Fortunately for you they've all signed an NDA. Regardless, you will keep yourself in check."

I bite the inside of my cheek, to prevent myself from telling Carl to go fuck himself, and nod my head in agreement, realising that I could jeopardise Drix's happiness if this arrangement were to somehow get out. That doesn't mean I have to accept his shitty behaviour though.

"Good. This Saturday evening is your engagement party. It's a black tie event with a black and white theme. I expect you to be dressed accordingly given we have over two hundred guests attending."

"Of course it is. It's as though you're allergic to colour," I mutter.

"It's classic, sophisticated and perfectly fitting."

"Yes, if you're attending a *funeral*," I can't help but say. "Though I suppose it's apt. Being tied to this family *is* the death of my happiness after all."

"I suggest you curb your attitude, young lady, or we may have a problem," Carl adds.

"I think you've made your point," Dalton interrupts, his voice low and controlled.

Standing up from my seat, I meet Carl's challenging stare head-on. "I am not some doll you can dress up to fit your idea of perfection," I declare, my voice steady despite the adrenaline coursing through my veins. "And I certainly won't be moulded into your narrow-minded image of what a perfect wife should be."

Carl's jaw tightens, his face turning a dangerous shade of red as he rises from his chair, towering over me. "You forget your place," he seethes, his voice a low growl. But I stand my ground, refusing to cower.

"I know *exactly* where I stand," I retort, my tone unwavering.

"And it's certainly not beneath you or anyone else who seeks to control me."

With that I stride from the room, letting the door slam shut behind me. As I drag in a steadying breath, I hear raised voices from inside the dining room.

"You had better get her in line, Dalton! I will not have her embarrass us," Carl shouts.

"Daisy is a free spirit, always has been. I can no more control her, than I can the fucking weather," Dalton responds angrily.

"You're a Gunn, you *will* get her in line."

I don't bother to listen to anymore, instead I stride off down the corridor, fuming.

"Daisy, wait!" Dalton calls, his footsteps echoing down the hall as he chases after me a moment later.

"He's a complete jerk!" I seethe as Dalton catches up, his fingers wrapping around my elbow.

"I agree, he was out of line," Dalton says, cupping my other elbow as I turn to face him.

"I will not change who I am to suit him. I'm giving up enough of my happiness already!"

Dalton nods. "I will speak with him tomorrow once he's had a chance to calm down."

"You really think he's going to listen to you?" I scoff, shaking my head.

"If he wants to ensure that he has access to his grandchild when he or she is born then he's going to need to respect you, quirky clothes and all," he replies, dropping his gaze to my sweater. If I didn't know any better I swear there was humour in his gaze, acceptance even.

"I'm surprised you didn't agree with him. I know you don't like what I wear."

"I never said that," he replies, his hands dropping from my elbows as he tugs at the hem of my sweater.

I lift my brows. "What did you say to me the other night? Wasn't it, *I prefer sophistication over a circus?*"

"I did, and it was wrong. I apologise," he says, meeting my gaze.

I nod, accepting his apology even if I don't entirely believe he means it. "I'm sorry for saying that you looked like you stepped through a storm cloud. Even if it was true."

Dalton's lips quirk up into a smile. "And there's me thinking I was looking suave."

"A bit of colour wouldn't go amiss," I offer.

"What would you suggest?" he asks.

I hitch a brow. "You really want to know?"

"I wouldn't have asked if I didn't. Go on, enlighten me."

I look up at him, chewing on my lip as I consider his question. "You have nice eyes, so something to bring out the shade. A royal blue, perhaps?"

"You think I have nice eyes?"

"Don't let it go to your head, Dalton. It's just an observation."

His chuckle fills the hallway, a sound that warms me towards him more than I'd care to admit.

"So, royal blue it is then. Any other colour suggestions?"

"I think that'll do for now. Got to ease you in slowly before I start suggesting cerise pink or coral."

"Not in a million years. I'll leave those colours to you," he replies, a horrified look on his face that soon fades as we stand in awkward silence, having run out of things to say. "So what now?"

"I'm pretty beat after all the excitement," I reply. "I just want to watch some trash TV and switch off for a while.".

"Can I join you?"

"*You* want to watch trash TV?" I ask, aghast. "Aren't you more interested in counting your piles of money or watching porn?"

"Porn could be classed as trash TV, I suppose," he muses. "Though that really depends on the calibre of porn you're watching. Sounds like you haven't been watching the right kind."

I wrinkle my nose. "I'll leave that to you, thanks."

"So you're a prude?"

"I am *not*," I protest. "I just happen to prefer my imagination, if that's all the same to you."

"Whatever floats your boat," he smirks. "We have a cinema room in the basement that's quite comfortable."

"A cinema room? Of course you do," I reply, blowing out a breath.

"And with high definition, *and* surround sound, it makes watching porn all the more... *intimate*," he adds with a smirk.

"I bet you just *love* that, Mr I-Can't-Keep-It-In-My-Pants," I retort.

Another laugh bubbles up his throat as I pull a face. It's not as if I haven't watched porn before despite what I just said, but I don't ever intend on watching any with Dalton Gunn, thanks very much. Can't have him getting any ideas. Not that he'll need any. I'm pretty sure Dalton is the type of man to film a sex tape. He's probably got a whole raft of them to keep him occupied for the entirety of our marriage.

"So... Trash TV instead then?"

"Fine," I huff, glad at least for the change of subject. "Lead the way, but be warned, my taste in TV shows is questionable at best."

"Drix has told me as much," Dalton replies, his hand briefly pressing against my lower back as he guides me along the hallway. "Pretty sure he said you binged watched an entire series of *Bikers with Tats* in one afternoon."

"What can I say, I'm partial to a biker with tattoos," I retort with a shrug.

"Then aren't you lucky you're engaged to one," he replies, smirking as my cheeks flush a deep pink.

"You're not *that* type of biker," I counter.

"I ride motorbikes. I have tattoos," he points out, opening a door to his left that leads to a stairwell into the basement. "I think that qualifies."

"You also live in an obnoxious mansion big enough to house the entire town, drink Veuve Clicquot like it's water, and own most of the businesses in Princetown."

"Minor details."

Five minutes later we're seated next to each other on the plush leather recliners sipping sparkling water and watching a reality TV show about aspiring designers battling it out in a high-pressure fashion house. When the first episode comes to an end, Dalton reaches for the remote control and pauses the screen.

"So when did your interest in fashion start?" he asks, shifting in his seat to face me.

"You really want to know?"

"We're supposed to be communicating, right? I'm communicating."

"I guess."

"So..." he prompts, folding his arms across his chest as he waits.

"I fell in love with fashion when Hubert took me to a children's clothing store the first week me and Drix moved in with him. Neither of us had much when we arrived, apart from the hand-me-down clothes we were provided with by our foster parents."

He winces at that, and his reaction makes my stomach coil with anxiety. I'm not ashamed of the fact I was adopted or the fact I was poor, it just serves to remind me how different we truly are.

"Go on," he encourages.

"I remember walking into the store and being so overwhelmed by all the colourful outfits," I explain, smiling softly at the memory. "We were there for hours."

"I can imagine Drix *enjoying* that," Dalton says with a smirk.

"He hated every minute, but me, I was in heaven."

"So that started your obsession with fashion?"

"With colour, actually. It wasn't so much the clothes, although they were lovely. It was the vibrancy, the patterns, the way bright colours made me feel when I was wearing them."

"And how did they make you feel?" he asks, looking at me curiously.

"Happy," I respond honestly. "Colour makes me happy."

"Why?" Dalton asks.

I chew on my lip, dropping my gaze as I debate whether to tell him the truth. "It's not really important," I lie, knowing that I'm not ready to go there, that I may never be. Dalton might be trying to make an effort here, but I don't trust him enough with my truth. I don't think that I ever will.

"It's important to me to know what makes you happy," he counters.

"Why?"

He regards me for a moment, a frown pulling together his brows. "Because if I know what makes you happy I can earn some brownie points when I get you the perfect gift for your birthday coming up in a few months," he eventually responds. "Got to make sure my future wife has everything she needs."

"Right," I reply, unable to hide my disappointment as I flick my gaze away and stare at the screen in front of us, feeling let down by his response.

Dalton seems to think that he can buy my happiness, that material possessions will somehow make up for the emotional distance between us. What he doesn't understand is that what I truly crave is a deep bond that goes beyond expensive gifts and extravagant gestures. I would happily choose a modest life with someone I love over a lavish one full of gifts but lacking any real love and connection.

Silence expands between us, and I can feel the heat of his stare as he looks at me. "Daisy, what did I say?" he asks, reaching for me, his fingertips brushing against my arm.

"Exactly what I expected. I'm going to bed. Enjoy the rest of your evening, Dalton," I retort, pushing upright and striding towards the door.

He rises to his feet, following me. "Daisy, talk to me," he persists, gripping my arm.

I shake off his touch, feeling a surge of frustration and hurt bubbling within me as I turn to face him. "There's nothing to talk about," I reply, my voice sharp and final.

His eyes widen in surprise, clearly taken aback by my sudden change in demeanour, but despite everything I said earlier in the car, I can't bring myself to explain why I'm reacting the way I am. How can I tell him that I love colour because I was kept locked up in a dark room for the first five years of my life? That my birth parents treated me so badly that I can't sleep without a light on, that his comment earlier about sleeping on a dirty mattress was dangerously close to a truth that haunts me still, or that his father's reaction to my choice of clothing shook the foundations of the carefully constructed walls I've built to protect myself.

"You wanted us to be open and honest, and yet here you are doing the exact opposite," he protests. "I'm trying here."

"Are you though?" I ask, still feeling as though this is all just his way of paying lip service to my request to communicate. I'm not confident that he really means it, that he would actually care enough to listen and process my story, to empathise even.

"I wouldn't be sitting here watching shitty reality TV shows if I wasn't!" he snaps back.

"I didn't ask you to join me," I reply, just as heatedly.

"You said you wanted us to find some common ground," he reminds me. "Or has that conveniently slipped your memory too?"

I heave out a sigh, feeling suddenly heavy with sadness. "Look, I don't want to fight. I just want to go to bed."

"You don't want to fight?" he replies with a scoff. "I'm pretty sure that arguing with me is at the top of the list of things you like to do to piss me off."

"This isn't about pissing you off," I whisper.

"Then what the hell is it? One minute we're having a conversation, then the next you're storming off like a goddamn child!"

"I just..."

"What, Daisy?" he prompts, scowling at me.

"I just really need to sleep. It's been a long day."

He stares at me, frustration evident in his eyes as he processes my words. After a tense moment, he lets out a breath, running a hand through his hair in exasperation.

"Fine," he mutters, his tone filled with a mixture of anger and resignation.

Too tired to engage further, I turn on my heel and make my way back towards my bedroom. When I enter, the bed sheets have been turned down, and the soft glow of the bedside lamp illuminates the room as I remove my clothes and slip under the covers.

Despite my exhaustion, sleep eludes me and I toss and turn, my mind replaying the tense exchange with Dalton. Minutes stretch into hours before I hear the creak of the bedroom door opening. Pressing my eyes shut, I feign sleep, instantly aware of Dalton's presence, his familiar cologne giving him away. Keeping my breathing even, I remain still with my eyes pressed shut, hoping that's enough to convince him that I'm deep asleep.

"I promised Drix I'd take care of you, and I'm already fucking it up," he whispers, his tone laced with remorse as he sits down on the edge of the bed.

The vulnerability in his voice tugs at something deep within me, stirring up a conflict of emotions. I almost open my eyes, but when he leans over and brushes a strand of hair off my face, his fingers lingering on my cheek, I keep them shut.

"Sleep well, Daisy," he says, and a moment later he's gone.

CHAPTER EIGHT

"I'm terribly sorry, Sir, Madam. I'm happy to provide you with complimentary meals in our restaurant for the remainder of your stay," Daisy says to the couple standing before her at the reception desk at the hotel a few days later.

My footsteps still, hidden by the large marble pillar that brackets either side of the reception area. I listen in on the conversation taking place between Daisy and the disgruntled couple glaring at her.

"That's not good enough, my husband and I expect our suite to be spotless, and our dry cleaning to be delivered in a timely manner. This is supposed to be a five-star hotel. Quite frankly, what you're offering as compensation is ludicrous," the snobbish woman replies, her nose lifting in the air as though she's smelt something she doesn't like.

"There was a *slight* misunderstanding with regards to when you'd need your dry cleaning returned, so I took the liberty of delivering it personally to the laundry team," Daisy replies. "It will be ready within the hour and returned to your room in good time for this evening's event. I have also inspected your suite myself, and I'm happy to say that it is spotless. As for your disappoint-ment, I'm offering you complimentary meals, to include alcohol, for the remainder of your stay," Daisy persists, her smile widening as she tries to hide the glint of annoyance in her eyes.

"Regardless, we are regular patrons of this hotel and as I've already explained, we are *very* good friends with the hotel owner, Carl Gunn. I'm sure he would be disgusted at the lack of customer service provided, as well as the very apparent disregard of our complaint," the woman's husband says, a man who I do not recog-nise, and given his apparent friendship with my father, I probably should. Either he's lying, or he is a newly acquired *friend* that I haven't yet had the displeasure to meet.

Daisy turns her attention to the man. "I'm sorry you *still* feel disappointed with the service you've received despite myself and my team members ensuring that your complaints have been listened to and any issues you have raised, rectified."

"Are you suggesting that we're being difficult?" the woman asks.

"Not at all," Daisy replies, her voice saccharine.

I know her well enough to know she's losing her patience fast, and as she opens her mouth to continue, I step out from behind the pillar and stride towards them.

"What seems to be the problem?" I ask.

"And who might you be?" the woman replies, her lips pursed as I approach.

"I am the manager of the hotel, Dalton *Gunn*," I explain, as Daisy mutters something indistinguishable under her breath. "Though given you know my father so well, I'd assume you'd already know that."

The couple's attitude instantly changes upon hearing my name, and dare I say it, the man looks more than a little uncomfort-able, telling me that he does not in fact know my father at all.

"Mr Gunn, it's a pleasure to meet you," the man says, holding his hand out to shake.

I take it, making sure to squeeze his hand tight. "And your name?" I ask, releasing him.

"Geoffrey Sinclair. This is my wife Octavia."

"Geoffrey and Octavia Sinclair?" I question, pausing for a moment as I pretend to recollect their names. "And did I hear you correctly when you said that you're both *very* good friends with my father?"

"I—" Geoffrey begins, but I cut him off.

"Which is interesting because I don't think I have ever heard him mention either of you."

Out of the corner of my eye I see Daisy smother a smile, her eyes widening at my very obvious ploy to catch them in their lie. There's nothing more that I hate than someone name dropping to gain special treatment.

Geoffrey clears his throat uncomfortably, exchanging a quick glance with his wife before plastering a fake smile back on his face. "My wife and I attend the same golf club as your father, have done so now for years," he stammers, beads of sweat forming on his brow.

"Golf club? My father hasn't played golf for at least ten years, he's been too busy building a billion pound empire," I counter, folding my arms across my chest and arching a brow. "Interesting then how close you are with him," I add.

"It must've slipped his mind mentioning us, but we do appreciate all your efforts to make things right, Mr Gunn," Octavia interjects smoothly whilst her husband turns a deep shade of red.

"I have made no effort at all, but Daisy clearly has. In fact, as far as I can tell she has bent over backwards to assist you, and I think what would be appropriate right now is for both of you to thank her for all her efforts, then graciously accept her rather *generous* offer of complimentary meals in our five star restaurant for the remainder of your stay."

"Well... I... This is most—" Octavia blusters, her face draining of colour.

"Awkward?" I finish for her.

Geoffrey and Octavia exchange nervous glances, clearly caught in their web of lies. I glance at Daisy who stands silently behind the desk, a mix of amusement and satisfaction flickering in her eyes.

"Well?" I persist, not letting them get away with their rudeness.

"Thank you, Daisy, we appreciate what you have done for us," Geoffrey mumbles.

I stare at Octavia until she gives her apology too. "Thank you," she says tightly.

"Excellent, have a good day," I retort, turning my attention away from them as they both scurry off.

As soon as they are out of earshot, Daisy bursts into laughter, unable to contain her amusement for a moment longer. "That was well played," she giggles, but her smile falters when I glare at her. "What?"

"How often have you been offering freebies to arseholes who pretend to know my father?"

She blanches. "Are you seriously getting angry at me for trying to manage this situation in a professional manner? Would you have preferred it if I told them to fuck off and take their business elsewhere?" she replies, bristling.

"Of course I don't expect you to tell them to 'fuck-off', Daisy, but I will not tolerate people trying to manipulate freebies with lies."

"And somehow their behaviour is my fault? I'm just doing my job," she hisses as the lobby door swings open with new arrivals checking in. "What's that saying, the *customer* is always right?"

"You don't need to bend over backward for those kinds of people who think dropping my father's name will get them special treatment. This is a business, not a free-for-all," I counter, not sure why I'm pissed off with her given she's done nothing but try to handle the situation diplomatically.

"And how, *exactly*, should I have handled the situation?" she presses, folding her arms across her chest.

"How about running it by me first?"

"I tried to. I sent an email earlier today when the complaint first came to my attention, and I also tried calling you, but you didn't respond to that either. I had to make an executive decision."

"You're not in a position to make an *executive* decision," I retort sharply. "You man the reception, not run the bloody hotel."

"Why are you being such an arsehole?" she snaps, her eyes flicking to the people approaching.

"In future, make sure you come to me first," I snap, striding off towards my office wondering why the fuck I'm so angry.

AN HOUR later I hear a knock at my door. "Come in," I say, my eyes fixed on my computer screen, not bothering to look up.

"What the hell was that all about earlier?"

My head snaps up as Daisy steps into my office, slamming the door behind her. She's clearly not gotten over our earlier interaction given the furious glint in her eye, but rather than give her an apology for acting the way I did, I find myself narrowing my eyes at her, enjoying her anger a little bit too much. It's always been fun to push her buttons, and even though I know I shouldn't, I can't help myself. After last night and the way she cut our conversation short, it's the least she deserves.

"It's not your break time yet," I say, folding my arms across my chest and leaning back in my chair, eyeing her.

"Since when did you pay attention to when I have my break times?"

"Since the moment I took over running this hotel. It's my job to know where my staff are at any given point in the day."

"Oh, don't get your knickers in a twist, I've swapped my break with Samantha," she retorts just as sharply as she takes a seat opposite me. "So?"

"So what?"

"So why were you a complete dicksplash earlier?"

"Firstly, what the hell kind of cuss is 'dicksplash', and secondly, I told you why I was pissed off. I don't like you making decisions like that without my approval, and especially not to people who name drop. We're a business—"

"That was called customer service," she snaps, cutting me off. "It's my job to resolve issues."

"Your job is to check people in and man the reception area," I remind her.

"*And* to deal with customer complaints, but I don't expect you to know that given you've never taken an interest in my role before now."

"I stand corrected, but in future leave those kinds of decisions to me."

She huffs out an angry breath. "What's really the issue here? Are you still pissed at me for not wanting to talk last night?"

"No," I lie, hating the way she's so easily able to read me.

"Because if that's the case then just say so, and stop acting like a—"

"Dicksplash?" I offer, my eyes narrowing on her.

"I was actually going to say *twat*, but given you're being both it really doesn't matter either way."

"If you're just going to sit here and insult me, then you can leave."

"If you're just going to ignore the fact that you acted out of line, I think I'll stay until you apologise, thank you very much!" she counters, her voice rising in frustration.

"You'll be waiting a very long time," I retort, turning my attention back to the screen.

"I don't understand you," she says, throwing her hands up in the air.

"There's nothing to understand," I reply with a shrug. "I'm your boss, and what I say goes."

"Fine, you need to have final say on how I choose to accommodate unhappy guests, I hear you loud and clear, but that isn't what I meant, and you know it!"

"I don't," I reply, leaning forward on my desk. "Care to enlighten me?"

"Dalton!" she snaps, but despite the anger in her voice, it's the way her eyes glisten with tears, which she furiously blinks away, that keeps my attention. "I don't understand why you would get those arseholes to apologise to me, and then treat me with the same contempt. Make it make sense."

Dragging in a deep breath, I pinch the bridge of my nose. She's right. If I were in her shoes, I'd be fucking confused, and angry, too. "Look, it just threw me, that's all."

"What, the fact they pretended to know your father?"

"No, the way they spoke to you. It pissed me off." I admit, surprising myself with the confession, because up until right now I didn't actually realise that was the issue. I thought I was still pissed off about her reaction last night, but I see now that's not the case.

"You've got a funny way of showing it."

"It's the truth," I admit.

The way they looked down on her, like she was shit on their shoe, angered me, just like the way my father spoke to her last night pissed me off. Both times I let her down. Instead of telling those arseholes to get the fuck out of the hotel, I'd allowed them to give her a half-hearted apology and keep their fucking freebie. I was more angry at myself than her, and rather than explain that, I took my anger out on the one person who didn't deserve it because I'm incapable of communicating my feelings.

"And yet you spoke to me in the exact same way," she points out, shaking her head in frustration. "Can you see why I might be confused?"

"I was out of line, I'm sorry. There, feel better?" I offer.

Jesus fuck, I can't even apologise without being an arsehole.

"Not particularly, no."

"What do you want me to say?" I question.

"I want you to communicate with me because you aren't making any sense!"

"Like you communicated with me last night?"

"So this *is* about last night?" she counters, huffing again.

"It has shit all to do with that. I'm just making a point." Again, another lie, because it is, partly.

"Whatever you say," she grumbles.

"I didn't like how they treated you, and I'm sorry I treated you poorly too. I'm sorry. Okay?"

Yep, still an arsehole.

"You know what, forget about it. I'll go back to work *checking people in, and manning the reception area,*" she says with more than a little sarcasm, "And you can go back to..." Her voice trails off as she waves her hand at my computer screen. "Whatever it is you're doing."

Pushing up from her seat she strides to the door, and as her hand wraps around the door handle, I say, "Daisy, wait."

"What, Dalton?" she snaps, her voice dripping with venom. "Are you going to tell me how you promised Drix that you'll take care of me like you did last night like a fucking creeper when you came into my bedroom? Because I can tell you that you're doing a terrible job at it."

My face drains of colour as I struggle to find the words to defend myself. "You were awake last night?"

"Yes, and I can also tell you that you *are* fucking up your attempts to take care of me. For a brief moment back there I thought you'd turned over a new leaf until you messed it all up," she adds with a bitter laugh. "How could I ever think that you of all people could change? You've spent your whole life treating people just like that couple treated me."

"Why didn't you say something?"

"I just did?!" she shouts in frustration.

"I'm talking about being awake last night, Daisy."

"Probably for the same reason you're not telling me everything now," she retorts, her voice laced with bitterness.

"And why's that?" I ask, feeling a knot form in my stomach. A knot that has no business twisting up my guts.

"Because I think we can both agree that we can't trust each other with anything, let alone the *truth*," she spits out, before yanking open the door and storming out.

CHAPTER NINE

"It's good to see you, Daisy," Daphne, the owner of The Rock Cafe, says as she plops down in the seat opposite me, fanning herself.

"Are you okay, you look a little flushed?" I ask, taking a sip of my Earl Gray tea as I look across at my friend.

"It's been a very busy day, that's all. Luckily for this old woman, the lunch time rush is well and truly over," she replies, the lines around her eyes deepening as she smiles.

"You really need to get some help. You work too hard," I reply, reaching over and patting her hand as I glance over at the couple seated at the back of the café. Fortunately for me they've already been served and are deep in conversation, which is a good thing because I could really use some of Daphne's advice right now.

She waves away my concern. "I haven't got any children of my own to fuss over, so I like keeping busy. How are you anyway? Settling in with Dalton, okay?"

"So you've heard?" I ask, knowing that Drix must've told her about my new arrangement given he loves Daphne as much as I do. As an old friend of Hubert's, she's been a constant in our lives, and ever since he passed away we've both spent a lot of time in her cafe, not just because she makes delicious food and neither of us can cook all that well, but because she's such a kind woman.

"Drix might've mentioned something," she replies.

"How much has he mentioned exactly?" I ask, lowering my voice.

"That you're engaged to be married, and that you've moved into the Gunn mansion."

"And..." I press, knowing she's aware of more.

"I know it all, Daisy, and I have to tell you, whilst I understand your decision to marry Dalton, I think you're making a mistake."

"Believe me that thought has crossed my mind on several occasions," I reply, blowing out a breath. She opens her mouth to speak, but I already know what she's going to say, so I cut her off with a shake of my head. "But I'm not changing my mind. I'm doing this for Drix and Lia. Besides, there really is no going back now."

She gives me one of her looks, but she refrains from saying anything further, which I'm grateful for because right now I'm feeling especially vulnerable given everything that's happened these past few days.

"You have always been a kind girl, and I know that what you're doing is an act of love for your brother," Daphne says, patting my hand comfortingly before leaning in closer, her voice barely above a whisper. "But I also know Carl Gunn, and he's a cruel man, Daisy. He uses people and discards them as soon as he gets what he wants. He conducts his personal life in the exact same way as he conducts his business dealings, and that is viciously with little regard for anyone but himself."

"I'm well aware of the kind of man Carl is, and I know what I've gotten myself into," I add, trying to reassure her, but failing given the look she gives me.

"And I've known Carl as long as I knew your father, God rest his soul, and he has chewed up and spit out three wives and count-less women over the years. And as for Dalton..." Her voice trails off as she shakes her head.

"It's alright, you can say what's on your mind, because I doubt very much what you think of him is any different to what I think of him. He's a clone of his father."

"Carl would like to think so, I'm sure," Daphne says. "But Dalton is more like his mother than he realises."

"You knew her?"

"I've lived in Princetown my whole life. I have served many people in this café, and I've learned a lot of things. Dalton's mother was a lovely woman."

"I don't think I've ever heard Dalton say anything kind about his mother. Anything at all, come to think of it."

"She left when he was a young boy, that can't have been easy on him," Daphne says, and I nod, mulling that over. "And I suspect his father hasn't encouraged their relationship in any way. I'd bet my retirement nest-egg that man has made it very difficult for her to have any contact with her son."

"You think he's somehow stopped her from seeing him?"

"I think Carl Gunn is capable of many deplorable things."

"Wow. That's... *horrid*."

"What I can tell you is that the Claudine I knew was sweet and kind, but unfortunately not very strong emotionally. At least not strong enough to stand up against Carl Gunn."

"Well, I can tell you that Dalton doesn't take after his mother," I point out. "Frankly, he's a jerk."

"I'm sure he can be, but I wasn't talking about that part," she says, squeezing my hand, before resting back against her seat.

"You're saying he's not emotionally strong?" I can't help but laugh. "Dalton *doesn't have* any emotions unless you include vanity. In fact he excels at being vain. The man *loves* himself. He's cocky, arrogant, self-centred, selfish—"

"And why do you think he might be vain?" Daphne asks, cutting off my tirade.

"Because he has an ego the size of the moon, and he thinks he's God's gift to women."

"Vain people are very often insecure, Daisy. They seek attention, validation and admiration from others to make them feel important because somewhere along the line they've been made to feel the exact opposite."

I puff out a breath, frowning. "I hadn't even considered that perspective."

"I'm not saying I'm right, I'm just saying that sometimes how people present themselves is a mask to cover up a multitude of hurts. Put it this way, if you had the misfortune of having a father like Carl Gunn, wouldn't you want to hide away any perceived flaws and suppress emotions that man would deem worthless?"

"So what are you saying exactly?"

"I'm saying that you need to be careful around Carl. People like him have a habit of pulling the rug out from under you when you least expect it."

"I promise, I will be."

"And with Dalton..." Daphne's voice trails off as she cocks her head at me.

"Yes?" I question.

"A person's vulnerabilities can be the very thing that shapes their character, both the good, and the bad. Those vulnerabilities can also be the key to unlocking someone's *true* nature and motivations. Something worth remembering, don't you think?"

"I'll bear that in mind."

"Good. Now, you enjoy the rest of that sugared bun, and I'll get back to work," she replies, getting up and dropping a kiss to my forehead, before heading towards the back of the café to clear up some plates left behind on a table there.

FOR THE REST of the afternoon, I wander through the streets of Princetown and stop by some of the local stores, picking up a couple of tops and a skirt from the charity store that caught my eye. Feeling a little thirsty, I head over to Bandits Bar for a drink. Despite still being relatively early, there are quite a few regulars inside, and I take a seat on one of the barstools waiting for Ben, the owner, and one of Drix and Dalton's good friends, to serve me.

"Hey, Daisy, what can I get you?" he asks, giving me one of his signature smiles that lights up his striking green eyes as soon as he spots me.

"Just a lemonade, I'm driving."

"Coming right up," he replies, grabbing a glass and filling it before adding some ice and a slice of lemon.

"Thank you," I say, taking it from him.

"So, where's your other half?" he asks, flitting his eyes around the bar in search of Dalton, no doubt.

"Counting his obscene amounts of money back at the mansion, I guess," I reply with a shrug, taking a sip of the sweet liquid.

Ben smirks. "Does he know you're here alone?"

"No, besides it's really none of his business where I choose to spend my time."

"He's your fiancé, Daisy, I think that makes it his business, don't you?"

"So you know then?"

"I received the invite to your engagement party."

"I haven't even seen them," I reply, huffing out a breath.

"That figures. Carl is–"

"A domineering bastard?" I finish for him.

"That's one way to describe him," Ben concedes with a wink. "Plus you've got a rock on your finger the size of Gibraltar, and I happen to be best mates with your brother *and* your fiancé, so I have some insider knowledge."

"I bet you do," I reply, rolling my eyes, and refraining from asking how *that* conversation went down.

"I can already tell you're running rings around Dalton. Bet he's loving the chase," Ben smirks.

"I never said that I'd make this easy for him," I shrug.

"You shouldn't, he could use a little humbling."

Despite being an heir to the Pike's family fortune, Ben's a lot more down to Earth than Dalton is, and I've always liked him. You wouldn't find many billionaire heirs serving drinks behind a bar.

"Dalton is used to getting what he wants, and I'm not in the business of allowing that," I reply. "If I want to have a drink, then I will."

"Daisy, maybe you should just–" Ben begins but the door to the bar swings open and a group of about twenty men walk in. One of them is wearing a huge penis hat and the others are pushing and shoving him in jest. Clearly they're on a stag do. "Ah fuck. Sorry, Daisy, looks like I'm going to have to cut this conversation short."

"Don't worry about it. I'm just going to drink this and then head out anyway."

Pushing off my stool, I head to a corner table to get out of the way of the group of men who are clearly a little worse for wear. For the next few minutes, I watch them with mild amusement, sipping on my lemonade when my phone vibrates in my bag. Fishing it out, I notice I have several text messages from Dalton, more appearing as I read.

"Oh for goodness sake, can this man be any more infuriating?" I mutter, casting my eyes over them.

Ben texted. What the fuck are you doing at Bandits Bar?

I glance over at Ben and shake my head, regretting my decision to have a drink here. They're all in cahoots together. Urgh.

Daisy, answer me.

Daisy, I swear to fuck if you don't answer me.

You know if you're trying to piss me off, you're doing an excellent job at it.

Kudos to me, I suppose. Daisy one, Dalton Nil.

Daisy!

You are my fiance, and you should not be there alone.

I roll my eyes at that. *Asshat.*

In fact you shouldn't be there at all!

This man is a nightmare.

Daisy, so help me. Get your arse home NOW!

I read his last message and let out a frustrated laugh. Who the hell does he think he is, and what exactly does he think is going to happen? I've been coming to Bandits Bar ever since I was old enough to drink, and it's not as if I can't handle myself.

"What a jerk!" I exclaim, dropping my phone back into my bag, my attention drawn to someone standing to my left. I slowly look upwards, taking in a pair of light denim jeans and a smart blue shirt, before settling on a pair of dark brown eyes set in a handsome face.

"Is this seat taken?" the man asks as one of his friends gathered at the bar hollers something provocative.

I raise a brow.

"Sorry about them, stag do. My friends are a little drunk."

"I figured."

"So, can I sit?" he asks, pointing to the seat opposite me.

"There are plenty of other seats available," I point out.

He shuffles on his feet. "Yeah, I know, but I saw you sitting alone and I thought, maybe..."

"I'd want company?" I fill in, arching a brow.

"Honestly, I could use a break from them," he says, jerking his thumb over his shoulder. "We're on a bar crawl. It's already been a long day, and the way these guys are going, an even longer night."

I chew on my lip, unsure whether I want to engage in conversation with a stranger, but there is an earnestness in his eyes that makes me feel sympathetic towards him. Besides, I'm only staying until my drink is finished. What possible harm could it be?

"Sure, why not," I find myself saying.

He smiles gratefully and sits, glancing over at his friends who are currently shouting orders at Ben. "So who's the groom?" I ask.

"Steven, the one wearing the knob hat," the guy explains.

"Of course he is, and what's your name?"

"Paul."

"I'm Daisy," I reply, offering my hand for him to shake.

"Nice to meet you, Daisy," he replies, his hand holding onto mine a little longer than necessary. I give him a tight smile before pulling my hand back.

"Do you live around here?" he asks, leaning forward, his arms pressing against the table as his legs stretch out beneath it.

"I do, and the bar owner over there," I say, pointing to Ben, "Is my friend."

Paul nods, his gaze coasting over to the bar and Ben trying to manage his rowdy friends. "What do you do for a living?"

"I'm a receptionist, you?" I ask, taking another sip from my drink.

"I work in logistics."

"Logistics?" I ask, acutely aware of how his gaze keeps dropping to my chest. Prickles of awareness, and not the good kind, scatter down my spine.

"Yeah," he replies, his countenance changing as he stares at me. "Okay, so let's cut to the chase."

"Cut to the chase?" I question, trying to shift my legs between the table as his thighs cage mine, my hackles rising.

"My friends and I have a little wager going, and right now I'm the only one here who hasn't managed to pull," he says, lowering his voice and licking his lips.

A wager? Really? I'm *so* done with men.

"Can't imagine why that might be," I reply, not bothering to hide my disdain as the atmosphere shifts, tainted now with an uncomfortable tension. I subtly inch my chair back, creating some physical space between us as I try to formulate an exit strategy in my mind.

Paul leans in closer, dropping any kind of pretence now as his eyes narrow. "Come on, you must be picking up what I'm putting down."

"Oh, I'm very aware of what you're doing," I reply, pressing my palm against the table as I move to stand. "And I'm not interested."

He reaches out and wraps his fingers around my wrist, squeezing tightly. "You're here alone, I'm here alone. Why don't we make the most of it?"

"You can't be serious?" I retort, trying to tug my wrist free. "Ben is my friend, and the second he sees what you're doing he'll be over here."

"Ben is very distracted right now," Paul replies, smiling lasciviously. "Just a quick kiss, yeah? Then I'll leave you alone."

"Not a chance!" I hiss back.

"Listen, I'll buy you a drink. Stay and talk some more," he says, attempting to make himself look less of a dick with an offer of a drink, as if that somehow makes his behaviour okay.

"Paul," I say, bending over so that my face is just inches from his.

"Yes," he smirks, dropping his gaze to my lips.

"FUCK OFF!" I shout, before lifting my handbag and smacking it into the side of his head.

Paul's smirk fades as he's shoved sideways from the force, the sound smothered by his friends whooping and hollering.

"You bitch!" he snarls, his fingers still wrapped tightly around my wrist as he pushes back his chair and stands.

"The fuck you just say to my fiance?"

Three things happen at once. I stiffen, Paul's eyes widen, and Dalton's fist meets the arsehole's jaw in a sickening thud. Releasing me, Paul stumbles backwards from the impact of Dalton's punch, and I grip my wrist, rubbing it.

"Daisy, are you okay?" Dalton growls, his eyes dropping to my hand wrapped around my wrist.

"I'm fine. Let's just go," I whisper, heat flooding my cheeks as the men Paul came in with all fall silent.

"Not until I've dealt with this prick, we're not," he says, twisting on his feet.

"He's with a lot of people," I hiss, reaching for Dalton's arm, but he just throws me a glare.

"I don't give a fuck. If they want a fucking brawl, then I'm more than willing to give them one," he says, his voice rising with every word as his attention focuses on the crowd, then back at Paul who he stalks towards. "You, arsehole, touched what's mine, and now you have to pay."

"Mate, it was a misunderstanding," Paul says, holding his hands up as he backs away.

"Dalton. Just leave it!" I protest, catching Ben's eye who has now come out from behind the bar and is holding a baseball bat. The other regular's stand, moving towards the pair in support of Dalton and Ben, and in warning to the group of drunken men.

"You thought you could come on to my woman and get away with it, did you?" Dalton snarls.

"I swear, this was just a huge misunderstanding. I didn't know she was with anyone, she never said."

"You prick!" I snap, stepping towards him. "I never gave you the impression that I was interested in you whatsoever. Where do you get off?"

"She has a fucking engagement ring on her finger, arsehole. Pretty sure that tells you she's already taken!" Dalton adds, gripping the man by the throat and forcing him backwards roughly until his back hits the wall.

"Woah! Let's just all calm down," one of the other men from the party says.

"I will calm the fuck down when you've all gotten the fuck out of my town!" Dalton growls, his fingers tightening around Paul's throat. He's already turning a deep red from lack of oxygen.

"Dalton, just let him go," I plead, gripping his arm, feeling the tension radiating through his muscles as Paul gasps for breath.

Dalton's gaze flickers between me and Paul, his jaw clenched tightly. After a moment of intense silence, he releases his grip on Paul's throat, who doubles over, coughing. The other men quickly move in to help their friend up as Dalton stands there, seething with anger.

"You're lucky Daisy stopped me," Dalton growls, his voice low and dangerous. "If I ever see you in this town again, you won't be so fortunate. Now get the fuck out of this bar!"

Paul nods frantically, his eyes wide with fear as he stumbles away with his friends, leaving the bar in a hurry. A moment later, Ben approaches us, setting the baseball bat down on the nearest table.

"You good?" he asks Dalton.

"I'm fucking pissed off," Dalton replies through gritted teeth, the muscle in his jaw flexing. "I should've killed the fucker."

"I had no idea Daisy was in trouble. I couldn't see past the group of men," Ben explains, flicking me a look of guilt.

"It's fine, Ben," I say on a soft breath.

"It's not *your* fault," Dalton says, glancing at Ben before lifting his hand to rub his forehead.

"I hope you're not suggesting that it's—" I begin.

"But it is *my* responsibility to keep you safe," he cuts me off, his eyes darting over me, checking for any signs of further harm as he steps closer.

"I'm fine. I was handling it," I protest, but he just closes the gap between us and cups my face, his fingers curling into my hair.

"Hitting him around the head with your handbag is *not* handling it," he replies tightly. "I told you to come home."

"You can't tell me what to do!" I hiss, aware we have an audience.

"Clearly, someone has to," he snaps back.

"I was just grabbing a quick drink."

"You were avoiding me, and look what happened, some fucking cunt tried to molest you. You are my fiancé, Daisy," he mutters, his gaze dropping from my eyes to my lips and back again. "And it's my duty to take care of you."

"Take care of me?" I snort with laughter, annoyed at the way he's trying to control me as I lower my voice and say, "Didn't we recently establish that you're not doing a particularly good job at that?"

"That's not fair. I came here, didn't I?" he asks, chest heaving with residual anger.

"To drag me home, like you have any right to do that."

"I think I'll leave you to it," Ben says, chuckling as he walks away.

"It's just as well that I did come," Dalton grinds out.

"I was handling it!" I repeat, trying to rip out of his hold, but he reaches up with his free hand and yanks me against his body.

"You were not!" he snaps.

"You're making a scene!"

"I can't fucking take care of you if you're swanning around doing fuck knows what," he says, completely ignoring what I've just said.

"I was visiting Daphne at the café, then I went shopping, then I came here to have a drink. It's my day off, I was not swanning around," I reply tightly, my hands pressing against his chest in an attempt to push him away, but it only seems to fuel his ire further, and he just tightens his grip. "Dalton, people are looking," I protest.

His eyes spark with defiance as his lips curl up in a smirk. "I'm *very* aware that we're in public, Daisy," he warns.

"Don't you–"

His lips slam against mine, swallowing my protest with a fierce kiss, and this time I can't knee him in the balls because we're out in public with an audience, and we have to act like a couple in love, albeit a couple in love who're fighting.

So I let him kiss me. I let him plunder my mouth with his tongue, and fist my hair so tightly that my scalp tingles with pain-pleasure that somehow makes this whole kiss more electric. This kiss is an act of defiance against my need for personal space. It's an act of possession that has me questioning his motives, and I hate myself for succumbing to the physical rush it elicits. I'm suddenly hyper aware of the way his body is pressed so tightly against mine, how his thick arms hold me, how he tastes of peppermint, how his familiar scent fills my nostrils, and how *I* kiss him back.

The people around us fade into the background as I find myself melting into his embrace, my initial anger giving way to a confusing mixture of desire and frustration. I *hate* this man, and yet my body seems to think otherwise. It's an uncomfortable feeling to say the least.

Yet, I don't make any effort to push him away, and like that time back at 'M' when he'd proposed, I find myself leaning into the kiss, my fingers curling into the thin material of his shirt, holding on tight when I *should* be letting go. Telling myself this is all for show, that this kiss is nothing but a stipulation in a contract. That it means nothing.

But this kiss is like a hurricane, whipping up a storm around us, between us. I imagine our feet lifting off the ground, carried by the wind as we hold on to each other tightly. My fingers bite into my palms, the material of his shirt doing nothing to prevent the deep grooves forming in my skin. And that's what it feels like to be kissed by Dalton, pricks of pain and anguish, the tiny crescents marking me in a way that hurts. Despite the pain, I find myself craving more of Dalton's touch. His kisses are like a drug, intoxicating and addictive.

It's not until I feel Dalton's cock thickening between us that I manage to gather my thoughts together enough to break the kiss. With a gasp, I push against his chest again, this time with more force, my cheeks flushing furiously at his arousal.

"Dalton, *please*, let me go," I manage to whisper.

He doesn't immediately comply, his grip on me loosening slightly but still keeping me close. His eyes blaze with intensity as he studies my face, looking as dishevelled and affected by the kiss as I feel.

"I would've broken his legs for you, Daisy," he says roughly.

"That doesn't make me feel any better," I reply, my cheeks flushing a deeper pink as I untangle myself from his arms and put much needed space between us.

"It wasn't supposed to."

CHAPTER TEN

The rest of the week passes without incident, thank fuck. My father has restrained himself from making any snide remarks towards Daisy during our dinners together, even though it's obvious her clothes still bother him.

In contrast, I've grown to secretly enjoy seeing what outfit she'll pick out each night, all of them carefully chosen to defy my father. I particularly liked the rainbow striped mini skirt she wore last night paired with a red t-shirt, bare legs and fluffy yellow socks. There was something both frustratingly sexy about her outfit and insufferably cute. Not that I'd ever let her know how much she's beginning to affect me, mostly because it's been almost three weeks since I've had sex and I'm starting to get major fucking withdrawal symptoms. In fact, that kiss we shared at Bandits Bar after that prick tried to molest her has only added to my discomfort, and has made things even more strained between Daisy and me.

I probably shouldn't have kissed her, but I was angry.

No, fuck that. I was *incensed*.

She'd ignored me all day, refused to answer my texts, and I couldn't fucking stop myself from storming out of my home in search of her. Yes, her defiance had angered me, but when I walked into Ben's bar and saw that man's hands on her, I'd seen red. It was as though a veil of violence had fallen in front of my eyes, and all I wanted to do was rip him apart for daring to touch her, to scare her like that. Because underneath her anger, I'd *seen* her fear, and it did something to me. I would've done a lot worse than hit the bastard if we didn't have so many witnesses. Luckily for him he wasn't alone.

Deep down, I know I acted no better than that jerk had towards her, and if I were a better man I wouldn't have attempted to kiss her at that moment, but fuck me, this possessiveness had unfurled inside of me and I couldn't fucking stop myself.

Truth be known, I don't regret kissing Daisy. Not one bit. That kiss was electric. It was potent, and I've not stopped thinking about how she'd felt in my arms, how she'd moaned and kissed me back despite her anger.

The mere thought of her lips on mine has my balls tingling and my cock hardening. Daisy might drive me fucking crazy with her sharp tongue and infuriating stubbornness, and I know she fucking hates me, but my cock? My cock hasn't gotten the fucking memo.

I've since tried making conversation with her, but she's become even more unreachable, and has avoided being alone with me at all costs. Like today, she's gone out of her way to avoid me at work, refusing my offer of a lift this morning even though we're working the same damn hours.

Truthfully, it's not something I'm used to. Most of the women I've been with in the past are willing to at least pass the time with surface level conversation before we fuck, and whilst I'm well aware that's never going to happen between us, we're going to be married soon and the least she can do is keep to her word, given she made such a big deal about it.

But Daisy remains closed off, and frankly, it's beginning to grate on my patience. After all, it was she who wanted to find common ground, to communicate, but despite my attempts of doing exactly what she suggested, I've been met with bland responses and curbed emotions. Where has the snarky woman who enjoyed nothing more than putting me in my place with her witty comments and sharp retorts gone? Fuck, I'm beginning to miss our spirited interactions.

Shutting the lid of my laptop, I decide that enough is enough, and reach for my phone, making a couple of quick calls. Then, ignoring all the jobs piling up on my desk, I go in search of my fiancé, finding her sitting alone in the staff break room.

"Daisy, we need to talk."

"My lunch break is over. I need to get back to work," she replies, placing her half eaten sandwich back on her plate.

"Caroline has agreed to cover the rest of your shift. I want to clear the air."

"So it's okay for you to rearrange my breaks, but not me. That figures."

"I'm not below using my powers as the manager of this hotel to my advantage. We need to talk," I repeat.

"There's no need."

"I beg to differ," I reply, refusing to back down. "Come with me."

"No."

"No?" My nostrils flare at her stubbornness.

"Like I said, I have work to get back too. Caroline shouldn't have to cover for me."

"She was happy to do so. Besides, this is non-negotiable."

Daisy stands, lifting her chin defiantly as she glares at me.

"What are you going to do, Dalton, throw me over your shoulder like some caveman?"

"If I must," I retort, blocking her path as she tries to sidestep me.

"Get out of my way!" she insists, trying to skirt around me.

"You really are a stubborn woman!" I grind out.

"And you're an arse. I have nothing to say to you," she snaps back, shoving her palm against my chest. "Now move!"

I smirk at her aggressive tone, enjoying that spark lighting between us once more. I'd take her anger over avoidance, any day.

"Dalton!" she warns when I grin mercilessly at her.

"You asked for this," I say, and before she's had a moment to react, I bend at the waist, wrap my arms around her thighs and haul her over my shoulder.

"DALTON GUNN PUT ME DOWN THIS INSTANT!" she screeches, her fists bashing against my arse and thighs as I storm across the staff room, kicking the door open with my foot. I'm not sure what has possessed me, but what I do know is that I'm not backing down, damn the consequences.

"If I put you down will you come with me?" I ask, striding towards the exit that leads to the staff car park at the back of the hotel.

"No, but I *will* punch your lights out!" she screams in response, slapping her hands against any spot she can reach.

"Then I guess I won't put you down," I reply snarkily.

"You're breaking our agreement to respect each other's personal space!" she argues.

"And you broke it by ignoring me," I retort in frustration.

"With good reason, you jerk!"

"Still angry about our little tiff, I take it?"

"Which one? We've had a few," she snaps, thumping my arse with her fist.

"Just let it go, already."

"Fuck you, and put me down this instant! People will see!" she protests, her body wriggling as she tries to free herself.

"Let them."

"But the contract!" she hisses out.

"Fuck the contract," I reply, pressing my shoulder against the door that leads outside, more than ready to show her just how far I'm willing to go. We might've gotten lucky that there was no staff in the hallway, but I'd bet a year's wage that there's at least one person outside this very door, given that's where all the smokers gather to have a sneaky cigarette break.

"You're an imbecile!" she growls.

"I just want to clear the air between us. Is that really too much to ask?" I reply, nudging the door with my shoulder.

"Okay, okay!" she replies, pressing her hands against the small of my back, and pushing upright. "I'll go with you. We'll talk. Just, please, put me down!"

"Is this just a ruse? Are you going to run off the moment I put you back on your feet?" I ask her, unable to hide the teasing tone to my voice. "Because, believe me, I rather like the chase."

"Dalton. Just. Put. Me. Down!" she replies, enunciating each word.

"I need your word, Daisy," I urge her, not in the least bit hurried to put her down. In fact, I'd go as far to say that I rather like having her pert arse in such close proximity to my face, and her hands on me, even if it is with violence.

"I promise, we can talk."

"Excellent," I reply, reaching for her waist, allowing her to slide down my body. My hands fall to her hips, steadying her as she drops to her feet. "You're cute when you're angry."

"And you're an ignoramus," she counters, glaring up at me, her face flushed pink, her body trapped between me and the door.

"Another one to add to the list," I muse, our breaths mingling as I inch my face closer to hers.

For the briefest of moments her eyes flare with heat, and this intense kind of connection snaps to life between us. Whatever the fuck is going on, I'm pretty sure I like it.

"You'll pay for that!" she suddenly shouts, shoving me on the chest before fixing her dishevelled blouse and skirt, breaking the tension.

"I'd expect nothing less. Shall we?" I ask, pulling myself together as I reach behind her and push open the door.

A member of staff greets us, his eyes widening in shock as he exhales a puff of cigarette smoke, and wafts his hand in the air to dissipate it. "Mr Gunn, I was just—"

"It's fine," I snap as he steps aside.

Daisy strides past him, wrapping her arms around herself tightly to ward off the cold air as I fall into step beside her. "We'll be taking my car," I say, gesturing towards the spot where my black, Aston Martin Valour is parked.

"Fine," she mumbles. "You can drop me back off later to pick my car up."

"No need. I've arranged for one of the staff to collect it."

"I don't have my bag or coat," she counters, her teeth chattering as she waits for me to unlock the door to my car.

"I took care of that too. They're in the trunk," I explain, opening the passenger door and motioning for her to get inside.

"You've got this all worked out, haven't you?" she asks, settling into the seat.

"Drastic times call for drastic measures," I reply, shutting the door and rounding the car.

"So where are we going exactly?" she asks, as I pull out of the car park and drive down the winding lane towards the main road.

"It's a surprise," I reply.

"I don't like surprises," she retorts, pressing her palms against the leather beneath her arse, presumably to warm her hands on the heated seat. Either that or to prevent herself from punching me just like she had threatened.

"I know that's a lie," I counter. "Drix said that you love surprises."

"So you're back to being friends again?" she asks me, not bothering to deny it.

"Not quite, but we've known each other for years and have had plenty of conversations during that time. Believe it or not, some of them were about you. He mentioned once that you love surprises, so here we are."

"Chucking me over your shoulder was a surprise. I *didn't* like that," she snaps.

"To be fair I wouldn't have done it if you hadn't mentioned it yourself. Perhaps it was a Freudian slip on your part."

"Are you actually suggesting I wanted you to throw me over your shoulder?"

"You tell me," I reply, smothering a smile.

"I can categorically tell you I did not."

"Noted," I reply. "Won't happen again, unless of course, you change your mind. I've been known to throw plenty of women over my shoulder in my time."

"You wish," she huffs.

Half an hour later we're pulling up to a quaint, ivy-covered storefront on a quiet cobblestone street in a neighbouring village. The dressmaker's boutique has a beautiful window display showcasing two stunning tailored gowns. One is a deep purple with crystal beading across the bodice, and the other is a pale green with layers of chiffon skirting and thin beaded straps.

"Why are we here?" Daisy asks, as we step out of the car.

"You'll see," I reply, pushing open the door, a tiny bell tinkling with our arrival.

Inside, the boutique is scented with lavender and rose, and

gowns in every shade imaginable line the walls. The dressmaker, and owner of the boutique, is an elegant woman with silver hair tied up in a neat chignon.

"Are you Mr Gunn?"

"Yes, thank you for fitting us in at such short notice."

"It's my pleasure," she replies, before turning her attention to Daisy. "And you must be Mrs Gunn."

"Not yet," Daisy replies softly, her attention drawn to the stunning array of gowns.

"Of course, how silly of me. You'll have to forgive me, my mind is not as sharp as it used to be. This appointment is to find you a dress to wear for your engagement party tomorrow night, is that correct?"

"It is?" Daisy frowns, cutting a look my way.

"Whatever you want, it's yours," I offer, taking a seat on the armchair situated just outside the changing room.

"I'm sure there will be something suitable," the dressmaker says, the lines around her eyes crinkling as she smiles. "What colour were you thinking?"

Daisy chews on her lip, flicking her gaze between me and the rack of dresses to her left as she trails her fingers along the material. "The theme is black and white," she murmurs, staring wistfully at the colourful dresses.

"You'll wear whatever dress you choose, regardless of the colour," I say firmly.

Daisy's head snaps around. "But your father was very specific."

"I don't care. This is our engagement party. You should wear what you want."

"I'm not sure your father would appreciate his money being spent on a dress for me that doesn't meet his expectations."

"It isn't his money buying the dress, it's mine," I explain, pulling out my credit card and passing it to the dressmaker. "Apologies, I didn't catch your name."

"Matilda," the old woman replies.

"Well, Matilda, charge anything Daisy chooses to this card, please."

"Of course," Matilda replies, taking it from me, and heading towards the back of the shop where her cash register is located.

"Why, Dalton?" Daisy asks, uncertainty filling her voice. "I can pay for my own dress."

I look at her, my gaze never wavering from her eyes. "In answer to your question, you told me that colour makes you happy. So choose a dress that will make you happy. And in response to your statement, I know you can pay for your own dress but it's the least I can do given I seem to be doing a piss-poor job at making you happy."

"You don't have to buy me things," she protests softly.

"I know I don't, but I *want* to. Let me do this for you, Daisy."

"But—"

"I'll buy you every damn dress in this shop if that's what it takes to make you smile."

She stares at me for long moments, and it isn't until Matilda clears her throat that she finally nods in agreement.

"Okay."

"Wonderful. Now where should we start?" Matilda asks.

For the next couple of hours, I keep myself occupied by logging into my work email and responding to messages whilst Daisy tries on a multitude of dresses, her laughter lifting up in the air as she chats with Matilda. By the time she's made her decision the sky is darkening and my stomach is rumbling loudly.

"Thank you so much for all your help, Matilda. You truly are very talented," Daisy says as she emerges from the dressing room in her uniform.

"You're not going to show me what you've chosen?" I ask, pocketing my phone as I look up at her.

"It's a surprise," she replies, tucking a strand of hair behind her ear. Her cheeks are flushed and her eyes are bright, making her whole face light up. As much as I enjoy her snarkiness when she's mad, it actually feels surprisingly good to see her happy.

Behind her Matilda emerges from the dressing room holding a zippered garment bag that hides the chosen dress inside. She hands it to Daisy with a warm smile. "There we are, dear."

Daisy gratefully accepts the bag, gingerly folding it over her arm like a precious treasure. "Thank you again."

"You are very welcome," Matilda responds graciously, before adding, "I often believe that it isn't us who choose the dress, but the dress that chooses us. This one was made for you."

Daisy's beaming smile widens even more at this sentiment. "I couldn't agree more."

"ARE YOU HUNGRY?" I ask as I place Daisy's dress in the trunk, and hand over her coat.

Daisy nods, pulling it on. "I could eat."

"Let's find somewhere then," I suggest, scanning the quaint village street.

As we stroll along the cobblestone pathway, the delicious aroma of freshly baked bread and rich sauces wafts through the air, leading us towards a small Italian restaurant nestled between a flower shop and a bookstore. The restaurant's exterior exudes an old-world charm, with a worn wooden facade and string lights twinkling above a sign that reads *Trattoria della Nonna*.

"What about here?" I ask.

"Sure, I love Italian food," she replies, as I push open the heavy wooden door and we step inside.

The interior is adorned with chequered tablecloths, flickering candles in wine bottles, and soft music playing in the background. A friendly waiter greets us with a smile, leading us to a cosy corner table by the window.

"Today's specials are listed on the chalkboard," he explains, pointing to his left. "Of course, you can also choose from the menu."

"Thank you," I reply, scanning the menu he just handed to us both. "We'll need a moment to choose."

"No problem. Would you like some water, olives, bread?"

"Yes, to all three," Daisy replies, smiling up at him.

As the waiter walks away, I focus my attention back on the menu and not on Daisy, whose bright eyes, flushed cheeks and plump lips are, admittedly, becoming more and more of a distraction.

"Dalton..." Daisy begins, her voice trailing off as I meet her gaze.

"Yes?" I ask, sensing her unease as she fidgets with her napkin.

"Thank you for the dress."

"You're welcome," I reply, my cock stirring to life as she chews on her lip nervously. Fuck, I really need to get myself in check. "What is it?"

"You said that you wanted to buy me the dress because you wanted to make me happy."

"Yes," I agree.

"But *things* don't make you happy, Dalton," she says softly.

"I beg to differ. You looked pretty happy earlier."

"Because you were being *thoughtful*. It wasn't about the dress per se, it was because you're supporting my right to be an individual, to express myself with colour, *that* made me happy. I would've felt the same if you'd supported my right to wear one of my own dresses."

"Well now you have a new dress, *and* you have my support," I reply with a shrug.

"I do. Thank you for both, it means a lot." She hesitates, and I realise that she has more to say, so rather than interrupting her, I give her the space to continue. "I want to apologise too."

"For what?"

"For ignoring you. For being distant."

I cock my head to the side, regarding her. "I can't deny that it's pissed me off, but I do understand it," I reply begrudgingly.

"You do?"

"Of course. I think we both needed some time to come to terms with our... arrangement," I say, carefully. "I guess I'm not used to having someone—"

"Who doesn't follow your orders? Who refuses to fall at your feet the moment you give them your attention?" she offers, her lip tugging up into a smile.

"That wasn't quite what I was thinking. Though I guess there is some truth in that," I admit. "I guess, if nothing else, this whole situation is a test of my control."

"Control?" Daisy echoes, her brows furrowing. "What do you mean?"

"I mean that I'm used to being in control of everything around me. My work, my social life, and especially my relationships."

"Relationships?" she snorts out a laugh. "*Booty calls*, you mean?"

I give her a look but don't rise to the bait. "When you didn't respond to my texts the other day, I was angry, and then when I saw that prick manhandle you, I lost it," I explain, offering her the truth. "You defied me, and put yourself in danger."

"I'm my own person, Dalton. You can't control me. I won't let you, so you really should stop trying."

"You don't bend to my will," I continue. "And admittedly,

that's both frustrating and intriguing. It's not something I've had to deal with before."

"Do women *really* throw themselves at you?"

"Is that so hard to believe?" I counter.

"I know they must, given your reputation. I guess I just wonder what you get out of it, what *they* get out of it. I mean, apart from the obvious," she says.

"People like to fuck, Daisy. I like to fuck. I don't really need anything else."

"What about friendship?"

"I have male friends for that."

She frowns. "Okay then, what about connection? Don't you want *more* than just a long list of one night stands?"

Silence descends between us as I contemplate her question. "I think I've just never really found someone worth building a relationship with," I finally say, and whilst it's not the complete truth, it's as much as I'm willing to share in the moment.

"I see, and now here you are stuck with me," Daisy replies, her attention drawn to the waiter as he returns to the table, setting down a bottle of sparkling water, a bowl of juicy green olives smothered in oil, and some warm bread.

"Are you ready to order?" he asks.

"Ladies first," I offer.

Daisy briefly flicks her gaze to the menu. "I think I'll have the Capricciosa pizza," she says, handing the waiter her menu. "And a glass of Chianti, please."

"Make that two Capricciosa," I add, passing him my menu as well.

"Some wine for you, Sir?"

I shake my head. "No. I'm driving. Water is fine."

"Coming right up," he replies.

I wait for him to be out of earshot before I continue with our conversation. "Just for the record, I'm not stuck with you, Daisy.

Despite our differences, I *do* like you when you're not spitting and hissing at me like some feral cat," I add with a smirk.

"Feral cat?" She laughs at that.

"You have to admit you do have sharp claws. Despite that, I like you. Why is that so hard to believe?"

"Who are you, and what have you done with the real Dalton Gunn?" she asks, wrinkling her nose.

"I mean it," I insist.

"Look, I know Drix has warned you not to make me completely miserable, and I do appreciate the effort you've made today, but you don't have to tell me things you think I want to hear."

"I'm not declaring my love for you, but I'm not lying. I like you, even if you do drive me fucking crazy at times. Besides, anyone who has the balls to put my father in his place is someone I can respect."

"Well, then I want you to know that I like you when you're not acting like an obnoxious prick."

"Thanks, I guess," I reply with a chuckle, feeling some of the tension that has been building between us dissipate.

She nods and reaches for an olive, popping it into her mouth. "These are delicious."

"I'll take your word for it."

"You don't like olives?"

"Not particularly."

"You don't know what you're missing," she says, popping another one into her mouth, her lips glistening with oil.

I have the sudden urge to lean across the table and kiss her, willing to taste the tangy bitterness on her lips just to feel her soften against me like she did for the briefest of moments the other night, but I curb that desire with a mouthful of icy water instead. It does nothing to cool my desires.

"Given we're being honest with each other, I need to explain why I reacted the way I did the night we watched TV together. I think I owe you that much at least."

"Go on, I'm listening," I say, glad for the distraction given my dick seems to think it's getting some action tonight.

"That night, when I asked you why it was important for you to know what makes me happy, you replied that if you knew, then it would earn you brownie points when you buy me the perfect gift for my birthday."

"And that's wrong? Explain," I ask, genuinely bemused.

"Because you wanted to know purely to make yourself look good. It didn't come from a place of genuine care," she finishes, her eyes searching mine for understanding.

I lean back in my chair, taking a moment to process her words. She's right, I was more focused on scoring points than truly understanding her. "I see your point," I admit. "I never meant for it to come across that way."

"Today, even though you bought me something, it came from a place of care. Can you see the difference?"

"I can," I admit begrudgingly.

"That's why I accepted this gift, and why it means something to me. So thank you for thinking of me."

"And I apologise for my lack of understanding before," I say, reaching across the table to gently grasp her hand. "If nothing else, I'm learning some things here."

"The right way to treat women, you mean?" Daisy asks, smiling a little.

"No, the right way to treat *you*," I reply, squeezing her fingers before releasing her hand.

"Because I'm your best friend's little sister, and he'll murder you if you treat me badly?" she questions.

"No, because you're my fiance, my soon-to-be wife, and the future mother of my child, and I don't want to be an arsehole to the person who is going to carry a piece of me inside of them," I reply.

Daisy's eyes widen, then she breaks out into a wide grin. "Seriously, have you been abducted by an alien and had your brain rewired?"

"Funny," I grin back as she chuckles to herself. "So, are we friends then?"

"We're a step up from enemies I think," she muses. "Frenemies?"

"I can live with that."

For now.

CHAPTER ELEVEN

Blotting my ruby red lips with tissue, I straighten up to survey my appearance in the full length mirror before me. Objectively, I know I'm not an unattractive woman, but I don't quite meet the expectations of the well to-do men and women of Princetown. I never have.

It doesn't matter that my last name is Hammer, I still carry the stigma of being adopted into the family and not born into it. Drix has felt the same judgement throughout his life, but when Hubert was alive it never hurt as much because he always made us feel so accepted, so loved. He's the only man, aside from Drix, who understood all the parts of me, who ever truly made me feel like I belonged, who wholeheartedly accepted me for everything that I am, who encouraged my individuality, and who loved me for it without restraint.

I miss him dreadfully.

Blowing out a steadying breath, I steel myself for the evening ahead. Mingling with the well-to-do families of Princetown has always been a daunting affair, but I'm well accustomed to the judgemental gazes and whispered criticisms disguised as polite conversation. Tonight, however, I'm determined to hold my head high and prove once and for all that I belong here just as much as anyone else. After all, I'm soon to become Mrs Dalton Gunn, and whilst the pain of knowing this is a marriage of convenience still stings, I refuse to let it show. This was my choice, and I will stand by it.

Downstairs I can hear the faint sound of a string quartet playing, signalling the beginning of this evening's event. Taking one last look in the mirror, I smooth down the fabric of my royal blue gown and adjust the silver necklace Hubert gifted me, drawing strength from it as though he were here with me too. For a moment, I feel a pang of self-doubt creeping in, but then I remember Hubert's words echoing in my mind. *"Stand tall, Daisy. You are a gift to this world, and to anyone lucky enough to have your love."*

With his words echoing inside my mind, I make my way downstairs to join the party unfolding in the grand hall. Gathering the material of my skirt, the multicoloured crystal-encrusted bodice shimmers under the glimmering chandeliers that hang from the ceiling, casting a cascade of prismatic light around me. This dress is probably one of the prettiest I own, and I chose it not just for the beauty of it, but for the way it makes me feel. Powerful, if not entirely happy. Beautiful, if not slightly out of place.

Forcing my shoulders back, and lifting my chin, I catch a glimpse of Drix standing at the bottom of the ornate staircase, his eyes meeting mine with an unspoken understanding. He knows me better than anyone else, understands the turmoil churning beneath my composed exterior.

"You look stunning, Daisy," he says when I reach him, taking my hand and squeezing it reassuringly.

"You don't look too bad yourself," I joke, eyeing him in his smart black tuxedo. "Where are Lia and Toby?"

"Talking with Sterling and Ben in the hall. We've missed you, Daise. How has it been this past week?"

"I've had better," I admit, wincing when he scowls.

"If Dalton has upset you, I'll..."

"Dalton has been fine. It's just taking me time to adjust, that's all."

He nods. "So, are you ready to face the vultures?"

I nod. "As I'll ever be. Let's get this over and done with, shall we?"

As we enter the grand ballroom, all eyes are on me, and I can feel the intensity of their scrutiny. My heart races and my palms start to sweat, but I ignore both and focus on projecting an air of confidence. Drix is my saving grace, his stoic expression betraying none of the discomfort I know he feels. He squeezes my hand once again before releasing it, and I give him a reassuring smile as we walk through a sea of people dressed in black and white. My marriage to Dalton might be a contract forged out of necessity rather than love, but I refuse to let it define me. I am still Daisy Hammer, with or without the prestigious name I am soon to be bound too. And tonight, as I pass through the ballroom filled with Princetown's elite, I hold my head high and remind myself that true belonging comes from within, and not from the expectations of others.

"Oh, here we go," Drix mutters as Mrs Fernsby approaches.

"Daisy, darling, your dress is... quite something," she exclaims with practised charm, her eyes flickering over my dress with a raised brow.

As a woman of her own wealth and standing, she has always looked down on both of us. This dress could've been encrusted with cut diamonds and she still wouldn't be impressed. Not that I care, her opinion means nothing to me.

"Thank you," I respond politely, refusing to be intimidated.

"Congratulations on your engagement. We were all so

surprised when Carl informed us of the news. You know, there was a time I believed Dalton was going to marry my own daughter, Clarissa, but alas, it wasn't to be."

My stomach coils at the mention of her daughter's name, given she was part of the group of people who treated me so poorly all those years ago at college. The sheer fact Dalton had spent any time with her makes my gut churn.

"I wonder, how *have* you managed to ensnare such a man?" she adds, lifting a perfectly arched brow as her gaze drops to my stomach.

I draw in a sharp breath, but before either myself or Drix is able to respond to her veiled accusation, a familiar scent wafts under my nose and a muscular arm wraps around my waist as Dalton appears at my side.

"Actually, it was me who ensnared Daisy," he says smoothly, dropping a kiss to the top of my head. "There isn't a woman here tonight that is more perfect for me. Daisy looks absolutely stunning, wouldn't you agree?"

Mrs Fernsby's gaze cuts to Dalton, her eyes narrowing. "Indeed. Well, I shall have to go and mingle. Good evening to you both," she says, completely ignoring Drix's presence and twisting on her heel.

As Mrs Fernsby sweeps away, Dalton's grip on my waist tightens imperceptibly, no doubt a silent warning to play the part of devoted fiance.

"You really do look beautiful," he says, and I don't quite have the courage to look into his eyes to see if he truly means it or if this is all part of his act.

"Of course she does," Drix replies, a note of anger in his tone. "Daisy is a diamond amongst coal, with the exception of Lia of course," he adds, his attention drawn to her as she walks towards us, stunning in a long-sleeved, black, form-fitting gown with Toby at her side. Sterling and Ben flank her.

"Lia, Toby!" I exclaim, stepping out of Dalton's hold and throwing my arms around Lia in a hug before crouching down and wrapping my arms around Toby.

"Your dress is so pretty!" Toby exclaims in awe as I draw upright, his small hands touching the delicate fabric of my skirt.

"Thank you, Toby. You look very handsome too," I add, beaming.

"We've missed you," Lia says, her smile sincere.

"I've missed you too," I reply, my chest aching a little at just how much.

"How about we get together soon?" she asks as Toby looks between us, grinning widely.

"Can I come? I promise I'll be good," he says, hopping on his feet.

"Of course! Maybe a play date at the park, followed by some food at Daphne's cafe in town?" I suggest, ruffling Toby's hair playfully.

"Yes please," he agrees, as Lia takes his hand in hers, and glances at Drix.

"We'll organise it soon," she says, giving me a knowing look that conveys her silent support. "I imagine we have lots to catch up on."

"We do," I agree.

"Daisy, you look good enough to eat," Ben says, stepping forward, his piercing green eyes casually perusing my dress before he grins at Dalton.

"Thanks, Ben," I reply, my cheeks heating as he leans in and presses a kiss against my cheek.

"Careful, Ben," Sterling interjects with a smirk as Dalton mumbles something under his breath, and his fingers dig into my hip. "You know how Dalton gets."

"Not with my sister, he won't," Drix grumbles.

Sterling smothers a smile, then drops his lips to my cheek. "You scrub up well," he adds with a wink.

"Thanks, Sterling. How are things with your family? Your stepmother and stepsister seem lovely," I say.

It was only recently, on New Year's Eve, that his father Robert married Melody Richards, a once famous Hollywood actress. I met her daughter, and Sterling's new stepsister, Harlow, for the first time at the wedding. She was incredibly gracious, and utterly beautiful. Not to mention a fantastic singer.

Sterling cuts a look to Drix, then clears his throat as he swipes a hand through his glossy brown hair. "They're settling in."

"Are you sticking around for a while?" I ask, knowing that he dislikes his father about as much as I like Carl, and since his dad divorced his mum and she moved out, his visits to Princetown are few and far between. Which is a shame because like Ben, Sterling is one of the few people who I actually like in this town.

"Of course, I wouldn't dream of missing your wedding," he replies, cutting a look at Dalton, who clears his throat pointedly.

"I hate to steal Daisy away, but there are other guests we need to greet. We'll catch up soon, yes?" he says to Drix, before looking between Sterling and Ben.

Drix doesn't reply, but Ben nods. "Actually, Harlow has agreed to sing at Bandits Bar, you should all come, might make her feel more at ease if there are some familiar faces in the crowd."

Sterling snaps his head around to Ben. "She has? When was this arranged?"

"Couple days ago. She's performing next weekend, in fact," Ben replies, his lips twitching up in a smile. "I asked her to fill in whilst the guys are doing some gigs in London."

"Princetown Bandits are gigging in London?" Drix asks, referring to the local band Ben manages.

"Yeah, a record label is very interested in them. I'm going to meet with the label and the guys when they return," Ben explains. "It's been a long time coming."

"That's amazing, they're really good," Lia adds.

"If you don't mind me coming too, I'd love to hear Harlow sing again. Her voice is stunning," I say.

"Oh me too," Lia adds. "She gave me chills when she sang at the wedding."

"Pretty sure she gave a few of us more than chills," Ben comments with a smirk, and I can't help but notice the way Sterling's jaw grits and his eyes narrow at Ben. I wonder what's happening there. Whilst Ben doesn't quite have the same reputation as Dalton, he's still single, handsome, and heir to the Pike family fortune. He's a catch. Perhaps he's made a move on Harlow, or maybe it was her who made a move on him?

"Anyway," Ben continues, "Of course you all should come. It'll be a great night."

"Well, I guess we better head off. I'll hopefully see you all soon then?" I say.

"You bet, Daise," Drix replies, pressing a kiss against Lia's forehead as she smiles up at him.

As Dalton leads me away to greet the other guests, I can't help but steal glances at Lia and Drix, feeling a bittersweet ache in my chest as I admire their genuine warmth and connection. In contrast, Dalton's hand on my back as we exchange pleasantries with the guests only serves to remind me of the charade we are playing, of the lies we are weaving to keep up appearances. Despite how uncomfortable that makes me feel, I play my part, smiling and nodding in all the right places. I even manage to keep myself in check when Carl finally approaches us both.

"Are you enjoying yourselves?" he asks, his cool gaze flicking over me. I see the annoyance in his gaze at my choice of dress, but thankfully he refrains from commenting.

"It's been a lovely evening, thank you," I reply, even though all

I want to do is escape to my room and hide. Honestly, I'm exhausted by all the pretence.

Carl nods, a polite smile on his lips as he glances between us both. "I'm glad to hear it. Daisy, do you mind if I steal Dalton away for a moment? There's a matter we need to discuss." His tone is casual, but there's an underlying tension that makes me stiffen.

"That's fine. I need to use the ladies room anyway," I lie, glad for the opportunity to escape, even if it's only for a little while.

"I'll come and find you in a moment," Dalton says, his fingers brushing mine briefly before he follows his father out of the ballroom.

The heat of his touch lingers on my skin as I slip through the crowd, and head towards the back of the manor, and the gardens beyond. I suddenly feel like I can't breathe and need some fresh air, a moment to recenter myself. As I step out into the cold winter air, I hear two women laughing, and my steps falter. Hidden by a marble statue, I listen in on their conversation.

"What about her dress? There's no accounting for taste," a familiar voice says. "Daisy looks like a Christmas bauble."

Heat floods my cheeks at the insult. It's Clarissa, Mrs Fernsby's daughter and someone I once considered a friend. That was before I found out that she was the one who'd dared my ex-boyfriend, Jonathon, to date me in college and then dump me in front of my peers at our graduation ball. Jonathon had pretended to be in love with me for months, took my virginity and then broke my heart, destroying my trust in people in the process. He was the reason Drix ended up in debt, because when Drix found out what Jonathon had done, he'd beaten him so badly he'd ended up in hospital. Carl paid the family off, and then used that debt to force Drix to be his enforcer.

A debt that will be fully written off once I marry Dalton and provide Carl with a grandchild he's so desperate for.

"I really don't understand what Dalton sees in her," the woman she's with replies.

"Oh, come on, isn't it obvious?" Clarissa says, her voice tight with bitterness. "He clearly pity fucked her and got her pregnant. If this isn't a shotgun wedding, I'll eat my hat."

The woman gasps. "Surely he wouldn't. She's a… *nobody.*"

"Exactly, just because she has the Hammer name, doesn't make her a part of this world. It never will," Clarissa replies. "Besides, we all know Dalton. There's no way he'd choose Daisy willingly. He was probably even drunk when they fucked."

Anger courses through my veins, and I can feel my fingers clenching into fists at my sides as I listen to their hateful words.

"Fuck this," I mutter, stepping out from behind the statue, my presence interrupting their conversation as I stride towards them, anger boiling like bubbling lava in my veins.

"Daisy…" Clarissa begins, taken aback by my sudden appearance.

"Save your breath, Clarissa!" I reply, holding my hand up, my voice cold and steady. "I have no interest in hearing what else you have to say."

The other woman looks on nervously, clearly regretting getting caught gossiping.

"We were just joking," Clarissa says, plastering on a fake smile.

"Joking?" I let out a bitter laugh. "Like you were joking when you, Jonathon, and the rest of your despicable friends humiliated me back in college? Just joking when you bet him to date me, to pretend he was in love with me only for him to dump me in front of everyone at our college ball, all for your entertainment?"

"I—" she stammers, backing off as I approach her.

"You are nothing but a spiteful, cold-hearted bitch who seems to have a lot of opinions about my life," I continue, my anger blazing now, "But let me make one thing perfectly clear, I am done letting people walk all over me because I don't fit into your world. You think you can be cruel, that you can judge me based on my past? That you're better than me because you were fortunate enough to grow up wealthy, with parents who love you? What kind of person would ridicule another for something that wasn't her doing? Are you truly that heartless?"

"I think we should go," the woman she's with says, but I round on her.

"Don't move, I'm not finished yet," I command, brooking no arguments before turning my attention back to Clarissa once more. "Back in college you may have hurt me, but believe me when I say, I'm not that girl anymore. I'm not afraid to stand up for myself. So, the next time you decide to spread rumours or talk behind someone's back, remember this moment, because if you ever speak badly about me again, or anyone else for that matter, I'll make sure you suffer. After all, it's *me* who's marrying Dalton, and it's my soon-to-be father-in-law who runs Princetown, and we all know that if you cross him, you're making an enemy of one of the most powerful men in this town, in the whole of England, in fact."

I lock eyes with her, my gaze unwavering as Clarissa steps back, fear flickering in her eyes as she realises the gravity of my threat. The woman with her edges away, sensing the need to distance herself from Clarissa, and the situation.

"You can't threaten me," Clarissa finally manages to say, her voice uneven.

"I just did," I reply with a steely resolve.

"My mother is close friends with Carl, there is no way he would—"

"I think you'll find that my father would indeed make your lives a misery if he were to find out about how you insulted not just my fiance, but *me*, and by extension, *him*," Dalton says, his words carrying a dangerous edge as he steps through the French doors behind her.

I take a deep breath, my heart hammering in my chest as Dalton's eyes meet mine. There's a moment of tense silence before he says, "And for the record, the only person I have *ever* pity-fucked is you, Clarissa. It is a night I regret immensely, though I barely remember it, it was so unremarkable."

She gasps, her eyes blinking in shock. "You don't mean that," she stutters.

"I believe we're done here," he says coldly, "Leave. Now."

The other woman scurries away, shooting him a fearful look before disappearing back inside, but Clarissa stands rooted to the spot, her expression a mix of fear and defiance. She opens her mouth as if to protest, but one glance from Dalton shuts her up.

"I won't tolerate this kind of behaviour, especially not towards my fiance," Dalton's tone is firm and unwavering. "Consider this your final warning."

Clarissa eventually seems to gather her senses and she brushes past Dalton, storming inside the manor. As she leaves, my breath whooshes out of my chest as hot tears threaten to spill from my eyes, but I refuse to let them fall in front of him. Instead, I turn away from Dalton and head towards the gardens, not wanting him to see how badly I've been affected by her hateful words.

CHAPTER TWELVE

"Daisy, wait!" I call, quickening my pace to catch up with her, but she gathers up the delicate folds of her exquisite dress and takes off into the darkness, the pale moonlight catching the stunning jewels that adorn the bustier of her gown as she disappears into the maze.

As I navigate through the twisting paths, the sound of her footsteps against the paved pathway grow fainter and the hedges loom high around me, casting eerie shadows in the moonlight. Straining my ears, I hear faint sobbing coming from somewhere to my left. Without hesitation, I change direction, following the sound. Drix had told me what happened with her ex-boyfriend, how the prick had humiliated her in front of everyone when she was in college, but I had no idea about the extent of the situation, or that Clarissa had been involved. If I had, there's no way I would have gone anywhere near her, let alone fucked her.

Just as I turn a corner, I see Daisy standing in a small clearing, her back to me, shoulders hunched over as if she's trying to contain an inner storm. Slowly, not wanting to startle her, I reach out a hand, and touch her bare arm.

"Daisy, you really need to stop running away from me," I say, hardly words of comfort, but it's all I can think of.

She lets out a tremulous breath, her pretty blue eyes glistening with tears as she turns to face me. "Why are people so cruel?" she asks, her vulnerability cutting me deep.

Wordlessly I take her hand and lead her to the stone bench situated beneath an arch of shrubbery. We sit together as I contemplate her question.

"Some people are just arseholes, Daisy. I could psychoanalyse them and say it's because they've got their own insecurities that causes them to act that way, and whilst it might be true, it doesn't excuse their behaviour."

"I've never done anything to hurt her. I would never do anything to hurt her like she hurt me, despite what I just said," she replies, swiping at the tears on her face. "At one time I thought she was my friend. I'd trusted her, trusted Jonathon. I was so stupid..."

Her voice trails off as she falls into silence, and I feel the urge to comfort her, to make this right somehow. It's a feeling I'm not used to, least of all equipped to manage. "Having a kind heart, and trying to see the best in people, doesn't make you stupid, Daisy."

"Really, because there have been times in the past when I distinctly remember you saying otherwise."

I flinch at her response, knowing it's true, and my hand tightens around hers. "If you hadn't already noticed, I don't always say or do the right thing, but I'm working on it."

She nods, her attention drawn to the moon hanging in the sky above us. As she looks up, her profile is bathed in a soft, silvery glow, highlighting the delicate curve of her jawline and the vulnerability etched on her features.

"Daisy," I start, clearing my throat, ignoring the pulse that beats in my bastard cock at how beautiful she looks. I've always seen her beauty. I'm not blind, but I've never allowed myself to really appreciate it, my friendship with Drix curbing those thoughts. Over the years I've encouraged our fiery relationship because it allowed me to keep my distance, to place her in the *never to be touched* category, and until very recently I've been okay with that.

Now, it's getting harder and harder to keep her there.

"You're one of the most genuine and caring people I know," I say, meaning every word. "It's not a weakness to believe the good in people, even when they disappoint you, it's *your* strength. I'm beginning to understand that now. But aside from that, I'm so fucking proud of you for standing up to Clarissa. I want you to know that."

She turns her head, her eyes meeting mine, a frown pulling together her brows. "I've not been very kind to you over the years. In fact, I've been pretty terrible towards you," she admits.

"I dare say I've deserved it," I reply with a shrug, my thumb drawing circles on the back of her hand. "I can be a self-centred, egotistical prick. I won't deny it."

A soft smile pulls her lips up at that. "Dalton, can I tell you something?" she asks after a moment, chewing on her lip as she looks at me.

"Of course."

"I've hated every second of tonight. Apart from the few people who genuinely like me, I've felt everyone else's judgement. I've felt their eyes on me, heard them whispering behind my back. It's like I'm back in college again, reliving that nightmare. Worse still, it drags up memories of my childhood. How can I expect anyone to like me when my own parents couldn't even love me?"

Her voice wavers, the pain of old wounds reopening before me. I know very little about her childhood, apart from the snippets Drix has revealed over the years, but looking at her now, I see that there's a deep well of hurt and trauma that I had never fully comprehended, that I'd selfishly never even tried to uncover.

"Do you want to talk about it, your past I mean?" I offer.

"Truthfully, I'm not sure how much help I'd be, but I'm willing to listen."

She considers me a moment, then shakes her head. "Probably best not to dredge all that up tonight. I'm feeling vulnerable enough as it is, but I do appreciate you standing up for me back there," she replies, and I can't help but feel like she's protecting herself from me. I've got to admit, that stings.

"And I'd do it again in a heartbeat," I say, choosing not to push her on the matter.

"Because you have to?"

"No, Daisy, because I *want* to," I say firmly.

"Is this real, Dalton?" she asks after a beat.

"What do you mean?"

"I mean how you're behaving towards me. Are you being sincere?"

"You think this is an act?" I question, unsure what to make of the fact that she believes me to be so disingenuous

"I don't know. You tell me."

"Like I said yesterday, I like you Daisy."

"Because I'm Drix's sister, and you have to?"

"You were Drix's sister before we entered into this arrangement, and we hated each other then."

"And now it's different? What changed?"

"Are you saying you still hate me? I thought we'd evolved into frenemies," I retort, avoiding her question altogether.

"This you, this person now. I could grow to *like* him."

"That's good to know. I'll do my best, but I can't promise I won't fuck up."

She wipes at her eyes, sniffling a little. "I expect you too, but I guess what I'm saying is that I'll try and do better too." She chuckles then, side-eyeing me.

"What is it?"

"Did you really pity-fuck Clarissa?"

"Put it this way, I regret ever sleeping with her."

"Why? I assume you enjoyed it. You like sex after all."

"Because she hurt you, that's why."

She looks up at me, her eyes searching mine. "Thank you, Dalton."

"For what?"

"For making this night almost bearable."

"It's not over yet," I say. "There's still my speech to go."

"You have a speech? Oh God, I'm not sure I'm ready to hear it."

"Yeah," I reply, swiping my hand through my hair. "My father wrote it. That's why he wanted to speak to me earlier."

"He wrote your speech?" She blows out a breath. "Now, I'm even more concerned."

I check my watch. It's almost nine pm. "We should probably head back inside soon. I imagine people will be wondering about our absence."

"Can't we stay a little while longer?"

"Tongues will be wagging. I wonder what whispers will be going around right now," I muse.

"Given your reputation, they probably think we're fucking," she mutters, laughing a little.

"Chance would be a fine thing," I reply, the ache in balls reminding me of how long it's been since I've had sex.

She laughs again. "Are you alright?"

"Alright?"

"In that respect. You clearly have uncontrollable urges."

"I won't lie to you and say that abstaining from sex hasn't been the hardest fucking thing I've ever had to endure," I reply, shaking my head ruefully. "But I have a hand, I use it."

She snorts, dropping her gaze to our entwined fingers. "I'm not sure you should be admitting that whilst holding *my* hand."

"What do you take me for, I'm not a complete animal. I do wash, Daisy," I reply, laughing with her.

"I don't know, you certainly act like one at times."

"Touché," I reply.

"Seriously though, this can't be fun for you. I *almost* feel guilty."

"Are you offering to relieve me of my *urges*, Daisy?" I ask her, cocking a brow.

"Now I know you're desperate. I'm not your type, remember? Or maybe you do just fuck anyone with a vagina."

"After tonight, I'm beginning to see the error of my ways."

"Well, that's a step in the right direction, I guess," she replies, moving to stand.

"Daisy, just wait a second," I say, pulling on her hand, not willing to let her go just yet. This isn't like me, I don't do this kind of thing. Talking with women is usually just a prelude to fucking, but I'm enjoying my time with Daisy and, admittedly, I don't want it to end.

"What?" she asks, sitting back down.

"I never told you how beautiful you look," I say.

"Actually, you did, back in the ballroom," she points out. "Unless of course that was all part of the act."

"It wasn't. I meant it, and I want to say it again. You look incredible tonight. That dress is perfect for you. You truly are the belle of the ball. I also happen to like the colour very much, it reminds me of something..."

"What?"

"Did you choose it because it matches the colour of my eyes?" I ask teasingly.

She rolls her eyes. "You really are extremely egotistical. I chose it because it made me feel good."

"Is that so?"

My gaze drops from her face to the sweetheart neckline of her dress, and the way her pale, freckled skin seems to shimmer in the moonlight, and I find myself wondering how she'd react if I reached out and trailed my fingers across her skin, feeling her softness. Would her breath catch? Would she flinch away, or lean into my touch? Would she want me to touch her as much as I want to touch her right now?

"Would it be so wrong if I kissed you?" I ask, the words tripping out of my mouth before I can stop them.

Her eyes widen, a blush spreading across her cheeks as our gazes clash. "You want to kiss me?"

"I said so, didn't I?"

"You asked if it would be wrong to kiss me, not that you want to."

"Okay then, can I kiss you, Daisy?" I ask, shifting closer, my hand cupping her cheek as I rest my forehead against hers. "Because I really fucking want to."

"Aren't you the kind of man who just takes what he wants?" she whispers back, her lips tantalisingly close to mine.

"Usually, yes," I admit.

"So why aren't you then?"

"Because I want you to *want me* to kiss you."

"That's new…"

"It is," I agree. "Maybe I *was* abducted by aliens."

"It would explain a few things," she replies, her soft laugh dying on her lips as I brush my lips ever so gently against hers.

"So, can I kiss you?"

"I don't want to make a mistake," she whispers back.

"It doesn't have to mean anything," I argue, wanting so badly for her just to give in, to let me taste her sweetness, to savour this moment and explore whatever the hell is happening between us, because something's shifting, and I need to figure out what that is. I need to know if this is just my desire to fuck burning brightly within me, or if it's because I've been spending so much time with her without the tightly bound constraints of my relationship with Drix keeping me in check, or if this is something else entirely.

She pulls back, putting space between us once again. "But that's where you're wrong. It *has* to mean something, Dalton, or what's the point?"

Sliding her hand from mine, she stands. "We should probably go inside now."

Gritting my jaw, I nod. "Yeah, you're right."

"WHERE HAVE YOU BEEN?" my father asks, his anger barely veiled by the thin smile he gives us both as we head back into the ballroom.

"I needed some fresh air," Daisy says before I'm able to respond.

"Well, we've all been waiting for you. It's time for your speech, Dalton," he replies curtly.

Next to me Daisy stiffens, but I take her hand in mine, tugging her into my side. "Come on," I encourage her. "Let's do this."

"Fine," she murmurs, falling into step beside me as we both follow my father onto the stage at the back of the ballroom that's been set up for this very moment.

"Ladies and gentlemen, can we have your attention, please?" my father says, plastering a smile on his face as we approach. "Dalton would like to address you all."

As we take our positions on the stage, the room falls silent, save for the soft instrumental music playing in the background. I steal a glance at Daisy, her eyes locked on to the crowd, the warmth of her fingers seeping into mine as she grasps my hand tightly. I squeeze her fingers briefly before reaching into my pocket and pulling out the speech my father has written for me, my eyes scanning the words. Yet none of them feel right for this moment, they're too stark, too perfunctory, entirely untruthful, and certainly not how I want to express myself to these arseholes. So, I pause, clearing my throat, before folding the paper up and sliding it back into my pocket. Daisy notices, her eyes widening a fraction.

"Ladies, and gentlemen," I say, my voice steady. "I stand before you all tonight, not just as the heir who will eventually take on the mantle of his family's legacy, but as a man who has been humbled by a woman willing to point out his flaws and marry him despite them."

"Dalton, the speech," my father hisses under his breath, but I ignore him, reaching for Daisy's hands, wanting to say this part directly to her.

"Daisy, I've known you for as long as I've been best friends with Drix. I've watched you blossom into a beautiful, resilient, *compassionate* individual despite the cruel treatment you've received from some members of this town, and the judgement of many others."

As I expected, there is an audible gasp from the crowd and a flurry of whispered comments erupts in the room. But I remain steadfast and pay no attention to them. Nor do I pay any mind to my father's obvious disapproval. I really don't give a fuck what he or any one else thinks for that matter. Right now, I need Daisy to know that I've got her back, that I will stand by her as my fiance, my wife, and eventually, the mother to my child. This might not be a declaration of love, but it is meant to be a declaration of my support, and I hope to fuck she sees it that way.

"I've come to admire you more and more with every passing day, and I'm grateful that you've chosen to be my wife despite knowing that we will have many more hurdles to overcome. I believe, wholeheartedly, if we face them together our relationship will only strengthen," I add, surprising myself.

"Dalton, what are you doing?" Daisy whispers, a question in her gaze as she glances out into the audience.

"Despite my past mistakes, of which there are many, I promise to honour our relationship, and the vows we will soon make to one another."

Stepping closer, I release her hands, and cup her face in my palms. She blinks up at me, uncertainty clouding her features, before a deep blush spreads across her cheeks.

With fierce determination, I lower my voice to a whisper and say, "I'm taking that kiss now, Daisy."

Then, without hesitation, I press my lips against hers with bruising force, causing her hands to fly up to the lapel of my jacket as she holds on tight, drawing her closer as her fingers dig into the fabric. Our kiss deepens as she melts into my embrace, and my fingers curl into her hair, tugging on the strands. She whimpers a little, and by fuck the sound is like music to my ears and a jolt of electricity to my cock. This kiss ignites the embers of my attraction, fueling them until they're fanning flames. I feel them lick over my skin as our tongues dance and my body presses against hers in an indecent embrace. I'm vaguely aware that we have an audience, but honestly as she whimpers into my mouth, I don't give a fuck about anything other than the taste of her glossy lips on mine, the feel of her silken body pressed against me, the heady scent of her skin, and the soft moans and whimpers that send me fucking feral.

"Well, Dalton," I hear my father say, his firm grip on my shoulder forcing me to break our kiss, as everything comes back into focus. "I think it's time you release your fiance, don't you?" he adds with a forced chuckle, mirroring the insincere laughter of the crowd. "A toast to Dalton and Daisy!"

Daisy's cheeks are flaming as she lifts her trembling fingertips to her mouth, her eyes as round as coins, shiny and bright as I slide my hand into hers, squeezing it tightly. She attempts to pull her hand away, clearly angry that I stole that kiss, but I refuse to let her go as my father's words cut through the air like a sharp knife, stinging me with their disapproval.

"To Dalton and Daisy," the crowd replies, raising their glasses, despite the glares of disdain and the palpable shock at my defiance.

I find myself searching the crowd, finally settling my gaze on Drix and Lia. Lia smiles in what seems like approval, and Drix acknowledges my gaze with a tight nod. I can tell he's pissed off that I kissed Daisy, but I'm hoping he at least trusts my promise, because despite selfishly stealing that kiss, I meant everything I said.

CHAPTER THIRTEEN

"So, that kiss..." Lia says, her voice trailing off as warm puffs of air release from her mouth. It's midweek, and we're sitting huddled together on the park bench whilst Drix and Toby run around the playground together, their laughter a balm to the churning feelings inside my stomach.

"...Was unexpected," I reply carefully, still not sure how I feel about it, in all honesty.

"From where I was standing it looked like you were enjoying yourself," she teases, nudging me with her arm.

"I can't deny that he's a good kisser," I mumble, my cheeks heating.

"But?"

"But it's all part of the act. We had to make our engagement look real," I reply, hating how good it had felt in the moment, knowing that it meant nothing.

"Well if that's the case, he's a *very* good actor," Lia muses.

"He's Dalton Gunn. He's been brought up to behave a certain way his whole life. Piling on the charm and putting on a show comes easily to him."

"And the speech, you think that was insincere?" she probes.

"I don't know..." I falter, my words trailing off. "It certainly wasn't the speech his father wrote for him. That I do know for sure."

"His father wrote an engagement speech for him? That figures," Lia comments, her feelings towards Carl about the same as mine. That is, she doesn't think much of him either.

"He did. They argued about it after everyone left the engagement party. It's been a tense few days," I admit.

"That doesn't sound fun."

"Not at all," I agree with a heavy sigh. "Dalton and Carl are barely speaking, which has made our last few evening meals together intolerable, and Dalton has thrown himself into work. I haven't really spoken to him much these past couple of days either." I heave out a sigh, feeling my chest tighten at the continued strain between us. "As soon as I think we're making headway together, something crops up and we're back to being distant again. I'm not asking to be best friends with him, Lia. I just want to make this whole situation as bearable as possible."

"Can I be honest with you, Daisy?" Lia asks carefully.

"Of course, I could use some honesty."

"I truly believe that Dalton was being sincere when he said what he did at your engagement party. I think that..." she hesitates, ruminating on her words.

"You think what?"

"That he *genuinely* likes you, and maybe he's struggling a little with that given the situation you're in, and his relationship with Drix."

"He's already told me he *likes* me, as much as a man like Dalton can like anyone," I add with a shake of my head.

"That's not what I meant," she continues.

"Then what are you saying?" I ask.

"Do you remember that time a few months back when you

found out that he fired Lewis for sleeping with someone else whilst dating you?"

"Yes, he was being an interfering arse," I reply, remembering the moment well. I'd been so angry at Dalton for sticking his nose in my personal business that we'd exchanged quite a few heated words in front of a restaurant full of people at the hotel, and then I called him an arsehole and stormed off.

"After you argued, I had a brief conversation with him," she continues on.

"You never said."

"You were so angry, and we were just getting to know each other. I didn't want you to think *I* was interfering," she explains, pulling a face.

"Lia, you're my friend. You're the love of my brother's life, I'd never assume you were interfering. So what was said during this conversation exactly?"

"That he fired Lewis because he was looking out for you."

I shake my head. "He would say that. He's a control freak. Besides, both him and Drix have always meddled with my past relationships. It's just what they do."

"He also went on to say that none of the men you dated have been good enough for you."

"He said that?" I ask, a little shocked to be honest.

"Yes," she nods her head, searching my gaze. "He told me that he sees you like a sister..."

For some reason that makes me feel worse, not better. "Fabulous," I mutter.

"But I didn't believe a word of it," Lia adds.

"So you think he was acting then, too?"

"No, Daisy, I think he *truly* cares for you."

"If he does, it's *because* I'm Drix's sister. Nothing more."

"There's something else I've never mentioned to you," she continues, flicking her gaze my way.

"Oh no, what?"

"Do you remember that night Drix took me to Bandits Bar to see the band play."

"The night when he tripped over his tongue because you looked so damn hot, you mean?" I respond playfully, remembering that moment well.

She grins. "Well, that night Dalton asked me to dance."

"I bet he did."

"It wasn't like that. He was very respectful."

"Okay, so you danced..." I let my voice trail off as I wait for her to continue.

"He asked for my advice about a woman he liked."

"I'm not sure I want to know," I admit. "It was bad enough that I found at our engagement party that he'd slept with my ex-friend Clarissa."

Lia's eyes widen. "That can't have been fun."

"It wasn't, but the fact he told her to her face that he regretted sleeping with her made up for it."

"Wait, when did that happen?" Lia asks, eyes wide with delight.

"At our engagement party. I overheard her talking about me unkindly, and I finally told her what I thought of her."

Lia grins. "Good for you!"

"Then Dalton came along and backed me up. He was... kind."

Lia grins, her eyes twinkling. "I knew it."

"You're reading into things," I say, brushing her off with a wave of my hand. "So... this woman that he asked your advice about. Who was she?"

"He never said, but given the conversation I had with him at the restaurant after you argued, I believe that woman is you."

"No way. Nope. Impossible," I reply, shaking my head. "Up until very recently Dalton and I hated each other."

"Look, I really don't know Dalton all that well," she says,

grasping my hand, and squeezing it gently. "But I do believe there is a lot more to how he feels about you than he's willing to acknowledge. The way he kissed you at the engagement party was not how a man kisses a woman who he sees as his little sister."

"Dalton and I are just playing a part," I argue, suddenly feeling very uncomfortable in my skin as my stomach does this weird flip-flop.

Lia tips her head to the side as she regards me. "But there *is* an undeniable chemistry between you. Even when you supposedly hated each other, I could sense it. You can't tell me you don't feel it?"

"I honestly don't know what I feel, or what's even real. I'm a little out of my depth here," I admit, recalling how it felt to have his hands on me that time in the spa, how it felt to have his lips on mine at Bandits Bar and then at our engagement party. But more than that, how he'd had my back when Clarissa had been cruel, and how he'd supported my choice to wear a dress of my choosing.

"Maybe you're just too scared to admit the truth to yourself."

"What truth?"

"That at the very least Dalton's attracted to you, and that maybe you're attracted to him too."

I heave out a sigh, shaking my head. "Dalton is a sex addict, Lia, and right now he's unable to indulge his desires. That kiss was a byproduct of all his pent up sexual tension. That's all it was, and I was playing along for the sake of our contract."

"Okay, if that's what you truly believe then I apologise for suggesting otherwise. But will you just do me a favour?"

"What?"

"If you do find yourself feeling something deeper for Dalton, and he reciprocates, don't close yourself off to the potential of something real. Don't be afraid to explore it. If I'd let my fear get the better of me, Drix and I might not be together today."

Her words linger in the crisp January air, mingling with the distant laughter of Drix and Toby as they continue to play. I watch them for a moment, their carefree joy a stark contrast to the turmoil gathering in my own heart. I honestly don't know what to believe. Could Lia be right? Could it be that Dalton really sees me more than just his best friend's younger sister? Could there be the potential for something more? And even if I did want something more, is Dalton capable of something deeper than just physical intimacy? I highly doubt it.

Before I can dwell on it further, Drix strides over to the both of us with Toby in his arms. "I think it's time we got Toby something to eat, he's worked up quite an appetite."

AN HOUR LATER, after dropping Lia and Toby home, Drix and I are sitting together in his car on the driveway of Highwood Manor Estate, an uncomfortable tension between us. Throughout lunch at Daphne's café he'd been thoughtful, quiet. I know there was a lot he wanted to say, but refrained given the cafe was full of people.

"So," Drix begins.

"So?" I retort, turning my body to face him. "Whatever you've been keeping inside, just spit it out, Drix."

He scowls, his fingers drumming on the steering wheel. "He kissed you, Daise."

"He did."

"I warned him not to touch you."

"It would've been a little weird if he hadn't kissed me, don't you think?" I reply. "We're engaged to be married after all."

"He could've pecked you on the cheek, not practically mauled you!" he says, side-eyeing me.

"We did what we had to do," I counter.

"He took liberties," he argues, scowling.

"You heard what Mrs Fernsby had to say, she was *surprised* to hear of our engagement. She doesn't believe it's genuine any more than the rest of the guests did. Everyone was whispering about us, Drix. Even Clarissa believed that the only reason Dalton is marrying me is because he must've gotten me pregnant. The sad fact is, they're suspicions aren't even that far from the truth," I reply bitterly. "God forbid a wealthy man like Dalton Gunn would ever choose to marry someone like me."

Drix runs a hand over his face, his features softening as he looks at me. "Don't do that," he says.

"What, speak the truth?" I reply heatedly.

"Put yourself down. Any man would be lucky to have you as their wife. You're an incredible person, Daisy."

"I'm not searching for compliments, Drix, I'm just stating the facts. They sensed something wasn't quite right, so Dalton and I tried to counter that. We have to make this believable, you know that."

"I do, but I don't have to like it."

"Well, you'd better get used to it, because this is how it's going to be," I reply, stoically. "I'm marrying Dalton in a little under a month."

"I know." His jaw grits as he looks out of the window, but he doesn't try to argue.

"Eventually Dalton and I are going to have a child together, and I need you to support me when that happens."

"Of course I'll support you, Daisy. I'll even be there when you give birth if that's what you want," he offers, reaching for my hand and folding his fingers around mine.

"Erm, I think that's taking it a bit far. I don't need you seeing my vagina, Drix," I chuckle.

"Yeah, okay, fair point," he agrees, then his expression darkens. "And neither will Dalton."

"He'll be the father."

"And he can wait outside the damn labour room with me," he mutters.

"Let's not think about that for now," I reply, waving off his concerns. "We haven't even gotten that far yet, let alone discussed the practicalities of it."

"Don't you think you should?"

"Yes, and we will. Don't worry, Drix. We've had several conversations about boundaries already," I say, trying to reassure him.

He nods, then falls silent for a moment. "Have you told him?"

"Told him about what?"

"What happened to you as a kid? Your fear of the dark."

I shake my head. "He doesn't need to know. Besides, I have a bedside lamp. I use it."

Drix stares at me, his eyes searching mine. "What about the nightmares?"

"I haven't had any in months, and if it hadn't escaped your notice Highwood Manor is huge. I doubt anyone will hear anything even if I do have one."

Drix's expression softens, his fingers still intertwined with mine. "I just worry about you, Daisy. You've been through so much, and I won't be there should anything happen," he says, his voice filled with concern.

"You've always looked out for me, but I'm okay, honestly," I say, squeezing his hand reassuringly.

"I know you're strong, but you don't always have to be. Call me, any time day or night, and I will come. You know I will," he says, reaching for me and pulling me into a tight hug.

"I know that, and I love you for it," I reply, hugging him back.

"Love you too, Daise."

"Now, you go home, go back to that beautiful family of yours," I say, untangling myself from his arms.

"Okay. See you at Bandits Bar this weekend?"

"Definitely," I reply, plastering on a smile as I step out of the car. Before slamming the door, I lean down and ask, "So, what's the deal with Ben and Harlow?"

He frowns. "Ben and Harlow? Nothing."

"I got the impression something was going on between them. Sterling looked pretty taken aback about the fact Harlow is singing at Ben's bar."

Drix blows out a long breath. "Yeah, he was."

"So?" I press, my curiosity piqued.

"So you're barking up the wrong tree," he replies cagily.

My brows furrow in confusion. "But...*wait*, are you suggesting...?" He gives me a pointed look that confirms my suspicions. "There's something going on between Sterling and his *stepsister*?"

Drix pulls a face. "I've said too much already."

"Wow, and here's me thinking my situation couldn't get any more complicated."

"My thoughts exactly."

CHAPTER FOURTEEN

"Are you ready, Daisy?" I ask, knocking on her bedroom door and pushing it open without waiting for an answer.

It's Saturday night and we're about to head out to Bandits Bar to watch Harlow sing. Christ knows that I could use a drink, it's been exactly one week since our engagement party and the first time we've been out together as an officially engaged 'couple' since I let the whole town know what I think of them. At least tonight we'll be surrounded by friends. For the most part, anyway.

"Dalton!" Daisy exclaims, covering her bra-covered chest as I stand on the threshold of her room. It takes me about five seconds too long to look away, and I have to smother a smile at the heat flooding her chest and neck, pretty sure the shade matches her bra.

"Apologies, I thought you'd be ready," I say, averting my gaze as I cross my arms and lean against the doorframe.

"You said be ready at seven-thirty, it's only quarter past," she reminds me.

"My bad," I reply, not feeling very bad about it at all.

"Then go wait for me downstairs!" she scolds, reaching for the red silk blouse that I'd bought her not too long ago.

"I'm fine right here," I say as she turns her back to me and pulls on the blouse, hurriedly doing up the buttons before tucking it into the rainbow striped mini-skirt that I happen to like a little bit too much.

"This is not respecting my boundaries," she reminds me, sitting on the edge of her bed and pulling on a pair of bright green, platform trainers.

I stare at them transfixed, or perhaps it's her slim ankles and shapely legs dusted in freckles that has caught my attention. I can't help but wonder if every inch of her skin is covered in them too.

"I'll work on it," I offer with a shrug.

"You're being obnoxious," she counters, but she doesn't insist on me leaving and so I take that as an invitation to stay.

"I'll try to refrain from being obnoxious the rest of the evening."

She snorts, shaking her head. "So we're back to talking now, are we?"

"I hadn't realised we were ignoring each other again. Is this about the kiss at our engagement party?" I reply, enjoying her sass.

Truth be known, I've missed it. I've been looking forward to tonight all damn week. Not because we're heading to Bandits Bar to hear Harlow sing, but because I'll get to spend some time with Daisy. I don't know what that means, and I don't care to look into it too deeply either.

"You tell me. You're the one who's barely said a handful of words to me this past week since the engagement party," she throws back, snatching up her bright blue, woollen coat. It grazes the tops of her ankles, covering up all that pretty skin.

"My dad has been busting my arse with a lot of work," I explain. "He's getting me back for going rogue, and not reading his damn speech."

"So that's your excuse?" she asks, lifting a brow, her lips thinning as she glares at me.

"I didn't realise you missed me that much. You should've said something sooner, I would've made the time, Daisy," I reply.

"I didn't miss you. I just..." She blows out a breath. "Nevermind."

"Don't 'nevermind' me. Tell me what you're thinking, Daisy."

Grabbing her bag, she slings it over her shoulder and strides towards me. "Nothing's on my mind," she snaps.

I throw my arm out, blocking her path as my fingers wrap around the doorframe. "I'm not going to let you leave until you tell me why you're so pissed off."

"Dalton!"

"Daisy..." I insist.

"You kissed me."

"I did."

"You said all of those things in front of everyone, then you kissed me," she accuses, folding her arms across her chest as she glares at me.

"Okay, so was it the kiss or the speech that made you miss me?"

"Neither, because I haven't missed you."

"You're feisty tonight," I observe, my lips flickering with a smile. "And very argumentative."

"Well, this is the Daisy you get when you act like you care, kiss me in front of everyone, and then ignore me all week."

"Let's break this down, shall we?"

She pouts her glossy lips, and I want nothing more than to kiss her. Instead I adjust my body, completely blocking her path. "Talk to me."

"You're not going to let this go, are you?"

"Nope."

"Okay, then. Did you mean what you said?" she asks, cocking her brow.

"I meant it. Yes. Every last word."

She considers me for a moment. "Lia thought you were being sincere."

"I knew there was a reason why I liked Lia so much," I grin. "And what about you, did you think I was being sincere?"

"In contrast, Drix thought you were taking liberties," she replies, ignoring my question.

"Well, they're both correct," I counter.

"You admit to taking liberties?"

"I wanted to kiss you. So I kissed you. I don't regret it," I add reaching out to pinch the end of the curl that's framing her face. "In fact, I rather enjoyed it. Besides, you seemed to like it too."

She slaps my hand away. "I kissed you back because it would've given the game away if I had kneed you in the balls, Dalton."

Leaning in closer, I lower my voice. "Do you know what I think?"

"What?" she counters, her gaze briefly dropping to my lips, before she quickly flicks her eyes back up again.

"I think you liked the speech I gave, and that you know deep down I was being sincere. I also believe that you enjoyed the kiss. Furthermore, I think you're pissed off because I haven't given you much attention this week," I observe.

Her eyes widen for a moment before narrowing again. "Are you trying to be funny?"

I chuckle, enjoying the banter between us. "I'm always trying, Daisy."

"Yeah, *very* trying," she retorts, jutting her chin out as she turns her face away from me.

Reaching for her, I rest my fingers against her chin, urging her to look at me. "Firstly, I'm sorry I haven't made time for you this week. You have my word, I will do better. Secondly, I want you to know that I meant everything I said. None of that was for show."

"But the kiss was?" she whispers.

"No it wasn't. That kiss was for me. I *wanted* to kiss you."

"Because you were trying to prove a point that you can take whatever you want and damn the consequences," she counters.

"No, because you looked stunning, and I knew that if I tried to kiss you when there wasn't an audience you wouldn't have let me. It was selfish, but I'd do it again just to get a taste of your lips, to feel your body melt against mine, and to hear those pretty little whimpers you make when I fuck your mouth with my tongue." I lean in closer, my breath mingling with hers as I murmur, "And I'm getting the distinct impression that you rather enjoy that side of me."

"That kiss..." she begins, her floral scent lifting up into the air and making me want to bury my nose against her throat.

"Yes?"

"Was good," she replies, her lips millimetres from mine.

"It was," I agree, smirking.

"But I've had better," she retorts, shoving me against my chest and striding past me.

She's had better?

No, she did not just fucking say that! Firstly, I'm a damn good kisser, and secondly, how many fucking men has she kissed exactly? Those thoughts run rampant through my head as I watch her storm away, and for a moment I have to gather myself, because my dick is doing its own thing again, and is straining against the zipper of my jeans, and my heart? That bastard muscle is pounding in my chest as if I've just run ten miles on the treadmill.

Fuck she's infuriating, not to mention entirely correct in her judgement of me.

I *have* been ignoring her this week. Not because I don't want to spend time with her, but because all I want to do is spend time with her. Why? *Fuck if I know.* I mean, she is fun to be around. I do like her, but I'm not used to this. The longest time I've ever spent with a woman before is a few hours before and during sex, and if they're lucky I stick around for the night just so that I can fuck them in the morning. But having actual conversations with them? Fuck, no.

Yet, I find myself wanting to pass the time with Daisy, and it's messing with my head.

"Fuck," I mutter, pushing off from the doorframe and striding after Daisy, knowing that tonight truly is going to be a test of my control.

"YOU LOOK like you've just swallowed a wasp," Sterling remarks, leaning his back against the bar next to me as I drag my gaze away from Daisy who is currently laughing animatedly with Riley, one of Drix's close friends and his employee at the gym he owns. He's a nice guy, we've all hung out together before, but right now I'm not feeling all that friendly towards him. In fact, I'm feeling slightly murderous.

"I'm fine!" I grind out, my fingers curling into fists at my side.

Sterling laughs, seeing right through me. "You're fuming."

"And you're drunk," I retort, noticing the glazed look in his eyes.

"Whatever," he replies, flicking his gaze towards Harlow, who is currently setting up her equipment on the stage.

Needing something else to focus on, I follow his gaze. Admittedly, Harlow's an attractive woman with long, silky blonde hair and sun-kissed skin, but there's something about her that just doesn't click for me. Maybe it's the way she's been giving Sterling the cold shoulder, or perhaps it's the fact that I am so thoroughly preoccupied with Daisy to even think about another woman in that way. One minute we're on the verge of being friends, and there's an ease between us that I could get used to, the next we're back to being enemies and throwing insults in each other's faces, and if we're not doing either of those things, I'm kissing her and she's kissing me back. All I know is that right now I'm on edge, and I'm not happy about it.

"I don't even know why I'm here," Sterling mumbles, drawing my attention back to him.

"Things not going too well in the Blade household I take it?"

"You're kidding, right?" he asks, knocking back another mouthful of scotch. "It's a fucking nightmare."

"Have you told Robert about you and Harlow?" I ask, lowering my voice.

"Yes, my dad was particularly pleased to find out that I had the best sex of my life with my step sister a few months before he married her mum," he hisses. "Of course I fucking haven't."

"Are you planning on doing anything about it?"

"About it?"

"You know, the fact you've still got a raging hard-on for her."

"Like what, exactly?" he groans, dragging out a long breath.

"She's not blood related," I offer with a shrug.

"It's not as simple as that," he retorts. "Besides, our one night stand started with her lying to me about her name, and ended with her sneaking off without a goodbye, let alone any way to contact her. She's refused to talk to me about what happened between us apart from telling me that it was a mistake. So despite pointing out that she's not actually my sister, there isn't a chance in hell that anything further could happen between us for a multitude of fucked-up reasons."

"Well that blows," I retort, twisting my body around, so I can order us both another drink. I catch Ben's attention and he strides towards me, a grin breaking across his face.

"Another one?" he asks, lifting a brow.

"Yes, for both me and Sterling," I reply, just as Harlow begins to sing.

"Oh fuck," Sterling mutters, tensing beside me as his eyes snap to the stage, instantly mesmerised.

"You think you should be encouraging him?" Ben questions.

"Listen, all is not well in the Blade household. He needs another drink."

"It's that bad?" Ben asks, pulling a face.

"Worse," I reply, my attention drawn to Daisy, and my own problems. She's stopped chatting with Riley, entranced by Harlow's singing as much as everyone else appears to be, but she hasn't moved away from him. In fact, I *do not* like how fucking close he's standing next to her right now.

"I meant Sterling," Ben says, following my gaze. "Though I'm guessing you're having a bad night too?"

"What do you think?" I grind out, my jaw clenching.

"I think you need to get laid," he retorts with a chuckle, knowing full well the predicament I'm in.

"Fuck you, Ben."

He straightens his features as best as he can, but there's no missing the spark of mirth in his eyes. "Might do you some good, abstaining from sex for a while. You could use the time to work on improving your personality. Silver linings and all that."

"Since we're talking about our sex lives, or lack thereof, how are things between you and *Mrs* Elodie Hoxton? Is she still married to that cunt?" I ask, referring to the woman he's obsessed with, and her marriage to the sleaziest, most corrupt man I've ever had the displeasure of meeting.

Ben's gaze darkens, his smile slipping into a scowl. "I'm working on it."

"Sounds complicated. Did he actually take you up on your offer?"

"He did, though we haven't finalised the details. *Yet,*" he adds, pouring himself a shot of scotch, and knocking it back before sliding the other two shot glasses towards me. "Though I plan on cashing in soon."

"Bet that went down well with Elodie," I remark. "Are you sure this is a good idea?"

"No, but if her husband is willing to accept two million pounds in exchange for me spending an uninterrupted month with her, then she's got to see what a bastard he is and divorce him."

"You don't think that she'll see you the same way for even suggesting this, let alone going through with it? That's one hell of an indecent proposal, don't you think?"

"It's a risk I'm willing to take," he replies, swiping a hand over his face. "Besides, what the fuck have I got to lose?"

"About two million pounds," I point out.

"She's worth it," he retorts without hesitation.

"Well, I guess we'll have each other to drown our sorrows with if everything goes tits up," I comment, eyeing Daisy once more.

Ben lets out a humourless chuckle. "How are things with you and Daisy, anyway?" he asks, just as Riley ducks down and whispers something into her ear.

My gut churns as I watch her turn her body into his as she listens, and even though I know it's probably because she can't hear him all that well over the music, a blaze of jealousy and possessiveness flares to life inside my chest.

"The fuck?" I snarl.

"Dalton..." Ben warns, but it's too late, because before he can stop me I'm already halfway across the room, pretty sure I'm about to cause a fucking scene.

CHAPTER FIFTEEN

"...And then Troy split his shorts right down the arse-crack when he bent over to pick up the weights he was lifting," Riley continues, breaking into a smile that has me snort-laughing.

"Oh my God, I bet the women at the gym loved that," I reply, giggling.

Riley smirks, dropping his mouth to my ear. "You bet they did, and a few of the men too, especially when he was completely starkers beneath them. Pretty sure the whole gym caught a glimpse of his family jewels, and a lot more besides."

I tip my head back and let out a raucous laugh, clutching my belly at the thought. "You're killing me, Riley!"

"Having fun?" a familiar voice mutters.

I snap my head around to find Dalton standing right behind me, his jaw clenched tight as he glares at us both. What the hell is his problem?

"Evening mate, I was just telling Daisy about Troy splitting his shorts at the gym yesterday. It was fucking hilarious," he says, good-naturedly, completely oblivious to the fact that Dalton looks like he's about to burst a blood vessel.

"Enjoying the singing?" Dalton asks pointedly.

"She's got a great voice," Riley answers with a grin.

"I agree, so maybe you should spend more time listening to it than flirting with my fiance!"

"Flirting?" Riley questions, flicking a bemused look my way. "We were just talking, weren't we, Petal?"

Dalton's nostrils flare. "*Petal?!*"

"Ignore him, Riley, he's had a little too much to drink, clearly," I interject with a scowl of my own.

"I'm not nearly drunk enough for this shit!" he snaps back.

"You've got it all twisted, Dalton. Daisy's a friend," Riley says, his tone conciliatory.

"You called her *Petal*," he growls.

"It's just a nickname," Riley shrugs, nonplussed. "All the guys at the gym call Daisy that."

"All the guys at the gym?!" Dalton counters, a muscle in his jaw flexing as he grits his teeth.

"It's cute, right?" Riley asks.

"Cute? It's fucking–" Dalton begins, but I cut him off.

"This is ridiculous. Maybe you should go outside. Get some air, and sober up a bit?" I suggest.

Riley clears his throat uncomfortably as he casts his gaze between us, eyes widening a fraction. "I should probably go and get that drink now," he says, but then hesitates, turning to face me. "Are you going to be alright?"

"Of course she'll be alright, what the hell do you take me for?" Dalton snaps at him, before reaching for my hand. "Come with me. Now!"

I take a step back from him, shaking my head. "With you acting like this, absolutely-fucking not."

"Listen, I can see you're pissed off," Riley interjects, "Though I've no idea why given we were just talking."

"You were flirting with her!" Dalton argues, his voice rising.

"You need to calm down, and consider how you're acting," Riley scolds, none too impressed with Dalton's behaviour.

"Fuck. Off. Riley!"

"Dalton, that's enough," I hiss, embarrassment heating my cheeks.

"You need to get your shit together, man," Riley argues, reaching out to grasp Dalton's shoulder, a mixture of concern and warning on his face. "This ain't a good look."

"Don't tell me what I should do," Dalton grinds out.

"Someone needs to!" I say, flicking my gaze across the room.

Thank goodness everyone is entranced by Harlow's singing and Drix is preoccupied dancing with Lia because I know for a fact he'll lose his shit if he sees the way Dalton is behaving right now.

"Come on, Dalton, have a little respect for Daisy. She doesn't deserve this," Riley adds.

Dalton grits his jaw, and for a moment I think things are going to escalate, but instead he nods sharply, swiping a hand through his hair, his expression falling. "Fuck!" he exclaims.

Riley frowns, genuinely concerned. "Seriously, though. Are you alright, man?"

"Apologies, Riley, Daisy. I'm being a dick," Dalton replies, blowing out a breath as he shakes his head. "I should probably go outside and get some fresh air."

"Yeah, seems like a good idea," Riley agrees as Dalton twists on his heel and storms off, shoving the door open before stepping outside. "What the hell was that all about?"

"Things are a little tense," I admit.

"Tense?"

"With the wedding plans," I lie.

Riley reaches out and squeezes my shoulder reassuringly. "I can see how that could happen. Looks as though you could both do with talking things through?" he says reasonably.

"Yes, you're probably right," I agree, chewing on my lip, though I'm honestly not sure how to handle the situation. Dalton had warned me he was possessive, but Riley is a friend to both me and Dalton, and I don't know how to feel about how he's acting. I don't like his behaviour, not one bit, but equally, I'm confused by it. His apparent jealousy would imply that he feels some type of way about me, but then again, perhaps I'm reading too much into it.

Riley gives me a sympathetic look before nodding. "Want some moral support?" he offers.

"Probably best if I do this alone," I reply, my attention drawn to Dalton through the window. He's standing outside, his hands shoved into his pockets, staring off into the distance. "I'll go talk to him now."

Riley offers me a smile before excusing himself to get a drink. I take one last glance out of the window before heading outside to find Dalton leaning against the wall, his gaze fixed on the ground.

"Dalton," I start tentatively.

"Just give me a moment, Daisy, or should I say, *Petal*?" he adds, cutting his gaze my way.

"He meant nothing by it," I find myself saying.

"It's too familiar," he counters.

"He's a friend. Yours too," I remind him. "Riley isn't like that. You know that."

"And the rest of the guys at the gym?" he questions. "Because apparently they all call you *Petal* too."

"Are just friends. I do have some you know," I point out.

Dalton pinches the bridge of his nose, muttering something under his breath. "I just—"

"You just what, Dalton?" I press, folding my arms around myself, white clouds escaping my lips from the cold.

"I was..."

"...Just super rude to both Riley and me? Acting insane? Trying to manhandle me? Should I go on?"

"I warned you I can be possessive," he retorts, a muscle in his jaw feathering as he side-eyes me.

"What I don't understand is *why*? Is it because you don't like someone else paying attention to one of your toys, is that it?" He opens his mouth to respond, but I hold my hand up, refusing to let him speak. "Firstly, I can talk to whomever I want, and secondly I'm a human being, Dalton, not some possession that you can pick up and discard at whim. You've pretty much ignored me all week, but the moment anyone else pays me any attention you act all possessive!"

"You're not a toy, Daisy, but you are *mine*," he retorts, taking a step towards me.

"We've been over this," I reply, exasperated. "I am not yours, I am my own person. After everything you said at the engagement party, I thought you were beginning to understand that! Clearly, you don't."

Anger blazes across Dalton's face as he reaches for me. One minute I'm facing him, the next my back is against the brick wall with his body pressed against mine.

"You're driving me insane!" he snaps.

"I think you'll find that you're already a little unhinged," I shoot back, trying to shove him off me, but he reaches for my hands, pinning them above my head with one hand whilst the other clasps my jaw. I gasp, a mixture of fear, and something else I don't want to look too closely at, scattering down my spine at the intense way he looks at me.

"You don't get it," he grinds out, his fingers curling tighter around my wrists.

"No, you're right, I don't get it," I heave out, my heart pounding as hard as his appears to be right now. "Now, let me go!"

We share a heated stare, our bodies communicating more than

words ever could. I don't want him to treat me this way, yet my body is betraying me once again as a flood of arousal pools between my legs at the *heat* between us.

"I think you want me to kiss you, not let you go," he accuses, his lips brushing against my cheek.

"You're delusional," I reply, my heart tripping inside my chest as he drags his lips across my jaw.

"You're turned on," he says, before pressing his mouth against the pulse in my neck.

"I'm not," I protest. "I'm angry."

And turned on, but he doesn't need to know that.

"I think you want me to trap your body like this," he continues, grinding his hips against mine as I drag in a sharp breath at his very obvious erection, "So you can feel what you do to me. So you know how much you drive me fucking crazy."

"You have an addiction, Dalton," I reply, not even trying to stop him as he slides his thigh between my legs.

"Yes, to you it would fucking seem."

"No, your need to be in control makes you possessive of me."

"You've no idea," he mutters against my skin, his tongue tasting me.

"Your need to fuck makes me attractive to you," I continue, biting down a moan at the unholy way he's licking my skin.

"That's not the only reason," he replies, gently biting down on the lobe of my ear.

"Your need to appease your ego makes me someone you want to toy with," I breathe, chest heaving.

"No," he insists, his teeth scraping over the tender flesh of my neck.

"None of this is what I need."

"But it is what you *want*," he counters, his lips grazing my collarbone as he releases my hands and reaches for the hem of my miniskirt. My hands fall to my side, just hanging there.

"I didn't say that."

"So why aren't you pushing me away, Daisy?"

"Because..."

"Because?" he murmurs, swirling his tongue over the dip in my neck.

Because I'm broken.

Bitter tears prick my eyes at the thought, and I hate that I feel so damn vulnerable. Logically, I *know* that the attention Dalton is giving me right now is a knee jerk reaction to my conversation with Riley, and a byproduct of his sexual addiction and possessiveness. I know that this isn't about him wanting *me*, but try telling that to the damaged little girl who still lives inside of me.

"Admit it, you can't fight this anymore than I can," he mutters. "*That's* why you're not pushing me away.."

"I have flaws too," I admit quietly, heaving out a tremulous breath, my eyes stinging with tears.

"I highly doubt that," Dalton replies, his lips sliding back up my neck, his fingers pushing up my skirt, the heat of his hand like a trail of flames licking across my skin.

A low, desperate moan escapes my lips as I whisper, "I do."

Dalton's hand glides over my hip with a possessive hold, his fingers digging in as he presses the firm muscle of his thigh against my aching pussy. The sensation sets me on fire, making me writhe and yearn for more.

"Oh God," I gasp, seeking pleasure, ignoring everything else.

"Tell me about your flaws, Daisy," he commands, his voice gravelly and intense, just like painful little stones beneath bare feet. "Tell me what you've been hiding beneath that sweetness you extend to everyone but me, and whilst you do, keep using my thigh to get yourself off."

With each word, his fingers squeeze and knead my arse, driving me closer to the edge as my body moves uncontrollably against his thigh, pleasure building as I rock against him.

It's wrong, but I can't stop. I can't.

"I ignore red flags," I whisper as he brushes his lips against mine, confessing my sins.

"I know, I've seen how many you've ignored over the years with other men. Fucking drives me crazy."

"I crave physical touch," I admit, my fingers curling into fists at my side as I try to stop myself from reaching for him and hauling him closer.

"Interesting," he replies, his free hand sliding up and over the centre of my chest and gently resting around my throat, his thumb stroking the thrumming pulse in my neck. "Anything else?"

"No!" I snap, refusing to let him get any more insight into my damaged heart.

"You're lying," he goads against my lips, his fingers tightening a little.

It only seems to add to the pleasure building in my core. My airways thin, forcing me to drag in more oxygen between my parted lips, intensifying the thrum between my legs. His touch is both a taunt and a seduction that leaves me dizzy with desire. The heat from his body brands mine, searing through the fabric of my clothes.

I gasp. "Don't..."

"Don't what? Don't hold your quivering pulse in my hand? Don't lick your skin? Don't taste your lips? Don't press my thigh against your dripping cunt? Don't what, Daisy?"

Don't stop.

I know that I should push him away, put an end to this reckless game before it consumes us both. Yet all rational thought evaporates into thin air as an orgasm builds, gaining traction with every rock of my hips, every gasping breath, every teasing burn of his lips against my skin.

"Tell me what you're hiding, Daisy. Tell me and I'll let you come."

"Don't make me say it," I whisper.

"Daisy, tell me. Tell me what's hidden beneath that pretty smile, and those bright clothes you wear."

"I can't."

"You will," he insists, his eyes glinting with determination, his fingers tightening on my hips as he guides me to rock faster, to chase the pleasure.

I tremble uncontrollably from his touch, from the orgasm building within me, from the heartbreaking, desperate truth hovering on my lips. My fists curl tighter as I try to find the strength to resist him, but the pleasure he's conjured is overpowering any semblance of sanity.

"Please," I croak, my voice shaking as stars pinwheel behind my closed eyelids and the first wave of my orgasm begins to crest, "D-don't make me say it."

He pulls back slightly. "Open your eyes and look at me," he demands.

My eyes snap open, and behind them tears tremble on my lashes.

"Daisy?" he gasps, the forcefulness of his need to know what I'm keeping hidden from him wavering at my distress.

I blink, and one by one my tears fall as I rip open my chest and admit the truth. "I seek out affection from the wrong type of man in my need to feel wanted, so I feel like I'm worth something, that I'm *loved*, because the right type of man never seems to want me."

"What?" he questions, pulling back, his body going rigid.

Everything comes to a screeching halt, my breath, his body, the sound of Harlow singing inside, the goddamn universe. Any pleasure I felt disappears and is replaced with a sense of deep loss. Then, like a bottle of champagne uncorked, my secrets bubble out of me, and I'm unable to stop now that I've started.

"I seek out comfort and kindness, care and affection, love and respect," I say, dragging in a tremulous, tear-stained breath, "So I can try to forget how badly I was abused and ridiculed, tied up and beaten, starved and abandoned by my birth parents."

"Daisy..." Dalton's voice softens, his eyes wide with shock.

"I was hurt so terribly by the two people who should've loved me the most that I accept the bare minimum from any man I've dated just to feel anything other than worthless."

"Fuck!" Dalton shouts, stepping back as cold air dashes across my skin from his sudden absence. There's a wild, almost unhinged look in his eyes as he stares at me. "Daisy, I didn't know..."

Gripping the hem of my skirt, I pull it back down my thighs, then press my eyes shut on the hot tears tipping over my lashes whilst the ache between my legs pulses. It's a dichotomy of pain and pleasure that tears me in two. "Why would you? We're not friends." I mumble, trying to find the courage to look him in the eye.

"Daisy, I've been an arsehole," he exclaims, swiping a hand through his hair as he paces up and down before me.

I wrap my arms around myself, trying and failing to seek comfort in my own arms. "All I've ever wanted was to be loved," I admit shakily.

Dalton stops pacing and stares at the floor, his face contorted with regret before he eventually lifts his turbulent gaze to meet mine. "I'm so sorry. I shouldn't have..." he swallows hard. "I never would've pushed things so far had I known. I let my own demons get the better of me. I was wrong. *I'm sorry.*"

"Demons?" I question, my heart heavy with pain, wanting to focus on something else. Anything else. He refuses to answer, casting his gaze away. "Dalton, I need to understand," I insist. "What's going on with you?"

"It's nothing compared to what you've been through. Daisy, why have you never said anything? Why hasn't Drix? Fuck!"

"Tell me what hurts you Dalton, *please,*" I beg.

He palms his face as if he wants to hide, but I reach for him, my fingers curling around his wrists as I drag his hands away.

"My father is a cold man, emotionless, and my mother left without a backward glance when I was just a kid. I've not had very good role models when it comes to affection, kindness, *fucking love*," he eventually admits, his voice barely above a whisper.

"Dalton..." I begin, but he shakes his head.

"I was jealous when I saw how at ease you were with Riley, how he made you smile and laugh because it only served to high-light what I lack," he explains.

"And what's that?" I ask softly.

"The ability to emotionally connect," he replies, rubbing at the centre of his chest. "I can't seem to get beyond the physical to anything deeper. Sure, I can pretend, but deep down I'm inca-pable, Daisy. I can't offer a deeper, more meaningful relationship because I don't know how. *I don't know how to love*," he adds, agony scoring deep grooves between his brows. He drops his head, his long fingers raking through his hair. I step towards him, my cheeks damp with tears, his confession stirring up a mix of emotions within me.

"Daisy?"

My head snaps around to see Drix striding towards us both. He takes one look at the tears streaming down my face and reacts.

"You motherfucker!" he yells, lifting his arm, about to throw a punch, but I step in front of Dalton, shaking my head.

"No. It isn't what you think," I say, pressing my hands against Drix's chest, forcing him backwards.

"You're crying, Daisy. He's obviously upset you," Drix argues, his whole body trembling with rage. "He's supposed to be looking after you. I fucking warned him!"

"Let him hit me. I deserve it for how I've behaved tonight," Dalton says, his voice low, broken sounding.

"No!" I argue, throwing a look over my shoulder at Dalton. "Go wait in the car. I need to speak with Drix alone."

"You'd better get out of here right the fuck now, or so help me," Drix warns.

"I'll take your punishment, Drix," Dalton says, stepping around me, but I turn to face him, placing my hands on his chest this time, forcing him backwards.

"Dalton, just go and wait for me in the car," I insist, hating that their relationship has come to this, hating how crestfallen he looks, how agony bleeds across his features.

"No."

"Please, for me?" I beg, my hand coasting up his chest, cupping his face. "We'll talk more, just give us a moment, okay?"

"Alright, I'll go," Dalton agrees after a moment, his voice barely audible as he locks eyes with me. I see the shame in them, the pain and anguish.

"Go," I urge him.

Nodding, he turns on his heel and heads towards the car. As the door slams shut behind him, I turn back to Drix. "I need you to understand something, Drix."

"Please do not make excuses for him. I *know* what he's like."

"I agree, you do, so you also know that he has his own issues, things that up until a moment ago, *I* didn't even see the truth of," I retort.

"That's why you're crying?" he asks, frowning as he flicks his gaze to the man he once called his best friend.

"I'm also upset because I told him a few things about me too."

"You told him about what happened to you as a kid?"

"A little." I heave out a breath, swiping at my face in an attempt to regain my composure. "But not everything."

For a moment, Drix seems to soften, his expression a mixture of concern and understanding, but then his anger flares once again. "Riley told me how he was behaving inside the bar, that's why I came out to find you. There's no excuse for that."

"You're right, and he apologised for it. He explained why he reacted the way he did. He has issues, Drix."

"Don't we all?" he counters.

"Yes, so you understand that he'll need time to work through them. We both do."

"And you want to help him to do that?"

I consider his question for a moment, and answer honestly. "Yes."

"Daisy, I don't think that's—"

"A good idea? So you think I should turn my back on him?" I challenge.

Drix pinches the bridge of his nose. "I just don't want you to get hurt-"

"I know that," I interrupt, "but equally, he's clearly struggling. No one's perfect, Drix. I've been unfair to him too."

"Especially not by Dalton," Drix continues with a sigh, rubbing the back of his neck, his voice tinged with resignation.

"I understand your concern, but I also believe that people are capable of change and growth."

"I've known Dalton a long time, and truthfully, I'm not sure he can change."

"Well, I guess we've got the time to find that out," I say with a half-smile.

"And what about you? Do you think he can give you the same care and thoughtfulness in return?" Drix asks me.

"Honestly, I've no idea," I admit. "But we have to find a way to live with each other. Maybe if we help each other to heal, we can at least be friends at the end of all of this."

Drix stares at me, his expression unreadable as he collects his thoughts. "Okay."

"Okay?"

"If you're willing to try, then I'll support you, but I won't hesitate to step in if he fucks up."

"I appreciate that," I murmur, throwing my arms around him, hoping to God that I don't end up regretting this decision.

CHAPTER SIXTEEN

My head is fucking scrambled. I don't know what to think, what to say, how to act, even. The whole drive home the tension between us has been suffocating as Daisy navigates the dark, winding roads that lead us back to Highwood Manor Estate. Tonight I told her something that I've never told anyone, not even Drix, at least not directly.

I don't know how to love.

It was the honest truth, and I don't feel any lighter after revealing it, I just feel the burden of it weighing heavily on my shoulders. But my issues are insignificant in comparison to the trauma Daisy has been through. How could I have been so fucking self-centred to not have realised that her upbringing had been as bad as that? Yes, I knew her parents abandoned her, but the cruelty she spoke of? Fuck, it makes my blood burn with a rage I've never felt before.

I'm angry at her parents for treating her that way. I'm angry at Drix for not telling me the whole truth. I'm angry at myself for the way I've acted towards her, not just tonight, but ever since I've known her. I'm an arsehole, the worst kind of person. All of the things she accused me of being are true. I should've let Drix hit me. Fuck knows I deserved it.

How do I even begin to make up for all of the shitty things I've said to her over the years, let alone how I've behaved towards her tonight? How could I have been so blind, so callous in my treatment of her? My mind is a whirlwind of guilt and regret as I grapple with the harsh truth of my own shortcomings. It's a terrifying realisation, one that leaves me feeling utterly lost and adrift.

As we finally pull up to Highwood Manor Estate, Daisy cuts the engine but doesn't make a move to get out. I know we need to talk about what happened tonight, about the bombshell that was dropped on us both, but where do I even begin? I'm not equipped for this.

Summoning what little courage I have left, I turn to face Daisy, who meets my gaze with a mixture of apprehension and resignation. Taking a deep breath, I search for the right words, words that can convey the depth of my remorse and regret. But as I open my mouth to speak, all that comes out is a choked whisper.

"I'm sorry," I say, the words tasting bitter on my tongue. "I'm so sorry for everything you've been through, and everything I've said or done over the years that has added to your pain."

"I appreciate that," she replies, before stepping out of the car, leaving me alone to face my thoughts.

I sit in the dark for a moment, trying to gather my thoughts before following her inside. When I finally catch up with her, Daisy is standing by the fireplace in the den, her silhouette illuminated by the flickering flames. She doesn't turn as I approach her, but I can sense her unease vibrating in the air between us as she takes a seat in the armchair by the fire. Sitting opposite her, I wait, hoping that she'll open up, that we can try to unravel the mess I've made of everything. Finally, she turns to face me, and in the dim light, I see the pain in her eyes, feel it as though it's my own.

"My parents used to keep me locked and tied up in a darkened room," she begins, her voice quavering.

My chest tightens at her words, another wave of guilt crashing over me. How could I have been so selfish in my own pain that I had failed to see hers? "Fuck, I'm sorry, Daisy. I want to make things right," I say earnestly.

"Then will you listen to what I have to say? Because after tonight I don't ever want to speak of it again," she replies softly.

"Of course I will, whatever you need," I offer, forcing myself to remain seated and not run from her vulnerability. She deserves to be heard. I owe her that much at least. Daisy takes a deep breath, steadying herself before she begins to recount the horrors of her past.

"I was just a child," she explains, her voice trembling. "Alone in the darkness for five long years, with only my thoughts and fears for company. They barely let me leave the room. They fed me scraps of food and gave me water to drink from a dog bowl like I was some kind of animal..."

As she speaks, her voice quivers with suppressed pain, each sentence a testament to the resilience she must have carried all these years. I can't equate what she's telling me and the godawful picture she's painting with the girl I've come to know. She's kept all of that trauma buried deep inside, hidden beneath her colourful outfits and sunny disposition. Her bravery floors me. Swallowing the lump in my throat I force myself to face her pain and not run from it.

"Daisy, I can't even begin to comprehend what you went through."

She gives me a small nod of acknowledgement, swiping at the tears on her face as she continues. "They beat me, called me names, and finally, when they'd had enough of me, they left me on a roadside in the middle of the night, malnourished, barely alive, and with nothing but a threadbare nightgown to keep me warm.

I've often wondered why they didn't actually just kill me..." Her voice trails off as she heaves out a sigh.

My fingers curl into fists at my side, the urge to rage at the world on the tip of my tongue, but I hold it in, not wanting to add to her distress.

"Eventually someone found me, took me to the local police station. A day later I was in foster care. That's where I met Drix. That's when I began to heal. His love saved me, and Hubert's kindness, patience and love helped me to grow into the person I am today."

"You've been through so much," I say, my voice hoarse as I struggle with my own emotional response to her harrowing story. Emotions I didn't know I had bubble to the surface like painful little blisters.

"I never wanted that experience to define me, and I've tried hard every single day to not let bitterness and hatred blacken my heart."

"I admire your strength, Daisy," I say, pushing up from my seat and dropping to my knees before her. Tentatively, I reach for her hands, clasping them within mine. She doesn't resist, instead she lets out another shaky breath.

"It's taken me a long, long time to get where I am today. Drix was so good to me, Dalton. I'm not exaggerating when I say he saved my life. He quickly became my anchor, the one person, until Hubert adopted us both, that made me feel safe."

"He's a good man," I say, missing his friendship even more in that moment.

"He is," she agrees with a soft smile.

"What happened to your parents, Daisy?" I ask, wanting to know that they paid for what they did to her, because if they haven't, I will do everything in my power to make their lives a misery.

"They were arrested and charged for child abuse and neglect. I'm told my father died in prison a month after he was sent there."

"And your mother?"

"Still alive. She'll never get out. Hubert made sure of it."

I nod. "Good."

"I try not to think about either of them. It's too painful."

"Have you had therapy? If you need anything like that, I can arrange it for you, Daisy. Anything you want, just ask, okay?"

"I've had a lot of therapy over the years, and for the most part I can function day-to-day, but at night, when I'm alone, it's a little harder for me."

"At night?"

"For obvious reasons, I was afraid of the dark. I still am," she continues. "I have to sleep with a light on, and on occasion I have nightmares. Though they have lessened over the years. Drix figured out early on that nighttime was worse for me. He used to sleep with me every night when we were in foster care. He used to wrap his arms around me and hold me until I drifted off."

"I'm so glad he was there for you, Daisy. That he still is."

"Me too," she replies, giving me a tremulous smile. "You know, even after we were adopted by Hubert, Drix would still come into my room if I had a nightmare or was feeling particularly vulnerable. He'd sit with me until the sun came up, never once complaining about being tired the next day." Daisy's eyes fill with tears as she recalls those memories. "He was my protector, my saviour. So when I found out about his debt, there was no question that I would help him. I agreed to this arranged marriage because his happiness means *everything* to me."

"I can see why he's so protective of you, and why he hates that I'm the one you're tied to now," I admit, scraping a hand through my hair at the realisation. "I wish things were different. I wish I could be the man you need..."

She grips my fingers. "I told Drix that I want you and I to be friends, I meant it. Can we at least try to be that, Dalton?"

"Yes," I reply without hesitation. "I want to be your friend, Daisy. I'm just so fucking sorry you've been drawn into all of this."

"Selfishly, I want something out of this arrangement too."

"A child?"

"Yes, someone I can shower with love. I want to give our child all the love I never experienced, that you didn't. I'm sorry you never felt loved either," she adds with a whisper. "I'm sorry I've been unkind to you too."

My throat constricts, and I nod, swallowing hard. "Then it will be my honour to help you to become a mother."

"Even if that means making this baby in an unconventional way?" she asks, a soft smile pulling up her lips.

"Even then," I reply.

A few minutes later I'm standing on the threshold of Daisy's bedroom as she steps inside and slips off her shoes, her toes curling into the plush carpet. When she turns to face me I can see the lingering vulnerability in her eyes.

"Thank you for listening, Dalton," she says, wrapping her arms around herself, looking more lost than ever, and before I've even had time to think my feet are moving of their own accord as I stride towards her.

"You're not alone, Daisy," I say, gently cupping her face.

Her body trembles as she leans into my touch, seeking comfort amidst the chaos of raw emotion. Every part of me wants to pull her into my arms, to hold her, comfort her, but I'm not convinced my body will react the way it should. Fuck knows I'm fighting the urge to kiss her again. The way I feel right now is confusing to me, and I don't know how to unravel it all. So we stand there for a moment, suspended in time, before she breaks the silence.

"Will you stay with me tonight?" she whispers.

"I'm not sure that's a good idea," I admit.

"All this talk of my past..." Her voice trails off as she catches the look on my face. "I shouldn't have asked. It's okay, I understand why you don't want to."

"I'm not sure that you do," I say, releasing her and swiping my hand through my hair in frustration. "I just don't trust myself right now. Earlier, I wasn't respectful towards you. I was caught up in my own head. I let my own selfish needs and insecurities get the better of me, and I'm not sure I have the willpower to ignore these urges I'm fighting against right now. I want you, and I wouldn't be a very good person if I wasn't honest with you about that."

"You want me?"

"You're a beautiful woman, Daisy. I'm trying my best not to fuck up here," I implore.

"You don't want to sleep with me?"

"If I lay beside you right now the last thing I'd want to do is sleep," I say, itching to draw her into my arms, wanting nothing more than to bury myself inside her until we both forget what's broken within us.

"What if I don't want to sleep either?" she replies, locking her gaze with mine. "What if I want you to touch me?"

"I'm a walking red flag, Daisy," I say. "Right now I'm everything you *don't* need."

"At this point, I'm not sure that I care," she says, stepping towards me as I take a step back.

"And that's exactly why this is a bad idea."

"Dalton, don't get a conscience now. I'm basically giving myself to you," she says, her voice cracking with emotion. "That's what you want isn't it, to fuck?"

"Yes..." I admit wincing. "Damn it, no!"

"What is it? Yes or no?"

"No, I don't... We're not fucking, Daisy. Not like this. I'm many things, but I am not a man who will abuse the situation. You're vulnerable right now, and if we fuck then I know you'll regret it in the morning. You don't want this. You don't want to have sex with me, you've made that perfectly clear already."

"But what if I tell you that I *do* want this? What if I tell you that I'm aching to be touched, to find release? What if I tell you that I want you to take the pain away? What then?"

"Jesus, Daisy, you're making this impossible."

"This is what you want, isn't it? You need relief, and I need to forget. You've used women before, so use me now. You know you want to. If it makes you feel any better, I'd be using you too."

"No," I shake my head adamantly. "That doesn't make me feel any better. Not by a long shot."

"I'm not asking you to love me, Dalton. We're two consenting adults. You fuck women all the time," she says in frustration.

"Not anymore. Not like this. No," I repeat, more firmly this time. Her expression falls and guilt climbs up my chest. "Staying here tonight would be a mistake, you know that deep down."

She stares at me for a long time, then eventually her shoulders drop and she heaves out a sigh. "Maybe you're right. Forget I said anything."

I fucking hate the way she seems to curl in on herself, how in my attempt to protect her, I've only appeared to make her feel worse. Part of me, the selfish part, is more than willing to do what she asks, to fuck her so that we both get respite from our demons. Yet, I know that's just a temporary fix, and despite how hard my damn cock is, how the air between us is swollen with desire, I refuse to take advantage.

"I was thinking of going to the track tomorrow. Would you like to join me?" I offer. It's my way of trying to fix things, to offer friendship.

"You want me to come to the track?"

"Yes. If you want to, that is."

"Sure, why not?" she agrees softly.

"Okay, then," I reply, reaching for the handle of the door,

needing to get the fuck out of her room before I change my damn mind. "Goodnight, Daisy."

"Goodnight, Dalton."

I gently shut the door behind me, wishing I could be the person she needs, hating that I've left her alone and vulnerable. So, instead of heading towards my own bedroom, I rest my back against the wall, and slide down the wooden panel until my arse hits the floor. If I can't give her the physical comfort she needs, the least I can do is offer her my support from a distance even if she's unaware of it.

"What the fuck now?" I whisper to myself as I sit in the hallway, listening to the muffled sounds of Daisy moving around in her room.

Closing my eyes, I try to make sense of the conflicting emotions within me, and fail miserably. Ultimately all I know is that I have to prioritise her well-being above all else. Despite the strange ache in my chest, and the gnawing tug of desire that refuses to dissipate, I make a silent promise to myself to be there for Daisy, no matter what.

CHAPTER SEVENTEEN

"How did you sleep?" Dalton asks as we step out into the winter sunshine.

There's a chill breeze in the air, but the sun is shining and the snow has long since melted leaving behind patches of damp earth and scattered twigs and leaves.

"Okay," I reply, winding my deep purple scarf around my neck as our footsteps crunch over the gravel drive.

Despite my response, I tossed and turned all night, plagued by memories I've spent years trying to forget, going over our conversation. Last night I'd offered myself up to him, and he'd refused me, and somehow that rejection hurt me more than I thought it would. In the end, I'd given up on sleep and had drawn a bath, lying in the hot water until the warmth had disappeared and my teeth were clacking from the cold.

"You're not a very good liar," Dalton says, his blue eyes searching mine as he opens the passenger door for me.

"Very gentlemanly of you," I reply, ignoring his comment and giving him a small smile as I slide into the seat. He gently closes the door, rounding the car.

Today he's wearing blue jeans, a thick grey woollen sweater, and a black leather jacket, his auburn hair catching the light as he settles behind the wheel. When he starts the engine, I catch a whiff of his cologne, a now familiar scent that only serves to remind me of that moment in the spa when his hands had been warm, and my body had been receptive to his touch.

Forcing that memory aside, I buckle in as the car hums to life. Dalton pulls out of the driveway, his fingers curling around the steering wheel as he concentrates on the road ahead. For a while we sit in silence, the only sound is the soft purr of the engine, and my pulse beating loudly in my ears. An undercurrent of tension crackles between us as I steal glances at Dalton, his profile outlined by sunlight streaming through the window. His jaw is set and there's a furrow between his brows, telling me he's preoccupied, no doubt with everything I revealed last night.

"Dalton, can we just forget about our conversation, and what happened last night? Can we just enjoy today?" I ask, making a decision to not dwell on the past, and the things I cannot change.

He glances at me briefly, his expression softening for a moment. "Whatever you need, Daisy."

"Thank you," I murmur.

"I just want to say one thing first though," he begins, clearing his throat.

"Okay."

"I know it wasn't easy for you to open up like that, but I'm grateful that you did. It made me reevaluate our relationship."

"Should I be concerned?"

"Not at all. Just know that I intend for things to be better between us. We can agree that we're friends now, right?"

"Yes we are, and that sounds good to me," I say softly.

I know that he's trying to process my revelations just as much as I'm struggling to navigate the aftermath of laying bare secrets I've long kept hidden, but in all honesty, I just want to put everything aside for today. A fresh start could be good for the both of us.

"Now that everything's out in the open, perhaps we can try to move forward?" I offer, pressing my palms against my red jeans to try and prevent my hands from trembling, not because he's making me nervous, but because I'm still shaken by the rawness of last night. Dalton notices my reaction and reaches out and wraps his hand around mine, his huge palm engulfing mine, the warmth of his touch seeping into my skin.

"Let's focus on today. Maybe if you're lucky I'll give you a ride on my motorbike," he adds jovially, a small smile playing about his lips as I glance over at him.

"Sounds positively thrilling," I reply, laughing softly.

"You've no idea," he retorts, squeezing my hand before letting it go.

After another twenty minutes of small talk that seems to lighten the mood, Dalton pulls up to the racetrack on the outskirts of Princetown. I've never actually been here before, and the sound of motorbikes revving fills the air with an exciting energy that crackles beneath my skin as we step out of the car.

"I'll introduce you to my friends," Dalton says, offering me his hand, a simple gesture of support as I slide my palm into his.

"You have some then?" I reply, smiling so he knows I'm only joking.

He chuckles. "As hard as that is to believe, I do. Truthfully, this is where I feel most at home."

"How so?" I ask.

"I'm just Dalton here," he shrugs. "I'm not someone who is the heir to a billion-pound fortune. There are no expectations for me to act a certain way. I can just be me. I'm respected for my skills on the track, and liked for who I am. Plus, when I ride, I'm free." He glances over at me. "It's hard to explain."

"I can understand that," I reply, frowning a little.

As we head towards a group of riders talking together beside a row of impressive motorbikes parked next to the track, I can't help but feel a surge of anticipation mixed with a touch of nerves at the thought of meeting Dalton's friends. But I needn't have worried as they greet us enthusiastically, clapping Dalton on the back and exchanging warm welcomes with me. Their easy smiles and banter immediately put me at ease.

"Everyone, this is my fiance, Daisy. Daisy meet everyone," Dalton says, throwing his arm wide to include the group of three men and two women.

"I'm Banks," a tall man with deep-set, hazel eyes and a flop of unruly black hair says. He points to his left to a guy with short blonde hair and a neatly trimmed beard, "And this is Milo, the best racer here."

Milo salutes me with a wink. "Alright, Daisy?"

"Hi," I reply, giving him a smile.

"Erm, excuse me," Dalton says, raising his brows. "We all know *I'm* the best racer here."

"Aside from me, of course," Banks adds, with a smirk. "You've got to admit it, your reflexes aren't as quick now that you're edging into your late forties."

"Fuck off, Banks," Dalton replies, lightly punching him on his arm. "I'm still a good seven or eight years younger than you, and we both know whilst you look forty, you're not quite there yet."

"Whatever, man," Banks replies, holding his hand out for me to shake.

"Nice to meet you."

"I'm Elijah," another imposing man says, he's slightly shorter than Banks and Milo, but no less intimidating with his tattooed face and shorn hair. I can't see the colour of his eyes, given he's wearing sunglasses, but his easy smile is welcoming.

"Hi Elijah," I reply.

"And that's Risk," Dalton says, pointing to the track as another one of his friends whizzes past at high speed, his red motorbike a blur of colour against the grey asphalt.

"Risk?" I ask, my eyes following him as he races off into the distance. I'm momentarily stunned by how close he leans to the ground as he rounds a corner, his knee hovering over the asphalt.

"It's his nickname because he has zero fear, and likes to scare the shit out of all of us with his moves around the track," Banks explains.

"Ah, I see," I say.

"Hey, I'm Tory," a woman with long multicoloured, braided hair says, stepping between Banks and Milo and holding her hand out to me. She's dressed in full leathers that match her rainbow hair.

"I love your outfit," I say, taking her hand and shaking it.

"Thanks. Gotta brighten up this place a little, right?" She smiles, the tiny lines around her eyes creasing.

"Right," I agree, instantly liking her.

"And I'm Swift," the other, younger woman says.

She gives me a once over, her cool blue eyes assessing me before she flicks her gaze to Dalton, then turns on her heel and strides off towards a stunning, sleek black motorbike, her long brown hair fluttering in the breeze behind her.

"Don't mind my daughter, she's a little cranky with newcomers," Tory explains.

"Your daughter? You don't look old enough to have a daughter," I say, surprise widening my eyes.

"Swift is twenty. I had her when I was seventeen. Been bringing her to the track with me since she was a kid," Tory replies with a shrug. "So you've come to race?"

"Oh no, not me," I admit, shaking my head vigorously. "I'm here to watch, Dalton."

"Well, enjoy. We're just having a practice run today," Milo

chimes in, patting Dalton on the shoulder. "You better bring your A-game if you want to beat me."

"Always," Dalton replies with a chuckle, exchanging a confident look with his friend.

As the group disperses to prepare for the practice run, Dalton takes my hand and guides me towards the sidelines of the track. The rumble of several motorbikes starting up intensifies, sending goosebumps erupting across my skin as I watch Risk zoom towards us at an incredible speed.

Dalton leans in close, his voice barely audible over the roar of the engines. "Impressive, isn't it?"

"How fast was he going exactly?" I ask, watching the others pull on their helmets and manoeuvre their bikes onto the track just as Risk pulls up, waving in our direction.

"Pretty damn fast," Dalton replies, before resting his hand over mine. "Do you mind if I go and join them?"

"Of course not, you're here to race," I reply, frowning as I drop my gaze to his outfit. "You're not wearing that are you? I mean, don't you have leathers or something to put on?"

"Are you afraid I'm going to hurt myself?" he asks me, but before I'm able to respond he adds, "I've got my things here. Don't worry, Daisy, I know what I'm doing."

"Come on Dalton, we're waiting!" Elijah calls, revving his engine.

"I gotta go," Dalton grins, releasing my hand, but I reach for him, my fingertips brushing his arm.

"Be careful, okay?"

He gives me a disarming smile. "I always am," he retorts with confidence, and then, almost reflexively, he presses a quick kiss against my cheek.

A rash of heat floods my face, and even though it was just a chaste kiss with no heat behind it, the disarming smile that he throws over his shoulder at me as he jogs away has my stomach fluttering with butterflies.

I quickly look away in an effort to hide my reaction, and a few minutes later he comes back out, head-to-toe in fitted black leather.

"Bloody hell," I murmur, unable to deny how good he looks. But it isn't just the fact he looks incredibly sexy in his leathers, there's an ease about him as he jokes and laughs with his friends, and it's something that I've never seen before. He seems really at home here, and it feels like I'm witnessing a whole different person as he pulls on his helmet and swings himself onto the seat of a beautiful silver motorbike, the engine purring beneath him as he revs it.

Moments later the group lines up at the starting line, their engines roaring in unison. The sound vibrates through the air, lifting the hairs on my arms, and my heart pounds in my chest as I hold my breath, waiting for the signal to start.

With a final glance in my direction, Dalton nods before shutting his visor. Seconds later a loud horn blares, and suddenly they're off, speeding down the tracks in a blaze of colour and noise, the scent of petrol and burning rubber in the air.

The wind whips at my hair as I track their progress, watching in awe as they lean into each turn with precision and grace. Risk takes the lead, his fearless manoeuvres leaving me in awe as he navigates the curves with skill.

Dalton isn't far behind, his focus apparently unwavering as he chases Risk and Milo who has just edged in front of him on the last turn. Hunching over the bike, his stomach almost pressed against his thighs, Dalton gains ground. The sound of their engines is deafening as they race past me, each rider seemingly pushing themselves to the limit in a display of raw talent and exhilaration.

As they complete another lap, Dalton throws a brief look my way and I grin at him, waving as the race continues on. My veins fizz with excitement and adrenaline as they jockey for position, each of them vying for the top spot, and as they approach the final stretch, Dalton pushes ahead with a burst of speed that propels him past Risk and across the finish line first.

I let out a triumphant scream as Dalton skids to a stop, his bike throwing up a plume of dust as he removes his helmet to reveal a wide grin, his hair sticking up in disarray. Dismounting his bike, Dalton kicks out the footrest as I rush towards him, unable to contain my excitement.

"Oh my God, you were incredible!" I exclaim, forgetting myself as I throw my arms around him in a tight hug, caught up in the thrill of the moment.

"Not bad for a man who spends his days behind a desk, eh?" he jokes, planting a kiss on my forehead that has my insides swarming with butterflies, and my cheeks heating.

It's a friendly kiss, with nothing more to it other than affection for a friend, but it sends a jolt of electricity through me nonetheless. Moments later, the others approach, offering congratulations and playful jabs at Dalton for beating them this time. Milo claps him on the back, grinning from ear to ear.

"Well done, mate! You had us sweating there for a moment."

Risk joins in, nodding in respect. "Impressive riding, Dalton. You've got some serious skills." He offers me a smile, pulling off his glove before shaking my hand. "I'm Risk."

"Nice to meet you, that was really incredible!" I reply, and he laughs, his deep brown eyes twinkling as his light brown hair is tousled by the wind.

"Not nearly as incredible as your other half," he retorts good-naturedly as he slaps Dalton on the back, the camaraderie between them evident even to an outsider like me.

As the banter continues, I take a moment to observe Dalton in his element, surrounded by friends, laughing and joking with them. It's a side of him I haven't seen before, and it adds another layer to the man I thought I already knew. Eventually the excitement from the race begins to ebb away, and the others steer their bikes back to the stand, but Dalton hangs back, pulling me into his side as he chuckles.

"What?" I ask, looking up at him.

"If I knew all it would take for you to throw yourself at me was a day at the track, I would've brought you here sooner," he says jokingly, but there's a warmth in his gaze that lingers, making me feel seen in a way I'm not quite used to.

"Funny," I reply, giving him a playful shove, both of us ignoring the fact that I threw myself at him last night.

"Would you like me to take you for a ride?" he asks after a beat.

"Back to that again, I see," I reply, hitching a brow.

"I meant on my motorbike," he flirts back, a lightness and ease to his tone that simply wasn't there before.

I laugh, shaking my head, before my smile drops and I stare at his beautiful motorbike. "I'm not sure. You go awfully fast."

"I promise to take it easy."

"You swear?"

"Of course, but you're going to need some protective leathers, and a helmet. You're about the same size as Swift, I'm sure she'd be happy to lend you something," he says, taking my hand as he tugs me towards her.

"You think she'll be okay loaning me something? I got the distinct impression she didn't like my appearance here today," I say, eyeing Dalton for any signs that he's had a past relationship with her given the look she'd thrown at him earlier.

"Swift takes a while to warm up," he explains.

My eyebrows lift. "Oh yeah?"

Dalton's steps falter as he turns to me. "Don't give me that look, Daisy. She's a friend, nothing more."

"Has she ever been more than a friend?" I ask, not sure why I want to know, but asking the question anyway.

"Nope. She's not interested in me, and I'm not at all interested in her. In fact I'm pretty sure she's got a huge crush on the guys."

"The guys?"

"Yes, Milo, Risk, Elijah and Banks."

"Oh, wow. That's... interesting. Do they know?" I ask, curious about the situation.

"Not sure. Possibly. They keep her at arms length though given their close relationship with Tory."

"Wait, Tory is with the guys?"

Dalton shakes his head. "No, Tory is just their friend. She's known them for the past couple years since she's been racing at this track. Besides, she prefers women."

"I see." I blow out a breath. "That's complicated."

"Frustrating for Swift given the guys are not the type of men to take advantage of a young girl's crush, especially not the daughter of their friend."

"Well, I already liked them. Now, I think I like them even more."

By the time we reach the group, Tory is chatting animatedly with the men, and Swift is checking over her bike, pointedly ignoring the group.

"Swift, you wouldn't mind lending Daisy some leathers and a helmet, would you? I want to take her for a spin on the track," Dalton asks as she flicks her gaze his way.

"Sure she doesn't mind," Tory answers for her, throwing a look over at her daughter before she can protest.

"Fine. You can borrow my old shit," Swift says, motioning me to follow her inside the brick building.

"Sorry about this," I say, trying to appease her because she's clearly pissed off.

"Don't worry about it," Swift mutters, rummaging through her box of gear, tossing me a leather suit and helmet as her gaze assesses me. "These should fit. Just make sure you don't fall off and ruin them, and we'll be good."

"Gosh, I hope not," I reply but she strides from the room, leaving me to change.

When I step out of the building with the helmet tucked under my arm, Dalton is waiting with his friends, his back to me. Risk lets out a low whistle as I approach, causing Dalton to twist on his heels. I can't help but notice a flare of heat flickering to life in his gaze, but he quickly recovers.

"Leathers suit you, Daisy," he says with a grin.

"You think?" I ask, genuinely surprised by his compliment because I feel pretty uncomfortable, given the leather is riding up my arse and is a little too tight around my breasts. I'm almost ten years older than Swift, and she's clearly a size smaller than me.

"Come on then, let's give you the ride of your life," he jokes, resting his hand against the small of my back as we head back on to the racetrack.

"I'm nervous," I admit as he takes the helmet from me and places it on my head. It's a snug fit, but at least my head will be protected should the worst happen.

"Don't be. I've got you," he says, his fingers grazing against my jaw as he clips the helmet in place and tightens the strap.

"I'm trusting you to keep me safe, Dalton," I say.

"I won't let anything happen to you," he replies with a reassuring smile, before he puts on his own helmet then swings his leg over the bike, patting the space behind him. "On you get."

I awkwardly climb onto the seat, my hands hanging loosely by my side as he kicks up the footrest and straightens the bike, causing me to wobble dangerously.

"Shit," I mutter, grabbing hold of his sides as my thighs grip tightly around his.

"You're going to need to hold onto me," he says, chucking a

look over his shoulder as he reaches back and grips my thigh, urging me closer.

"I am," I retort.

"Tighter, Daisy!" he orders, twisting the throttle briefly so that I'm thrown forward and have no option but to wrap my arms around his waist, and hang on for dear life, my *whole* body pressed tightly against him.

"Jesus, give a girl a warning," I mutter, my heart in my throat, all too aware of the heat between my thighs, and my entire body pressed against his.

"That *was* my warning, and for the love of all that's holy, don't let go. Drix will murder me if you fall off this motorbike."

"Don't you be worrying about Drix, I'll murder you if I fall off this motorbike," I reply, and Dalton chuckles as he accelerates across the asphalt.

"Holy shit!" I scream, but the wind takes my breath, drowning me out.

Digging my fingers into his leather jacket, I feel the powerful rumble of the engine beneath us vibrating through my bones. Despite my initial nerves, I can't deny the rush of adrenaline and the feeling of freedom it brings. Not to mention the way the vibrations hit in all the right places. My face flushes furiously from the sensation because the blood in my veins isn't the only thing pulsing wildly.

Relaxing into the ride, the world blurs into streaks of colour as Dalton leans into each turn, myself and the bike leaning with him as though we're an extension of his body. I cling to him tighter, my heart racing in sync with the engine's roar, the wind whipping around us both like a cyclone threatening to tear us apart. But, I just hold on tighter, soothed by Dalton's confidence as he handles the powerful motorbike with ease, a little distracted by how turned on I am.

As we zip around the track, the barriers between us seem to

dissolve leaving only the raw intensity of the ride, and the physical reaction on my body. I close my eyes for a moment, letting myself fully embrace the feeling, appreciating the freedom of tearing down the track at breakneck speed. Although it feels like we're going as fast as when he was racing solo, I know he isn't given that our knees aren't practically touching the asphalt as we turn into the bends. Nevertheless, I put all my trust in Dalton, and in that instant, I realise that this ride isn't just about speed or adrenaline, it's about trust, and about letting go of fear.

When Dalton finally eases the bike to a standstill, we're on the other side of the racetrack, alone but for the distant echoes of cheers and revving engines. Taking a deep breath, my hands shaking slightly, I slowly release my grip on Dalton, feeling the loss of his warmth as he kicks out the footrest and eases himself off the bike, offering me his hand as I sling my leg over the seat and stand on trembling legs.

"Did you enjoy the ride, Daisy?" he asks, his voice a little hoarse as we both remove our helmets.

"That was... amazing!" I reply, shaking my hair out as a wide smile spreads across my face. "I never thought I'd do something like that."

"Glad you enjoyed it," he replies, tucking my hair gently behind my ear as he looks down at me. My pulse thrums in my ear, and I don't know whether it's from the adrenaline, the way he's looking at me right now, or the fact that I feel so aroused. With my cheeks heating, the dull ache between my legs comes to life under his scrutiny. He cocks his head at me, eyes narrowing a little.

"What?" I mutter.

"You're flushed," he points out, swiping his index finger downwards from my temple to my jaw.

"Adrenaline, I guess," I reply, flicking my gaze away as I try to regain my composure, hoping he doesn't notice that I'm struggling with the ache between my legs.

"I guess," he retorts, picking up my helmet and slotting it back onto my head.

"What are you doing?" I ask.

"Taking you for another ride," he says, grabbing his own helmet and putting it back on.

"I think that's enough for one day," I begin, but he shakes his head, gripping me around the waist and plonking me back on the bike. I don't have time to get back off before he's straddling the bike and revving the engine once again.

Automatically I wrap my arms back around his waist, my thighs gripping him tightly, expecting him to pull off at breakneck speed once more. The vibrations from the revving hit me right in that sweet spot, and I can't help but moan.

"That's it, Daisy," he grinds out, just loud enough for me to hear over the engine.

"What's it?" I whimper, swallowing another moan, glad he can't see my face turning beetroot as he revs the engine over and over, yet not allowing the bike to move an inch.

Is he doing this on purpose?

Does he know what this is doing to me? Of *course* he does. This is Dalton we're talking about.

"Aren't we going to move?" I shout, trying and failing not to rock my hips as I search for what? For an orgasm?

Yes.

Fuck.

"I think you're doing that all by yourself," he grunts back.

"Dalton... This is..." I stutter, unable now to hide the tremble in my voice, my pussy growing slicker, wetter, hotter with every rev of the engine, at the wrongness of how easily I'm about to come, at the rightness of how it feels.

"Just let me give you this," he bites out, reaching behind me as his leather clad hand rests on my hip. He grips me tightly, urging me to move, to dry hump his motorbike.

"But I'm going to–"

"*Come?* I sure as fuck hope so," he replies.

I can feel the vibrations shudder through my body, cascading upwards from the tips of my toes to the top of my head, pleasure building in my core, urging me towards the edge.

"Oh God," I cry out, all sense of self, of respectability, seeping from me as I grind against the seat. His hand grips my hip as my fingers dig into his leather jacket. I'm just grateful he can't see my face, how my skin flushes with perspiration, embarrassment and pleasure.

So much pleasure.

I'm going to come, right here on the back of Dalton's motorbike, with his friends cheering and hollering from the other side of the racetrack. It's humiliating. It's thrilling. It's erotic and so, so dirty.

"Dalton, please..." I beg, and at this point I don't know what I'm even begging for more, my release or the scraps of my self-respect that drips from my pussy.

"This won't end until you finish," he grinds out. "So you'd better come quickly, or my friends are going to know exactly what's happening here."

"Jesus," I mutter, but that doesn't stop me from rubbing my aching pussy harder against the seat as my eyelids drop shut and I press my helmet covered head against the centre of his back.

"Come for me, Daisy. Let me do something right for once," he mutters.

And embarrassingly that's all it takes.

I come so hard that I'm scared his friends will hear my cry as I go rigid, my stomach muscles contracting as white hot heat bursts outwards from my core, circling my throbbing clit until eventually I go limp, my hot breath steaming up the visor with every panting breath.

"Good girl," he rumbles, releasing my hip and wrapping his hand around the handlebar. "Now hold on tight."

I don't get a chance to think as he pulls off. Instinct takes over as I grip hold of him tightly and he speeds off around the track and back towards the starting position, impossibly faster than before. I feel another rush of adrenaline spike in my blood, the unholy thrill still aching between my legs. It feels as though I'm letting go of the pain of last night, all the memories. I see them in my mind's eye, the remnants of my past like pieces of curled and worn pages torn from a book, flying up into the air with every second that passes. I'm not foolish enough to believe that they're gone forever, but right now, in this moment, as I hang on to the man that I never thought I could tolerate let alone become friends with, they float away giving me peace, if just for a little while.

It takes less than a minute to get to the other side of the track, and I've not nearly recovered from the exhilarating speed let alone my orgasm as he pulls up sharp and kicks out the footstand.

Sliding off the bike, he takes my hand and I stand, yet again on trembling legs. Reaching up, I pull off my helmet, needing to take a deep lungful of breath, gasping for air, thoroughly and completely overwhelmed as I watch him pull off his own helmet, a smirk pulling up his lips.

"Enjoy yourself?" he asks.

"That was... *thrilling*," I whisper, barely able to meet his eyes as a smile curves up my lips and more heat floods my already flaming cheeks.

"It was," he agrees. "But you know what's even more thrilling?"

"What?" I ask, slowly dragging my gaze up to meet his intense one, the deep blue of his irises lit with fire.

"Knowing I was the one to put that beautiful smile on your face."

"I think you'll find that was the motorbike," I mutter, choking on a smile.

CHAPTER EIGHTEEN

At breakfast the following morning, a bright smile paints Daisy's face in sunshine. Gone are the dark shadows of trauma that haunted her a couple of days ago, and in its wake is a lightness that seems to brighten up every corner of the dining room as she hums to herself. Even my father's austere presence is unable to penetrate the happy little bubble she seems to have wrapped herself in, or perhaps it's the canary yellow knitted jumper and purple leggings that's protecting her from his judgemental gaze. My ego would like to think that it's the memory of her orgasm that has her smiling so broadly. Either way, it feels good to see her smile. It feels good that she feels good. I don't even care that she hasn't even brought the subject up, her orgasm an erotic secret that's just between us.

But I can't deny it has affected me.

I went to bed last night fisting my cock and wanking off to the memory of her pretty mewls and high-pitched cry as she came all over my one-hundred thousand pound motorbike. With my hand covered in sticky cum, I vowed to myself that the next time she came it would be because my dick or my fingers were buried so deep inside of her that nothing else mattered but the feel of her pussy contracting around me.

As she nibbles on a piece of toast, her eyes scanning the newspaper laid out on the table next to her, my father clears his throat, causing both Daisy and I to look over at him.

"I have arranged for you both to speak with the vicar," he says.

Daisy pulls a face. "The vicar, what on earth for?"

"It's customary to visit with the vicar before you get married," my father responds.

"We're getting married in a church?" Daisy's eyes widen as she looks at me.

"Apparently so," I say, my jaw gritting at the audacity of my father to make arrangements without at least consulting either of us first. I should've known fucking better.

"It's tradition for all Gunn's to be married at St Augustine's," my father reminds me. "It will be no different for you, Dalton. The date has been set, and the invites have already been sent."

Of course they have.

"But I just assumed–" Daisy begins.

"That you'd be married in a civil ceremony?" my father replies, cutting her off.

"Well, yes, because I'm not religious."

"Irrelevant," my father snaps, dismissing her with a careless wave of his hand.

"Not to me it isn't," she retorts, her sunny disposition slowly fading beneath his persistence and disregard for our wants.

"Regardless, you will be getting married at St Augustine's and then you will have the wedding reception at my hotel. You're expected at eleven this morning. Don't be late," my father replies, standing.

"I'm not sure I feel comfortable lying to a vicar," Daisy says, frowning.

"Why? As you said, you're not religious, so what difference

does it make lying to a vicar when you've been lying to everyone else quite successfully so far."

I can see Daisy bristling with indignation, a spark of defiance lighting in her eyes. She sets down her half-eaten toast, glaring at my father.

"Daisy, there's no avoiding it," I interject quickly, not because I want to prevent her from giving my father a tongue-lashing— Christ knows he deserves it—but because I don't want her good mood to be ruined before the day has even begun.

"Exactly. Now, if you'll excuse me, I've got work to do," my father adds before twisting on his heel and striding from the room.

"Is he seriously going to make us get married in a church?" she hisses.

I hold my hands up in surrender. "I'm no more happy about it than you are, but we've got little choice, Daisy, you know that. Besides, you heard what he said, the invitations have already been sent."

Her shoulders sag in defeat. "I just assumed, *stupidly*, that it would be a civil ceremony with a registrar marrying us. I should've known better."

"What's really bothering you, Daisy? Is it the fact that we're getting married in a church, or the fact that this is becoming all too real?" I ask, rounding the table, and pulling out the chair next to her, sitting down.

Daisy's gaze drops to the table as she fiddles with her napkin. "I guess... it's just that I never imagined my wedding day to be like this. I had my own ideas of how it would look." She sighs, giving me a half-smile. "Stupid, I know, given what I agreed to."

"How did you imagine your wedding day?" I ask, cocking my head to the side as I wait for her to answer.

"As your father so ineloquently put it, that's irrelevant," she retorts, her expression falling.

"It isn't."

"But it clearly is," she persists. "Like you said, we can't avoid it. Your father is the puppet master and we just have to play along, right?"

"Just humour me, will you? Tell me what your dream wedding looks like."

"Do you really want to know?"

"I really want to know," I agree, because it's the truth.

"I always imagined a private wedding on a beautiful beach somewhere tropical, with only my close friends and family in attendance," she admits with a soft sigh. "I've always wanted to wear one of my own designs, reciting vows to the man I love as the sun's setting, with water lapping softly at our bare feet."

"Sounds beautiful," I muse, chewing on my lip as I watch her expression fall into thoughtfulness and longing.

She gives me a small shrug. "It's just a silly dream. I'll do what I have to do."

I study her face, seeing both conflict and resignation warring within her as she pulls her hand free from mine, then stands.

"I'm going to get some fresh air for a bit. I'll meet you at the car in an hour, then we can head over to the church, okay?"

"Sure," I reply, watching her walk from the dining room feeling an overwhelming sense of guilt rendering me immobile.

I know that none of this is what she wanted, not being married to me–a man she doesn't love, not being tied to a family who is using her for its own gain, and not getting married in a church to suit my father's wishes. But this is what we both signed up for, and there is little I can do to change it.

"WELL THAT WASN'T AS awful as I imagined it would be," Daisy says as we step outside of St Augustine's a couple of hours later.

"What were you expecting exactly, to go up in flames for pretending to be in love with me?" I ask, shooting her a half-smile.

"Actually, I admit I *was* expecting you to start smouldering a little," she retorts with a grin as we walk down the steps of the church.

I bark out a laugh, her humour amusing me. "Why?"

She arches her brow as a cool breeze ruffles her hair, sending her strawberry blonde and pink streaked strands dancing around her face. "You're seriously asking me why?"

"Go on, enlighten me," I insist, knowing exactly where she's going with this, but enjoying the banter anyway.

"Isn't sex before marriage a sin that gets you sent straight to Hell?"

"Not if it's with your fiance. I'm pretty sure there's a loophole for that," I tease, nudging her with my elbow, trying to make light of the situation, liking the way her lips quirk in a smile.

"You would say that," she retorts with a roll of her eyes, as she opens the passenger door to my car and slides inside.

"By your reckoning, coming all over my motorbike seat would also be a fast pass to Hell," I say, biting down on a smile that twitches my lips.

"If coming all over inanimate objects was a fast pass to Hell then every single woman on the planet would be lining up at the gates with their vibrators."

I throw my head back and laugh. "Now that's a little sexist, don't you think? I'm sure there are plenty of men who meet those requirements too."

"Well that goes without saying," she huffs, folding her arms across her chest as she feigns annoyance even as mirth sparks in her eyes.

A few minutes later we're heading back home, passing through town, when Daisy lets out an audible gasp. "What?" I question, glancing over at her.

"Look, they're playing Stardust at the cinema!" she exclaims excitedly.

"Stardust? Never heard of it," I reply, stopping at a red light as she turns to me with wide eyes.

"Are you kidding me, you've never watched Stardust?"

"Nope."

"You haven't lived. It's my all time favourite movie. *Ever*," Daisy replies, her eyes sparkling with enthusiasm as she continues to gush about the movie. "It's this amazing magical adventure with romance and action, and a beautiful unicorn!"

I arch a brow. "A unicorn? Don't tell me, that's when your obsession started! Am I right?"

"It sure is. Oh, I love the film so much. I think I've watched it a hundred times already."

"A hundred times?" I question incredulously. "It must be good then."

"It really, really is," she replies, almost a little wistfully.

"Well in that case, it looks like we're watching Stardust this afternoon," I declare, making a sharp turn towards the cinema.

"Wait, you're actually serious?" she asks, grinning over at me.

"I may regret this later, but yeah, why the hell not? You came to the racetrack with me, I'm going to watch Stardust with you."

"Haven't you got better things to do?" she asks.

"Apparently not."

Daisy lets out a squeal of joy, her laughter filling the car as I pull into the cinema's car park. "I'll buy the snacks and drinks, if you buy the tickets," she says.

"You're on."

Twenty minutes later we're settling into our seats at the back of the cinema, just as the movie begins to play. For the most part the seats are filled with children stuffing their faces with sugary treats, whilst their parents try to keep them quiet. Daisy is as excited as the children appear to be, practically bouncing on her seat as the opening scenes play out on the screen. I find myself watching her instead of the movie, a smile tugging at my lips.

As the story unfolds, Daisy is completely immersed in the story. You'd think this was the first time she'd ever seen the movie going by her reactions. There's something undeniably endearing about her childlike wonder, something I don't think I've ever experienced myself. Growing up with an emotionless man like my father, and a mother who was distant even when she was still married to my father, meant that I didn't have the opportunity to go to the cinema with my parents, let alone lose myself in a fantasy world like Daisy is doing right now. But watching her, I can almost understand the appeal of escaping reality for a little while, of believing in something magical and extraordinary. It's a refreshing change to my usual routine of work and responsibilities, and Daisy's enthusiasm begins to rub off on me as I relax into my seat.

"I love this part," Daisy whispers, an hour or so into the movie as her hand accidentally brushes against my thigh.

I clear my throat, ignoring the bolt of electricity racing down my spine from her touch. "It's good," I murmur, catching her fleeting smile.

"Told you."

As the movie nears its climax, I can't seem to take my eyes off Daisy. Every emotion that plays out on her face as she follows the twists and turns of the plot, fills me with a longing to touch her and absorb some of her joy. When she reaches for some popcorn from the bucket resting on my lap, her intoxicating scent envelopes me, tempting me to bury my nose in her neck and breathe in deeply. Enthralled by Daisy's company, I find myself unconsciously edging closer to her until our knees are touching. The warmth of her body seeps into mine, igniting desire deep within me that compels me to rest my hand on her thigh.

My touch seems to encourage a subtle shift in Daisy's demeanour, her breath hitching slightly as she turns her head to meet my gaze. Her expression is soft, her eyes filled with unspoken questions, but I don't remove my hand, instead, I begin to gently stroke her inner thigh with my thumb.

"Dalton," she whispers, the air between us crackling with tension, heavy with unexplored possibilities.

I can feel my heart pounding in my chest and my pulse rushing in my ears as Daisy's eyes flicker with uncertainty. Yet, she doesn't try to remove my hand, instead she waits, as if she's too afraid to confront the tentative connection blossoming between us. Fuck knows I am.

Drawn towards her, I lean in close, my lips barely brushing against her ear as I whisper, "You enchant me far more than any magic in this movie ever could."

"I think, maybe, you've had too much popcorn, the sweetness has gone to your head," she laughs softly, trying to temper the growing electricity between us with humour.

"I've not had any, I'm just getting high off of *your* sweetness, and your scent. It's… addictive," I admit, my nose brushing against the pulse point in her neck.

"I'm not wearing any perfume," she retorts with a soft chuckle, completely ignoring the movie now.

"You smell like daisies," I mutter, breathing her in.

A tremulous laugh escapes her lips. "Daisies don't have a scent."

"This one does," I reply, brushing my lips against her skin.

She sucks in a sharp breath, a charged silence settling between us, but for some reason I don't act like I normally would and steal a kiss. Instead, I want her to kiss me first. *Needing* her to.

"Was this the plan all along?" Daisy asks, turning her head slightly, her lips just inches from mine.

"Plan?" I question, struggling with the need to press my lips against hers and fuck her mouth with my tongue, but realising that now is not the time given her question.

"Yes, take me to see my favourite movie, ply me with sweet treats, and kiss me in a darkened cinema?" she continues softly, though there's no heat to her words like on previous occasions, just curiosity.

"I swear, I didn't have a plan. All I know is that I really want to kiss you right now."

"The other night you didn't," she murmurs.

"That was different," I retort.

"Perhaps," she replies as our lips brush, nothing more than a whisper of skin on skin, but it's enough to light me up like a blazing inferno.

I itch to claim her mouth, this need growing with every passing second. Just like the night of our engagement party, and the kiss we shared at Bandits Bar, everything fades into the background. The only sound is my blood pulsing in my ears, and her soft, popcorn-sweetened breath mingling with mine.

Kiss her, damnit.

I don't. I wait.

It's fucking excruciating. My cock thickens, my balls ache, my fingers flex and curl, my body fucking trembles. I've never wanted anything more, and yet... I wait. I fucking wait, caught in this intense moment. She shifts slightly, her scent tantalising my nose, making me groan, but I refuse to steal another kiss. I won't.

"Dalton," she whispers, her breath catching, but just when I think she's going to bridge the gap, the lights suddenly flicker on and the sounds of conversation break through the charged moment, disrupting the connection between us. Daisy quickly pulls away, avoiding my gaze as her cheeks stain with a delicate pink that only seems to make her even more irresistible.

God-fucking-damnit! I'm so fucking hard, it's painful.

"We should probably get going," she mumbles, gathering her bag as she stands.

I follow her out of the cinema, cursing myself for letting the moment slip away. The Dalton of old would've stolen that kiss regardless, but the person I'm becoming hesitated. This isn't like me, and I don't know whether that's a good thing or a bad thing. As we step outside, the cool air hits us, and Daisy wraps her arms around herself.

"Thank you for taking me to see the movie," she says, side-eyeing me.

"You're welcome," I reply, wanting to reach out to her, but I hold back, unsure of where we stand after that almost-kiss.

When we finally reach my car, she turns to face me, her eyes searching mine. "Dalton," she begins, her voice steady, despite the apparent turmoil in her gaze. "I don't want things to be awkward between us. Can we just forget about what happened back there, and at the racetrack too...?"

"Sure, it's already forgotten," I say with a shrug.

Liar.

"Promise?"

"Promise."

But later that night when I'm lying alone in bed, I break my promise to forget as I fist my cock, the memory of her scent and her captivating presence lingering in my mind as I come.

CHAPTER NINETEEN

"Thank you for inviting me, Daisy," Lia says with a wide grin, her fingers tracing over the wedding dresses hanging from the racks in this beautiful bridal shop just outside of Princetown.

Under different circumstances, Lia's happiness would be contagious. But right now, I can't seem to shake off the anxiety building up inside of me. This isn't about choosing a wedding dress to look beautiful for myself and the man I love; it's about picking out a dress for an arranged marriage to a man I used to despise, and now have complicated feelings for. To make matters worse, the ceremony will take place in a church filled with, for the most part, strangers I have no connection with and who've spent the best part of my life judging me for things that were not my fault.

"Of course, there's no one else I'd rather have with me," I reply, appreciating the exquisite selection of lace and silk gowns despite my inner turmoil.

"What about this one?" Lia asks, reaching for a stunning dress with layers of creamy chiffon making up the skirt and a bodice encrusted with tiny crystals.

"It's lovely..." My voice trails off as I heave out a sigh.

"But?" she questions, tipping her head to the side as she waits.

"But it's not really me," I reply, puffing out my cheeks as I blow out a breath.

"Then we'll keep looking. The perfect dress is just waiting for you to find it."

"That might be true if this wasn't all a charade," I whisper, my eyes flicking to the assistant waiting patiently at the back of the store whilst I choose some dresses to try on. Lia nods in understanding as she gently places the dress back on the rack and turns to face me fully. Reaching for me, she clasps my hands in hers.

"There's still time to change your mind, Daisy."

I shake my head, keeping my voice to a whisper. "There's a contract with my signature on it binding me to this agreement, and I'm not changing my mind."

She gives me a soft smile, her eyes filled with a mixture of sympathy and concern. "How are things with you and Dalton? Drix told me about what happened at Bandits Bar."

"Well we're no longer biting each other's heads off, and slinging insults at one another every chance we get. Things are... better," I say, struggling to find the right word to explain the shift in our relationship.

"Better is good," she agrees.

"I guess."

"You guess?" she queries, searching my gaze.

"Can we get out of here? I'm not really in the mood to pick out a wedding dress right now."

"Of course we can. Do you want to arrange an appointment for another day?"

"Perhaps if we come back later? I could murder a cup of tea," I offer, knowing that I must choose a dress today, given our wedding day is in just three weeks and the store needs time for any alterations needed.

"Sure let me just tell the assistant," Lia replies.

Once we're outside of the bridal shop, Lia links her arm with mine, offering her silent support as we search for a place to grab refreshments. Five minutes later we're settling down at a corner table in a nearby cafe, with a pot of tea and a plate of freshly baked scones with jam and clotted cream in front of us.

"So things with Dalton are better?" she asks, picking up a scone and slicing it in half before spreading cream then jam across the surface of each half. She plops one half on my plate, whilst placing the other on hers.

"It is," I nod, taking a sip of my tea.

"There's a but in there somewhere," she points out. "It might make you feel better if you talk about it?"

"After the evening at Bandits Bar when we watched Harlow sing, I told Dalton about what happened to me as a child," I explain, resting my cup of tea back on the saucer.

"And how did he handle that?" Lia asks. She's the only other person apart from Drix, and now Dalton, who knows the full details of my past.

"He was shocked at first, but then he listened to my story. There was no judgement at all, in fact he was kind. He offered to pay for therapy."

"I'm glad," she replies, reaching over to squeeze my hand.

"Then the next day he took me to the racetrack, introduced me to his friends and took me for a spin on his motorbike," I say, avoiding the fact that I asked him to fuck me the night before that, and he'd refused, and the fact I came all over his motorbike seat.

Lia's brows lift. "That sounds fun."

"It was," I admit. "Also, eye-opening."

"How so?"

"Dalton seemed different at the track. At ease. *Happy*. His friends were welcoming, he was fun to be around."

"You sound surprised," she laughs.

"I guess I was," I admit. "I enjoyed myself. I enjoyed his

company, and it felt good. Then yesterday after we went to meet with the vicar at St Augustine's church, we ended up watching Stardust at the cinema."

"Dalton agreed to watch Stardust with you?" Lia chuckles. "Wow, that's unexpected. I didn't peg Dalton for a cinema-going type of guy."

"Neither did I. He surprised me again..."

I shuffle in my seat, my body flushing with heat at the memory of his warm hand on my thigh, his nose pressed against the pulse in my neck and his lips hovering over mine. I've been thinking about that moment ever since it happened, about why he'd wanted to kiss me then, but hadn't wanted to fuck me the night I asked him to.

"Surprised you how?" Lia asks, her brows lifting as she studies me.

"We almost kissed."

"You almost kissed?"

"Yep," I reply, wincing a little.

"And the fact Dalton tried to kiss you is a surprise?"

"No, the fact that he didn't steal a kiss from me, was. The fact that I wanted him to kiss me was."

Lia gives me a knowing look, her scone forgotten on her plate, and I'm reminded of our conversation back in the playground the other week.

"So you wanted him to kiss you?" she repeats.

"Everything just felt... right," I confess, twirling my teaspoon nervously in my tea.

"So why didn't you kiss?" she asks.

"Because..."

"Because?" she persists gently.

"Because I didn't want to complicate our fledgling friendship." A friendship that has been blurred by me coming on his motorbike.

"Things are already complicated, don't you think?"

"You've no idea," I admit, chewing on my lip.

"There's something you're not telling me," she says, eying me.

"The night I told him about my parents and what happened to me as a child, I also asked him to sleep with me," I blurt out.

Lia's eyes widen. "*Sleep* with you or..."

"At first I just wanted comfort, but then I practically threw myself at him and he refused me. He said he didn't want to take advantage whilst I was feeling vulnerable, and so he didn't..."

"Sounds to me like he was being a gentleman, Daisy."

"But then he wanted to kiss me at the cinema," I add, frowning.

"You'd spent the day together having fun. You weren't feeling vulnerable then, right?"

"Right," I agree.

"So he didn't want to sleep with you and take advantage of your emotional state at the time, but he wanted to kiss you when you were feeling better emotionally."

"Yes..."

"So what's the problem? You were both in a better place. He wanted to kiss you, you wanted to kiss him..."

I let out a sigh, trying to unravel that for myself. "It was easier when we hated each other. I knew where I stood then. I could pack this whole arrangement up into a neat little box, and shove it to the back of my mind so that I could get through this whole ordeal."

"But feelings are creeping in?"

"For me, at least," I admit, before rushing on. "It's not as if I'm in love with him or anything..."

"There wouldn't be anything wrong with that even if you were," she says softly.

"I'm not," I insist. "It's just, there's more to him than I originally thought, and maybe you were right about the attraction between us. The trouble is, I don't know if any of it is real or not. I don't know if he wants to kiss me to keep up the charade of us being in love, or if he's so desperate for physical intimacy that I'm just another woman he can use like all the others—"

"If he wanted to use you, then he would've taken you up on your offer when you asked him to sleep with you, Daisy," she points out.

"I just don't know if he truly likes me for *me*."

"Okay, then ask yourself this, what if he does truly like you for you, what then? Would knowing that change things?"

"I'm not sure," I admit.

"Why?"

"Because I don't know if I like him for who he is, or if I like the kindness he's showing me, the *attention*, whether it's honest or not. I've always desperately wanted to feel loved, and I have a tendency to overlook the worst in people. I'm worried that my own past has screwed with me so badly that I can't trust what is real, and what is pretend, or even my own judgement for that matter."

"Oh, Daisy, I can understand that. It's difficult to unravel things, especially when it comes to matters of the heart, and especially when that heart has been so badly broken. Trust me, I know."

"What should I do?"

"I can't tell you what to do, Daisy. Only you know that. What I will say is that when I met Drix I was terrified that he would end up being exactly like my ex, even though I knew deep down that he was nothing like him. It took almost losing what we had, and your honesty, to set me straight. I guess it all boils down to what you want."

"I'm just so confused."

"Do you want to explore a potential relationship with Dalton that's more than being friends?"

"I don't know," I say truthfully.

"What do you know? I mean let's just lay it all out there. What thoughts come to mind when you think about Dalton. Forget the contract, the upcoming wedding, all of that complicated stuff. When you think about Dalton now, what do you know for certain?"

"That he loves to fuck," I reply, laughing a little.

"Okay, that seems apparent given his history. What else?"

"That he has a strained relationship with his father."

"Does anyone have a good relationship with that man?"

"True," I reply.

"He loves to race. He comes alive on the track."

"So he has an interest outside of being the heir to a billion pound fortune. That's good."

"He's a huge flirt."

"Again, goes without saying," she says.

"He's starting to become aware of other people's feelings, *my* feelings."

"Another positive," Lia agrees.

"Dalton's trying to be a better person. More thoughtful," I say. "His refusal to sleep with me might've stung a little at the time, but now that I think about it, I truly appreciate that he hadn't."

"Being thoughtful is important," she murmurs.

"He stuck up for me when his dad was being an arse about the clothes I choose to wear."

"That couldn't have been easy given his dad is the biggest arsehole on this planet, and incredibly overbearing," Lia says, wrinkling her nose in disgust at the thought of Carl Gunn. "But I'm glad he stuck up for you,"

"He didn't kiss me at the cinema even though I knew he really wanted to," I continue softly. "He could've just taken what he wanted, but once again, he didn't."

He gave me an orgasm without wanting anything back, I think, not quite ready to let that little secret out of the bag.

"That's an improvement for sure. Anything else?"

"He's ridiculously good looking," I add with a shrug.

"You've only just noticed?" she asks with a smile.

"Oh, I noticed, I was just never attracted to him because he was such an egotistical arse before."

"But he's not anymore...?"

"Not lately. No," I admit.

"And you admit you're attracted to him," she queries.

"Yes, I am."

Lia nods thoughtfully, taking in all the information I've shared about Dalton. After a moment of silence, she speaks softly.

"It sounds like Dalton is trying to show you a different side of himself, a side that perhaps you never expected to see. It's understandable that you're feeling conflicted, especially given your past experiences with him and his reputation, but I think it's worth giving him a chance to prove that he's sincere in his efforts to be a better person."

I consider Lia's words carefully. Despite my reservations and uncertainties, there's a part of me that wants to believe that he's truly capable of being more than the shallow playboy I once thought him to be.

Taking a deep breath, I look at Lia and say, "I think... I think I want to see if there's something genuine between us, but I'm terrified of opening myself up to the possibility of getting hurt."

Lia's kind smile is filled with encouragement and empathy. "It takes bravery to be vulnerable, Daisy. It's scary too, but sometimes that vulnerability can lead to surprising and wonderful results."

"So what now?"

"Well, right now we eat these delicious scones, drink this tea, and then you'll choose a wedding dress. And after that, I guess it's up to you."

BY THE TIME I've chosen a wedding dress that I'm comfortable wearing, and spent the rest of the afternoon catching up with Drix and Toby, it's past the time I usually sit down to eat dinner with Dalton and Carl. When I arrive back at the estate, rather than go in search of Dalton, I head to my bedroom still ruminating on my conversation with Lia.

Shrugging off my coat, and kicking off my shoes, I sit down at my desk and pull open my sketchbook, needing a distraction. Designing clothes has always helped to soothe my heart and calm my anxiety, and before long a stunning rainbow coloured dress has come to life before me. The colours are muted, but nonetheless striking. Pale pink, baby blue, soft yellow, subtle green and muted lilac swirl together in delicate layers of tulle and chiffon, creating a gown fit for a fairytale princess. As I add intricate beading to the bodice, my mind drifts back to Dalton and our future together. Would he appreciate the effort and creativity I've poured into this dress? Would he even notice the subtle symbolism of the colours representing hope, trust, happiness and new beginnings? Lost in thought, I don't hear the door creak open behind me until a voice breaks through my reverie.

"That's beautiful," Dalton says quietly, his eyes fixed on the sketch before me.

Startled, I glance up to find him standing behind me, his expression a mix of awe and curiosity. I quickly close the sketchbook, feeling a flush of embarrassment creeping up my neck.

"Oh, um, it's nothing. I was just doodling," I mutter, a flutter of nerves in my stomach at his sudden appearance. "Was there something you needed?"

"I thought I'd check in on you, see how your day went," he explains, his gaze lingering on the closed sketchbook. "But now I'm intrigued. May I take a look?"

"Sure," I say, passing the sketchbook to him.

He flips through the pages filled with my designs, his proximity sending a wave of warmth through me, and I struggle to focus on anything other than the way his presence fills the room.

"You're incredibly talented, Daisy," he murmurs, his thumb tracing the delicate lines of my sketches.

I feel a rush of warmth at his praise. "Thank you. Sketching designs help me to relax. I lost track of time."

"You need to relax? Did the wedding dress shopping not go well?"

"It was fine. I found something suitable to wear."

"Suitable?" he queries, passing my sketchbook back to me.

I slide it back in the top drawer of my desk. "It's not my dream dress, but it will work for the occasion," I reply.

"I see," he says, frowning.

"So, how was your day?" I ask, changing the subject.

"Pretty fucking awful," he replies, his gaze lingering on me as if searching for something in my expression.

"That bad, huh?"

"It wasn't the best," Dalton admits, taking a seat on the edge of my bed. "I was going to call it a night, but if you'd like some company, we could watch some trash TV if you'd like?"

"You know what, I'm feeling a little tired myself. I was going to get an early night too."

He presses his mouth shut in a firm line, nodding. "Well, then I'll let you get some rest," he says.

I watch him walk towards my door, and for the life of me, I don't want him to leave. "Dalton, wait," I say, following him.

"Yes?" he questions, turning to face me.

"I know I said that I wanted to forget what happened at the cinema and at the racetrack, but I..." My voice trails off as I chew on my lip.

"But?" he asks, taking a step towards me.

"But I haven't been able to do that," I admit.

"Me either," he replies, taking a step closer to me. "So what now?"

"This is probably a very stupid idea," I mumble.

"What's a stupid idea, watching trash TV? I mean, we'll probably lose a few brain cells in the process, but I'm still down for it, if you are?" he blurts out, and I can't help but notice his sudden nervousness. I shake my head, resting my hand against his chest.

"I was referring to the kiss... I mean the kiss that didn't happen."

"You want to talk about it?"

"No, I want you to kiss me," I whisper, my breath hitching as I look up at him.

"You *want* me to kiss you?"

"Yes."

"Are you certain?" he asks. There's longing and uncertainty in his gaze, something I feel just as powerfully.

"I'm not certain of anything, all I know is that I wanted you to kiss me in the cinema, and I want you to kiss me now," I say.

He nods, reaching up, his thumb tracing over my lips as he leans in slowly, giving me the chance to pull away if I want to.

But I don't.

I stay rooted to the spot, my heart pounding as his palm slides down my throat, gently cupping my neck as his lips meet mine in a soft, hesitant caress. Neither of us deepen the kiss, both uncertain of what this means, and despite asking him to kiss me, I realise that he won't truly do that unless I drop my barriers first.

"Daisy," he mutters, both hands on my hips now, his fingers flexing over my hips, as though he's battling with holding on and letting go.

Parting my lips on a soft exhale, I wrap my arms around his neck, pulling him closer, trying to erase the distance between us, and then he slides his tongue between my lips, and kisses me. I could be glaringly wrong about what's unfolding between us, but in this moment, right here and now, there is no past, no future, only the present.

Our tongues dance against each other's, teasing, tasting, stroking and licking. It's a searching kiss, exploratory, intimate, knee-shakingly perfect. He tastes of coffee and liquor, of frightening possibilities and unspoken desires. Every nerve ending in my body is alight, prickling with awareness, yet my mind is blissfully blank, consumed by the sensation of him, this moment, our kiss. He groans, his fingers digging into my skin as we stumble backwards until my back is pressed against the wall and his body is crowding mine. Heat licks over my skin as his tongue twines with mine and I can feel the undeniable ridge of his erection pressing against my stomach.

A kiss that began soft and tentative soon turns into passionate and raw, the shifting tides of our desire washing over the both of us, pulling us under.

I'm drowning in his embrace, overwhelmed by his commanding kiss, I'm weakened by it, helpless.

We... should... stop...

Those words are like shards of painful consciousness stabbing against my mind.

We. Should. Stop.

Stab. Stab. Stab.

This has gone too far.

I stiffen, chest heaving, my clit aching to be touched, my body alive and desperate for more. But this kiss is too potent, too overwhelming, and for the sake of my sanity and his, I rest my hands against his chest, feeling the thundering of his heart beneath my palm, then push against him.

"No more," I say, as firmly as I can muster. His lips part, his eyes snapping open as his chest heaves.

"Damn!" he mutters, still holding onto me, still caught up in the eddying attraction connecting us.

"No more, please," I beg this time, needing him to step back, to give us both space.

Dalton grits his jaw and with one firm nod of his head, releases me. Stepping back, he swipes a trembling hand through his hair.

"What the fuck was that?" he asks, eyes wild as a range of emotions scatter across his face.

"It was just a kiss," I whisper, knowing I'm lying, wondering why I am.

"It was more than a kiss, Daisy," he counters, exhaling heavily.

And he's right, because it wasn't *just a kiss*. He didn't steal it, we didn't kiss for show, we kissed because we wanted to, and that changes things. How stupidly foolish was I to think that giving in would lead to anything other than messy, complicated, heartache? Kissing is a prelude to something deeper, a taste of how good sex with Dalton could be. It's a stark reminder of the stipulations detailed in our contract, and everything I said I didn't want.

Except now? Now, I want more.

CHAPTER TWENTY

The next couple of days pass in a blur of wedding preparations and work commitments. Daisy and I have fallen into a frustrating new rhythm, and I'm trying my best to navigate our complicated relationship without fucking it all up. Since that kiss, we've reverted to circling each other, not knowing how to act, whether to reach out and hold on, or to sink back into what's familiar. That kiss was like the fucking sun parting a storm cloud, shining so brightly that I'm blinded by everything but the memory of it.

We've gone from enemies, to frenemies, to friends, to people who've kissed each other in anger, like lovers, who've kissed each other like it *meant* something. My head is spinning, and truth be known, I've avoided bringing it up, knowing that whatever lies beyond that kiss is too fucking scary for me to truly contemplate. All I'm capable of doing is work, and when I'm not working I'm counting down the days to when we get married, wondering what the fuck that's going to look like now that we've stepped over that line Daisy drew in the sand weeks ago when we signed the contract. In just a few week's time she'll be my wife, and the thought makes that possessive part inside of me prowl like a caged fucking animal.

To make matters even more excruciating, my attraction to Daisy has grown exponentially, and now that I've had a taste of the woman who, for a few blissful moments, kissed me back with as much hunger as I kissed her, I can't think of anyone else.

Believe me I've tried.

I've whacked off multiple times a day like a fucking hormonal teenager to try and temper these confusing feelings and curb my raging desire. Every time I force myself to think of other women, but each time I try, Daisy filters into my mind, and I come hard only to thoughts of her.

Whilst I'm well aware that abstaining from sex has complicated matters for me, there's this niggle deep inside that tells me this attraction is more than just my need to fuck. It's infuriating. It's complicated. It's fucking scaring the shit out of me.

"Mr Gunn, is there anything I can get you before I retire for the evening?" Fraser, our longest standing member of staff, asks as he steps into my office and jolts me from my thoughts.

I flick my gaze to my watch, noticing that it's almost ten o'clock in the evening, and I shake my head. "No, thank you. I'll be finishing up soon."

"Very well, Sir," he replies.

"Have you seen Daisy this evening?" I ask before he's able to leave.

"Briefly. She was watching television in the cinema room an hour ago. Though when I checked a few minutes ago, the lights were off. I suspect she has gone to bed."

"Okay, thank you," I reply, dropping my gaze back to my laptop as he exits the room.

By the time I head to bed, it's past midnight, and I'm exhausted from a long day of non-stop work, and a painful erection that has kept my body in a constant state of arousal. I'm ready to take a shower and relieve some of the building tension when I pass by Daisy's room and hear a soft moan. The door's slightly ajar, her bed-side lamp casting a warm glow through the crack in the door, and my feet still as I strain to listen.

When her moaning gets louder, concern for Daisy gets the better of me, and I cautiously open the door, stepping into her room and expecting to find her in the throes of a nightmare.

Except she's not in bed.

The covers are thrown back and the door to her en-suite is open. I pause, listening intently, but when she moans again, the sound of her pleasure is unmistakable.

"Fuck," I mutter, my whole body tensing as I realise what she's doing.

I know I should leave, that I should turn on my heel and get the hell out of her room, but my body is refusing to listen to sense. This time the thought of Daisy pleasuring herself is too much of a temptation to ignore.

Creeping closer to her bathroom door, I'm pulled inexorably towards her, and despite the warning voice screaming at me to get the fuck out, I do the exact opposite. Quietly stepping into the bathroom, my heart is in my throat as my gaze falls to her naked body. She's soaking in the bath, her eyes pressed shut as the water laps at her skin, her hand between her legs. Stunned by the sensual vision before me, all I can do is stare. Daisy's mouth is parted as she leisurely strokes her pussy, making my already hard cock desperate for relief. The sight of her in this vulnerable, yet incredibly sexy state has me rooted to the spot, struggling to rip my gaze away.

She's fucking stunning.

With rapt attention, I take in every curve of her body, marvelling over her creamy skin scattered with freckles, and the globes of her breasts just breaking the surface of the water. Her dusky pink nipples are hardened into points and begging to be sucked and licked. It takes every ounce of self-restraint not to do exactly that.

I find my own lips parting on a soft exhale of breath as my mind races with thoughts of what I should do. I mean, I know what I *should* do, and that's walk the fuck away, but I'm so consumed with desire that I can't. I fucking can't. So I stand there, an intruder on her most private moment, getting more and more aroused as the seconds tick by.

"Touch me," she whispers, and for a second I think she's talking to me, aware that I'm in the bathroom with her, but she doesn't open her eyes, lost to whatever fantasy she's imagining. "Make me come."

Jesus fuck.

As if on its own accord, my hand falls to my aching dick as I grip myself tightly. It's been so long since I've been with a woman that if I stay for much longer I know I'll come from just watching Daisy pleasure herself. Yet, I can't seem to move. Enraptured, I imagine it's my hand between her legs, and my fingers exploring the soft folds of her pussy as I stroke my cock over the material of my trousers.

Yes, I made her come on the back of my motorbike. Yes, it was fucking thrilling knowing she let down her guard long enough to enjoy the pleasure even if it wasn't strictly by my hand, but fuck this is different, this is a thousand times more intimate. I'm fully aware that I'm crossing a million boundaries right now, but selfishness and overwhelming attraction overrides common sense.

"That feels so good," she continues, lost to her fantasy, and I feel a sharp stab of jealousy at this imaginary person she's thinking about. Still I remain where I am, my breath catching in my throat as I watch Daisy's face contort with pleasure, her soft moans echoing through the steam-filled bathroom.

A bead of sweat trickles down my forehead as I struggle to contain the impulse to reach out and touch her, to coast my fingers over her pebbled nipples, to replace her hand with mine and bring her to orgasm. And as Daisy's moans grow louder, I step closer, my heart racing as she fingers herself, this primal urge to witness her undoing an addiction that I'm helpless to fight against. With a heaving chest, my gaze falls to her hand as her fingers swirl and tease her clit. Mesmerised, I fail to notice that the catch in her breath is anything other than her mounting desire until it's too late.

"W-what are you doing here?"

My gaze snaps to hers, my eyes widening as I fumble for words. "I heard you moaning. I thought you were having a nightmare," I say, realising how fucking ludicrous that sounds. "I just... Fuck, I'll go."

Daisy bites on her lip, her cheeks heating as her fingers slip from her pussy and she draws upright in the bath, trying to cover herself as water trickles over her skin. I watch the droplets fall, feeling a sudden jealousy at the way they get to glide over all the places I want to touch.

"Dalton, this is..."

"Wrong. So fucking wrong."

She sucks in a breath, her gaze dropping to my dick that's spectacularly tenting my trousers. "You're turned on," she whispers, flicking her gaze back up to my face.

"Beyond measure," I reply, wondering why she's isn't telling me to get the fuck out.

She swallows hard, her gaze fixed on mine, and for long moments we just stare at one another until eventually she unfolds her arms from across her chest and slowly sinks back beneath the water.

"Daisy, what are you doing?" I ask, my voice hoarse, thick with need as she rolls her head to face me, strands of her hair sticking to her neck and chest, the rest fanning out in the water around her.

"I'm trying to figure that out myself," she admits, her chest heaving as she bares herself to me.

"I should go."

"I..." she falters.

"What, Daisy?"

"I don't want you too," she whispers.

"Why?" I choke out.

"Because I don't think anyone has ever looked at me the way you are at this very moment," she admits. "It feels... *good.*"

"Jesus, Daisy," I reply, running a shaky hand through my hair. "You have to understand, my self-control is paper thin."

"What will happen if you lose control, Dalton?" she asks me, her fingers gently swirling the water as she waits for me to answer. There is nothing in her gaze but raw vulnerability, and I'm floored by it as she willingly bares herself to me.

I grit my jaw, pressing my eyes shut briefly, if only to give myself a moment to gather every last shred of self-control I can muster. "I refuse to let you find out."

She nods, giving me a wavering smile. "It's for the best, I guess."

"Daisy..." I plead, fighting with myself as I wobble on my feet, my whole body trembling in my need to go to her. I can't decipher how much of this is my addiction to the female form, my growing connection with Daisy or just pure animal need.

"You had no reservations making me come on the back of your motorbike," she counters, spearing me with her gaze. Daring me to object.

"That was different."

"How?"

"It just was," I reply lamely.

"Do you *want* to see me come?" she asks, her voice a mere whisper.

Her question burns like a brand, igniting fire in my belly.

"Yes," I choke out, my voice barely audible as she blinks up at me. "But I don't know if I can stop myself from taking you in my arms and fucking you right here and now if I do."

"If you touched yourself too, would that stop you from doing that?"

"You want me to touch myself?"

"If that would help?"

"Daisy, we're crossing a boundary here," I say, not understanding why in this moment I'm the voice of fucking reason. Not so long ago I was intent on making her mine in every way possible. My selfish need would've overridden any sense of right and wrong, but now that I know her like I do, I'm questioning everything.

"We're going to be married soon, Dalton, and after that we need to make a baby."

"Without fucking. You said that, remember?" I remind her.

"I do." She sighs, glancing up at me, her eyes filled with a mix of embarrassment, confusion and desire. "But what if we... Never mind."

"Say it. Just say what's on your mind," I demand, realising how close I am to saying *fuck it* to it all.

"I know what I said about you donating your sperm in a cup, but that was before," she says softly, wincing a little.

"Before?"

"When we weren't friends, Dalton. When I hadn't told you about my past, and you hadn't revealed your own pain. When you hadn't put me first, and walked away when I'd offered myself to you. When we hadn't spent time together, when we hadn't kissed the way we did..." Her voice trails off as she frowns. "It seems so clinical now. Wrong somehow."

"What are you saying?" I ask, my head fucking spinning.

"If we can't make a baby because we're in love with one another, by *making love*..." she adds, her voice wobbling. "At the very least I want us to both feel mutual pleasure, even if it's by our own hands," she continues on.

"This isn't something I can do," I say.

"Yet you can make me come on your motorbike," she argues, hammering the point home.

"That was for you."

"You don't pleasure yourself?"

"All the fucking time," I admit, with a shake of my head. "But I've never masturbated with a woman that hasn't then led to fucking them. That's the part I'm struggling with."

"Will you at least try. For me?"

Jesus, she really doesn't understand what she's asking. "And if I can't do this without wanting to step over the line you insisted on, one that has us both trapped in an impossible situation?"

"But what if I've changed my mind?" she whispers.

"You're regretting saying it?" I ask.

"All I know is that I can't bear this tension between us any longer. It's too much, too overwhelming. You need release. I need release. For now, maybe this will be enough?"

For long moments I consider her request, oscillating between wanting to leave, wanting to stay and do what she's asked, and wanting to haul her out of the bath, bend her over the lip and fuck her hard and fast.

"Dalton?"

Making a decision, I nod my head. "Okay, Daisy. We'll try it your way," I agree, my resolve crumbling.

With that, I begin to unbutton my shirt, revealing my bare chest covered in a multitude of tattoos as I pull my shirt free, dropping it to the floor. Daisy gasps, her eyes dropping to my heaving chest as my fingers fall to the zipper of my trousers, coasting over the dark trail of hair that leads to my groin.

"Are you certain?" I ask, giving her one last chance to change her mind.

"Yes," she whispers, her trembling fingers drifting to her throat as she watches me kick off my loafers, and slide my trousers and boxers down my legs until I'm standing naked before her.

Daisy's gaze roams my face before trailing down my body with a searing intensity that has my fucking pulse racing a hundred miles an hour, before finally coming to rest on my throbbing cock. She swallows hard, her throat working as she gulps down her nerves, and lifts her gaze to meet mine.

Gripping myself, I stroke my fist upwards, my eyes locked with Daisy's. Her breath hitches as I moan, fucking lost to this raw, churning feeling inside my chest. Desire and lust battles with longing, creating a storm of sensations that threaten to consume me as her fingers trail down her chest, over her stomach finally coming to rest between her parted thighs. I can barely hear her soft, breathy moans over the sound of my own ragged breathing.

"Fuck, Daisy, what are we doing?" I groan, my balls tightening as my hand moves faster, mirroring the increased pace of her fingers stroking her clit.

"Don't stop, Dalton, please," she begs, and it's as if my own hand is giving her pleasure right now.

"I couldn't even if I wanted to," I reply, my voice strained as I struggle to maintain control, the sound of her moans mixing with the blood pounding in my ears.

"I need to come," she moans, and with reckless abandon, I begin to stroke myself harder and faster, my body singing with a wild, untamed energy as my pleasure gathers at the base of my spine, sending bolts of electricity to my aching balls and throbbing cock.

"Then come, Daisy. Come for me, like I'm going to come for you," I say, my voice hoarse and ragged, my cock leaking pre-cum.

Daisy's eyes flutter shut, and her fingers quicken their pace, her hips jerking as she begins to lose herself to the sensation. A low, guttural moan escapes her lips, and she arches her back, pressing her palm harder against her clit as a wave of pleasure washes over her. I watch, transfixed as her stomach muscles contract, and she lets out a high-pitched cry, her body shaking as her orgasm crashes over her.

Seeing her come undone sends an electric current through my body, detonating my own orgasm. I let out a primal roar, my hand pumping fast as I push myself over the edge. With nothing to hold onto, I double over as I come, my body convulsing as hot spurts of cum explode from my dick, and into the palm of my hand. Jesus, I don't think I've ever come as hard. Gasping for air, I slowly straighten up, the room fucking spinning as I stumble a little.

"Fuck!" I groan, my hands sticky with cum.

"Are you okay?" Daisy whispers, pushing upright, water sloshing over the edge of the bath as she moves. Her cheeks, neck and chest are flushed pink as beads of water trail over her too hot skin.

"I'm good," I mutter, heat creeping into my cheeks as I stride towards the basin, and wash my hands. Fuck knows I need the distraction.

Once I'm cleaned up, I grip the basin, taking a deep, steadying breath, trying to regain my composure, but try as I might I can't seem to catch my breath. I feel raw, exposed somehow, and the feeling is uncomfortable to say the least. Behind me I hear Daisy rise from the water, and out of the corner of my eye, she reaches for a bath towel, wrapping it around her body.

"Dalton?" she questions softly. "Are you okay?"

Forcing myself to look at her, I lift my gaze to meet hers in the mirror. "I'm good, Daisy," I lie, not understanding what the fuck is wrong. Why, at this very moment, I want to run from the fucking room.

"You don't seem okay," she replies, stepping towards me, her fingertips tenderly brushing my back, setting off a cascade of electricity down my spine.

"That was..." I can't seem to find the words to describe how I feel, because I don't understand those feelings myself.

"Intense?" she offers.

"Yeah," I agree, turning around to face her as I lean against the vanity unit. I'm still naked, and instead of feeling relief, I just feel out of sorts, exposed in a way I've never felt before.

"Dalton, talk to me," she whispers, stepping closer, her hand coasting up my arm, leaving a trail of flames in her wake. "Have I ruined what we've taken so long to build?"

"No, Daisy," I reply.

"What then?"

"I... just... *fuck*," I mutter.

"Dalton?"

"It's not enough," I blurt out.

"What?"

"This isn't enough. Not for me," I reply, gripping the vanity unit so I don't reach for her. "I want more. I want to fuck you, Daisy. I want to fuck you now."

"But you've just..."

"Come? Yes, I have, and yet I'm still hard. Look at me. Look what you're doing to me. I'm aching for you," I say, my fucking voice cracking as I drop my gaze to my cock, the tip shiny and wet from my release. "I'm still hard, and if I don't leave now, I'll do something we both might regret later..."

"Then stay," she whispers, reaching for her towel, and pulling it free.

It drops to the floor in a puddle at her feet. My eyes widen, my mouth parts as I stare at her naked beside me. Unable to help myself I turn to face her, reaching up to trace my fingers down the centre of her chest, mesmerised by the way her nipples peak from my touch.

"You don't want this," I protest, even though her body tells me otherwise, her eyes flaring with more heat.

"I want this," she says firmly. "I want you."

"Daisy, I'm still that man you once hated. Nothing's changed," I say, my hand falling away, balling into fists at my side.

"You're wrong. Everything's changed," she whispers, her hand pressing against my chest, branding me with her touch. I wonder if she feels how my heart thumps for her? "I *don't* hate you. I *want* this."

"But I can't make love to you," I add, hoping that my honesty will put her off. I wish I could give her that. She deserves to be loved, to be made love to, but I can't give her that. I've never been able to give that to anyone.

"I don't need you to make love to me. I need you to fuck me," she says, reaching for my hand and placing it over her breast, holding it there.

My throat bobs as I swallow, and my cock gets impossibly hard at the feel of her softness beneath my palm, the heat radiating from her skin. She's so warm, so tempting.

"Daisy," I warn, trying to pull my hand away, but her grip tightens, holding me in place.

"I thought that this would be enough too, but it isn't. I've been telling myself that I can live without sex, but I need it just as much as you do. I want more. People have sex all the time and they're not in love, so why can't we?"

"But I thought you said..." I murmur, stepping closer, my feet moving of their own accord.

"I know what I said, and in an ideal world we'd make a baby by making love. But I'm not asking you to love me. This is just sex. We both want it. So why can't we just take what we want?" she asks softly, the confidence of her words belies her nervousness as her fingertips tremble against my skin.

"And yet when I asked to kiss you that night of our engagement party, and I said it didn't have to mean anything, you said that it *should* mean something. Why is this any different?"

"Back then I didn't..."

"Didn't what?"

"I didn't know you as well as I do now. I like you Dalton. You like me. Our relationship has evolved. We're going to be married soon."

"We are," I agree.

"We both want sex..." Her voice trails off as she chews on her lip, no doubt considering what to say next. "And I want you to know that having sex with you *does* mean something to me."

"What does it mean to you?" I ask, my hand gently massaging her breast. The way she feels in my palm, the way her body presses into my hold. Fuck, it's...

"It means mutual pleasure. It means release, *relief* for the both of us. But more than that, regardless of whether we love each other or not, it means the possibility of conceiving a child, *our* child. That means so much to me," she replies, her fingers coasting over my skin, feathering against the trail of hair leading to my cock.

"Our child," I whisper, my fucking heart squeezing at the thought.

I know that's what Daisy wants, what my father wants, and before this whole situation came about, being a father wasn't something I'd ever truly considered, but since Daisy agreed to marry me, to bare my child, I knew I wanted to be a part of that child's life in a way my father and mother have never been for me. It could be my opportunity to make things right.

"Yes. No matter what, we'll have a child together, Dalton."

"We will," I agree, "But I still need you to be sure that you want to have sex with me, Daisy, because even though it would be difficult for me, I'm willing to jack off into a jar to protect your heart. I don't want to put your emotions at risk by having sex with you. This is sex for the purpose of mutual pleasure, to conceive, but we're not making love, okay?"

"I know that. I'm okay with that," she insists.

I nod, searching her gaze for any hint of uncertainty. "There's no going back after this," I warn, reaching for her, my palm sliding into her hair as I tug on the strands, arching her neck back.

"I understand," she breathes, pupils widening as the hard ridge of my cock slides against her belly.

"I will fuck you until you're breathless, until you come so hard you'll forget every other man who's been inside of you. You'll be mine, and you won't be able to tell me to forget about this, because I won't be able to do that. I will want you tomorrow, the next day, *every* day. You need to understand what you're asking of me."

My chest heaves and I try to tell myself to put an end to this, that this could all just be her way of papering over the cracks despite everything she's said, but when her warm hand circles my cock, all rational thought leaves my fucking head.

I'm done for.

"I'm sure, Dalton. Please just fuck me," she begs, and her hand on my cock and those words are like a bullet obliterating my self-control.

"Let go of me," I grind out, releasing her from my hold.

She sucks in a breath, her fingers slipping from my cock. "Dalton, I told you that I *want* this."

I stare at her for long moments, long enough to see her confidence begin to crumble, long enough to know that I can't walk out of this bathroom without burying myself deep inside of her.

"Fuck it," I grind out on an exhale of breath.

"What?"

"I said put your hands on the vanity unit, and spread your fucking legs.".

For a beat, all I can feel is the pulse of my dick throbbing in time to the beat of my heart, and her soft breath against my skin. Endless seconds tick by as I wait for her to change her mind.

Except she doesn't.

She turns around and does exactly what I've asked, her eyes

locking with mine in the reflection of the mirror as her wet hair hangs in unruly curls around her face.

"Good girl," I murmur, loving how that sounds, how she shudders from my touch when I reach for her waist, my hands gliding over the curve of her hips. For a moment all I can do is stare at Daisy, admiring the freckles scattered across her creamy skin, the swell of her arse, the two tiny dimples in her lower back.

"You're so fucking stunning," I say as I lean forward, swiping her hair from her neck, then sink my teeth into the tender flesh of her shoulder, claiming her.

"Dalton," she whimpers, dragging in a sharp breath as our eyes clash in the mirror.

"There's no going back now," I repeat as my lips find her ear. "Bend over, Daisy. Bare yourself to me."

With a soft exhale she leans forward and presses her forearms either side of the sink, giving me a full view of her peachy arse and her glistening slit.

"That's it," I croon, my hand reaching forward to run my palm down her spine. She quakes beneath my touch, her pussy wet with arousal as I slide my fingers down her arse crack and between her parted folds. "You're so fucking wet. You want me badly, don't you?"

"Yes, I want you," she whimpers, pushing back against my hand, moaning as my finger circles her clit. I rub against the tiny nub until her mouth falls open and her breath begins to hitch.

"Every part of you belongs to me now," I say, gripping my cock and fisting myself as I slide my fingers inside of her pussy, fucking her with them. "From this moment on, there won't be any part of your body off limits to me. I will claim your mouth, your pussy, your arse. I will take you in every possible way, Daisy. I will pinken your skin with my hand. I will suck on your beautiful tits until you come. I will lick every inch of your skin. I will fuck you until you can't take anymore, and then I will fuck you again, and again, and again."

"God, stop teasing me," she whimpers.

"Say *my* name, Daisy," I command, slipping out of her and pinching her clit roughly.

She gasps, eyes flaring wide, her body tensing. Our eyes meet in the mirror as she says, "Dalton, just fuck me."

I lose it.

Every single thought that tells me that I'm making a huge fucking mistake leaves my head as I grip my cock, line myself at her opening, then slam into her with one firm thrust, shunting her body forward.

She cries out, pressing her hand against the mirror to prevent herself from colliding with it as I fuck her hard and fast. I'm not gentle. There's no tenderness. This is weeks and weeks of built up tension as I sink my cock deep inside of her.

"You wanted this!" I accuse, slamming into her over and over as she pants and groans, her cries echoing around the bathroom. "You wanted me to fuck you. This is what it feels like, Daisy!"

"Yes," she hisses as I ram into her, my hand reaching for her hair as I tug on it, her neck arching as I drive into her over and over and over again.

This is as far from making love as two people can get, and I'm mindless, my ability to be a thoughtful lover going out of the fucking window. Every part of my consciousness hones in on the way her pussy squeezes my cock, how she cries out as though in blissful agony. My free hand grasps her hip hard enough to bruise, and I should care, but I don't.

I want to mark her.

I want her to feel what I feel. Frenzied. Out of control. Fucking *mindless*.

I give in to everything we've both been fighting so hard against.

"Oh, that feels so good," she cries, driving me insane. "*You* feel so good."

"I. Can't. Love. You," I counter, thrusting inside of her with every word, warning her of everything I'm incapable of.

Except they don't feel like a fucking warning at all, they feel like a goddamn lie. So I say those words again in an attempt to blot out the riot of emotions in my chest at how it feels to finally be inside of her.

"I."

Thrust

"Can't."

Thrust.

"Love."

Thrust.

"You."

Thrust.

Sex has never been about feelings, it's only ever been about pleasure, and I'm angry at her for drawing something out of me that I'm not willing to give up. So I push those thoughts away and bury myself so deep inside of her that I feel the crown of my dick hitting her cervix.

"I don't love you either," she cries back, pushing against me, taking everything I give and meeting the frantic rock of my hips with a frenziedness of her own.

Her words anger me. They shouldn't, but they do because she didn't say she *can't* love me. She said she *doesn't* love me when I know she's more than capable of loving others.

Inexplicably, that *hurts*. It fucking hurts.

So I go harder, faster, driving her forward, rutting like a mindless beast. My cock throbs with fury as I slam into her over and over, the sound of our bodies colliding echoing around the bathroom. She's taking it all, every thrust, every harsh whisper, every primitive grunt as I lose myself to the animalistic need to possess her, own her, ruin her until she's mine.

The words 'I can't love you' bounce around my head, seeming as hollow as the air we're breathing. They were spoken reflexively, a reaction to this moment, but they resonate within my chest, a nagging reminder of the lies I've been telling myself, *her*, and I hate myself for it.

I try to drive away those thoughts by wrapping her hair around my clenched fist and fucking her mercilessly. Every stroke brings a mixture of agony and pleasure that threatens to consume me whole. Her cries fill the bathroom, mingling with the sounds of our bodies slapping together, driving us both to the edge.

"I'm going to come!" she cries and I feel her muscles clench around me, signalling her oncoming release. I'm right behind her, unable to hold back any longer.

"Come for me. Come for me, Daisy. Milk my fucking cock!" I roar, and with one final, powerful thrust, I spill inside her, our bodies shaking with the intensity of our union.

We collapse together, gasping for air, our hearts beating in sync as the aftershocks of our orgasms ripple through us. My chest is against her back, my heart slamming against my ribcage, her body quaking.

For long moments, we simply remain joined together, my body over hers as we bask in the raw, unbridled passion that has consumed us. Then, as the last pulses of our pleasure fade, reality seeps back in, and I find myself growing ashamed of my own actions. The words I spoke to her, the way I lost control and fucked her in a way I've never truly done before, and I'm not talking about being rough, I'm talking about the feelings she's conjured within me. Too much emotion whirls inside my chest, and it all feels like a nightmare I can't wake up from.

Pulling out of her, I step back on shaky legs, running a hand through my hair as she pushes upright, turning to face me. Her face is flushed, her pupils blown wide, her chest heaving as she stares at me, a host of conflicting emotions rushing across her features. My eyes drop to her thighs, and the red line that crosses the tops of them from me ramming her against the vanity unit.

"Daisy, I'm sorry. I shouldn't have been so rough–"

"Don't apologise. I wanted this. You wanted this. I'm okay. Are you?" she asks tentatively.

Am I okay? The truthful answer is, no. No, I'm not fucking okay. I might have come, but I don't feel relief, I feel fucking churned up inside.

Raw. Confused. Fucking lost.

"Can I hold you?" I blurt out, needing to pull her close, not understanding why, but wanting to hold her more than anything.

This isn't what I do. I don't hold women in comfort after sex. I avoid affection like it's the fucking plague, but right now I *want* to hold her. I need reassurance, and that's something I've never, *ever*, needed before. What the fuck is wrong with me?

"Of course," she replies gently, pressing her body against mine as I wrap my arms around her back. She leans her cheek against my bare chest, her warm breath causing goosebumps to scatter over my skin as her arms circle my waist.

"Jesus," I whisper under my breath as I try and fail to make sense of my emotions.

"What?" She looks up at me, her eyes searching mine.

"It's nothing," I say, dropping my head and pressing my lips against her forehead in a tender kiss, my thoughts reeling. I don't know what the fuck we're doing, what the fuck *I'm* doing.

"Okay," she whispers, but we both know that something fundamental has shifted between us and neither of us are ready to face what that means.

CHAPTER TWENTY-ONE

"This is the amusement arcade," I point out as Dalton wraps his arm around my waist and grins, his cheeks a little pink from the chill evening air as we step inside the building.

It's the first time we've been able to have some alone time together after having sex a few days ago, and whilst I love the arcade, it wasn't where I was expecting him to take me when he said we were going out on a date. I'm pleasantly surprised.

"It is," he agrees, guiding me towards the machine that churns out coins when you insert a note. He reaches into his back pocket and pulls out his wallet, sliding a fifty pound note into the machine, the sound of children's laughter and childish squeals lifting up into the air around us.

"I love the amusement arcade," I say, smiling.

"I know that too," he replies, gathering up the coins into two separate cups and handing me one. "I thought we could have a competition."

"A competition?"

"Yes, whoever wins the most tickets gets to choose what we do next," he explains, wiggling his brows in the most ridiculously cute way that I can't help but laugh. Dalton has never been cute. He's suave, charming, sure, but never cute. Today he's revealing a playful side that I never knew existed. It looks good on him.

"You do realise that I spent my childhood in this place?"

"Maybe so, but I'm very competitive, and I'm not about to lose," he warns with a smirk, tucking his wallet back into his pocket, grabbing my hand and dragging me over to the motorcycle video game where two kids are arguing over which bike they get to ride on.

"Wait, no fair, you have an advantage," I protest.

"I'll try not to lap you more than twice," he replies, smirking, before turning his attention to the young boys still bickering, and tapping the older one on the shoulder. "Hey, I'll give you ten pounds each if you let us go first."

"Ten pounds? *Each?*" the boy repeats, eyes widening.

"Yes," he replies, pulling out two crisp, ten pound notes from his wallet.

They snatch them from his hand, grinning, before running off to the coin machine.

"Are you going to do that all night long, pay off the kids so we can go first?"

"I'm not a particularly patient man, Daisy," he replies with a shrug.

"You're incorrigible," I reply, choosing the red bike over the blue one.

"Hey, I wanted the red bike," Dalton says, popping out his bottom lip in faux disappointment.

I reach up and tug on it. "Too bad, too sad. Now come on, sling your leg over the bike, and prepare to get your arse whipped."

"I think you'll find that it will be you who'll be getting your arse whipped if you lose," he replies, and there's not a hint of a smile on his face as he gives me a salacious look. His eyes drop to my legs, my pink woollen skirt having ridden up over my knee to reveal my deep purple stockings.

"Is that a promise?"

"No, it's a certainty," he grins, tugging on a strand of my hair. "Especially if those are stockings and not tights."

"Take your mind out of the gutter, racer boy, and get your head into the game," I retort, grabbing two pound coins from my cup, and sliding them into the slot.

He laughs, settling onto the blue motorbike.

As the screen comes to life, and the game lights up, Dalton and I exchange competitive glances before the countdown begins.

3...

"Get ready to lose, Daisy."

2...

"Get ready to eat your words, Dalton," I counter with a wink.

1...

The sound of roaring engines fills the air, blending with the laughter and excitement of the other patrons as I grip the handle-bars tightly, turning the throttle. Determined to show Dalton what I'm made of, I take the lead, laughter bubbling up my chest as he grumbles something unintelligible, the weight of his body making the mechanical motorbike groan as he leans from side to side. He might be an expert on a real race track, but he doesn't realise that I hold the highest score on this particular game, and have done so for years.

With a determined set of my jaw, I navigate the twists and turns of the digital race track, Dalton hot on my tail as we speed through virtual city streets, neon lights flashing as we race.

"The fuck?" Dalton laughs, as he realises a little too late that I'm beating his arse.

Weaving through the traffic effortlessly, I dodge obstacles, hitting speed boosts with precision. Dalton's grin falters as he struggles to keep up, his bike crashing into virtual cars left and right in his haste to catch up with me. I can't help but laugh as a stream of curse words erupt from his lips. With one final burst of speed, I surge ahead, crossing the finish line way ahead of Dalton. The machine dings loudly, signalling my victory with onscreen fireworks and flashing lights.

"You've got to do better than that, racer boy," I tease.

Dalton stares at his screen in disbelief before turning to me with a mixture of admiration and amusement. "Okay, okay, you won *this* game," he concedes, a playful glint in his eye, "But just you wait until the next game. I won't go easy on you. This was just a warm-up. I was testing you."

"Sure you were," I laugh.

"Get ready, Daisy, because I'm not about to lose again."

"You're on," I reply, slipping off the motorbike.

With a smile tugging my lips, I slide my hand into Dalton's as we head to the next game, more than ready to whoop his arse once more. An hour later I have one hundred more tickets than he does, and I smother a smile as we wait in line at the kiosk to exchange those tickets for a nominal prize.

"Well, shit," Dalton mutters, side-eyeing me as I slurp happily on my blueberry slushy.

"What was that?" I ask, cupping my ear with a smirk. "Did you have something you wanted to say?"

"I didn't realise you had so many hidden talents."

"Oh, I have *many* hidden talents," I reply with a raised brow, wrapping my lips around the straw provocatively before sucking the sweet liquid into my mouth.

He groans, and I step forward, smiling sweetly at the attendant.

"What can I get you?" the teenager asks, his eyes flicking to

Dalton, who wraps his arm around my waist and tugs me into his side as he buries his nose into my hair.

"What can I get for three hundred and fifty two tickets?" I ask, my eyes grazing over the plastic toys, stuffed animals, and sweet treats lining the shelves behind him, my cheeks heating at the way Dalton coasts his hand over my arse then lower as he feels the ridge of my stockings.

"Thought as much," he mutters, and I smile internally.

"Anything on the middle shelf," the attendant says, pointing to a row of stuffed toys, completely oblivious to the fact I'm being felt up so indecently.

My gaze coasts along the shelf, before noticing a small crystal unicorn tucked onto the end of the top shelf. I point to it. "What about that?" I ask, swallowing a moan as Dalton's hand slides back up over my arse and squeezes.

"That's worth five hundred tickets," he replies, giving me a shrug.

"Ah, never mind, I'll grab the pink teddy instead," I say, handing him my tickets.

"Here, take mine. That's more than five hundred together," Dalton says, shoving his tickets at the boy.

"Don't you want your own prize? That toy Ferrari would look great on your desk at work," I tease.

"I've got a real one in the garage back home," he counters, winking at me before turning his attention back to the attendant. "The unicorn, please," he insists.

"Sure thing," the attendant replies as he retrieves the crystal unicorn from its spot on the shelf, and hands it to me. "Congratulations on your win. Enjoy your prize!" He gives us both a practised smile before turning his attention to the people waiting patiently behind us.

"So what next, champion?" Dalton asks me as we slowly weave our way through the arcade, his arm still around my waist.

My gaze flicks to the back of the amusement arcade and the House of Mirrors. "How about we get lost in there," I say, pointing to the entrance.

"The House of Mirrors?" Dalton chuckles. "Well, I can't say I've ever had the pleasure. Why not?"

"You've never been inside?" I ask, my brows lifting in surprise as I tuck the crystal unicorn into the pocket of my skirt.

He shrugs. "Nope."

"I mean, I have to say I'm surprised given how much you like to look at yourself," I joke, and he gives me a pretend hurt look before tickling my side in punishment.

"Low blow, Daisy. Low blow."

I squeal, untangling myself from his hold and batting his hands away. "Don't! I'm ticklish!"

He grins wickedly. "Good to know."

When we reach the entrance, the bored looking attendant guarding the door gives us both a once over, then says, "It's shutting for the evening. I'm just waiting for the last people to exit. Sorry."

"Oh, never mind," I reply with a shrug, twisting on my heel, but when Dalton isn't beside me, I turn to look over my shoulder to find him surreptitiously handing the attendant a wad of notes, and muttering something in his ear.

"What are you doing?" I ask, looking about to see if anyone has noticed him paying off the kid.

"Paying over and above the fee to get inside," he replies nonchalantly.

"It's not worth *that* much money," I point out, as the attendant pockets the roll of notes and steps aside as the last few people exit the room.

"I haven't looked at myself in a mirror all day. I rather miss my face," Dalton replies with a grin.

Laughter bubbles out of my throat as the attendant holds open the door, and we slip inside the darkened entrance. I'm immediately enchanted by the labyrinth of illusions, each mirror reflecting our images in a myriad of ways as we follow the path through the maze. I burst out laughing when I catch Dalton's distorted reflection in one particular mirror, his body made tiny and his head impossibly huge.

"So handsome," I joke as he frowns.

"I look like one of those plastic toys Drix loves to collect," he protests, shifting his body to see if his reflection changes.

"It's a good look on you, matches that huge ego you have," I reply, grinning as he grumbles something under his breath. "Come on Mr Vanity, let's keep going."

Following me, we pass through a corridor of mirrors, lit up in different coloured neon lights, each one playing tricks with our eyes and leading us further into the maze. We can't help but stop and admire the distorted versions of ourselves, each mirror reflecting elongated limbs, shrunken heads, and exaggerated features that has us both giggling like children. We keep going, weaving through the maze as we try to navigate our way to the centre. Dalton's hand finds mine, his fingers tangling with my own.

"This is fun," he admits.

"Don't sound so surprised," I reply as we pass more mirrors and head deeper into the maze. "Oh, if I remember correctly we should be near the centre. I love this part."

And as we turn the corner, we step into a room of mirrors that is designed in such a way that it makes us appear as if we are floating in a sea of stars, our reflections shimmering in the dim light.

"Now this is cool," Dalton says, his eyes widening in wonder.

"*Cool?*" I snort with laughter. "That is not a word I ever expected to come out of your mouth."

"I'll have you know, my vocabulary is vast and diverse. I'm

particularly good at dirty talk," he replies, his fingers tightening around mine as he tugs me against his chest.

"Is that so?" I tease, arching a brow as he runs his hand down my back and grabs my arse, squeezing it.

"Definitely. Want to hear some?" he asks, dropping his mouth to my ear.

"Why not? Let's see what you're made of," I reply, tingles of excitement rushing down my spine as he chuckles softly.

"Dirty talk doesn't really have the same effect if we're not actually being dirty," he retorts, capturing the lobe of my ear between his teeth and nibbling gently. A smile spreads across my face as he pulls me into his body.

"We're in public, Dalton," I protest weakly, my voice breathless as his lips trail down my neck.

"We're in a maze of mirrors with no one else about," he counters, his tongue trailing circles over my pulse point.

"There might be cameras," I argue.

"There are, but I paid the attendant to turn them off. See," he says, pointing to a camera I can just about make out in the corner of the room, "No red light."

"You have this all planned out."

"What can I say? I really want to sink my cock inside of you and feel how wet you are for me right now."

"Dalton," I caution, but my tone lacks any real conviction. In fact, it comes across more as a plea than a threat.

"Are you dripping for me, Daisy? Is your clit aching to be touched?" he asks, drawing his lips back up my neck and across my jaw, his mouth hovering over mine. "Are you as turned on as I am right now, knowing I'm about to fuck you so hard that your screams will be heard all the way down the street, let alone in the amusement arcade?"

I gasp as his words send a jolt of desire straight to my core, everything heightened by his dirty mouth and his touch. "You're very sure of yourself."

"Stop trying to delay the inevitable, we both know you're desperate for me," he accuses against my lips. "Show me, Daisy. Show me just how wet you are."

Without thinking, I slip my hand beneath the waistband of my skirt, then my knickers, brushing my fingers through my drenched core. My eyes stutter shut briefly as I tease my clit.

"I didn't tell you to finger-fuck yourself," Dalton warns, gripping my forearm and dragging it back up. Holding my arm, he smirks, eyeing my glistening fingers. "Thought so."

With a growl he captures my fingers with his lips, drawing them into his mouth, humming around the taste. I stare at him, my mouth popping open as he twirls his tongue around my fingers, sucking them clean.

"Fucking delicious."

"I'm—"

"Going to fuck you now," he grinds out, and without another word, he spins me around and pushes me against the nearest wall of mirrors, his hands grabbing my hips. "Palms against the mirror. Eyes on me."

As Dalton's hands grip my hips, I obey, pressing my palms against the cool surface, meeting his eyes in the reflection before us. I feel the heat of his body behind me, his breath hot against my neck.

"When I slide my cock inside of you, I want you to know that every sound you make, every word you say, every thrashing beat of your heart and thrum of your pulse is because of me and what I'm doing to you," he grinds out.

"Yes," I whisper.

"You're pleasure is mine," he says, gripping my skirt, gathering the material and rolling it over my hips, tucking it into my waistband. Then he grabs my arse, and says "This delicious arse is mine."

"Yours," I agree.

"This pussy," he says, reaching between my legs and cupping me over the fabric of my knickers, "Is mine to fuck."

"That too," I whimper, as he pushes the material of my knickers to one side and presses two of his fingers inside of me. I gasp, eyes fluttering shut as he finger-fucks me steadily, the motion making me moan, making me wetter, hotter, needier.

"Eyes. On. Me," he repeats, and my eyelids snap open, our gazes clashing. "Does that feel good, Daisy?"

"Yes."

"Do you like the way I stroke you, how I bury my fingers deep inside your dripping cunt?"

"Yes," I hiss, rocking against his hand. I like it way, way too much.

"Pull your top up, let me see your beautiful tits," he commands.

I push off from the mirror, following his command as I gather up my top and bra, freeing my breasts, and tucking the material of my top beneath the elastic of my bra. His free hand comes up to cup me, his fingers pinching my nipple. "These tits–"

"Are yours to play with," I finish for him.

"Damn right," he grumbles, groaning as he presses a wet kiss to my cheek, still pumping his fingers inside of me.

I can feel my core throbbing with need, his expert fingers sending waves of pleasure through me, his words edging me higher. With growing urgency, I grind myself against his hand, wanting more. He adds another finger, stretching me further, and I cry out, arching into him.

"What do you want, Daisy?" he rasps, his voice low and husky. "Do you want me to make you come with my fingers first, or should I just plunge my cock into your pussy right now?"

His fingers crook inside of me, touching that spot deep inside that makes me cry out in bliss. "I want both," I gasp, my breaths becoming shallower, my hips bucking against his hand.

"Then that's what you'll get."

His fingers pump faster, and I feel my core tightening, my whole body tingling with sensation as my head falls back against his shoulder. "Yes, just like that," I groan, my oncoming orgasm building deep inside as my internal muscles ripple, then tighten.

"My cock aches to be inside of you. Can you feel how hard I am?"

"Yes," I retort, feeling the hard ridge of his cock pressing into my lower back.

"I think about being inside of you all the time. It's all I fucking think about, Daisy. The way you whimper and moan, the way your pretty tits swell when you're turned on, how your nipples peak. I think about your plump lips, and the taste of your tongue. "

"I think about you too," I admit. "The way you fucked me, like you couldn't hold back, like you would die if you didn't fuck me."

"I would die a happy man deep inside your cunt," he growls, his fingers pumping harder, his thumb edging the rim of my arsehole, making me gasp then whimper as he pushes his thick digit inside of me. "But not before I've claimed your arse. I want that too. I want your mouth on my cock, I want my lips on your pussy. I want to fuck you in every position imaginable. I would die if I couldn't have that. Say you'll let me."

"Yes, take it all," I groan.

"Then come for me, Daisy. Come for me now, because I can't hold out a second longer," he demands roughly.

And just like the other night, I come on his command, splintering around him, my internal muscles gripping him tightly as pleasure rocks through me, making me arch and shudder. My breaths come in short, sharp pants as I struggle to catch my breath.

"That's it," he croons, still stroking me deeply. "So wet for me."

"Oh God, oh God, oh God," I pant, head dropping forward as he gently pulls his fingers free.

I sway on my feet, my legs feeling wobbly from the intense orgasm as his snakes around my waist and he holds me steady.

He lifts his fingers, wet from my arousal, to his mouth and sucks on them. "You taste so fucking good," he says.

"Dalton..." My voice trails off as he reaches up and grips my jaw, turning my head to the side as he shifts position, kissing me deeply. I can taste myself on him as he licks into my mouth, and I twine my fingers in his hair, kissing him back, nipping his bottom lip.

"Fuck, Daisy," he mutters, pulling back. As our gazes clash I falter, feeling a wave of... lust *and* affection. I wonder if he feels that too. "I'm so turned on. I've been hard for days ever since we fucked in your bathroom. I've wanked off thinking about that moment, how you bent over for me, how your pussy dripped for me, how you squeezed my damn cock so tight I saw a blaze of stars —just like these ones—behind my eyelids."

"Then fuck me, Dalton. Make *me* see stars," I say, begging for more, my core contracting, desperate for his cock.

"Believe me, I'm gonna give you the whole fucking universe by the time we're done," he murmurs, reaching between us to unzip his fly and pull out his erection, allowing the length of his cock to rest against my arse as he shoves down his jeans and boxers past his hips.

"Palms back on the mirror," he orders. "Now, Daisy!"

When I don't do as I'm told immediately, because I'm still recovering from the aftershocks of my orgasm, he raises his hand and slaps my arse.

"Ow!" I cry, the sting spreading out across my arse and the base of my spine, making me jerk away from him.

"Don't do as I say when I command it, and that's what will happen," he warns with a growl, gripping my hip with one hand, whilst stroking the other over the stinging burn from his slap. My core tightens from the sensory overload, my clit throbbing as though that slap was sent straight to the tight bundle of nerves pulsating there, and his gentle strokes only add to the intensity. Pain, pleasure, it all rolls into one, heightening everything.

"Dalton..." I murmur, shocked by my reaction, because I *liked* the sharp sting of the slap, but more than that, I love the blissful way my body reacted to it and the way he's soothing me afterwards. I like it a lot. So I don't put my hands on the mirror, my gaze locking with his in our reflection with challenge.

"So you liked that, huh?" he asks softly, tipping his head sideways as he studies me.

I don't reply with words, I simply arch my spine, giving him my arse. Needing to see if I truly do like it. Given my history, I'm not sure why that is.

"There you go again, surprising me, Daisy Hammer," he murmurs, his hand hovering in the air as he eyes me. "I'm going to spank you once again on each cheek, then I'll soothe the sting, okay? If it's too much, you tell me to stop and I'll stop."

I nod, bracing myself.

Shifting his body sideways, he wraps one arm around my waist and then he slaps my right arse cheek, pausing a moment to see if it's too much. The pain is intense and immediate, but I don't tell him to stop, I simply wait. He spanks me again on my left arse cheek and the soothing way he strokes me afterwards sends me into an almost catatonic state. My mouth pops open, my eyes roll into the back of my head, my knees turn to jelly, and my body quakes. If I was dripping for him before from the orgasm he drew out of me with his fingers, then I'm soaking for him now.

"Hmm, I can smell your arousal from here," he says before reaching between my legs and swiping his fingers through my folds. "Just as I thought. Do you get enjoyment from me spanking you?" he asks, looking intently at me.

"I don't know. Yes, maybe..." I say, trying to figure that out. "It hurts, but then... it feels good, especially when you stroke me afterwards," I stutter out, still trying, and failing, to focus on anything more than holding myself upright. It's just as well he has his arm tightly cinched around my waist.

"I like to see your skin pinken from my hand," he admits. "I like discovering what turns you on."

"I think I like that too."

"Fuck, Daisy, where have you been all my life?" he asks.

"I've been right here, Dalton," I reply softly.

"You have, haven't you?" he whispers, pressing his body against mine, still keeping me upright. "We'll bench this discussion for later, but right now I'm going to fuck you. Hands on the mirror , widen your stance."

This time I do as I'm told, and as our gazes lock, he lines up the head of his dick with my entrance and slowly pushes himself inside me until I'm lifting up onto my tiptoes, trying to adjust to our height difference. My eyelids stutter shut as I feel him twitch inside of me, slotting into place, as though he is a puzzle piece I didn't realise I was missing.

"Fuck, Daisy, the way you fist my cock. I don't think I'll ever get enough."

He groans as he seats himself fully, filling me with his length, and it feels... *He* feels so right. My heart soars, and try as I might I can't contain the rush of emotions. I try to push them aside, pressing back against him so that I'm distracted by how his cock swells inside of me, and not how it feels to be in his arms. Like it's the only place I'll ever find true happiness.

"You're everything," he whispers, his hips slowly rolling against me as he begins to set a steady rhythm.

"Everything?" I murmur back, my breath catching.

"You fit me perfectly, Daisy."

I moan, feeling the pleasure building inside of me once again, the heat between us growing more intense. "Fuck me harder," I beg, pushing my hips back to meet his thrusts, as my cheek presses against the mirrored wall.

He obliges, his arm tightening around my waist as he curls over me, grinding into me deeper. "That's it, Daisy," Dalton praises, his voice rough, bathed in lust. "Take my cock, take every last inch. Let me hear you scream my name as you come for me."

"I'm already so close," I cry out, shocked at how easily he seems to draw out my orgasms, at how my body responds to him.

He glides his cock steadily into me, his cock hitting that sweet spot deep inside, over and over, and I can feel myself nearing the edge, the intensity of my impending orgasm building with every thrust.

"Then come!" he orders, slamming into me.

That's all it takes, and I shatter, my mind blanking out for a moment as white-hot pleasure courses through me, and my internal muscles ripple around his dick, milking his cock.

"Fuck, Daisy. Fuck! You're so tight," he shouts, his thrusts becoming erratic as he fights against his own release. His breathing is ragged, his face contorted as he curses under his breath.

"Come for me, Dalton!" I reply, loving how that command sounds, how powerful it makes me feel to demand *his* release just like he's demanded mine from me.

"Fuuuucccckkkk!" he groans, his body tensing as he surges forward, pressing me harder against the mirrored wall. I can feel him unloading inside of me, his cock pulsating as his sperm coats my insides in long, hot spurts.

Our hot breaths steam up the mirror until, eventually, Dalton presses a chaste kiss against my cheek, and withdraws out of me, tucking himself away with shaky hands.

"God-fucking-dammit, that was intense," he mutters, staring at the ground, unable to meet my eyes as I turn around to face him.

"I'm not sure he's listening. Pretty sure you're on his shit list."

"Shit list?" he questions, a look of utter bewilderment on his face.

"For sinning," I joke, pressing my lips together as I try not to laugh.

"What the hell are you doing to me, Daisy?" he asks, shaking his head. I can't interpret the look on his face, and my smile fades. It's though he's caught somewhere between regret and bliss, confusion and longing.

I can relate to that, because I feel the exact same way. What exactly is happening here?

When we fuck, I'm there with him in the moment, enjoying every second, and yet afterwards there's this weird, uncertain energy between us. It was the same the other night.

"I could ask the same of you," I reply, my voice barely above a whisper as I ease my bra and top down, before adjusting my underwear and skirt. The woollen material of my skirt feels rough over my sensitive skin, our combined release soaking my knickers.

"Daisy?" he questions, stepping towards me and cupping my cheek, as a deep groove forms between his brows as he frowns.

"What?"

"This is just sex, right, just like we agreed?"

I pause for a moment, trying to dive deep into myself and search for the truth, my feelings as tumultuous as this moment between us appears to be. "It's just sex," I finally agree, plastering on a smile.

The relief in his eyes hurts more than it should, given our agreement, yet the way his fingers trace the curve of my jaw almost reverently makes me question everything, the deceiving tenderness igniting a fiery ache in my chest that's impossible to ignore.

"A man could get used to this," he murmurs, brushing the pad of his thumb over my lips.

"Get used to what, fucking in a hall of mirrors?" I ask, laughing softly, trying for a lighthearted response.

Dalton chuckles, but the sound is strained. "Yeah."

"Well it's just as well, because we're going to be married soon," I reply, my heart aching with each word, because despite all the laughter today, the incredible sex, he can't ever love me.

"Yes we are," he agrees, and I have to remind myself that we're just two friends fucking, two people who are contracted to marry each other, and will eventually have a child together.

We're not in love, but when he drops his mouth to my lips and kisses me with tenderness, my resolve to keep him firmly in the 'friends who fuck' category starts to crumble.

CHAPTER TWENTY-TWO

"A word, son," my father calls from his home office as I stride past his door a few days later.

"What now?" I mutter as my footsteps still, resenting how much of my time he's taken up these past few days with business matters, when all I've wanted to do is to spend it with Daisy.

I consider pretending I didn't hear him. I've been walking on cloud fucking nine since my date with Daisy and, despite his attempts, so far he hasn't managed to ruin my good mood. But I know ignoring my father will only piss him off more, so I turn on my heel and head into his office.

"Yes?"

"Shut the door behind you. Take a seat," he commands, looking up from his computer screen as he points to the chair opposite him.

"What is it? I have a busy day," I counter.

"With work?" he questions, seeing right through me, because I have every intention of spending the rest of the day with Daisy.

"Actually, no. I was going to take Daisy out before everything gets too chaotic before our wedding on Saturday," I retort, meeting his gaze challengingly.

"What, on another trip to the amusement arcade?" he asks, lifting an unimpressed brow. "And before you ask, I have eyes everywhere."

"So you were spying on us?"

"That's hardly a befitting way for the heir of this family to be spending their time, don't you think?" he retorts, ignoring my question. "You're not a damn child!"

"We were having fun, a concept you clearly struggle with," I counter.

Fun is a concept he's *never* understood. His idea of fun is corporate takeovers, firing people and turning the businesses they once put their blood, sweat and tears into into something lucrative yet unrecognisable.

"Fun?" he laughs. "Are you forgetting the purpose of this marriage?"

"I've not forgotten," I reply tightly.

"It seems to me like you're enjoying this arrangement a little bit too much," he questions.

I lean back in my chair, holding my father's gaze as I weigh my words carefully. "What harm is there in finding friendship in a situation that was forced upon us both? It works in your favour if Daisy and I have found a way to make this work."

My father's eyes narrow, his lips forming into a thin line of disapproval. "This is not about friendship. Your personal feelings are irrelevant. Your behaviour and how you both represent this family, however, matters immensely. Stop fucking about, and *focus*."

"Spending time with my fiancé is not fucking about," I reply through gritted teeth.

My father leans forward, disapproval etched deep into his features. "Need I remind you that this whole arrangement is about securing the future of our family, about maintaining our legacy *and* standing in society. It is your duty as my son and heir to uphold it with respect and responsibility. Your actions reflect not only on you but, more importantly, *me*, and I'll be fucked if you think you can continue to act with such blatant disregard to my—"

"Your what? *Feelings?* Would you prefer it if I act like you? Cold, calculating, ruthless? Is that the legacy you want me to uphold?" I challenge him, my voice holding a mix of defiance and frustration.

My father's eyes flash with anger, his composure cracking just slightly before he regains control. "Firstly, do not mistake pragmatism for lack of feeling, boy. Everything I do is for the good of this family," he responds icily. "And secondly, you think you're none of those things too? I've watched you fuck over and discard women time and again. You might be doing a good job at pretending with Daisy, but I see you."

I flinch at that. Maybe once I had been that man, and that stings, but now? I don't want to be that person anymore.

"Family? We've *never* been a family," I cut back, unable to contain myself. "We are no more than business partners that share the same blood."

He barks out a laugh. "If we're going to be truthful, *son*, a business partner would imply equal standing, and we can both agree that isn't the case."

Despite being a grown fucking man, I can't deny that my father's words cut me deeply, and are a stark reminder of the power dynamics between us. His expectations, and continued lack of care and any form of affection stifles any sense of individuality or happiness that has dared to bloom these past few weeks in Daisy's presence. Everything that I'd begun to feel starts to wilt inside my chest, and I fucking hate him for it.

"I don't have to listen to this shit!" I snap, moving to stand, needing to get the fuck out of his office and as far away from him as possible, before he turns everything inside of me into nothing but dust.

"Sit the fuck down," he retorts, struggling to contain his anger as he leans back in his chair, the leather creaking beneath him. "You've always had a sharp tongue, but watch what you say to me. Do not forget who you're speaking to."

"I've learnt from the best, and I know exactly who I'm speaking to. You're someone so consumed by power and control that you've forgotten what it means to truly care for another human being."

"Being this way has gotten me to where I am today. I'm not ashamed of that fact, and you will do well to remember that this lifestyle you live, this mansion you've been brought up in, the doors that have opened so easily for you, is because of *my* unwavering desire to secure your future and that of the Gunn family name. Without it, you have nothing. I could cut you off as easily as that," he retorts, snapping his fingers. "So don't ever think you can disregard my wishes without facing the consequences of your actions."

"And without me and Daisy you don't have a family or the possibility of continuing the Gunn family name. Perhaps *you* would do well to remember that," I reply just as sharply.

My father's jaw tightens at my words, his face contorting with a mix of rage and disbelief, his knuckles turning white as he clenches his fists on the desk. Tension crackles in the air between us as we stare each other down. I hold his gaze steadily, refusing to back down even in the face of his intimidating presence.

"Your point is noted," he concedes after a moment, despite his tone still holding a dangerous edge. "Have your fun with Daisy, but don't forget what's at stake here. You're not the only one who's future will be ruined if you fail to fulfil my wishes. Drix's debt is only paid in full if Daisy has your child, or have you forgotten that part?" he adds with a cruel smile.

My blood runs cold at the reminder of Drix's precarious position and my father's insidious hold over *all* of our lives.

"Well?" he insists, arching a brow.

"I'm well aware of what's at stake," I respond through gritted teeth.

"Good," he replies, the tension leaving his body as he realises he's won this argument. "Now do what you need to do to ensure that everything is proceeding according to plan, but don't let sentimentality cloud your judgement. Treat this as a business deal, nothing more, understand?"

I nod my head, dropping my gaze as defeat creeps up my spine. He's got us all over a fucking barrel and he knows it.

"Oh, and one last thing. I've arranged for the press to attend the wedding reception party."

"You've done *what*?" I ask, snapping my head up.

"You and Daisy will pose for pictures as a happily married couple, which shouldn't be too hard given how you've enjoyed spending so much time together, no?"

With that, he dismisses me with a wave of his hand, and as I step out of his office my head spins with anger and resentment towards my father. In just a few minutes he's managed to strip away any semblance of happiness I've begun to feel, and has reminded me of my own shortcomings. I was a fucking fool to believe that I could ever get the upper hand, and the weight of that knowledge is a heavy burden to carry.

"DALTON, WHAT IS IT?" Daisy asks, as she falls into step beside me, our feet crunching over the frostbitten leaves that litter the path leading towards the old ruins a few miles outside of town. It's a place I've often frequented when I've needed to get away from my father, and today I wanted to share a quiet moment with

Daisy without prying eyes watching our every move to report back to my father.

"It's nothing," I lie, forcing a smile on my face as we step beneath the vine-covered archway into the ruins.

"You can talk to me, you know," she says, gently pressing her fingers against my arm.

"There really isn't much to say. It's just... business," I add, wincing at my choice of words given what my father had said to me earlier about our arranged marriage being nothing more than a business deal. Maybe in the beginning it had been, but now? Now, standing in the shadows of these ancient walls with Daisy's concerned eyes searching mine, I feel a surge of guilt for ever thinking of our relationship as nothing more than a transaction. She deserves better than that.

"You know I never even knew this place existed," Daisy says, sensing that I'm not willing to talk any further on the subject. "It's beautiful, if not a little creepy."

"It's been my secret sanctuary for as long as I can remember," I confess. "Not even Drix knows I come here when I need a moment to think."

"I guess there's a lot to think about with our wedding only a few days away," she murmurs, stepping over some rocks, her breath visible in the chilly air.

"You know legend has it that this place once belonged to a powerful witch who was said to have the ability to see into the future."

Daisy turns to face me, her lips quirking up into a smile. "Something I'm sure you'd love to make use of right now, huh?"

"I'm not sure that knowing what's coming would be a good thing. I'd rather be blissfully unaware," I reply honestly.

"Really? That surprises me," she says, cocking her head to the side as I approach her.

"Surprises you? How so?" I ask as cool air swirls around us, picking up some scattered leaves and tossing them in the air.

"Well, for someone who needs to be in control, I would've thought you'd want to know every detail of what's to come," she explains, a teasing glint in her eyes. "Personally, I believe a little mystery is good for the soul."

"Is that so? What mysteries are you hiding from me, Daisy Hammer?" I ask, brushing an unruly curl off her face as we stand within the crumbling stone walls.

"None in particular. There isn't much more to me than you know already," she replies, shrugging her shoulders.

"Perhaps there are depths to you that even you're not entirely aware of," I reply, referring to the fact that she appeared to enjoy being spanked in the House of Mirrors. It surprised me greatly, and turned me on.

"Go on," she murmurs, her cheeks colouring a little as she looks up at me. "What is it that you think I'm unaware of?"

I lean down, capturing her lips in a soft kiss before whispering against them. "The depths of your own desires, Daisy. The ones you keep hidden, even from yourself."

"Is that why you brought me here today, so you could have your wicked way with me?"

I smirk at her playful challenge. "Do you want me to have my wicked way with you?" I ask, my hand trailing down her back as I draw her closer, the air around us eddying with anticipation.

"Perhaps," she replies, a mischievous glint in her eye as I brush my lips against hers, unable to stop myself.

Without a word, I take her hand and lead her further into the centre of the ruin where shadows twirl and contort around aged stones, whispering secrets only the ghosts of the long dead inhabitants can hear. As we step into a covered archway, I pull Daisy close, the late afternoon light filtering through the cracks in the stone wall.

"Do you feel that?" she asks, her hand tightening around mine as she shudders. "It's as though we're being watched. Maybe that witch you spoke of haunts these ruins."

"I dare say she does," I reply, "But I'm not afraid of ghosts, Daisy."

"What are you afraid of?"

"Nothing," I reply, stiffening a little at the way she searches me with her gaze.

"Everyone is afraid of something," she insists.

"Not me."

"Liar. Tell me."

"I think you know the answer to that already," I whisper, pressing her back against the stone wall and crowding her body with mine.

"I'm not sure that I do," she murmurs, tipping her head back as she looks up at me.

I grind my hips against hers, my cock thickening with lust as I try to blot out the truth hovering between us.

"Do I need to spell it out to you?"

"You're afraid of love?" she whispers.

"Yeah, that," I admit.

"No one should be afraid of love, Dalton," she replies, reaching up, her fingers delicately brushing against my jaw.

"And yet here I am, admitting that to you. Love is a concept that terrifies me, Daisy."

"Why?"

"Because when you love, you open yourself up to pain, disappointment and heartache. It makes you vulnerable, weak. I don't ever want to be in that position. Nothing good can come of it."

"That's true, loving someone can make you vulnerable, but I disagree about it making you weak. Love gives you strength. Strength to battle your demons, strength to *live*. There are so many wonderful things about being loved, about loving someone, Dalton," she says gently.

"Like what?" I ask, leaning into her hold, unable to help myself as she cups my cheek, drawn to the warmth and care emanating from her. It's so effortless for Daisy, and I'm envious of that.

"Happiness. Joy. Loyalty. A sense of belonging," she answers with a gentle smile, her thumb caressing my cheek softly. "And passion... intense, unbridled passion," she continues. "The kind that makes your heart race, and your body ache for the other person."

"I can feel that without needing to be in love," I counter.

"Can you though, *truly?*" she questions.

"Yes," I argue.

"Fucking someone can feel passionate, I agree, but when you really boil it down that's just the bodies response to a rush of plea-sure hormones."

"That's what passion is, isn't it? A rush of hormones."

"I disagree. Real passion isn't just a physical reaction, it's an emotional one too. It's so much more fulfilling when there are feel-ings involved."

"I wouldn't know," I mutter.

"That makes me feel sad for you, Dalton," she replies, and my fucking throat constricts.

The encounter with my father earlier has left me raw, in need of someone to talk to, but words lead to truth, and truth uncovers feelings, and... Well, we've already established that I'm not any good at those.

"Don't feel sad for me, Daisy. I don't deserve your sympathy," I retort, shoring myself up as I press my lips against hers in a hard kiss, wanting to dominate this moment with sensation not feelings.

For the briefest of moments, she responds, parting her lips, allowing me to sweep my tongue into her open mouth. My fingers wrap around her throat as I hold the beat of her pulse in the palm of my hand. She tastes of sweetness and light, and everything someone like me can destroy. But before I can take things further she twists her head to the side, her hands pushing against my chest gently.

"It's not sympathy, Dalton," she whispers, a frown deepening between her eyebrows. "It's empathy. I can see that you're guarded, and I can understand why you might be afraid of love, but do you know what else I see?"

"What?" I find myself asking, aching to kiss her again, yet needing to hear what she has to say.

"I see the potential for something beautiful in you, *for* you, even if you can't."

My breath catches, my fucking heart squeezes painfully. How? How can she see something that simply isn't there? I'm not someone deserving of anything beautiful, least of all her.

"And yet all I can think of right now is taking you against this wall and fucking you. I don't feel anything other than the desire to sink my cock inside of you, to feel your pussy clench me tight, and to come so hard that I'm lost to the physical sensation. Love has nothing to do with it," I say, refusing to listen to that nagging voice deep inside that is quietly calling me a fucking liar.

"I see," she whispers, her hand falling away, disappointment flickering in her gaze.

"Daisy, I told you about my failings, and you accepted them," I say, scrambling to regain control of the situation.

She nods. "You're right. I did…"

"But?" I ask, crowding her in as she tries to step out of my hold.

"There's nothing more I want to say. Perhaps we should go?"

"I don't want to go. I want to fuck you."

"And what if I don't want to have sex? What then, Dalton? Are you that heartless that you could take something from me that I'm not willing to give right now?"

"Of course not!" I exclaim.

"Then let me go."

"You're angry," I accuse.

"A little, yes."

"Because I told you the truth?"

"No, because your inability to look inside of yourself is only hurting you. Don't you see that? At the very least you should love *yourself*."

"You've already told me on many occasions that I do that already," I counter darkly.

"And I'm sorry for that, truly. That was cruel. But that's not what I'm talking about. I mean accepting yourself, embracing your flaws, making peace with them. Perhaps once you do, you'll be open enough to let love in, to love someone else."

"I know who I am, Daisy, and I know who I'm not. More importantly, I know my limitations," I reply tightly.

"And that's the issue right there," she sighs, her eyes pleading with me to see the truth. "You're so focused on your perceived limitations, that you're missing out on the person you *could* be. You have so much wasted potential."

"I already have everything I need, Daisy. There is no wasted potential."

"On the surface, yes. You live in a beautiful home, you have a wonderful lifestyle, and all the material things. But what about your happiness? What about that?"

"I *am* happy," I say a little too forcefully.

"No, all I see is a man holding himself back out of fear, and for what exactly? To live the rest of your days in a mansion filled with things, to surround yourself with piles of money? That's a very lonely life, Dalton. At the end of the day, when all is said and done, nothing is more important than love. It's the only thing worth living for."

With that, she ducks out of my arms and strides away, once again leaving me fucking reeling.

CHAPTER TWENTY-THREE

I'm here again, in this nightmare, my adult self watching the memory as it unravels before me. Both a part of it, and separate. Before me a tiny child who's never known love, doesn't yet know the healing warmth of being loved, is curled up in a tight ball, her tiny hands pressed over her ears as she tries desperately to drown out the hateful words cascading over her.

I feel every one of them. I remember the pain they caused, they still cause, and I wish... Oh, how I wish I could tell her that it won't be much longer, that very soon she'll be free.

I wish I could wrap myself around her, protect her from the abuse, but I can't. All I can do is watch, a silent witness to my past, forever a part of it, always haunted by it.

Never, ever, free from it.

There on the dirty mattress, my younger self presses tiny hands against her ears as she tries to drown out our father's voice, but they're useless against the onslaught as he spits fire at her, burning her body with spite, and incinerating her innocence one hateful word at a time.

"Useless little wretch... Snivelling little shit... Worthless bag of bones..."

He knows.

He knows that the words he uses hurt her the most. That somehow her tiny little body can switch off and go someplace far, far away when his meaty hands crush her skinny little limbs and his knuckles bruise her fragile body. So he uses his words like a blade, slicing through her body, cutting her up until she's nothing more than a pulpy, hollow mess.

Broken, trembling, she wraps herself up into the tiniest of balls hoping he'll leave her alone, that he'll tire of being evil, and he'll just leave her to rot in this disgusting room. She hopes for release, and an end to this cycle of horrible, incomparable abuse, not knowing that it's death she's wishing for.

This time, however, he's at his worst. A cruel creature wanting nothing more than to inflict pain with hateful words that shatter her very soul. Those times... they're the worst.

"You're not wanted," he sneers, looming over her, a monster made of fire and brimstone, daggers and blades, lancing at her skin, sinking his hate into the very innermost parts of her, of me. Her fragile innocence is no match against his brutality. "No one will ever want you. No one could ever love you. Your mother should've had you aborted. Instead we're stuck with you. I can't bear to look at you. You dirty little bitch. You should be dead."

"Please stop, please stop, please stop," she chants, crying, her eyes sore from the acidic tears, from the lack of sleep, from the years of relentless abuse. I hear her say those words, my own voice hoarse and cracked as I say them too...

"Please stop, please stop. PLEASE STOP!"

The scream that rips out of my throat, yanks me out of my nightmare. Thrashing at the covers, I fight against the ghost of the memory, and the very real horrors that haunt me still.

"Daisy?!"

The door to my bedroom slams open as my chest heaves and I sob uncontrollably now. Tears stream down my face, giving me little relief from the harrowing, debilitating grief that pulls me to shreds and scatters me into tiny sharp-edged pieces.

Broken. I'm broken.

"Daisy? Jesus, are you okay?" Dalton asks, rushing to my side, hauling me into his arms as I beat my fists against him, caught between wakefulness and nightmares. My father's claws are still buried inside my chest, squeezing the life from my heart, making me question what's real and what isn't.

"Please no, please no, please no," I cry, sobbing uncontrollable as Dalton grasps me to his chest, holding me as I tremble. I'm nothing more than metres and metres of brightly coloured thread, unspooling and unravelling into a messy, tangled heap, colour leaching from the strands.

"Daisy, you're okay. You're okay. I've got you. It's just a nightmare," he says, doing his best to soothe me.

It's just a nightmare.

Only it isn't. It's a memory. It was real. I lived it, breathed it... I survived it.

I survived. I hold onto that.

"I'm here. I'm here. It's just me. It's just me," Dalton repeats, his voice harrowed, hoarse, affected by my pain as I curl into his body and hold on tight. My limbs wrap around his body as I press myself against his chest, anchoring myself to him. Needing him, a man who can never soothe me, not really, not truly, not deep down. He can't mend my shattered heart. He can't fix what's broken. He can't ever *love* me.

"I'm going to be sick," I cry, sobbing, shaking, feeling my stomach churn and twist violently.

Pushing out of his arms, I scramble off the bed and run towards the bathroom, hot scalding tears blinding me as I lift up the toilet seat and retch. My body tries to rid itself of the gut-churning, acidic memories, but my stomach is empty and nothing comes up as I choke and heave.

"Daisy, fuck," Dalton stutters out, dropping to his knees behind me as he pulls back my hair with one hand and rubs my back with the other.

I retch and retch, trying to purge the memories and those hateful words, imagining them releasing from my throat and into the basin, wishing I could see the physical expulsion empty into the bowl instead of air and bitter sobs. When I'm spent, I collapse onto my arse, breathing heavily, inhaling oxygen as I try to regain control.

"I've got you," Dalton repeats, wrapping his arms around me, holding me close as I curl into him. Seeking comfort. Desperate for it.

"I'm sorry. I'm sorry. I'm sorry," I cry, curling my fingers into his t-shirt, my tears soaking into the material, wanting things from him that he cannot give me. Yet, here I am trying to steal them anyway, sapping him of his strength so I can try to gather my own.

"Don't be sorry, Daisy," he croons, stroking my hair, rocking me in his arms. They feel protective, I feel safe in them, and that only makes me cry harder.

I cry and cry for what seems like hours, but lasts only minutes, until eventually the tears dry up and I'm a hollowed out mess.

"I–" I begin, but the words won't come. There are no more tears, there's just an empty, shattered shell, tattered and bleeding from the wounds my parents inflicted on me all those years ago.

"What can I do? What should I do?" he asks, pressing a kiss against my temple, cupping my face as he stares at me, eyes wide, afraid, concerned.

"I–I need to w—wash it away," I hiccup, blinking up at him, my teeth chattering, my bones rattling as my body tries and fails to find strength from somewhere, anywhere.

He nods, pushing upright, helping me to stand on shivering,

shaky legs. He leads me to the edge of the bath, pushing me gently downwards to sit on the lip.

"Let me run a bath. Just sit there, okay?"

"Okay," I whisper, my hands falling to my lap as I teeter on the edge, not just of this bath, but my grip on reality, my father's voice still whispering cruel words in my mind.

Beside me, he turns on the taps, unaware of how close I am to free falling into a terribly dark place. He plugs the hole, before dropping to his knees before me. His hands are warm as he cups my bare knees, looking up at me.

"Just concentrate on me, okay? Just breathe. I'm here."

Our gazes clash as I nod, doing as he asks. He breathes with me, dragging in deep breaths through flared nostrils, blowing air back out of parted lips. We do that for long minutes, our breaths mingling as the bath fills and steam curls up into the air, eddying between us, covering our skin in a sheen of dampness. It's as though my whole body is weeping, oozing with past hurts. Every second that passes is another second where I try to mentally lock up the nightmare, but it lingers like a nasty stain, darkening everything with bitterness.

"What time is it?" I eventually ask, noticing the shadows beneath his eyes, his mussed up hair. Needing to hold onto his image, needing to remain in the present, forcing myself not to spiral further.

"Early hours of the morning. Just after two am, I think."

"I woke you up. I'm sorry," I mumble.

"Don't be. I'm not," he replies, reaching up to gently rub my arm, his eyes flicking to the bath. "It's almost full. Do you want me to leave?"

"No!" I reply on a panicked breath. "Please, don't leave me. I'm not ready to face the rest of the night alone. I can't. *I can't.*"

"Then I'll stay. I'll do anything you need, Daisy," he reassures me as I reach for the buttons of my pyjama top. My hands are shaking so much that I can't seem to undo them. Dalton covers my hands with his. "Let me."

Caught in the warmth of his concern, my hands fall away as he slowly unbuttons my top. Cool air pools over my bare skin as the material parts, revealing not just my naked skin, but the heart of me, the damaged, broken core.

I wonder if he sees it, what he thinks of me now?

"Stand, Daisy," he gently commands, taking my hands as I lift up onto my feet robotically.

Silently, he slides the material off my shoulders, his warm hands coasting over my skin as the material falls to my feet. He drops his gaze to my sleep shorts, and I just nod, giving him permission to remove them. Unable to do much more than that.

Dalton drags in another deep breath, his fingers brushing my hips as he starts to slide the fabric down my legs. My heart hiccups at his tenderness, and I sway on my feet as I step out of them. For the briefest of moments, he captures me in his arms, holding me close as I bury my face in his chest, breathing in the heady scent of him, my stupid, foolish heart desperate to find solace there.

"Let me help you into the bath," he offers, taking my hand as I gingerly step over the lip, sinking below the surface as he turns off the taps. Despite the heat of the water I shiver, unable, *incapable* of getting warm.

"Get in with me?" I ask, but it's more of a plea than a question.

Dalton nods, stripping off his clothes, revealing his lean, tattooed body before climbing into the bath, facing me.

"I'm sorry," I repeat, hating the pity I see in his gaze as I draw up my knees and wrap my arms around them.

"Stop saying that. Stop it, Daisy."

"I can't... I... Oh, Dalton..." I whimper, and his hands press against my crossed arms, gently prying them apart.

"Come here," he whispers, pressing his hands beneath my

armpits, hauling my body against his as water spills over the ledge and onto the floor.

My legs slide over his thighs, my chest pressed against his chest as I fall into his embrace. His hands glide over my back, gentle fingers gingerly tracing my skin as he rocks us both.

"Close your eyes, Daisy," he whispers. "Turn off your mind, just concentrate on my touch."

I try to do as he asks, but every time I close my eyes all I can see is that monster who hurt me so thoroughly. The memory isn't tightly locked away. It hovers still, waiting for the opportunity to drag me back under.

Snivelling little shit...

My father's voice is loud in my head, and more wracking sobs bubble up my throat, spilling out of my mouth, staining him with tears.

"I can't. I can't. I can't," I cry.

"Then look at me, Daisy. Look at me," he commands, his hand coming up to the back of my head, his fingers curling into my hair, tugging hard.

My scalp tingles with sharp pain, blotting out my father's voice for one blissful moment. I hiss out a breath, focusing on the man before me, revelling in the pain.

"Dalton..." I whimper. "Make it go away."

"But–" His fingers loosen in my hair, and the darkness creeps back over me.

Worthless bag of bones...

"Please, Dalton. Make it go away."

"How?"

"The pain..." I mutter.

"What?" His voice catches, body stiffening beneath me.

"*Hurt* me," I whisper, the words tripping from my tongue.

"Hurt you? I don't want to hurt you, Daisy," he replies, shaking his head.

Useless little wretch...

I reach up, placing my hand over his, curling my fingers around his hand, forcing him to tug once more. The sharpness erases my father's voice, every thought, every feeling of despair. I cling onto that, needing escape. I can't unravel why the pain causes my mind to blank out, but it does, and right now I crave oblivion most of all.

"It helps to blot it out, the pain I mean..."

"Pain helps you to blot out the memories?" he questions, confused by my request.

"Yes," I reply, voice quivering.

"But your parents hurt you too. I don't want to do that."

"You spanked me in the Hall of Mirrors, I liked it... I don't know why, but... I...I *liked* it," I admit, clinging onto that feeling, that almost catatonic state I went to.

"I'm not sure this is a good idea, Daisy. You're so vulnerable right now."

"I need this. *Please.*"

"Fuck," he mutters, his gaze piercing mine. "I know that there can be pleasure in pain, *release*. I know this, but..."

"Don't deny me. Please, Dalton. Don't deny me this."

"This isn't something we should be experimenting with right now, Daisy. You've just woken up from a terrible nightmare. This isn't how this is supposed to happen. There's too much at stake. You're not emotionally fit enough for this right now. I could make this worse, not better. No," he shakes his head, "I can't."

"Dalton, he's still in my head. I can hear his voice," I say, pressing my palms against my temples, trying and failing to drown out the sound. "When you tugged on my hair, his voice disappeared. For the briefest of moments, I didn't hear him anymore."

"Jesus, Daisy. I'm not sure I'm equipped for this..."

"I trust you not to take it too far. I trust *you*," I say, meaning it.

For long moments he just stares at me, battling with himself, but as he reflexively tugs on my hair more, that simple act has my mouth dropping open in bliss. I let out a soft mewl, everything going blank.

"Please," I whisper.

"Fuck," he mutters.

"*Please.*"

"Okay," he relents, releasing me from his hold before placing his hands on my hips and urging me to rise. "Lean your body over my shoulder, Daisy. Grab the back of the bath to steady yourself. I'm going to spank you five times, but that's it, that's all I'm prepared to do. Don't ask any more of me."

"I won't," I agree, rising out of the water and draping myself over his shoulder as he wraps one arm around the back of my thighs.

Grasping the edge of the bath, I bite down on my bottom lip, my father's voice getting louder and louder inside my head with every passing second.

"I'm going to count them down, okay. Ready?"

"Yes..."

"One!" he says almost immediately, and then his palm lands across my arse, slapping me so hard that for a moment all I'm aware of is white-hot heat. It's painful, blissfully so, and I cry out, my fingers curling around the bath. The sharp sting fades as quickly as it came, and behind it follows a soothing blankness that envelops me right before he spanks me again.

"Two!"

Another sharp slap. More pain. More bliss.

"Three!"

Tears burst from my eyes, my body stiffening then relaxing as the sting spreads out, reaching every crevice, filling up the cracks with a sense of relief as my father's voice fades into the distance.

"Four!" he grinds out, his arm tightening across my thighs, as my body turns liquid.

My cries become mewls of pleasure, the pain transforming into a peaceful kind of euphoria, a dizzying, buffeting lust, that I willingly fall headfirst into.

"Five!" he finishes, and the second his palm meets my sore arse, he reaches upwards, dragging me back down onto his lap. The warm water hits my stinging skin and I hiss from the pain as I fall into him, my body limp, my mind empty as I drag in deep lungfuls of air, quivering against him.

"Daisy?" Dalton questions, his voice gravelly, thick, as he gently nudges me upright, cupping my face as my eyes try to focus. "Are you okay?"

"Yes," I whisper.

I'm more than okay, I feel... free.

I feel... turned on.

My pussy contracts, my clit throbbing as the stinging fades, one intense feeling merging with another as pain gives way to pleasure.

"Kiss me," I demand, my fingers gliding up his chest, my pussy pressing against the thick ridge of his cock.

With his gaze never leaving mine, Dalton nods once, his eyes glittering with fire, with empathy, with something else I can't quite decipher, as he presses his lips to mine and kisses the air from my lungs, and any lingering memories from my mind.

This kiss is fervent, desperate, heightened in a way I haven't experienced before, and I sink into it, caught up in this incredible connection forming between us. I trusted him enough not to hurt me, and he cared for me enough to give me what I craved.

Clinging onto him, my fingers glide up and over his shoulders, tangling in his hair as I pull him closer, hold him tighter. Between us his cock thickens, and he groans, jerking his hips against my pussy that I shamelessly rub against him. Heat gathers, building, growing, expanding as my body weeps for him, and my heart aches to be loved.

"Daisy," he warns, his voice rough, like boulders falling over a cliff.

"Don't stop. Please, don't stop," I beg, reaching between us, my fingers wrapping around his length, stroking him.

His mouth drops open, his eyes rolling in the back of his head as I fist him, needing him to want me as much as I want him.

"This is..." he gasps.

"Exactly what we both need," I whisper, lifting up as I hover over his dick.

"You're hurting," he replies, his cheeks flushed and his pupils dilated as he gazes up at me. I can see him questioning the morality of our actions, but it's too late for that now. We've already crossed that line, and all I need at this moment is him.

"Not any more," I say. "I need you to fuck me. *Please*, Dalton."

CHAPTER TWENTY-FOUR

"Not any more," Daisy whispers, her red-rimmed eyes locking with mine. "I need you to fuck me. *Please*, Dalton."

I can't deny her.

God-fucking-help-me, I can't deny her this anymore than I could the pain she begged I inflict on her not moments before, not when she looks at me the way she is doing now, as though, somehow, I'm worthy enough of fixing her, of healing her pain.

When I'd heard her screams, I'd been lying awake unable to fucking sleep after our conversation at the ruins earlier. She'd told me that she sees something in me, something that I don't, that others never have. For the first time in my fucking life I felt hope, hope that I can be a better man and not end up like my father. Ruthless, callous, heartless.

I don't want to be like him, alone with nothing but his riches to measure his worth. It's a sad life, fucking lonely, I see that now. I understand what she was trying to tell me.

"Dalton," she whimpers, her nails digging into the flesh of my shoulders. "Please."

Rightly or wrongly, her brokenness has given me a twisted

sense of comfort, and that maybe, somehow, I can find peace in it, and more importantly, that she can find peace in me. So I don't deny her, I simply nod, and as she lowers herself onto my dick, inch by torturous inch, my eyes stutter shut at how her body fists mine, at the blissful awareness she draws out of me.

Everything feels heightened, my senses, my... feelings.

Feelings.

Christ, she drags them all to the surface with her whimpers of pleasure, with her tears of pain, with her faith in me as a man. I don't know when her opinion of me shifted from one of hate and annoyance to affection and acceptance. Was it that night she revealed her past and I refused to fuck her? Was it when she clung onto me tightly around the racetrack, putting her trust in me to keep her safe? Was it before either of those times when I brought her a dress and supported her right to wear colour because I understood how much it meant to her? When I stood up for her in the garden of this very mansion? Was it at the arcade when we'd laughed so much our bellies hurt? Was it when we fucked that first time, overcome with need for each other? Or was it a culmination of all those moments?

I guess it doesn't matter now.

What matters is that she isn't hurting any more. What matters is that the happiness and joy my father tried so hard to extinguish is still alive inside my chest. It's *still* there.

And it's because of her. Daisy.

The girl I once loved to hate has become the very reason I want to feel joy, happiness, acceptance... Maybe, eventually, love. Is that really possible for me? It's a question I've asked myself over and over again. I still don't know the answer.

Right here and now, confined by the walls of the bath, all I can do is hold her in my arms as she rocks against me, the soft mewling sounds releasing from her parted lips making my cock thicken and grow within her. The way she grinds against me, using my body as a talisman to ward off her demons, only makes me more protective of her. She can fuck me like this forever if she wants, and I would welcome it.

My hands find their way to her breasts, cupping them, and beneath my palms I feel the steady thrum of her heart thrashing against her rib cage, a reminder that it still has the capacity to beat despite her trauma, and the people who tried so hard to break it.

I'm in awe of her, swept up in her courage as she grinds against my cock, taking everything that I give her willingly. Mouth parted, her gaze never leaving mine, she rides me harder. Gripping my shoulders, she anchors herself to me, and my hands fall to her hips, supporting her, my pelvis rocking in time to her rhythm.

Minutes pass, and I'm in no hurry to come. This isn't the frantic, all-consuming fucking we've shared before, where we've both sought the welcome release of orgasm. This is different, it's more... and I'm not able to fully comprehend what's happening between us. I don't even want to. I need to just live in this moment, wrap myself up in it, let it consume me, guide me.

As we move in sync, the horror of her trauma has faded to bliss as her features soften, and this sense of belonging washes over me. She needs me, and God help me, I need her, need this, whatever this is.

She's my friend, my lover.

She's a woman unafraid to point out my flaws.

She's brave, and stubborn. Fierce and kind.

She's colourful and bright. Determined and focused.

And in just a few days time she'll be my wife.

My wife.

"Dalton," she murmurs, caressing my cheek, her lips lowering to mine in a kiss that begins to unravel everything I've built to protect myself.

My arrogance is torn to shreds by her vulnerability.

My selfishness is pulled apart by her courage.

My isolation is destroyed by her affection.

At this moment, I'm not just helping to heal her pain, she's helping to heal mine too. Just by existing, by being herself, she is shaping me into someone new, someone I could be proud of.

Sex has never been like this for me. Never.

I can *feel* everything, her heart beating wildly as she plasters herself to my chest, her breath catching in her throat as we kiss, the little gasps of pleasure that escape her lips and cascade over my skin in a soothing balm.

I'm lost, utterly fucking lost in her.

She takes and I give.

But this isn't one way, I fall into her as much as she falls into me.

Her wounds are mine, and we stitch them back together with every kiss, with every gentle thrust of my hips, and every downward stroke of her pussy.

Time seems to slow down as our joining fuses us together, soothing sharpened edges, grinding pain into dust. We've become one, and as I continue to hold her, to wrap my arms around her back and press kisses against her chest. I can't help but marvel at the strength she possesses. She's carried this burden of her past for so long. A smothering heaviness that has broken her heart but has also built resilience, a determination to not let it rule her life.

I'm in awe of her.

So completely and utterly in awe.

Our gazes meet once more as I arch my neck to look up at her, and in that moment I see the unfiltered truth of Daisy, of the woman I'm about to marry, and in turn I see the man I can become with her by my side.

"Look at you," I whisper.

She smiles down at me. It's just a gentle curve of her lips, a caress of joy that warms every single part of me. This moment, as

I'm nestled between her legs, my cock buried deep inside of her, feels so fucking *right*.

"I'm going to come," she murmurs, her breath quickening, her core gripping my cock so tightly that I'm drugged by the feel of her.

Pleasure ricochets up and down my spine, expanding outwards to every taut muscle, seeping into my bones, gathering in the tightness of my balls, loosening the breath from my lungs, smashing through the barriers around my heart.

"I feel it," I say, and I don't just mean the way she grips me so tightly, or how my body responds to hers.

I feel... *more*.

I feel the first fluttering of something bigger than me and my selfish needs, something worth exploring, something indescribable, something special.

As her hips buck against me, and her inner muscles clench and release, milking my cock, I feel my own orgasm taking hold, gathering and swirling deep inside. The sensation is exhilarating, intoxicating as she jerks against me, her mouth dropping open, whimpers releasing from parted, kiss-bruised lips. I reach between us, pressing the pad of my thumb against her thickened nub, adding more pleasure, wanting her to come undone. Needing to be the man who makes her fall apart, so I can put her back together again.

"Yes," she hisses, as I rub her clit and thrust up into her, matching her stroke for stroke.

"Fuck, Daisy," I groan, my own orgasm looming near as the world around us fades and collapses, until there's only us. Two bodies drowning in pleasure, two people connected by lust and desire, by friendship and affection, by pain and *hope*.

I'm almost there now, on the very edge, teetering on the precipice of my release. "Now, Daisy," I pant. "Come... Now... With me."

I thrust one last time as our gazes clash, and our hips collide. She jerks, clamping down on my dick with a cry, and I explode, my orgasm barrelling out of me like a bullet from a gun, obliterating every thought that enters my head and replacing it with a white-hot, lightning strike of bliss. Our bodies stiffen, slick with sweat, both of us are caught up in the moment as she falls into me, gasping, sucking in deep breaths as we hold onto each other, caught in our little bubble of peace and pleasure.

Which bursts the moment she pulls back.

"Dalton, I..." she begins, her lip trembling, her eyes wide and gleaming with tears that trickle down her cheeks.

Fuck.

My throat constricts, fear shuddering through my body. Have I done the wrong thing? Have I taken advantage of her vulnerability? Did I make this worse, not better? Oh, fuck, what have I done?

"What is it?" I ask, as she lifts off of me, her gaze flicking away as I run a shaky hand through my hair.

"It's nothing. I'm fine," she whispers, giving me a quivering smile as she shakes her head.

A better man than me would haul her back into their arms and deal with this moment with kindness and empathy, but I'm still finding my feet, grappling with my own emotions. If she was raw and bleeding from her nightmare, then I am a reflection of that right now. I feel as though my chest has been ripped open, my heart stuttering behind the raggedy bones of my ribcage. So I don't press her. I let her tend to herself, as I do. We wash ourselves in silence, no longer touching, cleaning our bodies distractedly. Whatever had connected us in those intense few minutes evaporates alongside the steam curling up into the air.

"Daisy," I begin, but she just gives me a broken smile and rises upwards, stepping out of the bath.

"It's late. I should go to bed," she says, gathering a towel and wrapping it around herself, as though protecting herself from me.

I nod. "You're right."

She slips out of the bathroom, disappearing into the bedroom. By the time I've dried myself and dressed, she's lying on her side on the bed, the cover pulled up beneath her chin. For a moment I stand beside her, uncertain what to do. My skin feels too tight, my breath too shallow. I itch to touch her, to make her talk to me, but I don't know if I have the right words to soothe whatever it is she's feeling. Perhaps it's better if I leave?

Yet my body refuses to, even as my fight and flight instincts kick in.

Not sure if I'm doing the right thing, I climb onto the bed and lay down beside her. I don't know what to say. I don't even know if my closeness is welcome now, but despite all of that I spoon her body, pressing my chest against her back, dropping my arm over her waist.

She heaves out a sigh, and the sound guts me, because it doesn't sound like a sigh of contentment, it sounds like an exhale of sadness. I feel it thicken the air between us, shrouding what has just come to pass in grief, and even worse, regret.

We lay like that, together yet distant. I'm not sure how much time passes, but as the sky outside begins to slowly lighten, turning the black of night into the grey twilight of dawn, I lean over and press a kiss against Daisy's temple, then leave.

CHAPTER TWENTY-FIVE

As I sit gazing at my reflection in the mirror, my eyes accented with warm shades of gold, my lips adorned with soft pink, and my hair cascading in curls around my face, I release a quiet sigh.

It's finally our wedding day, a day when I should be filled with joy and excitement, ready to start a new life with my husband. Instead a heaviness weighs down my heart, settling in my stomach like a lead balloon.

I chose this.

I chose to sign the contract to marry Dalton Gunn.

A man who I have a complicated relationship with. A man who, for a long time, I hated. And now? I don't even know what we are.

Over the past couple of months we've fought, insulted each other, laughed together, been awkward in each other's company, spent time together, shared secrets and past hurts, kissed out of obligation, kissed each other in lust, made ourselves come whilst the other watched.

We've fucked...

Our relationship is complicated to say the least. We're hesitant, uncertain, and of late have been oscillating between friends that fuck and something... *more,* something neither of us can define. Like the first buds of spring pushing up through frost-dusted soil, feelings have begun to grow, delicate yet fragile.

Oh so fragile.

We're attracted to each other, that much is clear. We've begun to open up, slowly revealing ourselves bit by bit, but is it foolish to hope that something deeper could bloom from such a tumultuous foundation? I can't deny the yearning in my heart for something real, something everlasting, something I'm not certain we can give each other despite the vows we're going to make today.

The other night when I'd awoken from that awful nightmare, Dalton had held me, he'd soothed me, he'd helped me to obliterate my father's cruelty with pain, he'd fucked me, and yet... It felt like more than just sex. It felt like coming home. But afterwards when all I'd felt was relief, when I'd cried tears of release, I'd seen *fear* in his gaze, and even though he'd laid down beside me, there was a distance between us, a chasm. Eventually I'd fallen asleep, and when I'd awoken and found myself alone, I'd felt bereft.

Why had he left? Did he not feel what I felt?

Maybe I was hoping for something that simply wasn't there. Maybe I'm just a fool.

"You can do this, Daisy," I say to my reflection, shaking off those feelings, refusing to wallow in self-pity.

I have to remember why I'm doing this, it's the only thing keeping me from curling up into a ball and letting a torrent of tears wash away the makeup I've spent the morning trying to perfect. As I pick up a deep brown eyeliner to add the finishing touch to my eyes, a faint knock at the door interrupts me. I glance at my phone resting on the dressing table, it's a quarter past twelve, in a little over an hour I will officially become Mrs Dalton Gunn.

"Come in," I reply softly, placing the kohl liner back on to my dressing table.

Tessa, a kind woman with dark hair and gentle eyes that I've briefly chatted with a few times since I moved in, stands at the door. She's been a maid for the Gunn family for years, and whilst I've not had the chance to get to her know her fully, she's always offered me a kind smile and whispered hello's whenever we've crossed paths in this huge mansion I now call home, even if it's far from homely.

"Mr Gunn asked me to bring you this," Tessa says, stepping into the room, holding onto a cloth garment bag, the white material zipped up so I can't see what's inside.

"Carl?" I ask, frowning.

"No, Dalton," she replies, stepping into my room as she hangs it up on the open door of my wardrobe, right next to the wedding dress I bought with Lia, a beautiful cream and gold embroidered gown that now seems to mock me with everything it represents.

I turn back to Tessa, frowning. "What is it?" I question.

"He said it was a gift to you, something *new*," she explains softly, her eyes darting to the wardrobe where the bag now hangs. "He also wanted me to give you this."

Reaching inside the pocket of her dress she pulls out an envelope, handing it to me. "Would you like me to stay and help you with your dress?"

"Thank you, yes, I'd appreciate that..." I reply, my voice catching.

Lia had offered to come this morning, knowing I'd have no one else, but I'd told her that it wasn't necessary. Truth is, I couldn't face another conversation about Dalton and our relationship, despite how supportive and understanding she's been. Opening the envelope, I find a handwritten note from Dalton, his neat cursive a blur of words that make my heart clench with unexpected emotion.

Dear Daisy,

As you already know I tend to say and do the wrong thing and fuck things up, so instead I wanted to give you something that I hope will, at the very least, make this wedding bearable, it begins, the words so simple yet so laden with unspoken feelings. *But what I will say is this; whilst I can't give you your dream wedding, I can give you your perfect wedding dress.*

"What?" I whisper, my eyes flicking to the cloth garment bag, before I drag my gaze back to the letter.

I took the liberty of contacting Matilda a few days after you showed me your drawing, and she very graciously agreed to bring your beautiful design to life. I hope it's everything you wished for. Even if I can't make you truly happy like a husband should, then I hope this dress will give you some happiness, however fleeting, Dalton.

"He didn't?" I say, my eyes brimming with tears as I fold the letter up and slide it back into the envelope.

"Is everything okay?" Tessa asks me, concern etched in the gentle lines of her face as she looks at me.

"Have you seen what's inside?" I ask her, trying to compose myself as I reach for the garment bag.

"No, Miss, I haven't," she replies.

With trembling fingers, I unzip the bag, gasping at the beautiful layered chiffon that reveals itself to me. The dress is breathtaking, a vision of pale pink, baby blue, soft yellow, subtle green and muted lilac that seems to shift and change colour as I run my hands over the delicate fabric. An exact replica of my design, the dress is like a rainbow woven together, each hue blending seamlessly into the next, creating a stunning ombre effect that takes my breath away. More tears blur my vision as I run my fingers over the coloured gems that adorn the bodice catching the sunlight that filters into my bedroom.

"It's..."

"Beautiful," Tessa says, as my own words fail me.

"It's my design," I whisper, my throat clogged with emotion as

I'm faced with a decision. Do I wear this beautiful gown, the dress of my dreams that Dalton has gifted me, or choose the wedding dress that would meet the expectations of his father and everyone else who will be in attendance today?

I flick my gaze between the two dresses, knowing that my decision will be a pivotal moment in defining my own sense of self. The dress I had chosen with Lia, though stunning, symbolises my marriage into a family who have certain expectations of me, and only serves to remind me of that moment I signed the contract to save my brother from a life he didn't deserve, and binding me to a man who had once only ever thought of himself.

Yet within the delicate threads of the gown Dalton unexpectedly gifted me lies a glimmer of hope, a shard of kindness and understanding amidst the chaos of my emotions. In this singular act of generosity, Dalton has given me something far more precious—a reminder that even in moments of heartache and uncertainty, there can be grace and unexpected beauty.

There really is only one choice I can make, and so with a deep breath, I slip off my dressing gown and reach for the ombre dress, a warm smile pulling up my lips.

DRIX IS WAITING for me on the steps of St Augustine's church as I step out of the chauffeur driven car, his expression a mixture of love, admiration, and fleeting concern that he hides with a beaming smile. I know today is hard on him, but having him here means everything to me.

"Daisy, you look incredible," he says, as his eyes fall on my stunning wedding dress.

"Thank you," I reply, offering him a small smile as I walk towards him, the cool breeze causing my dress to flutter around my legs in a cascade of colours.

"Your dress is exquisite," he exclaims, grinning broadly. "Lia said it was beautiful, but this is just... So *perfectly* you."

"This wasn't the dress I chose with Lia," I reply.

"It's not?"

"No. This is a dress I designed. Dalton surprised me with it this morning. He had it made for me," I say softly.

Drix's eyes widen. "He did? That's... thoughtful."

"It is," I agree. "Despite everything, Dalton is really trying, Drix. Maybe it's time you two sorted things out?"

Drix flicks his gaze away, his expression unreadable, his jaw clenched as he processes my words. "Let's not worry about mine and Dalton's relationship today, okay? I'll talk to him once this wedding is out of the way and I've had time to process."

"Okay," I nod, taking his proffered hand.

"Are you ready to do this?" he asks, giving my fingers a squeeze.

"As I'll ever be," I say as we walk towards the entrance of the church, the soft melody of a string quartet drifting through the air.

As we step inside the church, our entrance is hidden by a huge marble pillar, and wooden panelling. Nerves churn in my stomach at the soft murmur of people talking but with Drix by my side, I feel more grounded, more capable of facing what's to come.

As we stand there, waiting for the music to change, signalling my entrance, I steal a glance at Drix. Our eyes meet and I give him a soft smile, silently thanking him for always being my rock.

"We're ready," Drix says, noticing the choir boy waiting for us, and with one brief nod the processional song begins to play.

It's not a melody I recognise, chosen by Carl like everything else about this day has been, but it is beautiful regardless. Taking a deep breath, I slide my arm through Drix's and we step out from behind the pillar as a sea of faces turn towards us both. Some people gasp softly, others whisper words under their breath, no doubt commenting on my wedding dress, but as I walk down the aisle, all I can focus on is Dalton waiting for me at the altar, his gaze fixed intently on me, an unreadable expression on his face.

After what feels like the longest walk of my life, we finally reach Dalton who's wearing a beautiful tailored, navy-blue suit, and a silk tie that matches the colours of my dress. I can't help but smile at that, my cheeks heating as I raise my gaze to meet his.

"You look so fucking beautiful," he murmurs, and my breath catches at the sincerity in his voice.

I swallow hard, feeling a surge of conflicting emotions that only add to the intensity of the moment as we stare at one another. Beside me, Drix releases my arm, gently taking my hand in his before offering it to Dalton.

"Daisy is precious to me," he mutters under his breath. "Do right by her."

They exchange a look, and for a moment I think Dalton is going to say something he'll regret, but instead he takes my hand in his and says, "I promise to do everything in my power to make Daisy happy for as long as she'll let me."

My stupid heart skips a beat at his words.

With one last kiss to my cheek, Drix steps away leaving us alone at the altar, and as the vicar begins speaking, the sound of his voice is dulled by the thrumming pulse of my blood thumping in my ears. Dalton faces me, his fingers gently clasping mine as his thumbs run gentle circles over the back of my hands. I'm confused by the look in his eyes, it makes me feel like I'm drowning and flying all at once, and I tear my eyes away stealing a glance at the stained-glass windows of the church, the sunlight casting a kaleido-scope of patterns across the stone floor.

"Daisy?" the vicar prompts, and I realise he's been waiting for me to answer, that I've missed minutes of him speaking.

"S-sorry," I stutter, blinking up at him.

"It's time to recite your vows. Would you please repeat after me?" he asks before continuing.

I nod, swallowing hard as I listen intently, trying to focus.

"I, Daisy Hammer, take you Dalton Gunn to be my husband..." I repeat, my voice wavering as I look up at Dalton, feeling the gravity of this moment pulling at my soul. He squeezes my hand, his gaze unwavering as his eyes reflect a myriad of emotions that mirror my own tangled feelings. "To have and to hold from this day forward..."

"For better, for worse, for richer, for poorer, in sickness and in health, to love and to cherish, until death do us part," the vicar continues.

"For better, for worse, for richer, for poorer, in sickness and in health, to..." I say, my throat tightening, my heart bashing against my rib cage as I swallow hard.

"To love and to cherish, until death do us part," the vicar reminds me.

"To love and to cherish," I whisper, tears pricking at my eyes at the words, "Until death do us part."

Dalton's eyes flare with heat, with a potency that makes my breath catch as I take the ring offered to me by our page boy—the child of one of Carl's friends— and slide the wedding band onto his finger. I drop my gaze to the simple platinum ring, a sign of our commitment, and a reminder of this lie we've woven.

As Dalton repeats his vows, a tear escapes my cheek, the lie feeling heavy and burdensome. Dalton notices, and he raises his hand, his thumb brushing away the tear, his touch gentle, loving, which only confuses me more.

None of this is real.

It's not real, I have to remind myself.

"To love and to cherish. Until death do us part," Dalton finishes, his voice clear, unwavering, as he slips the ring onto my finger.

"You may now kiss the bride." The vicar smiles, nodding at Dalton who steps forward, the heat in his gaze blazing brightly.

Cupping my face, he draws me towards him, and I step into his embrace on trembling legs as he drops his face to mine. For a moment I'm caught up in the tangled web of our deceit. My stupid heart desperately holds onto the lie, whilst my head is screaming at it to protect itself.

"You're mine now, *wife*," he says, and though his words are a soft, gentle caress there's no denying that they're filled with possession, with longing, with the kind of searing passion that has no place in such a sacred building, or directed at me, a woman he doesn't love, who he's incapable of loving by his own admission.

I gasp as his lips press against mine, and for the moment I forget the lies we've told, the deception woven into our vows. All I can focus on is the eddying heat between us, the crackling electricity as he kisses me like a man who's as desperate to belong to someone as I am.

I'm at the mercy of his kiss. It's indecent, provocative, and toe-curlingly beautiful, and all I can do is melt into his hold, unable to fight the connection between us, weakened by it.

The guests begin to clap as the vicar clears his throat. Dalton steps back and my cheeks are flaming, my heart pounding. If it wasn't for Dalton's arm wrapped around my waist I'm certain that my knees would give way beneath me.

It takes me a moment, but I pull myself together enough to step forward, wanting to leave, to catch my breath before I have to face everyone for photos outside, but Dalton pulls me back, clearing his throat as he raises his hand.

"Can I have your attention, please?" he says, and the clapping stops, as people turn to look at each other, as confused as I am.

I glance over at Drix, Lia and Toby. Drix is frowning, Lia has tears in her eyes and Toby is waving at me frantically, completely unaware that this isn't what usually happens at this stage of a marriage ceremony. We should be halfway down the aisle by now.

"My wife and I will be heading directly to our honeymoon.

The reception party will still go ahead, and of course you must all attend to celebrate our marriage, but we won't be in attendance."

"Excuse me?" Carl says, standing from his seat in the front row, glowering at us both. "We have the press waiting, Dalton!"

The press? Oh please, no.

"This isn't up for discussion. We're leaving now," Dalton replies firmly.

"The hell you are!" he seethes.

"Dalton, what are you doing?" I whisper, glancing at Carl, his face turning a deep, angry red.

"What I should've done the second my father ruined your idea of a perfect wedding," he replies, dropping a kiss to my head before addressing his father directly. "Daisy's happiness is my priority, and staying here for a second longer so the vast majority of you can all pretend to be happy for us both whilst gossiping behind our backs is something that I will not tolerate. I will also not allow the press to invade our privacy. I don't give a fuck about the deals you've made without our permission, *father*," he snarls.

"Why you ungrateful–" Carl begins, but Dalton holds his hand up, cutting him off.

"Enjoy your evening everybody," he says, before clasping my hand and guiding me back up the aisle as everyone breaks out into disgruntled conversation.

We rush out of the church, Dalton's hand tight around mine. I stumble a little on my dress, almost falling down the steps outside, but he reaches for me, sliding his arm around my back and knees, picking me up with a determined set of his jaw as he cradles me in his arms.

"Dalton, I can walk," I say, more heat flooding my cheeks as he carries me swiftly towards the waiting limousine.

"We need to leave before the press catches wind of what's happened," he bites out as I steal a glance at his profile, his jaw clenched in resolve, his eyes focused ahead.

"But where are we going?" I ask, as he gently places me back on my feet and opens the waiting car's passenger door. "I don't have anything packed."

"Somewhere we can be alone," he replies cryptically, as I slide onto the seat, making room for him beside me. "And I took care of your clothes. Don't worry, you'll have everything you need."

"But your father... the guests, the reception party he's organised," I say, a little helplessly.

"Fuck my father. Fuck the guests. Fuck the reception party. The only person I give a shit about is you," he replies, before turning his attention to the driver. "Take us to the airport, my private jet is waiting for us."

CHAPTER TWENTY-SIX

Twenty-four hours later, Daisy and I are walking along a stretch of a private, white sand beach on the island of Koh Phi-Phi Don, situated just off the coast of mainland Thailand. The beach is empty save a few people scattered in the distance, and the sun is setting on the horizon, painting the sky in a stunning sunset of startling burnt orange, crimson red and delicate gold-edged pinks. Beneath us, the waterlogged sand cups our feet as the turquoise sea laps against our bare ankles.

After arriving late last night, and settling into our bungalow on the exclusive resort which will be our home for the next ten days, Daisy has been, for the most part, quiet and thoughtful.

"So, what do you think?" I ask, glancing at her, marvelling at how the setting sun douses her in a warm halo. She's wearing a pale yellow cotton dress that grazes her knees, her bare shoulders dusted with a slight pink, her freckles darkened by a few hours in the sun. I make a mental note to remind her to wear more sunscreen tomorrow.

"It's beautiful here," she whispers, her gaze drifting out to sea as her footsteps still.

"It is probably one of the most beautiful places on Earth," I agree, my feet sinking into the warm sand as I stand by her side.

"Have you been here many times?" she asks softly, a gentle breeze lifting the skirt of her dress as she glances at me. It flutters against my thigh, and I get the urge to haul her into my arms and kiss her.

"A handful, yes."

"Have you brought other women here?"

"No. I come here to get away from everyone, Daisy," I admit, hating that she thinks I would take her to a place I've fucked other women. "I thought you would appreciate some peace and quiet."

She nods, her eyes drifting back to the ocean as we step up onto a jetty that rises out of the water, our feet padding across the warm wood. String lights are hanging from the handrails, some of them blinking on as the sky begins to darken.

"I didn't realise just how much I needed to get away until we arrived. Thank you for bringing me here."

"You're welcome," I reply, as we fall into a comfortable silence the further we walk away from the shore.

"I had no idea you were arranging this. When I spoke to Drix earlier, he was taken aback too, but he's glad I didn't have to face the press. I think, maybe, he's softening to the idea of talking to you again," she replies as we come to a standstill on the platform at the end of the jetty, the ocean a deeper, more azure blue here.

"My father's an arsehole. I couldn't let you go through that, and whenever Drix is ready to talk, I'll be there. We've been friends for a long time Daisy, I miss him," I admit.

"I think he misses you too. This is just... hard on him."

"I get that."

"Dalton...?" Daisy questions, her voice trailing off as she drags in a deep breath.

"Yes?"

"I haven't thanked you for the dress. It meant a lot to me. So, thank you."

"Did seeing it at least make you smile?" I ask.

"It made me *happy*," she replies, my fucking heart clenching as she reaches for my hand and squeezes it gently. "It made me feel like me."

Before she's able to pull her hand away, I wrap my fingers around hers, needing to touch her, fucking desperate for physical contact. "You deserved something that *you* wanted after my father decided to make our wedding into a fucking performance," I say, stepping around her so that we're face to face.

"It was always going to be a performance, Dalton," she whispers, her brows creasing together in a frown as she drops her head, refusing to look into my eyes.

"What I said at the wedding wasn't a performance, and that kiss we shared to seal our vows wasn't either," I admit, drawing her chin upwards with my fingers. "You're my *wife*, Daisy."

"On paper, yes," she agrees, her words like a knife stabbing my gut.

"I wish..." My voice trails off as I try to articulate what I'm feeling.

"What do you wish, Dalton?"

"Fuck, Daisy, I don't even know what I'm trying to say," I reply, my insides all churned up.

I never thought that getting married would make me feel the way I do. I'm *proud* to be her husband. I want to make her happy more than anything. Nothing seems as important as her happiness.

"Do you wish that things were simpler? That you could go back to your life before this exploded in our faces? she asks softly, misinterpreting me.

"No, that's not what I'm saying at all," I insist.

"What then?"

"We're friends, right?" I ask, needing her reassurance, hating how fucking vulnerable that makes me sound.

"Yes," she agrees.

"Then we can build on that, can't we?" I ask, reaching up to cup her face, my thumb lightly brushing against her bottom lip.

"Into what exactly? What are you asking?" she asks, blinking up at me, her lips parting as her pupils widen, eating up the light blue of her eyes and pitching her gaze into pools of glistening darkness.

"Honestly, Daisy, I don't fucking know. What I do know is that I like spending time with you. You make things brighter. You make me *happy*, and fuck knows no one has ever made me feel that way. You infuriate me. You challenge me. You turn me on."

"Because the contract says that marital affairs aren't allowed, and I'm the only one available to you now?" she counters softly.

"Jesus, no! I'm hard for you, Daisy, not because I'm desperate to fuck just anyone, but because I want *you*," I admit. "I think of nothing else but being inside of you again. That's all I think about. I can't get enough."

Which is a lie, because I haven't just thought about fucking her, I've thought about how I don't *ever* want to fuck anyone else, but I don't tell her that. I'm not sure I'm ready to lay my shit bare.

"What are we exactly? Friends who fuck?" she whispers.

"Aren't most married couples that?" I counter with a wry grin.

"Most married couples are hopelessly in love, Dalton."

"And I love how it feels to be buried so deep inside of you that I don't ever want to be anywhere else. I love how your skin pinkens with desire when I touch, kiss and lick you. I love how you whimper my name when we fuck like I'm the only man on this Earth made for you. I love how you're always so wet for me, how your body grips my cock," I reply in a ragged breath, my filthy words making her gasp.

I can't help it, I slide my thumb between her parted lips,

wishing it was my cock she was tentatively pressing the tip of her tongue against, wishing she was tasting the pre-cum that's jewelling on my dick right now. Our gazes clash and I step closer to her, my free hand running up the bare skin of her arm as she shudders.

"You're messing with my head, *wife*," I say, enjoying the way that sounds, how she belongs to me now. We're bound together in a way we weren't before; the vows we promised to each other and our wedding bands binding us more tightly than the dried ink on the contract tucked into my father's desk. "I want you so fucking badly, it's all I can do to breathe."

She lets out a whimper, her eyes drifting shut as she sucks my thumb into her mouth, and this time it's me who's trembling, who's barely hanging on by a thread.

"Fuck, Daisy, I haven't been able to get you out of my head. All I've thought about is making you smile, making your cheeks and chest flush that pretty pink colour when you come. I want nothing more than to take you in my arms and hold you. *I* want to be the man to make you feel safe," I admit, meaning every word, knowing that's a truth I can't hide from. I feel protective of Daisy, and if the truth be known, I always have.

"I want to feel your lips around my cock. I want you to taste how turned on I am right now. I want you to moan as you suck me off. I want to taste you too. Fuck, how I want to taste you, Daisy. Are you wet for me now? Do you want me as much as I desperately, inexplicably, want you?"

My thumb slips from her mouth, as I grasp the back of her head, my fingers curling into her pretty strawberry-blonde hair. Tugging gently, I urge her head backwards so that I can drop my lips to her forehead.

"I'm afraid that you're going to break my heart," she admits, her words nothing more than a whisper.

"I don't want to," I reply, pressing another kiss against the tip of her nose, the back of my hand coasting upwards over her stomach, up to her delicious pert breast. "I'll do everything in my power not to."

"I want to believe that," she gasps, not pushing me away, but leaning into my touch.

"Believe me when I say that I've never wanted to be a better man for anyone else. You do things to me, Daisy, things that fucking terrify me. But I'm willing to walk into the unknown with you."

"Dalton..."

She shudders as I gently cup her, feeling the heaviness of her breast in my hand. I can't help it, I can't seem to stop as I tease her nipples, pinching them delicately between my finger and thumb. They're hard, fucking desperate to be licked.

"But you can't love me, Dalton. You said so yourself."

"I've said a lot of things, things I wish I could take back, and I've done a lot of things I wish I hadn't..."

Those words hang as heavy as the humidity that beads on our skin, and my hand glides upwards, cupping the base of her throat gently, my thumb rubbing against the thready pulse in her neck.

"This is..." her voice trails off as I brush my lips against hers.

"...Our honeymoon," I murmur against her mouth. "You're my wife, Daisy, and I want to be a good husband to you, starting with making you come right here and now on this jetty in the middle of paradise."

Her gaze flicks between my eyes and my lips, and back again, her whole body shaking in earnest now. There's so much vulnerability in her gaze, so much lust, I feel it billowing between us. It churns me up, makes me want to do so many, dirty, dirty things to her. I know there are things we need to talk about, mostly what happened that night she had a nightmare, but right now I need to taste her, I need to gather my strength with her pleasure so that I can find the courage to be honest and open.

"I want you to make me come, Dalton," she whispers. "Please, make me come."

"Yes," I hiss, monumental, overwhelming desire burning in my veins as I smash my lips against hers.

Lust, passion, need, want, I feel it all in that moment as our mouths collide in a soul-searing kiss. It all comes pouring out of me as I wrap my hand around her back and curl my fingers tighter in her hair. This kiss, fuck. This kiss is like a match being struck against jagged rock. It's flammable, *consuming*, marking my heart with scorching heat. Flames lick against my tongue as I fuck her mouth, taking ownership, feral in my need to claim her as my wife, as mine. She whimpers, clawing at my chest, her fingers curling around my t-shirt as she kisses me back, matching my desire, meeting me stroke for stroke.

This kiss is dangerous for all the reasons I've been running from. Daisy is no longer my best friend's off-limits sister, she's not just the girl I used to love to hate, she's not only my friend, she isn't just my wife, she's so much more.

So much more.

And all the words I cannot say come pouring out of me in this kiss. All the feelings I've been avoiding, that I've kept guarded, are unleashed as I kiss her with every fibre of my being. I don't hold back. I couldn't even if I wanted to, and before long we're both dropping to our knees, collapsing under the undeniable weight of our feelings as we ravage one another. Feelings I can't seem to untangle, feelings that are alien to me, yet I don't run from. Don't want to.

"Fuck, Daisy, the things you do to me!" I groan, gently tugging on her bottom lip with my teeth, drugged by the heady scent of her, the beautiful way she moans against me, the way her fingers curl into my hair tightly as though she can't bear to let go of me, anymore than I can her.

But I can't fight it. I can't fucking fight it anymore.

I'm lost to her.

My whole fucking body is alight, aware of every touch she blesses me with, every desperate kiss, every moan and whimper. Her flowery scent fills my nostrils as I drag in a deep breath, my hands roaming her sun-kissed skin, this need in me to consume her is overwhelming.

"Dalton, please," she begs, and that's all it takes for everything to fall away. Our messy past dissipates as we kiss and lick, as we fuck each other's mouth with our tongues.

Before long she's lying on her back and I'm pressing the hard ridge of my cock against her core, showing her just how much I want her, no *need* her. Placing one hand in the warm wood beside her head, I push upwards, staring into her beautiful eyes. Her hair is spread out around her, tangled and dusted with speckles of white sand from spending the day at the beach.

"Fuck, you're beautiful, wife," I murmur, rocking my hips, my cock rigid against her warmth, as she parts her legs further and presses up against me in a slow, sensual rock of her hips.

"My husband," she whispers, and it's the first time I've heard her call me that as she reaches up, her hand cupping my check, the gentleness of her touch making a shiver run down my spine.

God, hearing those words does something powerful to me, and I lower my mouth to hers in a soft, whispering kiss, my fucking heart punching a hole against my ribcage. Her hand slides into my hair as she offers me her neck, moaning breathily as I slide my lips across her jaw and press an open-mouthed kiss against her thundering pulse, wanting to capture the beat of her heart, consume it, keep it safe.

"Look at you," I mutter, feeling the heat between us, the pooling liquid between her thighs as I rock against her, desperate, fucking aching to be inside of her.

If I've learnt anything sleeping with a multitude of women, it's not just the feral act of fucking that brings a woman to orgasm, in most cases it's the build up, the foreplay. But I am ashamed to admit that in the past I've been so consumed for the need to fuck, to bring women sexual pleasure that I never took the time to care about the emotional connection.

Daisy has taught me how to *care*, to have empathy, to be kind. She's opened something up inside of me that I don't want to let go off. Seeing her laugh, catching her smile, feeling the warmth of her joy is as much a turn on for me as the way her body is so receptive to my touch now.

I want all of that and more, but the way Daisy seems to submit to me now, I get the feeling she wants to give herself over to me in this moment, and I'm more than happy to take the lead.

Shifting lower I press my mouth against her clavicle, swirling my tongue over her sun-kissed, salty skin. I draw my teeth lightly over the tender bone, edging my mouth lower as I cup her breast over the soft cotton of her dress, my fingers sliding beneath the thin strap so I can pull the material lower. Slowly, I reveal her skin, inch by beautiful inch, until her tight pink bud is millimetres from my lips. I blow across the puckered nib, and she groans, arching her back, pressing herself into the wet heat of my mouth.

"Dalton," she whimpers as I swirl my tongue around her areola. She clasps me against her chest, urging me to take, to give, so she can receive.

So I suck on her, dragging my teeth gently over her sensitive skin, licking my tongue over her flesh, hollowing out my cheeks as I pull her nipple into my mouth, the gentle sound of waves buffeting against the jetty, is a melody matching the rhythm of our hearts.

"Oh God," she cries, lips parted, her cheeks and chest colouring a soft pink.

She liquifies beneath me, and this sense of intense pride floods my system as she unravels. No, as she *blooms*.

Daisy, my beautiful flower.

"Mine," I mutter against her chest.

Releasing her breast, I edge lower, pushing up the skirt of her dress and bunching it up beneath her breasts as I blaze a trail of kisses over her freckle-splattered stomach. One day I intend to kiss every single freckle, but right now I want to make her come. I want to hear her call my name as I bring her to the edge of orgasm, as I keep her there hovering over the precipice, then allow her to fall so she can come, long and hard.

I don't know much about her past sexual experiences, but I do know that I want to erase every single memory of any other man she's been with and replace them with only thoughts of me. A possessiveness unfurls like an intolerant beast inside of me at the thought of someone else touching, kissing, licking, fucking what's mine, and I shuffle downwards, my head between her legs, my hands gripping her hips possessively. Dropping my gaze, I see the wet stain of her arousal seeping through the cotton of her knickers, hugging the lips of her pussy and I can't help myself, I drop my nose to the wetness, breathing in her heady, musky scent.

"Fuck, Daisy. I don't think I'll ever get enough of you," I grind out, my cock painful in my arousal.

But this moment isn't about me, and that in itself is a revelation. In the past I've always been guaranteed a release of my own, knowing that it will be a million times better when the women I've fucked have orgasmed before I have. Yet, right now, I expect nothing in return. This is all about Daisy, my focus is solely on her and not my need. At this moment, despite how much I want her, I'm not ruled by my addiction, I'm at the mercy of my developing feelings, and my need to give, not take.

"You're mine," I repeat as she rocks her hips involuntarily, her slit sliding over the bridge of my nose.

I react instantly, rearing upwards so I can curl my hands around her panties, and pull them free, wanting to give her everything she desires, needing that more than anything.

"Fuck, I can't believe I haven't tasted you yet," I rumble, staring at her pretty slit.

"You have," she mutters, as I swipe my fingers gently between her folds.

"Not like this I haven't," I reply, resting back between her legs, kissing her lower stomach as a joyful laugh bubbles from her lips.

I smile against her skin, the sun slipping below the horizon as nighttime begins to fall, slowly enveloping us in the welcoming blanket of darkness and blinking jewels of starlight. Sliding my arms beneath her thighs, I rest my hands on her hips, and lower my mouth to her neatly trimmed pussy.

The second my lips meet her tender flesh, she moans and her thighs fall open, giving me full access. Under the cover of a night sky, lit by a full moon, and the twinkling fairy lights hung along the jetty, she reveals herself to me. Her willingness to bare herself, to let go and allow me to taste her, drives me wild as I spear her hole with my tongue.

She shudders, her hands flying to my head, gripping tight, urging me closer, deeper, harder. And I give her everything she needs, her sweet, musky taste exploding in my mouth.

Fuck, she's delicious.

I groan. She whimpers.

I lick her from crack to slit, circling her clit, gently at first. Teasingly, I focus my attention on the tight bundle of nerves that has the power to take her to another place where pleasure replaces all our past mistakes. Her breath hitches, her moans releasing from parted, kiss-bruised lips as her body's lubrication merges with my salvia. It's erotic as fuck, and I'm more than willing to drown in her arousal.

Every stroke of my tongue brings her closer to the edge. Every moan, every gasp for air, the way she grasps my head tightly, only turns me on more. She's so wet, so responsive. She opens up to me completely, her trust bleeding into every pore, every muscle, as I draw circles around her clit slowly, teasingly. Somehow this seems far more intimate than fucking, because this time it's all about Daisy. Her orgasm, her pleasure, *her*.

Yes, I'm hard. So fucking hard, but I want to see her unravel more than I want to come.

"Dalton, I'm close. I'm close," she cries, throwing her head back as her thighs draw together, trapping me between her as she begins to tremble, approaching the edge of orgasm.

A wildness billows inside of me, her pleasure becoming my pleasure. My cock pulses, my balls drawing tight. I'm so fucking turned on. So in awe of her, of this eddying, blazing attraction between us that no ocean can cool.

If she is fire, then I am ash, burnt to a cinder by this woman, Daisy, my flower, my wife.

My wife.

She's my wife.

"Come for me, wife," I demand, my voice raw with need.

I feel her internal muscles tense around my tongue, her breath hitching as I increase my pace, my tongue probing deeper, faster, revelling in her responses.

"I'm going to come, Dalton," she moans, her nails digging into my scalp.

The sound of her so lost in pleasure, the sight of her so vulnerable and open, fills me with an inexplicable joy, and as she reaches the peak, her body shudders violently, her muscles clenching around my tongue as her cry of release buries itself into my soul. It's a beautiful, primal sound that resonates within me, echoing my own arousal.

I savour the moment, a rush of pride and possession sweeping over me as I lap at her until she slowly comes down from the high, her breathing easing into a steady, more even rhythm.

"That was..." her voice trails off as she sits up, flushed, dishevelled, overwhelmingly beautiful.

"Fucking perfect," I finish for her. "You're fucking perfect."

Taking her hand, I stand, pulling her up on trembling legs and haul her into my arms. Holding her close, her body melts against mine as I wrap my arms around her back, and in the peaceful silence a voice deep inside of me screams the truth. A truth that I've run from for so fucking long.

All the years we've spent hating each other, all the times she's been with other men, I've stepped in and interfered not just because I wanted to protect her, but because I didn't want anyone else to have her.

Because *I've* always wanted her.

The truth hits me hard right in the centre of my chest, but I welcome it. Welcome how she makes me feel, how fucking *beautiful* we are together.

"Dance with me?" I ask, as she leans her head back, starlight dancing in her eyes.

"Dance with you?" she questions back, another smile quirking up her lips.

"We never got to have our first dance. It's tradition," I reply, taking her hand in mine and pressing it against my chest.

"There's no music..." she whispers.

I press my mouth against her ear and begin to sing the chorus of *Stargazing* by Myles Smith. Badly, sure, but I sing it nevertheless.

"Who knew you could be so romantic?" she murmurs as we sway side to side.

"Not me," I reply, grinning, feeling more alive than ever before.

CHAPTER TWENTY-SEVEN

After spending the following day exploring our surroundings and swimming in the turquoise ocean, Dalton and I sit on the porch of our beautiful, secluded bungalow, eating ripened fruit and crudités, washing them down with sparkling champagne. The shade of the vine-covered pergola above us creates a mosaic of warm afternoon light that dances across our skin, and I feel slightly intoxicated. Not just from the single glass of champagne I've just consumed, but from a heady mix of emotions swirly inside of me, and the memory of Dalton's tongue and mouth on my pussy last night.

It was the single most erotic experience of my life.

Yes, we've had sex. Yes, I've come all over his cock, but this was different.

It was... *more.*

It wasn't just the way he brought me to orgasm with his lips and his tongue, and didn't expect anything in return. It wasn't just the way he called me his wife, or the way he'd pulled me into his arms afterwards and held me like I was someone precious to him. It wasn't just the way he kissed me like he'd never get enough of me, or the way he danced with me, *sung* to me. It was all of that, and it was so much more.

I felt *worshipped.*

Right there on the jetty, with stars sparkling above us and Dalton's baritone voice filling up an emptiness deep inside of me, I felt our connection strengthen into something powerful. That feeling of being utterly adored lingers still, and as I slowly chew on the sweet slice of mango, I feel Dalton staring at me, the heat of his gaze caressing me with sin. Everything seems so heightened, and I've spent the day walking around in a daze of arousal, wanting nothing more than to submit to the pleasure he can, apparently, so easily conjure within me. Instead, we've taken the time to just *be...* With each other, ourselves, and it's been such a beautiful day of hand-holding, laughter, and heightened awareness.

But my heart is yearning for more.

I want him to fuck me again.

No, I want him to make *love* to me.

"Daisy, what's on your mind?" Dalton asks, breaking the silence between us as a warm breeze coasts over my skin, the scent of the ocean only serving to remind me of the way I'd so willingly submitted to him last night.

"Do you want the truth?" I reply softly, turning to face him, my pulse thrumming in my ears, between my legs.

"Yes, I want the truth," he replies, his gaze locking with mine.

"I haven't been able to stop thinking about last night," I admit. "I feel..."

"You feel what, Daisy?" he gently prods, resting his empty glass of champagne back on the table, his strong fingers and wide palms pressed against his thighs as he waits for me to answer.

My gaze falls to his bare chest, and the way his open shirt reveals the beautiful tattoos that adorn his sun-kissed skin, darkened a little after a couple of days in the sun. He's cut to perfection, a Grecian god, made of marble, dipped in ink.

"I feel aroused," I whisper, my cheeks heating at all the other words on the tip of my tongue. Does he feel that closeness too, the beautiful connection between us? The joy of finding the other part of you?

"You're aroused now?" he says, his voice strained.

"Yes. I feel wound up tight, and..."

"And?"

Shit. A sudden wave of uncertainty washes over me. What if I've read this all wrong? What if he doesn't feel what I feel? What if this is all in my head? He's told me on countless occasions that he can't love me, that he doesn't know how. Then again last night he'd said he'd regretted a lot of the things he'd said, that he wants to build on our friendship. Do I trust what I felt between us? Do I listen to my head, or to what he's told me? Should I be truthful and open my heart, sharing my doubts with him, or should I keep them underwraps?

I chew on my lip, trying to decide.

"Daisy?" he questions, canting his head to the side, frowning a little as he stares at me. "Talk to me."

"I'm afraid, Dalton," I admit.

"Of what?"

"I'm afraid that my need to feel so desperately wanted is blinding me from the truth," I rush out as a sudden sharp pain lacerates my heart. I flick my gaze away, dragging in a shuddering breath.

"What truth?"

"That you—"

"Daisy, what truth?" he persists, reaching for me, his hand wrapping around mine, squeezing gently.

"That you truly are incapable of *ever* loving me."

He hesitates for a moment, a frown appearing between his eyebrows. "Do you want that, Daisy? Do you want *me* to love *you?*"

"I've always wanted to feel loved, Dalton," I say, blinking back hot tears, refusing to let them fall.

"But do you want *me* to love you? Do you want me to make love to you, *wife*?" he persists, and the way he calls me his wife makes me tremble with need.

"I want that more than anything. I want to be loved, Dalton. I want it so badly that it hurts," I whisper, rubbing my chest where my heart swells painfully. "But more than that, I want *you*, and it terrifies me that you only want me for one thing. Part of me still believes that I'm just a means to an end, an itch you need to scratch, an addiction you need to appease, and I'm scared that what I'm beginning to feel forming between us isn't real."

"Daisy, look at me," he demands softly, urgently.

I don't. I can't. More tears well in my eyes, and I hate that I'm so vulnerable.

"Look at me now," he repeats, more forcefully this time, and my eyes snap up to meet his.

I suck in a breath at the heat in them, at the way he seems to drink me in like a man desperate to quench his thirst.

"I'm *not* a sex addict, Daisy," he says, leaning closer and cupping my face, his thumb trailing over the tears that glisten on my skin. "Despite really enjoying sex, and despite what everyone thinks, it's more complicated than that," he explains, blowing out a shuddering breath of his own. "If I'm being honest with myself, it isn't the sex so much as..."

"What, Dalton?"

He levels his gaze with mine. "When I've fucked women before, for a brief moment in time, I was their everything. That made *me* feel wanted, adored, desired, loved," he adds softly. "And as much as everyone thinks I've used those women to get myself off, they've used me too for the exact same thing. No one has ever fought to keep me. No one has ever cared for me, not really, not in the way that matters. The women I've been with before have only ever truly wanted me for my money, for the notoriety of ensnaring the heir to a fortune. I walked away before they could do the same to me. Just like my own mother did. You're the only one who's stayed. I know you're bound to me, but the sheer fact you've not run, that you aren't interested in my family's fortune, that you want to be friends, that you trust me with your pain, that you see something in me that others never have, it means a great deal."

"Dalton, I didn't realise," I say, my heart aching for him.

"It's different with you," he continues, pressing on. "I want you. God help me, I do. But I don't just want to fuck you. I *want* to make love to you."

"You do?"

"Yes. So much, and I will, one day, when I truly understand the meaning of the word," he says, pressing his hand to his chest, mirroring me. His honesty both causes a crack in my heart, and simultaneously heals it.

"You truly want me, for *me*? You could love me?"

"Yes, Daisy. *Yes*," he replies emphatically, pressing a tender kiss against my knuckles, his lips lingering against my skin. "I think I've wanted you for a long time now, but I kept you at a distance. I encouraged the animosity between us because you were off-limits to me. I refused to look too closely at why it drove me crazy when I saw you with other men," he admits.

My heart rate kicks up a notch at the honesty of his confession, at the helplessness he so clearly feels. Like me, he's been cast adrift, consumed by the current of our developing feelings, helpless against them.

"What do we do now?" I ask, hopeful, willing to tread water, to keep afloat whilst we learn how to swim, together.

"Right now, I need you to bear with me, Daisy. Will you do that? Will you be patient? Will you give me the time to explore what's growing between us? Because the next time I sink inside of you I want it to be out of love."

"Yes," I reply without a moment's hesitation, wanting to give him that, wanting it more than anything. Then I push back my chair and stand, tugging on his hand. "Come with me?"

He nods, rising to his feet as he follows me into the lounge. I guide him towards the main bedroom suite where I've been sleeping. There are two bedrooms in this bungalow, but we haven't shared a bed since we arrived. Perhaps it was because we felt the need to give each other space, or maybe it was because we were both afraid of what sharing a bed for an entire night could mean. There's something about holding each other in sleep that is far more intimate than fucking, and I guess neither of us were truly ready for that, but none of that matters now as I stop at the end of the bed, turning to face him.

"What are we doing?" he asks. There's a wariness in his gaze, but also a willingness, and it emboldens me.

"Take your clothes off, Dalton," I whisper.

"Why?"

"Because loving someone isn't just about sex," I reply, feathering my fingers against his stubbled jaw.

"Yet you want me naked?" he asks, a soft laugh releasing from his lips.

"Loving someone also means taking care of them," I continue, gently. "Sex is wonderful, of course it is, but kindness, care, empathy, *tenderness*, that's a huge part of it too. I think you're beginning to see that, at least I thought you were when we..."

"When we what, Daisy?"

"That night when I had the nightmare. It was so... I felt.. It seemed as though you... *cared* for me," I say, choosing my words carefully.

"Christ, Daisy. I *do* care for you. I did what you asked of me because I care."

"But..."

"But, what?" he asks.

"After we had sex, when I looked in your eyes, I saw so much fear there, hesitancy, and it threw me. I thought perhaps you wished we hadn't had sex that night, that maybe I'd cornered you into doing something you didn't want, that you pity-fucked me."

"Fuck, no. I hate that you thought that," he exclaims, swiping a hand through his hair. "That wasn't what I felt at all. I wanted to ease your pain, Daisy. I wanted you to escape from your memories. I wanted you to feel good, but when it was over and you were crying, I was afraid I took advantage of your emotional state. That I made things worse, that I did the wrong thing like I'm prone to do."

"You didn't. You did exactly the *right* thing," I say, dragging in a deep breath. "You saw me at my worst, you held me with care and affection, you helped me overcome the memories by giving me what I craved. You *did* ease my pain. It was, and forever will be, a perfect moment in time. All of it, not just the sex, or the spanking, or the way you held me both before and after. Every single moment."

"Fuck, it was perfect wasn't it? It was as though... It was as if..." His voice trails off as he winces. "Why is this so damn hard for me to talk about? I'm sorry I'm not able to express myself very well. I should've explained how I felt at the time, but like now I couldn't find the words."

"I understand, and now that I do, I'll make sure I don't rush to any conclusions," I reply, feeling an immense sense of relief.

"So what now?" he questions, giving me a lopsided grin.

"Do you trust me?" I ask, sliding my palms up over the firm muscles of his chest, my fingers pushing the material of his shirt over his shoulder.

"Yes," he whispers, as I remove his shirt, allowing the material to flutter to the floor.

Reaching for the waistband of his swim shorts next, I slip my fingers beneath the material at his hips and slide them off until he's naked before me. His dick hangs heavy between his thighs, not completely erect, but not soft either. And whilst I want nothing more than to touch him and bring him to orgasm like he did for me on the jetty, I don't, I simply say, "Get on the bed, lie down on your stomach."

Without uttering a word, Dalton does as I ask. He lays down on the huge bed, resting his cheek on his folded hands. For a moment I just stare at his beautiful body, at his broad shoulders and back covered in stunning abstract black tattoos, that curl and loop around each other. I allow my gaze to coast over his strong muscular arms and legs, before finally resting my gaze on his profile.

"You're a beautiful man, Dalton," I say, climbing onto the bed, straddling his firm arse as I gently lower myself over him, my cotton dress gathered around the top of my thighs. "I've always thought so. I guess I was hiding my own attraction for fear of being rejected," I admit. "Now I don't have to."

Dalton sucks in a breath, and I know he must feel the dampness of my knickers, how I'm wet for him, but he doesn't try to move, and I don't grind against him to relieve the ache I feel. Instead, I rest my hands on the centre of his back, then gently run my fingers up and down the length of his spine, caressing him with fondness and affection, with care and tenderness.

"That feels good," he murmurs, as I stroke his skin, soothing him.

"I want you to feel good," I reply and as my fingers continue to glide over Dalton's skin, his muscles start to relax beneath me as the tension in his body begins to dissipate. "I want you to feel cared for."

Taking a moment to savour the sensation, I begin to massage his shoulders, kneading the muscles gently until I hear a soft moan escape his lips. I'm not doing this to get him off, to make him hard, though given the sounds he's making I suspect that's happening anyway. I'm doing it because I want him to feel taken care of. So I continue to massage him, interspersing the kneading of his muscles with soft strokes of my fingers over his skin. Then slowly, tentatively, I lean over and press soft kisses against his skin, imbuing tenderness into his flesh, wanting him to know that he is treasured, that I treasure him.

Part of me expects him to turn beneath me, to succumb to the sexual attraction between us, but he doesn't, he simply allows me to stroke him, soothe him, and as time passes his eyelids drift shut and his breathing settles into an even rhythm. When I'm certain that he's fallen asleep, I climb off him and lay by his side, my hand pressed against the middle of his back as I stare at the man I now call husband. Before long I'm drifting off to sleep too, thoughts of a happy, *loving* future with Dalton whispering across my mind.

THE NEXT MORNING I wake up to the press of firm, warm lips against mine, and my eyelids flutter open as Dalton reaches up and brushes a strand of hair off my face.

"Morning, wife," he says, rubbing the tip of his nose against the bridge of mine.

"Morning, husband," I whisper back, twisting in his arms that have somehow wound themselves around my body as he stares at me. "Did you sleep well?"

"Like a baby. Speaking of which..." he replies, his voice trailing off as he runs his hand over my hip, the warmth of his fingers dragging fire across my skin as he grins. "There's no time like the present."

"Dalton, I think maybe we should—" but my words are abruptly cut off as his hand reaches between my legs and he cups my pussy, making me forget everything I was about to say.

"I woke up to dirty thoughts of filling you with my cum," he says, dropping his lips to mine and kissing me as the heel of his palm presses against my clit. "Last night you bewitched me with your touch. I was so soothed by it that I fucking fell asleep. Believe me when I say, that will *never* happen again."

"There's nothing wrong with..." I moan, his hand moving over my tender flesh.

"Nothing wrong with what, wife?" he softly goads, nuzzling my neck.

"Feeling relaxed enough to fall asleep." I gasp as he gently strokes his finger over the fabric of my knickers.

"I was turned on, you know. So fucking turned on, I want you to know that, but I forced myself to remain still, wanting to know what would happen if I just allowed the moment to play out," he explains, his fingers sliding beneath my panties, a groan releasing from his lips as he finds me soaking for him.

"L–like I said, loving someone isn't just about sex, Dalton," I mutter, my words tripping awkwardly off my tongue as he fingers me slowly.

"Are you saying you love me?" he jokes, a sexy smile pulling up his lips as he pulls back slightly, looking down at me.

"There's so much about you worth lov–" I begin, but he dips his finger inside of me deeper, and I forget how to breathe, let alone speak.

"You don't need to say anything. I wasn't searching for any affirmations," he adds, his smile slowly fading as heat and lust glimmers in his eyes. "In fact, the only sound I want coming out of your mouth are those pretty little moans that turn me on so much. So will you let me touch you, kiss you, taste you?"

"Only if you let me do that to you in return. This isn't one sided, Dalton. If you're going to pleasure me, then I want to plea-sure you too," I reply, drugged by his attention, caught up in the moment, needing his touch, wanting his kisses, wanting to taste him.

"Good girl," he replies as he removes his hand from my pulsing core then sits up, sliding off the end of the bed. I can't help but stare at his beautiful body, at the way his erection bobs between his thighs as he stares down at me. "Take your dress off, wife," he orders.

I bite my lip, drawing upright to do as he commands, slipping off my dress until I'm left in just my lace knickers. I hadn't worn a bra yesterday, the humidity making it too uncomfortable, and Dalton's gaze flares with more heat at my bare breasts, his gaze slowly lowering to my knickers.

"Those too."

He holds his hand out to me and I wriggle out of my panties, passing them to him. Dalton bunches them up in his hand and lifts them to his nose, breathing in deep.

"Fuck, you smell delicious," he grinds out, before lowering his hand to his cock, and using my knickers to fist his length.

I gasp at the eroticism of the moment, how he stands there and fucks himself with my arousal-stained panties. "Jesus," I mutter, my body lighting up with desire.

"Do you like watching me pleasure myself?"

"Yes," I breathe, turned on beyond belief.

"Good, but we're both going to enjoy this more," he grinds out, dropping my underwear to the floor, and grasping my ankles with a wicked grin on his face as he pulls me to the end of the bed.

My legs hang over the mattress, my toes grazing the floor as he parts my knees, licking his lips as he stares at my pussy. As much as I want him to eat me out, I want to taste him more, so I push upright before he has a chance to drop to his knees.

"It's my turn," I say, grabbing his cock gently before he has time to protest.

"Fuck, Daisy," he mutters, his chin dropping to his chest as he looks down at me, at my fingers grasping him.

"This isn't just about me," I remind him, gently fisting his cock. "I want to make you feel good too."

"You already make me feel good, Daisy. Just being in your presence makes me feel so fucking good," he admits, resting his hand on my head, stroking my hair. "I fucking adore you."

My heart clenches as I drag in a sharp breath. "Are you saying you love me?" I whisper, half-joking, half-serious.

Our eyes clash, but when he doesn't answer, I simply smile then press a gentle kiss against the head of his cock.

"Fuck," he groans, jerking in my hands as his fingers slide into my hair and tighten around the strands.

Emboldened, I tentatively lick his crown, tasting the saltiness of his pre-cum, humming around the taste before I lick the round head of his cock.

"Jesus, fuck," he mutters, eyelids drooping as he looks down at me, and I look up at him. "Look at you. So fucking pretty, so fucking mine. My pretty, little flower."

"Flower?" I question, smiling as I brush my lips against his cock.

"You're not just a single petal, Daisy. You're a whole fucking flower, and perfectly, wholly mine."

His words fill me with pride, with lust, and I take him further down my throat, suctioning my lips around his cock as he thrusts gently into my mouth, groaning. The noises he makes turn me on, and I drag my lips and tongue back up his length, swiping the head of his cock over my lips before gently gripping him in my hand and licking him from base to tip, over and over again, making sure I pay particular attention to his crown and the thick vein running beneath his skin.

"I've never seen anything more fucking erotic than you sucking on my cock, Daisy. It feels so fucking good, so fucking right," he exclaims, palming the back of my head, urging me to take him into my mouth.

I smile up at him, a moan releasing from my lips at the almost feral way he stares at me as I take him into my mouth. He's trembling, but I can tell he's holding back, that he wants to sink himself deeper. He's so big, I don't know whether he'll fit without making me gag. As though sensing my thoughts, he gently strokes my hair as I caress him with my tongue.

"Put your other hand on my hip, Daisy. If I go too deep, tap me, and I will pull back," he directs me.

Following his instructions, I rest my hand on his hip, the other still stroking the base of his cock, which is now slippery and wet with my saliva.

"That's my good girl," he mutters, sliding his hands into my hair, behind my ear. "As you take me deeper, breathe in, it will help."

I nod softly, trusting him to not force himself down my throat, the feeling of power and control overwhelming me as his mouth drops open and his eyes roll into the back of his head. My mind is hazy with desire as I suck on him, tasting the saltiness of his pre-cum and the muskiness of his arousal. He continues to gently thrust into my mouth, his hips moving with a rhythm that synchronises with my breathing. Every now and then my hand presses firmly into his hip, letting him know when he goes too deep, but he's gentle and attentive, always pulling back when necessary.

Pleasure courses through my body, my pussy growing wetter with each lick and suck of his cock, and as much as I want to touch myself whilst pleasuring him, I keep my focus on his erection, wanting to please him, to make sure he enjoys this just as much as I do.

"That's it, wife, take my cock. You take me so well," he groans, his words only adding to the intensity of the moment. I whimper around him, my clit pulsing, aching to be touched as heat climbs up my chest and neck.

His eyes snap open at the sound of my whimpers, and with

blazing eyes filled with lust he says, "Do you like sucking my cock?"

I nod, the slippery sounds of me sucking him off turning me on.

"Good," he moans. "Because I fucking love it too. I love seeing my cock slipping between your plump lips, how your skin blushes a pretty pink for me. Look at you, so fucking willing to take me deep."

Encouraged by his praise, I take him deeper, the soft tip of his cock hitting the back of my throat briefly before he pulls back. My nostrils flare as I breathe in deep.

"That's it, just like that," he stutters out, his chest heaving as both of his hands gently hold my head, guiding my movement as his thrusts become more and more erratic.

"I'm close, Daisy. I'm so fucking close. You need to let me go. You need to let me go before I come down your throat," he gasps, a deep guttural sound ripping out of his chest as his dick seems to grow impossibly large in my mouth.

I pull back, panting as I stare up at him with wide eyes. "Dalton," I whimper, my hand falling to my crotch, needing to touch myself, to relieve some of the building pressure between my legs.

His eyes flare with heat, noticing what I'm about to do, and he growls, fisting his cock almost violently.

"Lie on the bed. Open your legs wide. Do it now!" he cries, squeezing his cock tight as I shuffle backwards on the bed, my cheeks flaming as I widen my legs, giving him a full view of my slick pussy.

"Fuck, look at your pretty cunt, so wet, so pink, so fucking beautiful," he groans, still fisting his dick as he kneels between my parted legs. My hand flies to my clit, but he shakes his head. "Don't you dare touch what's mine," he demands, glaring at me, fierce in his lust. "I'm going to cover you with my come, Daisy, then I'm going to use my fingers to fuck you with it."

"Oh God," I whimper as my hands fall away.

"Say my name, wife!" he demands. "I want you to say my name when I cover you with my seed, and finger-fuck you with it until you come so fucking hard it will obliterate every memory of other men and replace them with me."

"Dalton," I cry, wound up tight, almost coming from his words alone.

"That's it, say it again," he grinds out, the veins in his forearms and hands bulging as he relentlessly strokes himself.

"Dalton. Please come. Please come all over me," I say, gasping at how dirty that sounds. "I want you to come all over me."

"Yes, wife," he groans, a deep guttural sound that seems to vibrate the air between us as his hips thrust and his cum spurts into the air, splattering across my stomach and chest in thick, white streams.

The slickness of his cum, and the sound of his heaving rasps as he falls forward pressing his hands into the mattress either side of my head, makes my pussy throb with need. The sight of my husband, his cock still pumping, his eyes pressed shut in ecstacy and his face contorted in lust, sends my arousal soaring. Once again my hand moves to my pussy, and I press my finger against my clit, almost bucking off the bed from that slight touch.

"Don't you dare," he growls, his eyes snapping open as he reaches between us, knocking my hand away, replacing it with his own as he slides two fingers into my soaked core in one firm thrust. "This is mine as much as it is yours, and now I'm going to fill it with my cum."

"Yes," I hiss, writhing beneath him, not caring how desperate I must look.

As he continues to thrust his fingers inside me, he rises upwards and uses his other hand to scoop up some of his cum. Our eyes meet and the possession in his has my heart rate thundering, matching the building orgasm deep inside of me.

"I'm going to stuff you full of my seed, wife. I'm going to fill you up with every last drop, and you're going to take it all. You're going to take my seed and you're going to come so fucking hard that the stars behind your eyelids are going to be brighter than any in the night sky," he exclaims, chest heaving, arms flexing, eyes blazing.

"Fill me up, Dalton. Make me come," I growl, so close to free-falling. His words like fuel to the fire building inside of me, making my whole body clench in anticipation.

Dalton smiles wickedly and removes his hand from between my legs, replacing them with his cum-soaked fingers and plunging them inside of me. I gasp as he works them in and out with fervour. I writhe beneath him as he scoops up more cum and coats his fingers with the sticky liquid once again, alternating his fingers, making sure I take every last drop.

"Take what I give you," he says, his voice pitched in lust, his expression twisted with desire and dominance.

"Yes, Dalton. Yes!" I cry, trying to hold on to reality as my body trembles with the intensity of my impending climax.

"Call me your *husband*, wife," he commands.

"Fuck me with your cum, husband," I cry out, my orgasm barrelling out of nowhere, a cascade of bright white stars bursting behind my closed eyelids as I come.

My orgasm is intense. Powerful, and I feel it unravel deep inside as my internal muscles clench around his fingers, drawing his sperm deep into my womb.

"That's it," he soothes, as tears trickle from my eyes. "Take everything I have to give. Take it all."

I'm not crying because I'm sad. I'm crying because I'm so over-whelmed, so overtaken by lust and desire, connection and pure animal need. It's all that I've ever wanted.

I'm a mess of emotions, of rawness, as my orgasm ebbs away, leaving me satiated, depleted, and thoroughly and blissfully content as he drapes himself over me, his still hard cock pressing against my lower stomach.

"You're mine..." he says, his voice thick, and as I look up at him, at the almost shocked expression on his face, I know that I am his. That I belong to Dalton Gunn, and that he belongs to me.

"As you are mine," I whisper back.

CHAPTER TWENTY-EIGHT

The next week of our honeymoon passes in a haze of laughter, conversation, and shared orgasms. Daisy and I spend all of our time together, and not a minute passes without being in each other's company. We don't fuck, and it isn't because I don't want to, it's because the next time I bury myself inside of Daisy I want to do it out of love.

Right now I'm still learning, still grappling with my feelings, still trying to unravel years worth of trauma from never having felt love from my parents. All I know for certain is that if I could ever love someone, it would be her. Bottom line is, I'm willing to do whatever it takes to be the man she needs.

"Hey, Dalton, would you like to have dinner out tonight, or stay in?" Daisy asks, interrupting my thoughts as she steps out onto the deck, her hair piled up on top of her head, her body wrapped in a long white towel after taking a shower.

The sun has already slipped past the horizon, and the air seems cooler tonight than it has been since we've arrived. In the distance I can hear a rumble of thunder, and the first spots of rain begin to hit the deck in huge, fat droplets.

"I guess we're staying in tonight," I say, pushing back my chair and taking Daisy's hand in mine, leading her inside. "Looks like a storm's coming in."

"We can call for room service, or if you'd like I can throw something together? There's still plenty of cold cuts in the fridge and fresh fruit. I'm not all that hungry anyway, my stomach is a little bloated from all the overindulging," she says with a soft laugh.

"Or maybe it's the baby I've put inside of you," I joke, knowing it's a real possibility. She laughs, her eyes softening at the thought as her hand absentmindedly rubs her belly. "You really want this child, don't you?"

"You don't?" she asks, leaning against the kitchen island as she regards me.

"I want to make you happy..." My voice trails off as I consider her question.

"But?" She winces a little, and I hate seeing her expression change to one of uncertainty.

"No buts. I want to make you happy. I like the idea of you growing our child inside of you," I admit. "I also happen to like all the occasions we've been practising to make that happen these past few weeks."

"Me too," she agrees with a soft whisper.

"Want to try some more?" I offer, stepping towards her, my fingers trailing over the bare skin of her arm.

She cocks her head to the side, a smile tilting up her lips. "We've barely been out of the bedroom this past week. I'm beginning to wonder if you have any sperm left."

"Believe me, I have plenty."

"Is that so?" she laughs as my fingers edge beneath the towel, tugging on it.

"Uh huh," I murmur, easing open the towel, sucking in a ragged breath at her bare skin and tight nipples.

My fingers trail around her breasts, circling them, but not cupping them as I draw ever decreasing circles across the swell of her tits.

"You're very good at this," she says, her breath hitching as I pinch her nipples, tugging on them.

"I've had a lot of practice," I say, instantly regretting my words when she stiffens.

"Don't remind me."

"Are you jealous, wife?"

"A little," she admits.

"You've no need to be. No one has affected me the way you do," I reply, leaning over her as I stand between her parted legs, and brace my hands on the island on either side of her body.

"That's good to know... *husband*," she adds, knowing full well what hearing her say that does to me.

"I like being your husband," I say, pressing my lips against the curve of her neck, and my words into her skin.

"I like it too," she replies, sighing as I feather kisses over her shoulder blade.

"And I especially like making you come."

"I enjoy that as well. So, so much..."

Her breath catches as I dip downwards and circle her nipple with my tongue, before suctioning it into my mouth. She arches into my touch, her body responding beautifully as I cup her other breast, my thumb circling her nipples, eliciting another soft moan. Still sucking on her, I reach between her legs, swiping my fingers between her slit, gathering her wetness before circling her clit.

"Fuck, you're always so wet for me. Do you realise how much that turns me on, knowing what I do to you?"

"I hadn't noticed," she laughs, dropping her hand to my erection, squeezing it gently.

"I'm always so fucking hard for you, Daisy. I can't get enough."

She whimpers as I enter her tight cunt, plunging my finger in and out of her in a steady, even rhythm, loving how she blushes for me. It makes her seem so fucking pure, and yet she's a vixen, so eager to please me, to receive pleasure.

"Get up onto the counter," I demand, removing my hand from between her legs as I grip her around the waist and hoist her onto the marble countertop before she's even had a chance to do it herself.

"What are you doing?" she asks, as I round the counter and head towards the fridge, pulling open the door and gathering the freshly cut fruit left over from our lunch earlier, placing the plate on the surface beside her.

"You want to eat right now?" she asks, eyeing me with raised brows.

"Yes," I reply, picking up a slither of papaya, and returning to her. "Now lie back."

She doesn't hesitate, curious, yet willing.

Lowering the slice of papaya to her lips I say, "Open your mouth, taste."

She parts her lips and I slide the slice of papaya between them. She hums, her eyes never once leaving mine as she tastes the sweet juices.

"Don't take a bite, just yet," I order, pulling it free, remnants of juice on her lips as I lower my mouth and kiss her softly. She reaches up to grasp my face, deepening the kiss, but I pull back shaking my head. "You kiss me like you can't get enough."

"That's because I can't," she admits as I trail the papaya over her chin and down her neck, loving how the juice glistens on her skin, leaving a slick trail for me to taste.

"Good," I mutter, my attention focussing on her face as I swirl the papaya over her erect nipples, chasing the juice with my tongue. The sweetness explodes on my tongue as I draw her nipple into my mouth, sucking on her.

"That feels so good," she whispers as I pull back and drag the piece of fruit lower, dipping it into her belly button before heading to her slick pussy, my tongue lapping at the trail of juice.

"Open your legs for me," I order, and she gasps as I swipe the ripened fruit gently on either side of her pussy, right up high on the tops of her thighs.

"Now *this* is a meal fit for the heir to a billion pound fortune," I mutter, a wicked glint in my eye.

"*This* is filthy," she murmurs.

"Yes. Yes, it is," I reply, before lowering my mouth to the trail of juice, tasting the sweet papaya before licking her glistening seam. "Fuck, that's good," I mutter.

"Oh my, ahhhh..." she cries as I repeat the action over and over again, my tongue lapping at the juices the sweet fruit leaves behind, before swiping my tongue through her pussy, and the wetness her body produces from my attention.

Rising upwards, I slide the papaya into her mouth. "Eat. I'm going to feed you until you're full and you can't take any more, then I'm going to make you come."

She opens her mouth willingly, eating the slice of fruit as I reach for a strawberry, taking a small bite before I swirl it over each nipple.

I can't help but grin at her moans, lowering my mouth to her core, tasting, licking, fucking her pretty cunt with my tongue, all the while using the strawberry to soak her nipples before feeding the pulpy fruit to her. With each slice of fruit, I do the same until all we're left with is a thick slice of apple, the length and width of my finger. It's not as soft as the other fruits, and I lift it to my mouth, sucking on it, the tangy sweetness exploding on my tongue.

"I'm going to make you come now, wife," I say, pinching it between my finger and thumb, and dropping my gaze to her hole that drips so beautifully with her wetness.

She looks up at me wide-eyed as I gently slide the piece of apple into her mouth. She groans, her lips suctioning around the fruit, her skin flushing as I lower my mouth to her clit and suck on it, all the while gently fucking her mouth with the slice of apple.

"Dalton!" she cries, twisting her head to the side, the piece of apple discarded on the countertop as I grab her sticky breast and tease her clit with my tongue. "Please."

Her cries turn me on so fucking much that I reach between my legs and shove my hand into my swimshorts, fisting my cock, twisting it roughly. The taste of her, the sounds she makes, the beautiful way she trusts me, turns me on so fucking that it isn't long until I feel my own orgasm building at the base of my spine, my balls drawing tight against my body.

"I'm so close," she whines, grabbing my head, pressing herself against me, needing more, just like I need more.

I want her so fucking badly. So badly that I could give into my desire and fuck her now, but I don't. Instead I eat her out like a ravenous man, pushing two fingers inside of her with one firm thrust.

"Then come for me, wife," I grind out against her.

"Please... Oh, Dalton. Please, please, please!" she cries, as I crook my fingers and stroke that tender, spongy spot deep inside of her.

"Come. Come now!"

And she does, right when I demand her too.

Her internal walls tighten, her back arches as she cries out my name, coming long and hard. The sound is like a shot of pleasure straight to my dick, and I rear upwards, still finger fucking her as I awkwardly push down my swim shorts, and rise up onto the balls of my feet, white, hot strings off cum erupting from my cock as I empty my seed all over her pussy and lower stomach.

"Jesus," I groan, my whole body fucking trembling, my hips

jerking, my cock strangled by my fist as I milk every last drop of cum from my dick. "Look at the mess I've made of you."

Dropping my dick, I swirl my fingers in my cum, sliding it over her clit so it drips between her folds and onto my waiting fingers, then I push it inside of her, loving the slick sounds, and the desperate pants that fall from her lips.

"The way your pussy weeps for me. Fuck, Daisy, I can't get enough," I admit, my skin heating, my damn heart swelling in my chest as this feeling of euphoria washes over me. I've never, ever, felt this way before. It's an unfamiliar feeling, strange, frightening. That most of all. Yet despite the fear, I don't stop. I embrace it.

"Dalton," she whimpers, pushing up onto shaky arms, her tangled hair falling about her face in a halo as she blinks up at me.

"You're..." my voice trails off as I fail to find the words to describe how fucking stunning she is, how helpless I feel in the moment. All I can do is pull her towards me, needing her chest to chest. Placing my hands on her hips, I drag her to the edge of the counter. "Wrap your arms and legs around me. I'm going to clean you up."

Gripping her tight against me, I step out of my swim shorts, kicking them aside, then I lift her into my arms and stride towards the ensuite bathroom in her bedroom. She softens in my hold, her check pressed against my shoulder as I carry her.

I'm still hard, still fucking desperate to sink inside of her, and my dick is teasingly close to her entrance. All it would take is pinning her against the wall and one firm thrust of my hips and I'd be inside of her. It takes every last scrap of self-restraint not to do that. Instead, I step into the shower cubicle and reach for the tap, turning it on. As warm water falls from the showerhead over us both, I gently drop her to her feet.

"Dalton," she whispers, her hands pressed against my chest as she looks up at me, droplets of water cascading over her upturned face.

Yet she doesn't continue, captured in the moment as I am, the heat from the shower is nothing compared to the warmth between us. I drop my gaze to her freckles, slowly counting them one by one, needing a moment to centre myself, to calm the racing beat of my heart.

Thirty-eight. She has thirty-eight freckles dusting her nose and cheeks, each one as beautiful as the next. Then, when my heart has finally calmed to a more even rhythm, I lift my gaze to meet hers, only for it to skip a beat at the intense way she looks at me. I see something in her eyes, something that makes my heart stutter then stall, something I want to desperately lean into, to welcome, yet I shake my head.

"Don't say it," I whisper, cupping her cheek, brushing my thumb over her bottom lip.

"But I think I'm falling..."

"Please, Daisy. Not yet," I whisper, catching her mumbled words with my lips, kissing her deeply, overwhelmed by the eddying emotions swirling inside my chest. When I reluctantly pull back, her expression falls, and I see a hint of disappointment in her eyes.

"Let me wash you clean," I say, grabbing the bottle of shower wash and squeezing some into my hand, needing the distraction from my own tumbling thoughts as the scent of jasmine and coconut lifts into the air.

"Okay," she whispers, a soft sigh parting her lips as I slide my hands over her body, my touch gentle, my heart pounding, my chest heaving as I battle with myself and the tumultuous feelings that are beginning to overwhelm me. There's nothing sexual about the way I touch her, it's more of a comforting feeling, for me, for her, and somehow it's way more intense.

"Loving someone is also taking care of them," she had said to me, her words echoing in my mind as I lather up more soap and

gently wash her hair. "*Sex is wonderful, of course it is, but kindness, care, empathy, tenderness, that's a huge part of it too.*"

She's right. She's so fucking right.

The truth of her words hang sodden between us. They rain over my skin, cleansing me, washing away all the past hurts, the loneliness I've felt buried deep beneath my arrogance and vanity, my selfishness and greed. The old me, the man I was, is shredded with every water droplet, leaving someone shiny and new, someone achingly vulnerable.

"You're right," I murmur.

"What?" she questions.

"Nothing, just thinking out loud," I reply, tucking those thoughts deep within me, holding them close, keeping them safe until I'm ready to set them free.

Once she's thoroughly clean, I wash myself as Daisy watches. Her gaze is heated, filled with so much longing that I almost drop to my knees and beg for her forgiveness. There are so many unspoken words between us, but I don't need to hear her say that she thinks she's falling in love with me, when I *feel* it. I feel her tentative love, and it scares me to death. It scares me to death because, God help me, I think I'm falling too.

"CAN I GET YOU ANYTHING?" I ask half an hour later as I step back into Daisy's bedroom, dressed in a pair of loose linen shorts and a white t-shirt. She's lying on the bed, dressed in her cotton pyjamas, her bedside lamp filling the darkened room with a soft glow, a thin sheet pulled up over her body as she looks over at me.

Outside the air trembles with thunder as sheets of rain fall heavily, the sky through her window lit momentarily with lightning.

"I'm fine. I think I might just go to sleep if that's okay with you?" she replies softly.

"Daisy, I'm sorry…"

"Don't be. I understand. This is overwhelming for me too. I need to just sit with this for a moment. I need to…" She heaves out a breath, looking so fucking vulnerable that I hate myself for not being honest with her. I should tell her I'm falling too. Why am I so fucking terrified of speaking the truth?

Maybe it's because I'm still uncertain that what I'm beginning to feel is actually love. Maybe it's because I'm not certain that what Daisy feels for me is love, but simply a culmination of lust, desire and her desperation for it. I want her to be certain. *I* need to be certain, and I won't say those three words until I am. I won't make love to her until I am.

"Rest. I'm going to sit in the living room for a while, okay?"

"Okay," she nods.

"See you in the morning?" I add in hesitation.

"Sure," she replies, then she rolls over onto her side and closes her eyes.

For the next couple of hours, I watch the storm roll across the ocean. The waves churned up by the wind, crashing against the shore in a hypnotic rhythm as the sound blends with the rumble of thunder overhead. Lightning brightens the sky in erratic bursts, illuminating the darkened living room briefly, the only other light coming from the lamp that's still switched on in Daisy's room.

As I drag in a shaky breath, the air seems to be suffused with a heavy kind of tension, mirroring the conflict raging within me. I can't seem to shake the memory of Daisy's vulnerable expression, etched as it was with hurt and confusion. It makes me question everything. Am I truly falling in love with Daisy or is this just a fleeting infatuation that will fade with time? Even as I think those thoughts, my gut churns, the thought of Daisy ever leaving me causing a sharp pain in my chest as I'm reminded of my own mother walking away and never looking back. I loved her too... I see that now. I see that I had once loved, that I knew how, and my mother's abandonment turned that love into something bitter and painful until I couldn't help but run from it, closing myself off from the possibility of ever loving someone despite searching for the feeling every time I fucked a woman.

That's the truth of it.

"Fuck," I mutter, swiping a hand through my hair.

Needing some fresh air, I push up from my seat and open the patio doors, the wind whipping through my hair, carrying with it the scent of rain and storm-churned ocean. Just as I'm about to step out onto the deck, a sudden bolt of lightning strikes somewhere close by and the whole area is pitched into darkness, the lights in the neighbouring bungalow suddenly cut out. I glance over my shoulder, noticing the light in Daisy's room has gone out too. Seconds later I hear her scream out my name.

"Dalton!"

I bolt towards her, knocking into furniture as the fear in her voice propels me forward. With my heart racing in my chest, I burst into her room just as another flash of lightning lights up the space momentarily before pitching it back into darkness once more.

"No, no, no," she cries, reaching for the bedside lamp, flicking the switch on and off. "It's so dark."

"Daisy, I'm here. You're okay," I say, climbing onto the bed and reaching for her. She grasps for me, the darkness enveloping us both. "It's the storm. I think it's taken the power out."

"No," she cries, her fear palpable as she climbs into my arms, curling her body around mine as she presses her chest to my chest as though trying to bury herself beneath my skin.

"Shh, it's okay. I'm here. I'm here," I say, rubbing my hand up and down her back as I try to soothe her, to calm her fears, but she continues to tremble, a shuddering sob releasing from her lips.

"I c-can't go through this again."

She buries her face against my neck and I can feel the wetness of her tears as she sobs. The sound she makes is heartbroken as she clings to me. It terrifies me, her fear. It makes my throat close over and a tightness forms in my chest.

"Hold on to me," I say, feeling an overwhelming need to shield her from the demons that haunt her.

"Don't let me go," she whimpers.

"I'm not letting you go," I promise, holding her tighter against my chest. She lets out a shuddering sob, my goddamn heart aching at the sound.

"I'm scared."

"I know, but I'm here with you. Nothing can hurt you while I'm here. I promise," I murmur, meaning it, wanting her to know that I will protect her. I will. Whatever it takes.

"I hate this," she groans, trembling, her voice weak. "I hate that they did this to me."

"Oh Daisy," I whisper, pressing a kiss against her hair, wanting to take her fear away more than I've wanted to do anything.

"They hurt me so badly, Dalton. They hurt me, and I can't... I feel so lost sometimes," she chokes out. "I wish I didn't remember. I've tried so hard to forget. But here in the dark I'm thrown back into that room again, cold, alone, in pain, terrified..."

"Jesus, Daisy." My words are thick, raw, and I feel the prick of white hot tears in my eyes. I don't fucking cry. I never cry, and yet here I am feeling the sting, hurting for her, with her.

"Just hold me..." she whispers, her voice so quiet I can barely hear it above the thunder and lightning.

"All night long," I promise.

She nods, her body shifting with mine as I lay us both down, drawing her into my side, my body lined up with hers, chest to chest, breath mingling, hearts racing. Reaching up I cup her cheek, pressing a tentative kiss against her mouth.

She sobs, clutching hold of me, falling into the kiss. Just like that night she woke from a nightmare, I feel this intense need to replace her fear with something else, with *me*. And so I kiss her. I kiss her with a profound sense of needing to soothe her, to calm her, to show her that I'm here, that I won't abandon her like her parents did, that I won't hurt her like they did.

Our kiss deepens, and it's raw and beautiful and fucking heart-wrenchingly painful in a way that makes me quake for her. Not because it's wrong, but because it's so fucking right. I kiss her until her sobs become whimpers, and her tears stop falling. It's only then that I pull back, needing to stop, because if I don't I could so easily slip inside of her, and I made a promise to myself and to her that the next time I did that it would be because I was certain that I loved her.

Instead, I tug her against my chest and hold her. We stay like that, wrapped around each other for what feels like an eternity as the storm continues to howl outside. Gradually, Daisy's trembling subsides and she lifts her head from my shoulder.

"Thank you," she says softly, her voice barely above a whisper.

"I don't ever want you to feel afraid," I reply, cupping her cheek, barely making out the expression on her face as she looks at me with her cheeks stained with tears. "I want you to feel safe with me."

"I do, Dalton. These past weeks..." Her voice trails off as she heaves in a breath. "These past few weeks have been magical, and I do feel safe with you. I do."

"Good," I reply, pressing my lips against her forehead.

"Promise you'll stay with me tonight."

"Of course, I'm not going anywhere. You have me, Daisy. You have me," I promise vehemently, and it's the closest I've ever come to saying I love you.

She leans into me, her body relaxing as I hold on to her. Before I know it, she's fallen asleep in my embrace, her gentle breaths comforting against my skin. But I can't seem to drift off like she does. Instead, I spend the next few hours awake, my thoughts replaying the events of the past few weeks, hell, the past few years. Deep inside I know that Daisy has become an intrinsic part of my life, someone who has woven herself into the very fabric of my being, and ultimately, I can't see a future without her in it.

CHAPTER TWENTY-NINE

I wake up the next morning feeling a heavy ache in my stomach as bright, startling sunlight filters into the bedroom. It's as though the storm was just a distant dream and my fear was nothing but a nightmare. Groaning, I shift upwards, careful not to wake Dalton who is slumbering beside me, his soft breaths coasting over the bare skin of my arm. Reaching for him, I run my fingers lightly over his shoulder, so grateful he was there for me last night, feeling a swell of... *love*, expanding in my chest. It's a scary feeling, but I feel the truth of it nevertheless. Did I question myself about this feeling for hours before the storm took hold last night? Yes, I did. But do I know that it's real? Absolutely. This isn't lust decorated in false love. It's true and pure, and I won't deny it to myself a second longer.

I'm in love with Dalton Gunn.

Shifting, I feel a wetness between my legs, and despite the joy I feel, my heart sinks a little knowing without needing to look that I'm bleeding. Pulling back the covers, I slide off the bed, noticing a small patch of deep red on the pristine white sheets and the cotton of my pale blue pyjama shorts.

"Shit," I murmur, padding towards the bathroom, a deep ache from my period spreading across my stomach as I lift up the toilet seat and pull down my pyjama shorts and underwear.

My periods have always been on the heavy side, and this time is no different. When I think about it, I realise that my last period was just before I moved in with Dalton, over seven weeks ago now. They've always been irregular, but it's never really concerned me, it's just a part of who I am. Yet here I am staring at the blood, disappointment blooming inside my chest, and even though I know that it's foolish to believe that I could fall pregnant so quickly, I can't help but feel a little sad about it.

"Daisy?" Dalton calls, a question in his voice, and my cheeks flame as I realise that he's probably spotted the blood.

"Just give me a moment," I reply, relieving myself and wiping between my legs.

"Are you okay? There's blood," he says, approaching the bathroom.

"Don't come in. I need to clean up," I say quickly, sliding off my stained shorts, and reaching for a towel, wrapping it around my waist as he pushes open the bathroom door.

"You're bleeding," he repeats, concern etching his features with a frown.

"Dalton, I'm fine. It's just my period." My cheeks heat as I gather up my dirty clothes, but he doesn't leave. Instead he steps into the bathroom, eyeing me.

"You've got your period?" he asks, almost as if he can't believe it himself.

"I'm a woman. It happens," I shrug, smiling to cover up another rush of disappointment.

Dalton blinks a few times before shaking his head. "Of course it does. Sorry. It's just..."

"You've never spent long enough with a woman to have to deal with situations like this? Don't worry, I'll call room service and get them to change the bedding," I reply, wincing at how that sounds.

"That wasn't what I was thinking at all," he mutters, swiping a hand through his hair.

"What then?" I question softly.

"I guess I thought…" he mumbles, swiping a hand through his hair.

"That I'd fall pregnant straight away?" I smile then, trying to ease the sudden tension between us. "It doesn't happen like that. I mean, for most people anyway."

"Maybe… I… Shit, sorry. I'm not sure how to handle this."

"A cup of tea would be good," I offer.

"Of course, yes. Let me get that for you," he says, hovering in the doorway, sleep still lingering around his eyes. My heart tugs at that, at how I've seen him polished and smart in his business suits, confident and sure in his motorbike leathers, relaxed and playful in casual clothes, and mussed-up with sleep. I like knowing I've seen so many sides to him.

"What is it?"

"So, erm, are you in pain? Should I get you some painkillers?"

I nod, feeling another twinge in my stomach. "I'd appreciate that."

"Okay, sure. Do you need anything else?"

"Could you grab me some clean underwear and a sundress, please?" I ask him.

"Sure, hang on."

A moment later he returns with the items, passing them to me.

"Thank you," I murmur as he steps closer and presses a kiss against my forehead, his hand sliding into my hair. For a moment we stand pressed against each other with his lips brushing against my skin, his fingers coiled in my hair. I let out a soft sigh, wanting nothing more than to curl into him, to tell him that I love him.

I love you.

But I don't of course, knowing that he isn't ready to hear the words, that he isn't at the same place I am, even though last night it felt like maybe he was, maybe he is. I push that thought away.

"I'm going to take a shower now," I say, and he steps back, giving me one last lingering look before stepping out of the bathroom and closing the door behind him.

Fifteen minutes later I'm clean and dressed, thankful that I hadn't forgotten to bring some tampons with me. When I step out of the bathroom I notice that bedding has been stripped and warm air filters into the room as I go in search of Dalton. I find him sitting outside, nursing a cup of coffee as I approach.

Gently pressing my fingers against his bare shoulder as I pass him by, I take a seat at the table, noticing a couple of painkillers on a side plate and a glass of freshly squeezed orange juice, as well as the cup of tea I requested.

"Did the maid come already?" I ask, picking up the pills and popping them in my mouth as I wash them down with the orange juice.

"No. I stripped the bed, and left them folded by the front door. They'll be here in a few minutes to collect them and change the bedding."

"You stripped the bed?" I ask, a little surprised if I'm honest.

"It's no big deal, Daisy," he shrugs. "Besides, I didn't want you to feel embarrassed or anything."

"I'm not embarrassed, but you seem a little uncomfortable," I point out.

"No, I'm not. Sorry, this is new to me, that's all. Like you said, I've never been with a woman long enough to be around them when this happens."

"Ahh," I reply, trying not to laugh at the heat that creeps up his cheeks. "Well, I guess you'd better get used to it because this will be happening a lot more in the future."

"Not if my little soldiers have got anything to say about it," he replies, smirking a little as he peers over at me behind a swathe of auburn hair.

"Your little soldiers?" I snort out a laugh. "Are you talking about your sperm, Dalton?"

He grins. "What can I say, they'll be marching straight to your womb the second they get the chance."

"They will, will they?"

"Yep," he replies, popping the 'p' with a wink.

I laugh, feeling a rush of warmth at his playful teasing, finding myself so at ease in his company. After all the years of hatred between us I would never have believed this was possible, yet it feels almost effortless falling for him. Despite the slight sting when he asked me not to reveal my feelings last night, I understood where he was coming from, that he needs time, and now we have it. He wouldn't have asked for my help if he didn't want to explore these emotions and our growing bond, which gives me hope that one day he will reciprocate my love. I should be more scared than I am, but strangely, I'm not.

"Well, let's hope they're good swimmers then," I tease back, taking a sip of my tea, trying to hide the rush of heat flooding my cheeks at the thought of him filling me with his cum.

Dalton chuckles. "Trust me, my little soldiers are top notch."

I giggle. "I'll take your word for it."

We sit in comfortable silence for a while, enjoying our drinks and watching the ocean lap at the sea gently as though it wasn't trying to gouge out huge piles of sand last night during the storm.

Last night I'd spiralled fast and if it wasn't for Dalton, I dread to think where my memories would've taken me. I shiver at the thought, my past not quite locked back into that box I keep it in.

"Hey, are you cold? Do you need a cardigan?" Dalton asks me, interrupting my thoughts.

"It's ninety degrees, Dalton. I'm just fine," I say.

"You were shivering," he points out. "Are you in pain? Should I get a doctor or something?" He frowns, moving to stand as though he's about to storm off and do just that.

"No, honestly, I'm fine," I say, reaching for his arm and tugging on it so that he sits back down.

"Daisy..." he says, a warning note to his voice.

"Dalton. Please, I'm fine."

"Then what is it?"

I heave out a breath. "Last night... I..."

"You don't have to talk about it if you don't want to," he offers.

"It's not that. Just sometimes after that happens, it takes me a while to readjust, to slip back into feeling like myself and not that desperately broken child I once was. Doesn't help that I'm on my period either," I admit, wincing a little at the dull ache.

"I hate what they did to you," he says, anger laced within his words.

"I do too, but please, can we not talk about it anymore? It's better that way. I don't want to remember that time. I want to forget it."

"Of course. I'm sorry..." he apologies, his voice trailing off as his gaze drops from my face to my stomach where my hand is pressed gently against it. "It's our last few hours together before we have to catch our flight this afternoon. I wanted to take you somewhere, but if you'd rather stay here and rest, that's okay too."

"I don't need to rest. Let's do whatever you were thinking."

"But you're in pain."

"It's manageable."

"I don't want you to have to manage it," he says a little gruffly. "I don't want you to be in pain."

"It's no big deal. You get used to it. I'm okay, truly," I say, reaching for him, but as my hand presses against his, he reaches for me and tugs me into his arms.

"C'mere," he says, and I let out a surprised laugh as I drop onto his lap.

"Are you feeling okay, Dalton?"

"I don't like to see you hurting," he says quietly, and even as his large hand presses against my stomach gently I know he's not talking about my period pain this time, but how I was last night.

"You helped ease that hurt," I whisper, cupping his face and clutching him to my chest. "Thank you."

He nods, his fingers coasting over my stomach, rubbing gentle circles over the cotton of my sundress. "I feel protective of you, Daisy."

"I know," I reply, stroking his stubbled check, loving how his arm curls around my back, how comfortable I feel in his arms, how *loved*. Maybe I'm wrong to assume that, but I can't help it. I do feel loved in this moment, and even if he's not in love with me, right now his empathy and kindness is enough.

"I always have..." His voice trails off as he shifts a little, looking up at me.

"I see that now," I admit.

"You do?"

"Yes. Though, admittedly, every time you interfered with my love life before I thought you were just being an arse."

He lets out a soft laugh. "I can't deny that I was an arse too."

We fall silent, and I feel another surge of love unfurling in my chest, this connection between us tethered not just by the few weeks we've spent together since I moved into his home, but by years of shared memories. Somehow they've woven us together, I just hope they're strong enough to keep us that way.

"Thirty-eight," he murmurs eventually.

I frown. "Thirty-eight?"

"Yes," he replies, lifting his hand and gently swiping his finger across my cheek, over the bridge of my nose and across the other cheek. "You have thirty-eight freckles scattered across your face."

A smile pulls up my lips, as my heart doubles in size at his words. "You've counted them?"

"I've counted them," he agrees.

"You know you really are good at making a girl fall in–"

But he cuts me off with a gentle press of his lips against mine, and I don't protest, I simply curl into his arms, kissing him back.

"THIS IS STUNNING!" I exclaim, stepping onto the grassy area that leads to a dozen rocks circling a pool of crystal clear water, a waterfall cascading from a cliff face behind it.

"I found it the last time I was here. I'm glad you like it," he says, grinning. "I thought you might like to take a swim?"

"I'd love to. This is perfect."

He nods, and we drop our bags, stripping down to our swim-suits. I glance over at him, at the way the sunlight shines through his reddish-brown strands, the colour vibrant against the dark stone and green moss clinging to the surface of the cliff face behind him.

Taking my hand in his, Dalton leads me to a slab of rock that seems to act as a natural jetty. My gaze falls to the deep pool of water, and the way the sun seems to dance all the way down to the bottom, fracturing light into shades of turquoise, and crystalline blue. It must be at least thirty-feet deep.

"It goes down a long way," I comment.

"It does. Are you scared?"

"A little," I reply, wrinkling my nose, wondering if there are any creatures swimming in the depths that I should be aware of. I can't see any, but that doesn't mean they aren't there.

"Don't be. I've got you," he replies, squeezing my fingers. "We jump together, okay?"

"Together," I murmur, looking up at him as he gives me a soft, tentative smile. Somehow those words feel loaded, but I don't have time to question them as he tugs on my hand.

"After three. One, two, three!" he yells, and then we're both leaping into the pool and are under the surface in seconds.

We break the surface together, our laughter mingling with the sound of the waterfall behind us as we tread water for a moment, taking in the beauty of our surroundings. Then Dalton releases my hand and dives beneath the surface, appearing a few metres away.

"Come," he says, disappearing behind the spray of the waterfall.

I follow him, blinking my eyes free of water as I pass through the waterfall to find him standing on a submerged rock, the lower half of his body hidden beneath the water, glistening droplets sliding over his beautiful, suntanned skin.

When I reach him, he helps me to stand on the rock, and with his hair slicked back and an intense look on his face, he takes me in his arms, his cool skin pressed against mine.

"This has been the best ten days of my life," he confesses as I wrap my arms around his neck, the cool mist from the waterfall kissing our skin.

"I bet you say that to all the girls," I joke, but his eyes flicker with hurt, and I instantly regret my words. "Dalton, I'm sorry. I didn't mean that."

"I've never felt like this before, Daisy. *Never*. Please believe me," he urges, gripping me tighter, his expression serious.

"I do believe you," I reply as my gaze meets his. There's a mixture of desire and tenderness swirling in his deep blue eyes that makes my breath hitch. "You know I feel the same way."

He nods, thoughtful.

"It's so beautiful here. Thank you for bringing me."

"You're welcome," he says, then leans in slowly and presses a soft, whispering kiss against my lips that soon deepens, igniting the connection between us once again, setting my skin ablaze.

Eventually we pull apart, breathless, smiling, *happy*.

"You know..." he starts, hesitating a little as he brushes his lips across my cheek.

"What?" I whisper.

He pulls back slightly, staring into my eyes once more. "I have something I want to say," he says, a hint of uncertainty in his voice.

"Okay," I reply, waiting, my heart swelling, my breath hitching. Time stands still, and I can see how he fights with himself. I can barely breathe as he struggles to form words.

"I'm... I think... *Fuck*," he mutters, smiling ruefully.

"It's okay," I reply.

His smile falls. "Why is this so hard for me?"

"It's okay," I repeat, meaning it. "I can do this for the both of us."

"Do what?"

"You know what," I whisper against his lips.

"Daisy." He groans softly, bringing his head down to rest on my shoulder, and I reach up, caressing his damp hair. "I don't deserve you."

"Yes you do. You deserve to be loved, Dalton. *I love you,* and nothing and no one can take that away. Understand?"

He lifts his eyes to meet mine, startled almost.

"Seems I've let the cat out of the bag," I say, my lips tilting up in a smile, not at all concerned that I've told him how I feel. I don't even care that he doesn't say he loves me back. I'm willing to wait, to hear him say those words of his own volition. I don't want him to say them because he feels he has too. I want him to mean it.

"Say it again," he commands, tugging me closer as though he can't bear to have even a millimetre of space between us.

"Seems I've let the cat out of the bag..." I grin.

"Daisy!" he warns, his hand roaming up my back, his fingers

tangling in my wet curls as he tugs on my hair and tilts my head back. "You know what I meant. Say it again."

"I love you, Dalton," I say, cupping his face with my hand. "And nothing and no one can take that away."

"Nothing and no one," he agrees solemnly.

CHAPTER THIRTY

"You have a lot of explaining to do!" my father grinds out, pointing to the chair opposite him as he steeples his hands on the desk and glares at me. We've been home no more than an hour and he's already demanded I meet him in office like a naughty fucking kid, or worse still, an errant employee. Thank fuck Daisy went to rest after our long journey home, because she doesn't need to be here for this.

"There's nothing to explain. Daisy and I went on our honeymoon, and now we're back," I retort, settling in the seat and folding my arms across my chest. "Oh, and we had a great time, thank you for asking."

"Not much to explain?! You walked out on your wedding day and left me with over two hundred fucking guests to deal with!" he explodes, his skin flushing a furious shade of red. "Not to mention the press."

"*Your* wedding guests," I remind him as I level my gaze with his. "Apart from a handful, none of them were people that Daisy and I would've chosen to attend *our* wedding. As for the fucking press–"

"A wedding I paid for, alongside your damn honeymoon," he reminds me, cutting me off.

"Actually, I paid for *our* honeymoon. Not you," I retort, fucking bristling.

He barks out a laugh. "With the money I pay you to run my hotel. Don't get fucking smart with me, *son*."

I grit my teeth, hating how he always throws that back in my face, as if nothing I earn could ever truly belong to me. It's always his money, his business, his fucking rules.

"You brought the press to our wedding reception. There was no way I was putting Daisy through that bullshit."

"Why the fuck do you care? All you had to do was show up at the church, marry her, and act as a doting husband at the wedding reception."

"I *care* about Daisy," I say, meeting his gaze head on.

"Bullshit. She's a means to an end. You know that as well as I do. This is an arrangement, a marriage of convenience. The sooner you get her impregnated with my grandchild, the better. So, have you fucked her yet?" he asks, an evil grin sliding across his face as he leans back in his chair.

"That's none of your fucking business," I snap back.

"I think you'll find it's exactly my business. So have you?"

"No," I lie

His smile widens. "And there I was thinking you'd be happy to have some pussy on demand. Just fuck her, and get the damn job done."

"Enough!" I snap. "She's my *wife*, and I will not allow you to talk about her like that. She's not someone you can use and toss aside once you've got what you wanted from her."

He leans forward, his face contorted with anger. "You don't get to play the devoted husband now, Dalton. You went into this knowing full well how it was going to play out. Marry Daisy, impregnate her, divorce her once the child hits a year old, and, meanwhile, represent the Gunn family in the way I fucking expect!"

I clench my fists, rage like nothing else I've experienced before boiling my blood. "Daisy belongs by my side. So like it or fucking not, *that's* the way it's going to stay," I shout, pushing upright, my chair toppling over from the force of my anger.

He looks up at me, eyes narrowing. "Please don't tell me you've gone soft and fallen for her? She is not your future. We both know she doesn't belong in our world."

"That's where you're wrong. She *is* my future, and when we bring a child into this world, we'll be doing it together as a married fucking couple. There'll be no divorce, not in a year's time. Not ever."

He snorts, leaning back in his chair, regarding me with a mixture of disdain and contempt. "You really think you're capable of being with one woman for the rest of your life? Don't be so fucking foolish. You're my son, after all. The Gunn men aren't built for marriage, let alone spending our days with one person. You'll realise this soon enough.

"I may be your son, but I am *not* like you," I grind out, striding towards the door.

"You keep telling yourself that, but you forget I know you. You'll tire of her eventually," he throws back, and I don't need to see his face to know he's smirking. "Now, I'll be out for the rest of the evening. Make sure you get this done."

Reaching for the handle, I yank open the door before throwing a look over my shoulder. "You don't know me at all. You never bothered to take the time too, so do not sit there and think that you do, because, *father*, I will show you exactly the man I am if pushed too far. Enjoy your fucking evening."

With that I step out into the hallway, slamming the door behind me.

I CAUTIOUSLY push open Daisy's bedroom door, but hesitate in the doorway. Daisy is sound asleep, her face nestled in her hand and her legs curled up against her body. I long to join her in bed, to hold her close and wrap my arms around her, but I'm still fuming with anger from my heated argument with my father, and I don't think I have the energy to contain all of my emotions if I wake her up. She doesn't need to know about the argument. So, reluctantly, I gently shut the door and head to my bedroom at the far end of the hallway.

Right now I could really do with a friend, and making a decision, I pick up my phone and dial Drix's number. After a few rings he answers.

"Dalton?" he questions.

"We're home. I thought you should know."

"Where's Daisy? I've called but she hasn't answered."

"Asleep. She's tired after the long journey."

"Can you ask her to call me when she wakes up?" he says, and by the tone of his voice, I know he's about to put the phone down on me.

"Listen, Drix. Can we talk, clear the air?" I ask, heaving out a sigh as I pinch the bridge of my nose.

The line goes quiet, and I hear his muffled words as he says something to Lia, no doubt. "You've got five minutes. Make it good," he says.

"I–"

"What Dalton?"

My throat squeezes and I fucking drop my head, struggling to find the damn words. The fight with my father has affected me more than I thought it would. It's not like I haven't argued with him before, but this is different. The shit he said about Daisy... I'm ready to commit murder, and I just need to talk it out. Except I can't tell Drix what the bastard said because he'll come here and do the job before I can, and I need to be smart about how I deal with that fucking arsehole. I need to bide my time, play him at his own game, and when the time comes I will ruin his fucking life, just likes he's trying to ruin mine and Daisy's relationship.

"I miss you, man," I say instead, throwing it out there. It's the truth at least. He sighs, and I rise to my feet, pacing. "I know you still fucking hate me–"

"I don't hate you," he concedes. "But I do love my sister, very fucking much, and I'm worried for her, okay? I know you."

"Fuck, not you too," I say, gritting my teeth. "I'm not... I won't... I fucking..."

"Dalton, you have to look at this from my point of view. All the women you've been with, who you've fucked around over the years. I've seen it all," he reminds me.

"This isn't the same."

"What, because you're married now?"

"Yes. She's my wife, Drix. I won't do that to her," I say vehemently.

"I want to believe you, Dalton, but–"

"I love her," I blurt out, the words tripping off my tongue before I can stop them. Bending over, I drag in a deep lungful of air, winded by the confession. If it surprises me, then it sure as fuck surprises Drix given the long pause at the end of the line.

"Say that again," he eventually says.

"I'm in love with your sister, Drix. I fucking love her, and it's scaring the shit out of me," I admit, straightening up, forcing strength into my spine.

"You love Daisy?"

"Yes."

"Why?" he asks.

"What kind of question is that?" I throw back in frustration.

"I want to know *why* you love her. Tell me why," he insists.

"Because she's good, kind, *strong*. So fucking strong," I begin, feeling out the words, searching for the all the reasons why I love Daisy, and finding them easily. "Because she makes me laugh like no one else has. Because she challenges me to be a better man. Because she is so colourful that she makes my fucking grey world brighter. I'm not just talking about what she wears, even though I love her style, I'm talking about *her*. She's like a fucking rainbow on a stormy day, rare yet overwhelmingly beautiful."

"She is," he agrees, and I can hear the smile in his voice as he asks, "What else?"

"Because she looks at me like I'm someone worth loving. Because when I look at her everyone else just disappears. Because the thought of her carrying our child fills me with the kind of peace I've never felt before. Because she turns me on. Because I don't just want to fuck her, I want to make *love* to her."

Drix clears his throat at that, and I know it must make him feel uncomfortable at how attracted I am to Daisy, but honestly I don't fucking care. It's the truth.

"I love her. I love Daisy so fucking much and I'm terrified of messing this up," I say, my heart pounding so loud I can barely hear his response.

"That's the easy part," Drix eventually says.

"What is?" I ask, dropping to the bed, my legs giving way beneath me.

"Falling in love," he says. "That's easy."

"Not for me it isn't," I reply.

He hums, and I can imagine his expression as he deliberates my response. "Maybe so," he agrees. "But I'm telling you now, this is just the beginning. If you love her as much as you say you do–"

"I do," I reply adamantly.

"Then you have to be willing to love her through everything, and as contrived as it sounds, you have to love her through the good times, the bad, the mediocre, the everyday, because she deserves nothing less."

"I will," I say forcefully. "I will do that. I want to."

"Being in love, *loving* someone is like the ocean, Dalton," he says. "It can rage and it can be still, calm. You have to be prepared to weather the storm, to ride the wave. You have to be gentle, to be supportive and lift her up, because believe me when I say, she will need you to carry her when she's unable to do that herself. Love isn't fleeting, it's not a passing phase. Love is eternal, it is bottom-less. So when you say you love my sister, Dalton, do you truly mean it?"

"I mean it. I fucking mean it," I insist, pushing upright, feeling a surge of love for Daisy overwhelm me in that moment. It eddies through me, sets every cell on fire. It's consuming, exhilarating, yet peaceful, serene. "I feel it. I feel it, Drix. You have to believe me. I love Daisy. I fucking love her!"

He blows out a long breath. "Well, this changes things."

"It does," I agree. "What the fuck should I do?"

"Does she know?"

"That I love her. No."

"Don't you think you should tell her?"

"Yes, but how?"

"Use your words, Dalton. Then act upon them. Just love her."

"I'm going to. I do. I will," I say.

"Does she love you back?" he asks.

"Yes. She told me she loved me, and I swear to you, I swear on our twenty-year friendship that I've never felt more at peace when I heard her say those words to me. For the first time in my life, I felt wanted. It felt like coming home. *She's* my home."

"You're a lucky man, Dalton," he says with a soft laugh.

"I know that..."

He lets out a long breath. "Then make her happy, that's all I've ever wanted for her."

"I will," I say. Silence descends between us and nerves coil in my stomach. "Shit. How the hell am I going to do this?"

"Don't dwell on it, Dalton. Don't wait. If life has taught me anything, you have to live it now. Be in the present, don't second guess, just *do*. Go and claim the woman you love," Drix urges.

I don't bother to reply. I simply click off the call and stride towards Daisy's bedroom ready to open up, ready to lay everything bare, ready to make her truly mine.

CHAPTER THIRTY-ONE

Groaning, I let the warm spray of the shower glide over me, my head tipping down as I look at the trail of blood washing away. My stomach aches, the heavy pull of my period tugging deep inside. I've dealt with a heavy flow since I was fifteen, but this seems abnormally painful, and nausea washes over me. The whole journey home I'd felt unwell, and now it seems like the pain is getting worse, not better. Feeling lightheaded, I press my hand against the tiled wall and groan. What on earth is happening?

"Daisy?"

Lifting my head, I see Dalton enter the bathroom, his gaze dropping from my face to my hand pressed against my stomach, to the blood swirling down the drain. I swallow the urge to throw up, not just because of the blood, but because of how unwell I feel.

"Are you okay?" he asks, stepping into the room and shutting the door behind him.

"I'm fine. Just... Well, except for the fact my body is doing its best to rid me of every last drop of blood it would seem," I mumble, trying to laugh even as another sharp pain lances through my stomach, and takes my breath.

He steps closer, his hand pressed against the glass as he peers around the shower door at me. "Is this normal?"

"For me it is. Don't worry, it'll only last another couple of days and then I'll be good," I reply, trying to reassure him, but another wave of pain takes over, and I stumble a little.

"I'm getting in," he says, his voice urgent.

"You don't need to," I say, turning to face him, my cheeks heating as I feel more blood trickle down my leg. "This is kind of disgusting."

"Nothing about you is disgusting. I can deal with a little bit of blood, Daisy," he says, trying to reassure me as he reaches for his jumper, about to remove it.

"I think I'm going to throw up," I say, covering my mouth with my hand as I step towards him on shaky legs.

"Daisy, fuck!" Dalton exclaims, slipping his arm around my back to steady me as another wave of dizziness takes over.

I'm caught between wanting to throw up and wanting to faint as he leads me to the toilet. Vomit rises up my throat and I drop to my knees emptying my stomach into the bowl, feeling humiliated, vulnerable. Dalton swears again, and grabs a towel draping it over my back as he rubs his hand up and down my spine.

"Something isn't right," he says, helping me to my feet as black spots dance in my vision.

"Dalton, I think I'm going to..." my words trail off as darkness engulfs me. The last thing I capture is Dalton's expression of fear as I collapse into his arms.

"DAISY, CAN YOU HEAR ME?" Dalton's voice cuts through the haze of confusion in my mind, bringing me back to reality.

My eyes slowly flutter open and I take in my surroundings, the blinding light of what appears to be a hospital room coming into focus. I'm lying on a bed with crisp white sheets, hooked up to an IV as a heart monitor beeps steadily beside me.

"Dalton?" I croak, my throat dry and scratchy. I focus on his concerned face as he reaches out to gently stroke my hair off my forehead.

"Hey, Daisy," Dalton breathes, relief flooding his features as he stares at me. "You had me worried there for a bit."

"What happened?" I ask, trying to ease myself upright, but feeling the heavy throb in my stomach and thinking better of it.

"You fainted in the bathroom back home," he replies softly, his hand still stroking my hair soothingly. "Don't you remember?"

I frown, snapshots flooding my memory. I remember Dalton carrying me into my bedroom, calling out for help, then ringing an ambulance as soon as Tessa rushed into the room. I vaguely remember throwing up in the ambulance, and blood. So much blood. I remember lying on a stretcher, lights blurring above me as Dalton barked out orders. Then nothing, just this feeling of floating...

"How long have I been out?

"A few hours," he explains, wincing. "Daisy—"

"A few hours? What do you mean, a few hours?"

He leans over, pressing a tender kiss to my knuckles, eyes flickering with concern. "You had an emergency operation," he whispers.

"What kind of operation? What the hell is going on?"

"The surgeon will be here in a few minutes to explain everything fully. Drix is just getting us both a cup of coffee. He came the moment I called. He's been here this whole time too..." His voice trails off as he stares at me, dark circles ringing his eyes. "Fuck, Daisy, I thought I was going to lose you. There was so much blood."

"Drix is here too? Why was I bleeding so much? My periods have never been this bad before. Why did I need an operation? Is there something wrong with me?" I ask, question after question tripping off my tongue as I try to grasp what's happened.

Dalton blows out a breath. "I think we should wait for the surgeon to explain. I—"

"Dalton, tell me now. Tell me!" I demand, my voice becoming frantic and desperate, rising to a panicked pitch. Dalton's hesitation only seems to fuel my fear as his eyes hold a mixture of sorrow and empathy.

"You had a large ovarian cyst that ruptured on your right ovary," he says, his voice trembling with emotion.

My heart drops into the pit of my stomach as the words sink in. "A...a cyst? Is it cancer?" I choke out, my mind automatically thinking the worst as tears fill my eyes and fall down my cheeks. The thought of facing such a devastating disease is almost unbearable.

"No, you don't have cancer," Dalton quickly reassures me, but his tone does little to ease my terror.

"Then what? What is it?" I cry, tears escaping faster now, but as Dalton reaches up to wipe them away, his expression shifts to one of concern.

"Daisy..." His voice trails off, and I know something is terribly wrong.

Gripping his hand tightly, I can feel my heart pounding painfully against my rib cage as I wait for him to reveal the full truth. "Dalton, please tell me everything. Don't keep anything from me," I plead, searching his eyes.

He takes a deep breath, his gaze locking with mine. "The cyst ruptured and caused damage to your right ovary, they had to remove it, Daisy. I'm so sorry."

"They removed my ovary?" I whisper.

He nods. "They performed laparoscopic surgery so your recovery will be quicker," he adds, as if that makes this horrible, heartbreaking news any better.

My voice quivers with emotion as I ask, "Why did I have a cyst? I don't understand." More tears well in my eyes at the realisation of what he's telling me, of what this could mean for our future.

"It was an endometriosis cyst, Daisy," he explains gently, my heart sinking as he continues. "They also discovered some lesions around your left fallopian tube, and they removed them, but I'm afraid they've caused some damage to your fallopian tube."

"Lesions?"

"From endometriosis," he says.

Panic sets in as I realise the potential impact this could have on my chances of conceiving a child. "This can't be happening," I cry, tears streaming down my face at the thought.

"I'm so sorry," he whispers.

"What does that mean exactly?" I ask, trying to wrap my head around everything.

"Daisy there's more..." his voice trails off as he looks at me, pain in his eyes.

"What? What else could possibly be wrong?"

"They tested your blood and found high levels of the hCG hormone."

"What's hCG hormone?"

"It stands for human chorionic gonadotropin, it's... *Fuck*," he whispers, tears welling in his eyes.

"Dalton, please," I sob. "Tell me."

"It's the hormone produced by a foetus. You were pregnant, Daisy. It was very, very early. No more than a couple of weeks."

"I was pregnant?"

He nods. "I'm so sorry."

"I was pregnant?" I repeat, my voice catching as I sob uncontrollably now.

"Daisy, I'm so sorry. I'm so fucking sorry," Dalton says, pain lacerating my chest as he hauls me into his arms and holds on to me tightly, his own grief palpable as he tries to comfort me through my anguish.

"Why?" I cry, letting out all my pain and sorrow, the knowledge that I had been carrying a tiny life within me, a life that is now gone, cutting deeper than any physical wound ever could.

The revelation of losing our baby amidst the chaos of surgery and diagnoses leaves me shattered. I cling to Dalton, the reality of my situation and the loss of a future we'd barely begun to comprehend ripping through my heart by the cruel hand fate has dealt us.

"Shh, I've got you, I'm here," Dalton says, his hand rubbing up and down my back as he embraces me.

As my cries subside into exhausted whimpers, Dalton continues to hold me close, offering silent solace in the face of our shared tragedy. The room feels suffocating, filled with unspoken grief and unanswered questions that loom over us like a storm cloud ready to burst.

"Is there any hope?" I ask, my voice tremulous.

"The consultant said that you still have a functioning ovary," he explains, pulling back and brushing the tears from my face. "But because the fallopian tube connecting to your healthy ovary has been damaged by the lesions you might not be able to conceive naturally."

"No," I shake my head, as more anguish crushing me.

"I'm so so sorry, Daisy."

"Dalton, why is this happening? Our baby's gone..." I say, unable to comprehend everything as I drop my head and let out another choked sob.

"Shh, it's okay. It's okay, Daisy."

"But what if...? What if that was my only chance?"

"Don't think like that, we'll figure this out."

"But I *have* to conceive... I lost our baby...Oh my God, what are we going to do?" I ask, my thoughts tumbling, my emotions all over the place, my heart breaking.

"Listen to me now. You're the most important person here. I don't want you to worry about any of that. Do you hear me? We get you better, and we go from there, okay?"

"But what about Drix, the debt?"

"That is not something you need to worry about, Daisy," Drix says as he steps into the room, his own expression filled with sadness.

"Drix," I cry, looking up at him, at the worry in his eyes, the tenderness, the love. "But..."

"We'll figure this out. Like Dalton said, all you need to do is focus on getting better," he adds, placing the two coffee cups on a side table, and dropping into the chair on the other side of the bed as he reaches for my hand, squeezing it gently. "I'm so sorry, Daisy."

"What if I can't conceive again?" I whisper, pain lancing my chest at the thought. "It's all I've ever wanted, to be a mother, to have a child, and now that might not be a possibility. Why? Why did this have to happen?"

Dalton and Drix exchange looks before Dalton reaches out to hold my hand. "Daisy, whatever happens we'll face this together. But right now your health is our priority," he says gently, but firmly. "You're not alone in this. I will get you the best doctors, we will figure this out."

"What about Carl?" I ask, hating how my stomach twists in knots, how he holds all the power. "If he finds out I've miscarried, that I might not be able to conceive again, the contract will be null and void and Drix will have to become the families' enforcer once again. I can't let that happen. I can't."

"We'll deal with Carl," Drix says, gritting his jaw as he meets Dalton's gaze.

"Does he know?" I whisper.

"He wasn't there when the ambulance was called, but he knows you were taken to hospital and that you needed surgery. We haven't told him any of the details. We're just figuring out what to say," Dalton says, blowing out a breath. "One step at a time, okay?"

"Okay," I nod weakly. The thought of facing Carl, of dealing with the repercussions of this loss and its potential impact on our fragile arrangement, fills me with dread. But more than that, what if this changes things between Dalton and me? What if he doesn't want me after this?

Sadness and exhaustion creep over me, and I don't fight the pull of sleep, needing to fall into the darkness, needing to forget, if only for a little while. The last thing I hear before I drift off is Dalton's whispered words of comfort.

"We'll get through this together, Daisy. I promise."

THE NEXT DAY is a blur of tests, and numerous discussions with doctors about my condition. I had no idea I had endometriosis. My periods have always been heavy, irregular, but I've never had any of the other symptoms. Perhaps a little fatigue, some bloating, but I never, *ever*, questioned my ability to conceive, not once. I feel like my body has betrayed me, that I should've known, and the guilt I feel is immense.

I've been told that I should feel a lot better in a couple of weeks time, and provided I rest and don't do anything too strenuous, then I should be fully healed in about a month, and can resort to normal activities then. But right now I'm not sure what normal even means. Before this happened, 'normal' was being a woman able to conceive, to carry a baby, not someone who's ability to get pregnant has been drastically reduced. That knowledge is like a constant ache in my chest that has refused to ease, despite Dalton's unwavering support.

Truthfully, my head has been a mess as I've tried to process everything that's happened, and whilst I'm grateful for Dalton, and his presence by my side, I can't help but feel as though I'm letting him down. That I'm a burden.

On my third day in hospital, not long after Dalton has left to go and grab a change of clothes and a shower back home, I hear a gentle knock at the door.

"Come in," I say, pushing upright in bed. I'm no longer hooked up to any machinery, or on any fluids, I'm simply resting. In a day or so I should be able to go home to finish my recovery there.

"Hey, you," Lia says as she enters the room, her eyes soft as she smiles at me.

"Hey," I choke out, feeling an overwhelming rush of emotions in her presence.

"Oh, Daise," she says, rushing towards me and pulling me in for a hug. "What an ordeal."

I cling to Lia, grateful for the familiar warmth and comfort she brings. As she pulls away, she brushes a stray tear from my cheek with a gentle touch.

"I'm so sorry I couldn't be here sooner," she murmurs, her expression mirroring the concern in her voice. "Drix was insistent he come every day, and I didn't have anyone else to watch over Toby."

"I understand. Thank you for coming," I whisper, my voice thick with emotion as Lia takes a seat beside me, her presence a grounding force in the midst of my turmoil.

"How are you holding up?" she asks, her gaze steady and unwavering.

I take a deep breath, allowing myself to voice the fears and doubts that have been weighing me down these past few days. Things I haven't been able to voice to Dalton.

"I'm scared, Lia. I'm so sad," I admit, the words heavy on my tongue.

"I know. I know," she replies, her words choked as she tears up.

"Miscarrying is painful enough, but the thought that I might never get another chance to have a baby... It's unbearable."

Lia listens intently, her eyes filled with understanding. "You don't know if that's the case. You still have an ovary, and if you find that you can't conceive naturally, there are other options, Daisy," she says, trying to reassure me.

"Everything seems like such a mess. I feel like..." My voice trails off as I try to temper my emotions. "I feel like a failure. Like I've let everyone down."

"You are not a failure," Lia says vehemently. "And you've not let anyone down."

"I'm supposed to give Dalton a child. If I don't... Lia, what am I going to do? I'm worthless to him now."

"No, don't you dare say that," Lia says, reaching for me and grasping my hand. "Dalton doesn't see it that way. He's been out of his mind with worry. That man does not think you're worthless. Not in any way. Not at all."

"But Carl will," I whisper.

"Carl thinks you've had an appendectomy," she says. "He doesn't know. He won't know."

"He thinks I've had my appendix out?" I ask, shaking my head in disbelief.

"Yes, Dalton thought it was the best thing to do given the circumstances..." Her voice trails off as she winces.

"So Dalton doesn't believe I'll be able to conceive despite his reassurances and everything he's said to me these past few days."

"That's not what I'm saying. He's just trying to protect you, Daisy."

"Oh God," I cry, hating that he needs to lie, that he's probably thinking the same thing as I am, that I may never carry his child, that everything we've done is for nothing.

"Listen, don't do that. Don't spiral. Dalton cares about you so, so much, Daisy. Please know that."

I swallow hard, trying to tell myself that the connection we have is strong enough to weather this storm, but the truth is, I don't know if it is. I love him, and yet I don't truly know how he feels about me. On our honeymoon I'd felt his love, I've felt it here in this room these past few days, but there's a huge part of me that thinks he'll decide that I'm not enough, that his feelings will change. Why would he stay with me now? He could lose everything he's ever wanted, his inheritance, his lifestyle, his riches. Why would he do that?

"What are you thinking, Daisy?" Lia asks me as I shift in bed, trying to regain some control over my emotions.

"I love Dalton," I whisper, clinging onto these feelings I have, hoping that's enough whilst knowing that it might not be.

"That's good, Daisy. That's amazing," she replies, her fingers tightening around mine as she gives me a gentle smile.

"But I don't know if..."

"You don't know if he loves you back?" she asks tentatively.

"Exactly." I drop my chin, staring at our clenched hands, unable to look her in the eye. "On our honeymoon, I thought, maybe he did. But now... How can he love me now?"

Lia reaches for me, her fingers resting beneath my chin as she urges me to look at her. "Dalton has been here almost every hour of every day. He's rallied around you, Daisy. That man has questioned every doctor. He's made sure you've had the best possible care. He's fended off questions from his father. He's done everything in his power to keep you safe. If that isn't love, I don't know what is."

"But this changes everything," I say, my heart sinking. "Even if we weren't bound by this contract, why would he want to stay with me if I might not be able to have his child? Why would I take his ability to be a father away? I won't let him do that."

"That's not up to you, Daisy. You can't make decisions for Dalton based on what you think he needs or wants. You have to trust his feelings for you. You have to trust in your feelings for each other, and believe in the strength of your relationship," Lia says, her voice filled with conviction.

"You make it sound so easy, but we both know life isn't like that," I counter. "It's not that simple, you know that."

"You don't have to have all the answers right now," she says softly. "Just focus on healing and taking care of yourself. The rest will fall into place in its own time."

Lia's words echo in my mind as I lay in the hospital bed, my thoughts a tumultuous whirlwind of doubt and fear. All I know right now is that nothing seems certain. Not my future with Dalton, not my ability to conceive a child, and not his feelings for me.

CHAPTER THIRTY-TWO

"Mr and Mrs Gunn, it's good to see you both," Dr. Wigmore says, as we sit opposite him in the office of his private practice. He's the best reproductive endocrinologist there is, and he's been dealing with Daisy's case since she was rushed to hospital two weeks ago for emergency surgery.

"Thank you for seeing us," I say, curling my hands around Daisy's as she sits quietly next to me. "We appreciate it."

Since her discharge from the hospital, Daisy has become increasingly withdrawn, struggling to process everything that has occurred. I've tried to reassure Daisy that I'm with her, that I support her but, bit by bit, she's shut down, and I can't seem to reach her. I love her so damn much and I'm not ashamed to admit that this distance between us is killing me.

Yet, I *still* haven't told her how I truly feel, and that's not because I'm afraid of my love for her, but because I can't seem to find the right time. The last thing I want is for her to think I'm just saying it out of pity after what she's been through, and I get the distinct feeling that if I say those three words now, that's exactly how she'll feel. So I arranged for this appointment today to see how we move forward, hoping it will give us both some clarity, or at the very least encourage her to open up, so we can talk.

Dr. Wigmore looks between us both, "I understand that this has been a difficult time for you, and I want to reassure you that I am here to support you both on this journey."

"Thank you," Daisy whispers.

"As you're aware, the lesions we removed from your left fallopian tube have greatly affected its functionality," he begins gently, his eyes full of compassion as he looks between us both. "Combined with the removal of your right ovary, this will make natural conception extremely difficult."

Daisy's breath catches in her throat as her fingers grip mine tightly, and I feel my own heart breaking for her, knowing how much she's wanted a child of her own. As Daisy struggles to keep her composure, Dr. Wigmore clears his throat.

"But there are other options that we can explore, given you still have a functioning ovary," he says softly. "We can discuss the possibility of In Vitro Fertilisation if you're willing to consider it."

"Is that foolproof?" I ask. "IVF, I mean?"

"Nothing is foolproof, there are many factors that can affect the success of IVF treatment," Dr. Wigmore explains. "You need to consider the success rates, and emotional toil that the process can have on the both of you. It's a significant decision that requires careful consideration. I have some leaflets here that you should read through before making a decision."

"Is there absolutely no chance I can conceive naturally?" Daisy asks, her voice wobbling as she takes the leaflet from him.

"I cannot say with absolute certainty either way, but given my many years of experience dealing with similar situations as yours, it is unlikely," Dr. Wigmore replies.

Daisy's expression falls. "I understand," she says softly.

"I know that this is a lot to take in," he continues, his tone gentle. "Take some time to heal and discuss what course of action you'd like to take. If you have any further questions and want to schedule another appointment to discuss your decision, I'd be very happy to go through the process in more detail."

I nod, feeling fucking helpless as I look at Daisy's stricken face. She sniffles, composing herself before speaking up.

"Thank you, Dr. Wigmore. We'll take some time to think about it, and let you know."

"DAISY, ARE YOU HUNGRY?" I ask, flicking my gaze over at her as we drive towards Princetown, the trees lining the country road, a blur of green and brown behind her head. We've sat in strained silence for the past half an hour, both of us trying to digest the news Dr. Wigmore had shared.

"Not particularly," she replies, staring out of the window, her hand still clutching the information leaflet Dr. Wigmore gave her.

"You should eat," I say.

"I don't feel much like eating," she retorts, wrapping her arms around herself.

"I know, but you need to keep up your strength. You're still recovering from the operation, Daisy," I reply, determined to take care of her, especially since she's struggling to do that for herself. "We could stop at Daphne's café. Drix said she's been asking after you."

"I'm not sure I'm ready to face her just yet," she murmurs. "It's not as if I can tell her what's happening anyway. As far as most people are concerned I've just had my appendix out, not lost the ability to conceive a child naturally. I don't have the strength today to pretend everything's okay when it's not, and Daphne has an uncanny way of uncovering the truth. Nothing much gets past her."

"Of course, I didn't think," I reply, cursing myself internally.

"How about we swing by Drix's place? I'm sure he'd like to see you, Toby and Lia too."

"Okay," she agrees, before leaning her head against the window and closing her eyes, cutting off any opportunity to talk further.

Fifteen minutes later Drix is opening his front door, his tall frame silhouetted against the warm glow of the house's interior lights.

"Hey, this is a pleasant surprise," he says, drawing Daisy into his arms as she presses her cheek against his chest, her eyes shutting briefly as he throws me a concerned look. I shake my head, telling him without words that we should talk later.

"Sorry to just turn up unannounced," Daisy apologises, drawing out of his arms.

"Don't apologise, this will always be your home, Daisy. You can come by anytime you like, you know that," he replies, draping his arm over her shoulder and tucking her into his side. "Let's go inside, dinner is almost ready. I'm sure there's plenty to go around," he adds, guiding Daisy inside as I follow them both.

The scent of home-cooked food embraces us like a warm hug as we enter the kitchen. Lia looks up from the stove, her surprise quickly covered up with a welcoming smile as Toby jumps down from his seat at the kitchen island and throws himself into Daisy's arms.

"Daisy! You've come for dinner," he says excitedly, and I watch her forcing her lips up into a soft smile that barely hides the sadness in her eyes.

"Hey, Toby, haven't you got tall? I think you've grown at least an inch since I last saw you," she says softly, ruffling his hair as he grins up at her.

"Mama said so too, didn't you, Mama?" he replies, throwing a grin at Lia who nods, her brows pulling into a frown as she glances at me.

"I did indeed. I think you've had a growth spurt," she agrees, her eyes flicking to Daisy.

"Drix says I'll be the tallest at school when I start," he grins, hopping from one foot to the other.

"Without a doubt," I say, my smile falling as Daisy drags in a tremulous breath, busying herself with removing her coat and handing it to Drix who offers to take it from her.

"I've made spaghetti carbonara, a green salad, and some home-made garlic bread. Come on over and take a seat whilst Drix hangs up your coats," Lia interjects in an attempt to counter the heavy weight of sadness Daisy carries.

"Thank you, Lia. It smells delicious," I say, shrugging off my jacket and handing it to Drix who leaves the kitchen momentarily.

Pulling out the seat next to Daisy, I sit down, watching Lia as she dishes out the food onto five separate plates. By the time she's finished placing the salad and garlic bread onto the counter, Drix has returned. He briefly squeezes my shoulder as he passes by me, dropping onto a seat next to Lia.

As everyone begins to tuck into the food, Toby chatters excit-edly about his day spent at the park with Drix and Lia building a fort out of fallen branches and twigs, distracting us all from the unspoken tension hanging in the air.

Daisy barely touches her food, only managing to eat a few mouthfuls before pushing it around her plate absently, with-drawing into herself. Her mind is clearly elsewhere and I steal glances at her, noticing the way her eyes gloss over every now and then.

Fuck, I can't bear to see her like this.

Yes, Dr. Wigmore might've given us a glimpse of hope with talk of IVF treatment, and whilst we haven't had a chance to discuss it, I already know that hiding that process from my father isn't going to be easy. As far as he's concerned, Daisy is recovering from having her appendix out, and not trying to come to terms with the devastating news of her miscarriage and the prospect of fertility treatment. I don't even want to think about how he might react to the news, but if I know my father as well as I think I do, then it won't be good. He doesn't give a shit about Daisy, anyone for that matter. Sympathy for her situation will be the last thing on his fucking mind.

"Wanna see my new toys, Daisy?" Toby asks, interrupting my thoughts as he reaches over and pats Daisy on the arm.

"You've got some new toys, huh?" Daisy asks him after a beat.

The kid tips his head to the side as he looks up at her, and even though he's unaware of the truth behind her unhappiness, there's no doubt that he senses it and is trying, in his own way, to fix her heartache. He's such a sweet kid and a credit to Lia.

"Yes, they're in the den, do you wanna see?" he persists, his small hand wrapping around her fingers.

"Do you mind?" Daisy asks, looking between us.

"Of course not," Lia replies. "Toby's missed you. Go hang out whilst we clear away the dishes. The apple pie isn't ready to be served yet anyway."

"Thanks," she murmurs, flicking her gaze my way briefly before taking Toby's hand and slipping off the stool, following him out of the room.

"I don't know what to do," I blurt out, raking a hand through my hair as I look across at my friends helplessly.

"You went to see the consultant today, right?" Drix asks. "What did he say?"

"Pretty much what we know already. He said it's unlikely that Daisy will be able to conceive naturally. He suggested IVF as an option," I explain.

"I see," Drix replies, exhaling heavily. "That's a lot to come to terms with. Have you talked about this with Daisy?"

"We haven't had a chance. I wanted to, but in the car on the way over she shut down on me... I thought coming here and being with family, with people who love her, would help. Fuck, she doesn't deserve this, Drix," I say heavily.

"IVF can be very successful," Lia adds, reaching over and giving my arm a squeeze. "Try not to lose hope."

"I appreciate that it can be, but we have the added complication of my father, and keeping this from him..." I say, grinding my teeth in frustration.

"He doesn't ever have to find out. Women don't always fall pregnant immediately anyway," Drix says.

"Drix is right," Lia adds. "It took me six months to get pregnant with Toby."

"And what if the treatment fails, what then?" I ask.

"Then we cross that bridge when we come to it," Drix replies. "We'll figure this out."

"You make it sound so fucking easy, but we all know my father is a canny bastard. It's a fucking miracle he hasn't figured out what's really going on already. I keep waiting for the fucking guillotine to fall."

Drix leans back in his chair and lets out a heavy sigh, rubbing his temples as he contemplates my words. "Then I'll take the debt back on. I'll do it for you and Daisy. It was never meant to be yours in the first place," he says.

"Drix..." Lia whispers, gripping his hand.

"Absolutely not," I say, shaking my head. "That is *not* an option. You're my best friend, and there's no way I'm going to let my father rule over your life like he has done mine. I let him do that to you once, and I let you down. I refuse to do that again. No. I just need some time to figure this out."

With that I push back from the table, my mind whirring as I go in search of Daisy. I need to protect her, to shield her from my father, and one way or another, that's exactly what I'm going to do. I don't care what it takes.

"Daisy?" I say, pushing open the door to the den to find her sitting on the floor with Toby in her lap as she reads him a story.

She looks up at me, acknowledging my presence before continuing to read, and I lean against the doorframe, watching her, caught by her beauty, gutted by the sadness that lingers in her eyes. Eventually she finishes reading, and Toby throws his arms around her neck.

"Thank you, Daisy," he says, planting a kiss on her cheek before jumping up. "I'm gonna see if the apple pie is ready." With that he runs off, leaving us alone.

"You okay?" I ask, dropping onto the floor beside her, stretching out my legs, wincing at the stupid fucking question. Of course she isn't okay.

"Not really," she replies, heaving out a sigh.

I reach for her hand, wrapping my fingers around hers. "Do you want to go ahead with IVF treatment?" I ask her.

"I don't know, Dalton. I need time to think," she whispers.

"Of course, take all the time you need," I reply, squeezing her hand gently.

"Dalton?" she asks after a moment.

"Yes?"

"I'm sorry."

"For what?"

"For not being able to give you what you need," she croaks out, tears spilling over her lashes as she drops her head. "For putting your inheritance in jeopardy."

Shifting my body slightly, I reach up and cup her jaw, gently lifting her chin. "You're who I need. *You*, Daisy. Please believe that."

She nods. "Okay."

But I feel her faith in me, *in us*, slipping away, so I lean in closer, brushing my lips against hers gently, pouring all the love and reassurance I can muster into that one, simple kiss, hoping, for now, that it's enough.

CHAPTER THIRTY-THREE

"We're having a dinner party tonight. Some business acquaintances will be in attendance, alongside their wives. I take it you've recovered enough to attend?" Carl asks, looking up at me from across the table as we eat breakfast, his steely blue eyes narrowing.

My stomach drops. Despite another week passing since Dalton and I spoke with Dr. Wigmore, and despite feeling physically better, emotionally I'm not. The thought of having to be in the company of strangers makes my stomach coil with nausea. I'm not myself. I haven't even been able to talk openly with Dalton about possible IVF treatment, let alone our relationship, his feelings about everything, or our future for that matter. The last thing I want to do is entertain Carl's business acquaintances and their wives with small talk.

"I–" I begin, but Dalton cuts in.

"No. Daisy's still recovering," he says, eyeing his father with disdain.

"Forgive me," Carl says, narrowing his eyes at me and giving me a look that tells me he couldn't care less about my forgiveness, "But if you've been able to leave the house and visit with your brother since leaving hospital, then I think an hour or two sitting at a dinner table should be manageable, no?"

"I said she's still recovering," Dalton persists through gritted teeth.

"I wasn't talking to you," Carl retorts, levelling his gaze with Dalton before looking back at me.

Dalton's curled fist slams against the table, making the crockery and plates jump from the force. "And I don't give a fuck, she isn't going."

"Dalton, please..." I whisper, shaking my head at him.

"Daisy? Is there something you wish to share?" Carl asks, lifting a brow, his gaze falling to my red jumper with yellow embroidered daisies sewn across it. I wore it purposefully in the hope that it would make me feel better, it doesn't. Nothing is making me feel better. "Well?" he insists, and I don't like the way he's staring at me, as though trying to delve into my head and claw out my thoughts.

"I'm still a little tired, but I think I can manage a dinner party," I say softly, dropping my gaze back to my bowl of half-eaten yoghurt and fruit, wishing I was far, far away from here.

The need to run away has been building with every passing day. I hate that I feel that way, and I know it isn't fair to push Dalton away after he's repeatedly tried to talk with me, but I can't help feeling like this. I just need time to heal, to grieve, to figure out how to move forward. I love Dalton, that hasn't changed, but that love has been tinged with so much sadness and disappointment, and this dreadful feeling of not being enough. We both know that there are no guarantees with IVF and if I can't have his baby, where does that leave us? He can tell me all he likes that the contract doesn't matter, but we both know that it does.

"Excellent. It will be a semi-formal affair, so be sure to dress accordingly," he says, before pushing up from his seat and striding from the room.

"Daisy, you don't have to do this," Dalton says as I move to stand, wanting to get away, to go back to my room, curl up on my bed and sleep.

If Carl has noticed that we haven't been sharing a bedroom since our return from the hospital, then he hasn't said anything. I don't suppose he cares how we choose to sleep at night, because as far as he's concerned this is still a marriage of convenience, not a chance to indulge in an actual, healthy relationship. And even if this wasn't a marriage of convenience, then it's become very apparent that women to him are just trophies to parade around and vessels to impregnate. I can't imagine he's ever shared his inner sanctuary with a woman outside of fucking them.

"It's fine. It'll just be a couple of hours," I reply. "I'll see you later. I think I might just go and lie down for a bit."

"Daisy..."

With a heavy heart I ignore the pleading tone in Dalton's voice, and simply turn on my heel and leave.

"THIS IS DAISY, my son's wife," Carl says loudly, cupping my elbow as soon as I enter the reception hall and guiding me towards several men in suits who are standing with their partners on the other side of the room with Dalton.

"Daisy, I was just about to come and get you," Dalton says, traversing through the crowd towards me. He gives his father a dark look, taking my hand in his and drawing me out of his hold.

"There was no need. I'm perfectly fine," I reply, trying my best to act accordingly, when all I want to do is curl up on my bed and sleep.

Music is playing softly as we gather together, and some of

Carl's guests assess me with curiosity whilst the others look over at me with polite disinterest. I plaster on a smile, nodding my head in greeting as Carl introduces me to each of the couples in turn. When he said he'd be entertaining some business acquaintances, I'd expected maybe a handful of people at most, but there are at least twenty men here with their wives, and I feel a little over-whelmed with the sheer number of strangers I'm expected to engage with.

"And this is William Black and his wife Florence," Carl says, after reeling off several names, all of which I've forgotten. "He's overseeing the redevelopment of our very first hotel in Paris. It should be open within a month or so."

"A hotel in Paris?" Dalton questions. "I wasn't aware of this new venture."

"It was a fairly recent decision. We had to move quickly, and given you were away on your honeymoon, and apparently unreachable, I decided to go ahead and offer over and above the asking price," Carl explains. "Most of the hotel is already in good condition, I've just wanted to add the Gunn family flare, and William has been instrumental in securing the deal, and making sure the construction team and interior design staff are working to our very rigorous timetable. No point in wasting time, is there?"

Dalton's nostrils flare, and if looks could kill, Carl would be already six feet under.

William clears his throat, casting his gaze between father and son, sensing the tension there. "It's nice to meet you, Daisy," he says warmly.

"You too," I reply, offering him my hand as my gaze flicks to his wife, a woman several decades younger than him.

She dips her head, giving me a gentle, almost serene smile, and I feel Dalton's hand tightening around my fingers right at the same time I notice her other hand resting on her rounded belly. I try to ignore the stab of pain that shoots through me at the sight of

Florence's pregnancy bump, only serving to remind me of my own very recent loss.

"Congratulations," I offer weakly, plastering on another smile whilst inside I'm crumbling.

"Yes, wonderful news," Carl adds, turning his attention to Florence. "William tells me you're due to give birth in early summer."

"Four months, and our baby will be here," she replies, her cheeks flushing with pride as William presses his hand against her belly.

"Well, we certainly hope that it won't be very long before Daisy will be carrying my grandchild," Carl says, looking at me intently.

I blanch from his scrutiny, taking an involuntary step backwards.

"We've just recently married, father. There's plenty of time for that," Dalton says, his voice tight.

Carl raises a brow, before covering up his annoyance with a broad smile as hollow as the man himself. "There's no time like the present, wouldn't you agree, Daisy?" he says looking at me pointedly, reminding us both of the contract we signed all those weeks ago.

My cheeks heat, this entire conversation feeling like some kind of trap, but Dalton expertly steers the conversation in another direction, saving me from further humiliation.

After a few more minutes, I excuse myself, feeling Dalton's gaze on me as I wander across to the refreshment table and pour myself a glass of water despite Tessa offering to pour it for me.

"Mrs Gunn, are you alright?" she asks, her soft brown eyes looking at me with concern as my hands tremble.

"I'm just a little tired, that's all," I reply, taking a sip on the glass of water.

"Perhaps you should excuse yourself," she suggests.

"I'm not sure that would go down very well with Carl," I murmur.

"But you've just recently come out of hospital. Mr Gunn would understand," she says, frowning a little, her gaze drifting to Carl, who by all accounts is having a wonderful time charming his guests.

"That doesn't matter to him."

"Surely he realises that losing that amount of blood is an indication of—"

"No!" I snap, her eyes widening as I shake my head at her.

"You were bleeding heavily," she counters in a whisper, her face paling as my lips start to tremble. "I was certain that you..."

"Stop," I whisper, trying and failing to prevent the tears from slipping from my eyes.

"He doesn't know, does he?" she asks, lowering her voice as she reaches for me once again.

I shake my head, swiping at my eyes. "He thinks I had my appendix out. Please, you can't say anything."

"Oh no. No, I wouldn't," she assures me, squeezing my hand.

"Thank you," I whisper.

"They're coming this way," she adds quickly, "Go and freshen up. I'll make your excuses."

As Tessa smoothly intervenes, leading the others to the formal dining room, I retreat to the bathroom, grateful for a moment's reprieve as I lean against the vanity unit and close my eyes, willing the tears to stay at bay. But they come anyway, stubbornly tracing a path down my cheeks as I try to steady my breathing. It takes me a while to gather myself together enough to even consider joining the guests, but eventually I dry my eyes and wipe away the mascara staining my skin.

Moments later there's a soft knock at the door.

"Daisy, are you in there?"

It's Dalton.

"Just give me a moment," I reply, washing my hands and drying them.

I take a deep breath before finally opening the door to face him. He looks as harrowed as I feel, and it's all I can do not to fall into his arms and sob.

"I'm so sorry about earlier," he says, dragging a hand through his hair. "That must've been hard for you to see."

"It's not your fault," I reply. "I need to just deal with it. I'm going to be seeing a lot of pregnant women in the future."

"You shouldn't have to just deal with it. You shouldn't have to attend this damn gathering any more than you should have to hide what's happened to you."

"We don't have a choice," I say.

"What if I can get us away from here and out of sight of my father?"

"How? What are you suggesting?"

"He just mentioned the hotel in Paris. If I can convince him to give me a role as a manager, would you be willing to come with me? You could get treatment in France, we could make this work, and you won't have to worry about my father finding out. It needn't be a permanent move."

"What about Drix, Lia and Toby?" I ask, feeling the tiniest glimmer of hope, despite being more than a little sad at the prospect of leaving them, if only temporarily.

"I'm sure they'd be supportive, and it's not as if they can't come to visit. What do you think?"

"Will Carl go for it?" I ask, chewing on my lip.

"I can be very persuasive, Daisy. Leave it with me, okay?"

I nod, feeling a surge of gratitude wash over me at the prospect of escaping this suffocating situation, and the possibility of becoming pregnant via IVF treatment, and I cling on to it with all my might.

"I trust you," I say, and his eyes hold mine for a moment, a silent promise passing between us before he takes my hand in his and we head back to the party.

CHAPTER THIRTY-FOUR

It's been almost a month.

Three weeks, six days and seventeen hours have passed since the bottom fell out of Daisy's world, *our* world. Almost a month since we found out we lost our baby and that our chances of conceiving a child have drastically been reduced. Daisy may have recovered from her operation, the tiny incisions on her abdomen may have stitched back together, she may have gotten the colour back in her cheeks, but she's far from healed. And the tiny shred of hope I'd given her was destroyed the moment I suggested my idea of managing the hotel in Paris to my father who flat out refused. Despite spending the past fucking week trying to convince him, I've gotten nowhere, worse still, the bastard is getting suspicious, that much is painfully clear.

"Where are we going?" Daisy asks me as I drive through the twisting country roads.

Her voice is soft, and it pains me to hear the lingering sorrow within it, the shattered dreams and unspoken heartache. She's aware of my father's decision, and has withdrawn further from me, her hopes dashed, alongside mine.

"Sterling's place. He's invited us all over for dinner. Everyone will be there."

"Everyone?"

"Ben's got a night off from the bar," I say, eyeing her briefly, hating how she stares out the window as the evening light draws in and darkness seeps into the sky. "Drix and Lia are coming, of course."

She nods. "Yes, I recall him mentioning that when I spoke to him earlier in the week. Will Sterling's dad and stepmother be there too?" she asks.

"No, they've gone away for the weekend. Harlow's joining us though," I say, my fingers flexing and tightening around the steering wheel as I try to shake off this feeling of unease. "Sterling figured it would be good for us all to catch up seeing as we haven't managed to do that since we left for our honeymoon."

"I've kept you from your friends," she says, finally turning to face me.

I force a smile, trying to mask the turmoil bubbling inside of me. "*Our* friends, and no, Daisy, you haven't kept me from anything or anyone."

"When you've not been working, you've been stuck keeping me company," she counters. "Can't have been much fun for you."

"Daisy..." I warn, hating how she sees it that way. "I don't want to be anywhere else. You're my wife, and my place is by your side. I–"

"Hmm," she hums, staring back out of the window, her walls going back up.

"If you're not feeling up to this, we can go back home," I offer, all the other words I want to say dissolving on my tongue.

"It's fine," she says, shaking her head. "I could use the distraction."

"Distraction? Don't you think we should talk–" I begin, but she cuts me off, reaching for my thigh, and squeezing it briefly.

"What good would that do? We've run out of options, Dalton."

If the warmth of her touch didn't instantly remind me of how good it feels to have her hands on me, how I've longed over the past few weeks to get back to that easy affection we shared on our honeymoon, I would've argued back. As it is, I can barely stop myself from pulling the damn car over, hauling her into my arms and kissing the damn breath from her, to remind the both of us how good it got between us on our honeymoon, how easily she brought to life that part of me that I had suppressed for so long, that was so desperate for emotional connection.

Instead I keep fucking driving.

We haven't been intimate since our honeymoon, and I don't mean foreplay or sex, given she's still healing both physically, mentally and emotionally. I just mean emotional connection. I've had no expectations of her, but it's as though there's an invisible wall keeping us apart, it's unseen but very much real, tangible. Before Daisy I would've run from the kind of intimacy and connection that didn't lead to sex and shared orgasms. But since her, it's all I want, and I feel fucking bereft not experiencing the love she showered me with on our honeymoon. She's hurting, but I'm hurting too, and the truth is, I don't know how to fix us, or this situation, and I'm scared. I'm fucking terrified I'm losing her.

As we pull up at Sterling's stately home, the warm glow of the lights spills out of the windows, the sound of laughter and chatter drifting through the crisp evening air. Daisy sits beside me, her hands fidgeting in her lap, her eyes fixed on the windshield.

"Ready?" I ask, leaning over and taking her hand briefly, giving it a reassuring squeeze.

"Yes," she replies, unhooking her seat belt, opening the car door and slipping out before I can press her further.

As we make our way inside, we're greeted by our friends. Daisy is instantly wrapped in their warm embraces, and I'm met with concerned looks and firm handshakes. Maybe I'm just as incapable of hiding my real emotions as Daisy is.

"You got a minute?" Drix asks, pulling me to one side as Lia wraps her arm around Daisy's waist and they head over to Harlow, Sterling's stepsister, who's waiting in the lounge.

I watch Daisy slip into easy conversation with a gracious smile, keeping her pain underwraps. But I see her. I know her, and I don't know how much more of this pretence I can take.

"How about a drink in the billiards room?" Sterling suggests, noticing the look passing between me and Drix. "I don't know about either of you, but I could do with a shot, or five." He eyes Harlow, and I see the agony in his gaze. I'm pretty sure it matches my own.

"Yeah, same," Ben agrees, glancing at me. "Looks like you need a drink too, mate."

"Why not?" I shrug, throwing one last look over at my wife.

"Lia, Daisy, Harlow. We're gonna catch up for a bit. Are you good for a while on your own?" Drix asks.

"Sure," Lia replies for the three of them as Daisy's gaze rests briefly on mine. Her eyes flicker with something I can't quite interpret before her attention is drawn back to Harlow who smiles at something Lia says.

As we step into the dimly lit room, the scent of aged whiskey, cigar smoke and leather envelops me, and I follow the guys to the bar in the corner of the room. Sterling lines up four cut glasses, pouring a shot of bourbon into each.

Drix and Ben take a seat on the bar stools, and I lean against the counter, picking up my drink and knocking it back in one go, welcoming the burn of the fiery liquid as it slides down my throat. It will be my one and only drink tonight given I'm driving.

"Want to get shit off your chest?" Ben asks, swiping a hand through his tousled brown curls, eyeing me. "How's Daisy doing?"

Blowing out a breath, I feel the pain and confusion of these past few weeks settle over me. "She's trying to be strong, but she's struggling."

"It's a lot for anyone to handle," Ben replies, reaching for me and giving my shoulder a squeeze. "Have you talked with her about it?"

I glance at Drix, feeling fucking helpless. "Believe me, I've tried."

"She's just trying to process. Give her time. Just keep doing what you're doing, Dalton. Be there for her. Let her know with your actions that you're not going to give up on her," Drix says. "I know Daisy. She'll get there eventually."

"You keep telling me that, but as more time passes, the further away she seems," I retort, loosening the top button of my shirt, feeling as though my fucking throat is constricted. "Besides, if Daisy's inability to open up to me was my only problem, I could work with that, but it isn't. I think my father is beginning to suspect something is up. He refused my request to manage his new hotel in Paris."

"Paris?" Drix questions.

"I thought if I could convince my father to allow me to take over the managerial position at a new hotel he's bought there, it would enable Daisy to start IVF treatment without him finding out. But, of course, he denied me."

"Fuck," Drix retorts, exhaling sharply.

"My thoughts exactly," I reply in frustration. "I feel like a fucking failure. I've spent my whole life living off my father's wealth. I'm ashamed of myself, Drix. Now I can't even look after my wife. What kind of man am I?"

"You've made mistakes, Dalton," Drix says. "But haven't we all? What matters most is how you act from this moment on, yeah?"

I nod, gritting my teeth. "Yes."

"So let me get this straight, in order to pay off the debt, Daisy needs to have your baby, right?" Sterling asks, his eyes catching mine.

"Yes. Marry me, have our child. Only then the debt is written off. If we can't do that the contract is null and void, and Drix will need to go back to being the families' enforcer, jeopardising his happiness and relationship with Lia."

"How much is the debt?" Sterling asks, his eyes catching mine.

"Eight point five million."

"Damn," Ben whistles.

Sterling nods. "And if you can pay off the debt, will that solve your problem?"

"Not entirely, no. Whilst it will get Drix off the hook, I know my father, he wants an heir more than anything. If he finds out Daisy's predicament I know he'll want me to divorce her, and replace her with someone else. He doesn't give a shit about my happiness or anyone else's for that matter," I admit, wincing at how fucking awful that sounds.

"Fucking cunt," Drix mutters.

"Okay so I guess it all boils down to this, would you be willing to forgo your inheritance to be with Daisy?" Sterling continues.

"There's still the not so tiny matter of the eight point five million debt," I point out.

"Would you be willing to forgo your inheritance to be with Daisy," Sterling repeats, eyeing me pointedly.

Could I? A few months ago I would've answered no. I would've been a selfish cunt and thought only of myself. But things have changed. I'm so fucking in love with Daisy that the thought of losing her is too painful to comprehend. We could try IVF and hope that it works, but there's no guarantee. Ultimately she means far more to me than my inheritance, and she's worth every fucking penny I'd lose walking away from my father to be with her.

"Yes," I agree, knowing it to be true. I'd find a way to start over, for her, for us both. "I fucking love her, Sterling. I don't give a shit about my inheritance."

Ben whistles, and Drix leans over, gripping my shoulder. "Good man," he rumbles.

"Then I think I might have a solution," Sterling says.

"How? Your father will never loan me the money," I say. "Roger is as callous as my father."

"I wasn't suggesting that at all."

"What then?"

"My paintings," he says, swirling around the alcohol in his glass as he eyes me.

"Your paintings?"

"Yes. Believe it or not, people want to buy them, they *have* bought them. I've already got a tidy sum of money from sales over the past few years, and I have several more paintings that I could sell."

"How much money?" Ben asks.

"Currently about five million."

"Five fucking million?! You've kept that quiet! Who are you, Banksy 2.0?" Ben retorts, eyes wide as he looks across at Sterling who just shrugs.

"I can loan you the money, Dalton. I can get you the rest with the paintings I've got in my studio. It's yours if you want it."

"You're serious?" I ask, completely taken aback to be honest.

I know my friends come from wealthy families, but like me, I'd assumed their wealth was tied up in trust funds they couldn't touch until whatever age their father's deemed appropriate, or they'd need to jump through hoops like my bastard father set out for me. Looks like Sterling has been doing his best to get out from beneath his father's grasp, and I admire him for it. I fucking wish I'd had the foresight to do the same, but the old me was too selfish and too fucking lazy to strive my own path.

"Never more serious in my life. I was saving the money to get the fuck out of here and start a new life, well away from my arse-hole father—"

"Then I can't take your money, not if it's going to give you the ability to be free of him," I say, shaking my head.

"Things have changed," he says. "I'm not in any hurry to leave right now."

"Let me think about it," I mutter, scraping a hand over my face.

It's not that I don't appreciate his offer, because I really fucking do, but it's more than a little emasculating having to take a loan from one of my best mates. Then again, I'm willing to swallow my pride for the woman I love, and prove to her that I can be the man she needs so long as she gives me the opportunity to do so.

"Sure," Sterling replies with a nod.

"I'm guessing you're not in a hurry to leave because of a leggy blonde with a cracking pair of lungs, who happens to be your step-sister" Ben asks, smirking.

"Yeah, Harlow," Sterling agrees, reaching for his glass and downing his shot, before reaching for the bottle to pour another. "She's driving me crazy."

"You should probably keep it to just one shot," Ben warns. "Nothing good ever happens when you get pissed."

"It helps numb shit," Sterling mumbles, the liquid spilling into his glass.

"Numb shit?" Drix asks, giving him a concerned look.

Sterling blows out a breath. "You all know about my condi-tion," he says, looking at us in turn.

"Yeah," Ben replies. "Not in a good place?"

Sterling shakes his head. "Harlow has no idea how her singing affects me. How every time I hear her beautiful voice I'm bombarded with fucking colour, and this insane, unquenchable need to paint. I've got fifteen fucking paintings in my studio, all of them are of her. I've barely slept these past couple months since she came to live here. I'm exhausted, wired, enchanted, inspired, and I can't..." His voice trails off as he picks up his shot and downs it.

"You can't do what?" I press.

"I can't function properly. It's overwhelming. *She's* overwhelming," he admits. "When I'm not painting her, I'm thinking about all the ways I'd like to fuck my stepsister. I've thought about leaving, taking my money and running, but I *can't* leave, and I can't pursue her either. It's eating me up inside. I need to stay to figure this shit out one way or the other."

"Damn," Ben mutters. "There's me thinking I was the one with all the issues wanting a woman I can't have."

Sterling eyes him. "At least the woman you want isn't family."

"Yeah, but she is married to the biggest fucking prick, and we all know that cunt will never let her go... Well, at least not permanently, anyway."

"But temporarily?" I ask.

Ben meets my gaze, and anger blazes within them. "We drew up an agreement last week. She'll be mine for one month."

"When?" Drix asks, frowning.

"April. He's away on business the entire time. I'll get my chance then. That's partly why I can't help out with your situation, Dalton. I'm planning on taking Elodie with me to Los Angeles with the band whilst we're in talks with a couple of record labels. Get away for a bit. I've sunk most of my savings into getting alone time with her."

"Ben, I get it," I say. "You don't owe me anything. Least of all an explanation."

"Mate, that's fucked up," Drix says. "You can't just buy her time, or her for that matter. What you're doing isn't right. She'll hate you for it."

"You don't have to tell me that because I fucking know,

alright?" He counters angrily. "But I've got to try. There's no one else for me, Drix. I expect you of all people to understand that."

"This won't end well," Drix warns him.

"I know that too," Ben agrees, sighing heavily. "I've got one month to place a wedge between them, and to get her back."

"This is a dangerous game you're playing," I point out. "We all know what her husband is like. He's got a lot of connections, many of them with people you don't want to fuck with."

"He's a fool. I can handle him," Ben snaps. "And as for his connections, I'm not concerned, I have them too. If it comes down to it, I'm not afraid to call in some favours."

None of us try to persuade him to not go through with this. Firstly, Ben is stubborn, and secondly, Ben has power of his own. Like our own families, the Pike's have a sordid history of under-hand dealings and criminal activity. Ben's dad, Walter, might've stepped away from that life just like our own fathers' have, but that doesn't mean they don't still have the ability to fall back into that world should the need arise.

"So, have you told Harlow about your synesthesia? Does she know what hearing her sing does to you?" I ask, changing the subject. "Maybe she'll refrain from singing around you if she knew."

He shakes his head. "No. I don't want her to think I'm a freak, that I'm *obsessed* with her."

Ben lifts his brows. "Firstly, you're not a freak. You're a fucking talented artist, the five million pounds you have in your bank says as much–"

"Tell that to my father. You know how he feels about my art," Sterling throws back. "He couldn't give a fuck about how much I've earned from selling my paintings. The Blade's are born to be businessmen, not artists."

"Point taken," Ben concedes. "The obsession part, however..."

A smile pulls up Ben's lips that only seems to wind-up Sterling more.

"Oh, fuck off, Ben. You're one to talk," he grumbles.

"Hey, dinner is ready," Harlow says, her appearance making Sterling stiffen and the rest of us turn to face her.

She stands in the doorway, her long blonde hair piled up on her head in a messy bun, her gaze flicking between us as she waits. Out of the corner of my eye, I see Sterling straighten his spine, gathering himself to face her. Fuck, I feel for him.

"We'll be there in a minute," Sterling mumbles, barely able to look at her.

"Okay." She nods, her gaze lingering on Sterling for a few moments before she smiles at the rest of us, then she turns on her heel and leaves.

Sterling blows out a ragged breath. "So, do you want the money, Dalton?" he asks.

Making a decision, I nod. "I'll pay you back. Every last penny," I promise.

"I know you will," Sterling replies with a dip of his head.

"This isn't just on you, Dalton," Drix says. "It's on me too. I'll help. And if you need a place to stay then you have my flat above the gym. It's yours if you want it."

We exchange a look, and for the first time in weeks I can finally see a light at the end of the tunnel. "Thank you, that means everything."

"THAT WAS DELICIOUS," Drix says, leaning back in his seat as he throws an arm over the back of Lia's chair who is sitting beside him.

Daisy hums in agreement, despite barely touching her food. I don't comment, because now is not the time, but if she thinks she can stop taking care of herself and I'm not going to pull her up on it, she can think again. The minute we're alone together we're going to have a talk about that, about a lot of things, actually.

"Yes, thank you for having us," Lia adds. "This was all so delicious. Please pass on our thanks to your chef."

"Of course," Sterling replies, shifting awkwardly in his seat as Harlow reaches for her glass of wine.

"So are you settling in okay?" Lia asks Harlow, her gaze flicking between the two.

Fuck knows how Sterling has managed to keep his hands off her, I can sense the sexual tension between them from across the table, and I would bet my father's fortune that she feels it too given the slight flush to her cheeks, and the pointed way she ignores his presence beside her.

"Everyone has been very welcoming," she replies softly.

"Well, we're all happy to have you here, aren't we Sterling," Ben adds, his eyes twinkling.

Sterling throws him a look that could kill, and Ben just tips his head with a wink.

"So what now? A game of billiards?" Ben suggests.

"I'd really love to hear Harlow sing," Daisy murmurs softly. "You have a beautiful voice."

"I don't think that's a good idea," Sterling cuts in as he moves to stand. "I'll go and set up a game."

Harlow frowns, a hurt expression on her face at his dismissal.

"Personally, I would love to hear you sing again," Lia adds, clearly confused by Sterling's urgent need to leave the room. "Daisy's right, you have an incredible voice."

"I don't know..." Harlow hesitates, glancing at Sterling who looks like a deer caught in headlights, eyes wide, a terrified expression on his face that he quickly irons out with a tense smile.

"Yeah, maybe not tonight, eh?" Drix says, sensing Sterling's unease.

"Please, I'd really like it if you could sing for us," Daisy comments, looking at her brother as though he's grown another head.

I don't know if Harlow senses Daisy's sadness as much as the rest of us, but she nods in acquiescence. "Okay, sure. The parlour has a piano..." she replies, pushing back her chair and standing.

"You play the piano too?" Lia asks, clearly impressed. "Wow, I've always wanted to learn how to play a musical instrument."

"You still can," Drix says, supportively.

"I could teach you," Harlow offers.

"Really? That would be wonderful!" Lia exclaims, her eyes lighting with happiness.

"I guess we're listening to you sing then," Sterling mumbles as he throws me a pained look, and we all follow Harlow into the parlour.

Each of us settle on the large sectional that's big enough to comfortably seat twenty, let alone the six of us. Harlow pulls out the stool beneath the baby grand piano, and settles herself onto the seat. Silence descends as her fingers hover over the keys and I catch her briefly looking over at Sterling, her smooth, honeyed voice following shortly after as she begins to play the opening verse of *Someone You Loved*.

I steal glances at Sterling and notice a mix of emotions flickering across his face as she sings—longing, regret, desire, it all plays out in time to the melody. Recognising the turmoil he's going though, I know that he is unequivocably fucked. Next to me, Daisy's eyes glisten with unshed tears, as captivated by her voice as Lia appears to be.

"Wow," Lia whispers, leaning into Drix's arms as he hauls her into his side and she wraps her arm around his waist.

Daisy shudders next to me and I automatically reach for her, my hand resting over hers. She doesn't lean into my side like Lia does Drix, she simply remains focused on Harlow, and I can't help but feel the pain of her snub. It lances through me, gutting me in a way I never thought possible. Despite that, I continue to hold on. She's pushing me away because she thinks there's no future for us, but there is, and I'll be damned if I'll let her give up on us.

"Damn," Ben mutters, as affected as the rest of us by the raw emotion in Harlow's performance.

Tension crackles in the air as Sterling stares at Harlow intently, completely and utterly entranced. I notice how his fingers curl into the arm rest, knuckles white, his face paling as he's drawn in by the beauty of her voice, and I can't help but wonder what he sees when he hears her sing. He tried to explain to me once, and I still find it difficult to wrap my head around. All I know is that he translates what he sees when he hears music or someone singing into a masterpiece on canvas. Right now he looks like he's on the verge of running away from the torment. After the final note dissipates, there is a brief moment of stillness before Lia starts applauding.

"You're amazing!" she exclaims, jumping up from the couch and rushing towards Harlow, pulling her in for a hug as the rest of us murmur our agreement.

"Thank you," Harlow says softly, her eyes flicking to Sterling who remains frozen in his seat.

"I... I need some air," he manages to rasp, before getting up on his feet and striding from the room, ending the evening with his disappearance.

Half an hour later, after saying our goodbyes, we're pulling up to Highwood Manor. I put the car in park, but don't unlock the doors, needing to speak with Daisy to tell her about Sterling's offer and my decision to walk away from my inheritance. She reaches for the handle, ready to bolt, but when she realises it's locked she turns to face me.

"The door's locked."

"It is," I agree, unclipping my seatbelt and shifting in my seat to face her.

"Well, aren't you going to unlock it?" she asks.

"No."

"Dalton. Let me out."

"There are a few things I want to say first," I counter, determined to make her listen. "And if I have to lock you in this damn car in order to do that, I will."

"I don't want to talk."

"Regardless, we're going to."

"Dalton, please," she whispers, and I hate the way she presses her back against the car door as though trying to put as much space between us as possible.

"I know you're hurting, Daisy—"

"I'm dealing with it," she insists, lifting her chin in a feeble attempt to prove that she is.

"That's bullshit and you know it. You're not dealing with it, you're pushing me away, and it's killing me, Daisy."

"What do you want from me?" she asks with a sigh.

"I want to get back to how we were on our honeymoon. I want to kiss you. I want to hold you. I want to see a genuine smile on your face. At this rate I'd take your snark and your anger just to get any kind of emotion instead of unhappiness from you," I say, scraping my hand through my hair in frustration.

"I don't feel much like smiling and, frankly, I don't have any energy to be mad. So you're shit out of luck."

"And I *hate* that. I hate that you're so unhappy, and I haven't been able to do a damn thing about it, until now."

"What do you mean until now?" she whispers.

"Sterling is going to loan us the money to pay off the debt, releasing you from your obligations."

"My obligations?" She stiffens, going deadly quiet before she turns to face me. In a split second her apathy is replaced with a blazing kind of anger that hits me like a slap around the face. "You mean having a baby together? Is that what you mean by obligations?!"

"No! Fuck, no, Daisy!" I reply, shaking my head and cursing my stupid fucking mouth. "I just meant there would be no pressure anymore. No need to lie about what's happened, no need to do anything you don't want to do. You'd be free of my father, Daisy. He can't threaten to force Drix to become the enforcer once again if the debt is paid."

"And I suppose that means you'd be free of me too, right? You'd get to divorce me with a clear conscience. You'd get to cast me aside and walk away to marry someone new, someone who could give you a child and ensure you'd keep your inheritance, is that it?" she throws back, her voice cracking as tears tip over her lashes, and fall down her cheeks.

"You really think that little of me?" I ask, shocked by her outburst, gutted by it.

"Just let me out of the damn car. Let me go."

"No!" I shout, reaching for her, but she slaps my hand away.

"Don't fucking touch me! This has all worked out for you hasn't it? You've had a taste of me now. You've scratched that itch, and now you get to start over whilst I have to deal with a future alone as a worthless woman incapable of having a child."

And there it is, the truth of it. The lie she's been telling herself. How can she think that about herself? She's not worthless. She's fucking *everything*.

"The *fuck* you are!" I reply, gripping her chin and forcing her to look at me. "You're not worthless, Daisy. You're perfect, and you're mine. Fuck my father. Fuck the contract. Fuck my inheritance. The only thing that matters to me is you."

"But–"

"I'm your husband. I made a vow to support you through sickness and health, and I'm going to do that."

"But you don't have to now," she says quietly, her anger disappearing beneath her despair as her voice catches. "I'll help to pay Sterling back. Just don't feel obligated to stay with me, Dalton. I can't give you a family. You can walk away, I wouldn't stop–"

"Don't you dare say that to me, Daisy!" I seethe, frustration making me angry now too. "I'm not going anywhere. I will not abandon you, not today, not tomorrow, not ever. You. Are. Not. Alone. I'm right here," I remind her, gripping her hand and pressing it against my chest so she can feel how my heart beats only for her. The woman I love.

"But–"

"You told me you loved me. Was that a lie?" I ask, cutting her off before she's able to sabotage this conversation further.

"It doesn't matter now," she says, barely able to look at me.

"Of course it fucking matters. Do you love me, Daisy?"

"What difference would it make?"

"Daisy, do you love me or not?" I ask, my heart thumping so hard that I feel it pound against my ribcage violently.

"Yes, *of course* I love you," she whispers, her lips trembling.

A flood of intense relief pummels my body, and I do the only thing I can in the moment, I lean over and pull her into my arms, kissing her with the kind of passion that is born from a desperate need to show her how much I fucking love her too.

CHAPTER THIRTY-FIVE

His kiss burns. It's potent, life-altering. It has the ability to rage through my sadness and turn it to ash. I'm helpless against it, my body leaning into his, our connection snapping to life as I kiss him back.

Tears pour from my eyes, tipping over my lashes in scolding rivers. I can taste the salt of them as we kiss, and it reminds me of the turquoise ocean on our honeymoon, and the love that blossomed within me a thousand miles away from the constraints of his father's demands. There we had been free to explore our connection, sink into the blissfulness of each other, unravel the past and accept it for what it was. But real life slapped us both in the face, tainting that time with something neither of us had bargained for.

"Daisy, fuck. Daisy, I—" Dalton rattles on, grasping my face and leaning back slightly as he stares at me, his gaze harrowed. "Fuck, I thought I'd lost you."

"I'm sorry. I was so cruel just now," I whisper, reaching up and stroking my fingers against his stubbled cheek.

"Don't be sorry, not for anything, you hear me, Daisy?" he

demands, searching my face. "You were scared, and I didn't do enough to reassure you. I'm sorry, I'm still learning here."

"It wasn't just you, Dalton. It was me too. I pushed you away. I'm so sorry for that, for everything." My voice trails off as I drag in a quivering breath and he hauls me closer, his hand running up and down my back, comforting me.

"Dalton, can I ask you something?" I eventually ask.

"Of course," he says, leaning back and brushing his lips tenderly against mine. "Anything."

"Do you... Do you love me?" *There, I said it.*

"Do I love you?" he repeats, shaking his head as though in disbelief. "You really need to ask me that?"

"I–"

But my response is cut off as he slams his lips against mine and kisses me roughly, with more emotion, with a force that comes from somewhere deep within.

I feel it... his love.

I feel it in this kiss, it's undeniable.

My chest heaves at the desperate kind of aching I've felt this past few months, the fearful kind of wanting, and now at the unending sense of rightness, of belonging. Every doubt, every fear, every insecurity melts away in his embrace. The world narrows to just the two of us, lost in each other, suspended in time as we kiss and kiss and kiss.

When we finally break apart, our breaths mingling, cheeks flushed, mouths parted on soft exhales, he holds my gaze with a fierceness that steals my breath.

"Fuck, Daisy, don't you know that I already do? I *love* you," he says, pressing a kiss against my cheek. "I love you," he repeats, kissing the tip of my nose. "I love you," he murmurs against my mouth once more.

"I love you too." My voice quakes, a breath releasing from my lips in a soft puff of relief.

"I love everything about you, Daisy, my beautiful wife. My perfect fucking flower," he insists, pressing another kiss against my lips and taking my breath away with his confession before pulling back and laughing softly. "Do you know how incredible it feels to say those words, Daisy, to feel that love?"

"I have an idea," I reply, smiling through my tears.

"God, I feel like I could accomplish anything knowing that you love me, that I love you."

"Even now?" I ask.

"Even *more* so now," he adds vehemently.

My heart soars, thumping back to life. This past month it's felt bruised, and I've tried my best to keep it safe, to keep it from feeling much of anything really. Dalton was right, I'd allowed myself to wallow in sadness because I couldn't let it feel hope. Hope that what I sensed from him on our honeymoon was love. Hope that he could love me despite the fact I may never be able to carry his child. Until I heard those words right now, I'd still been uncertain, afraid that he was with me out of obligation.

"I've felt helpless, Daisy, not knowing what to do, knowing that my fucking father has this damn hold over us. I've been angry at myself for not doing more to distance myself from my father earlier, of finding my own way in life instead of sitting back and acting the damn playboy, living off his money. I'm ashamed of that man, Daisy," I admit.

"That's in the past now. I believe in you, Dalton. You'll find your way, we both will. If Sterling truly is able to help us, we can start again, can't we? We can live our life the way *we* want to," I say, faltering a little at the thought of what's to come. It won't be easy, I know that.

"What is it?" he asks, sensing the change in me, the lingering fear.

"Dalton, your father..."

"Listen to me, Daisy. Let me make it perfectly plain. I don't care about the contract. I don't care about my father or what he wants. I only care about you, about us. No matter what happens it will only ever be about us."

I nod. "I do. I *hear* you..." I whisper, smiling through my tears, feeling better than I have in weeks.

"Good," he replies, his eyes flaring with heat.

"So what now?" I ask.

"Honestly, Daisy, I just want to be with you. I want to lay down next to you and kiss you all night long. I want to hold you in sleep, and wake up with you cradled safely in my arms, and then tomorrow we're going to face my father together. We're going to start over, we're going to begin the rest of our lives. I'll get a job, any fucking job, and I will work from the ground up. I'll make you proud."

"I'm already proud of you Dalton, and I need you too," I add with a whisper.

As we enter my bedroom a few minutes later, Dalton gently shuts the door behind him, then taking my hand he leads me to the end of the bed. Slowly he begins to undress me, removing every item of clothing until all I have left on is my underwear. His fingertips gently, reverently graze over my skin, tracing lines over my clavicle, down my arms, beneath my rib cage, across my stomach. Gently he caresses me, and I reach up onto my toes, kissing him.

"Lie down on the bed, Daisy," he says against my lips, his voice low, hoarse, as he begins to undress too.

Climbing onto the mattress, I lay down on the centre of the bed, propping my head up on the pillows as I watch him strip down to his boxers, drinking in every inch of his strong, masculine body. The dark tattoos that I've traced with my fingers, and kissed with hungry lips seem to twirl and dance as he inhales deep, steadying breaths.

"Spread your legs, Daisy," he commands roughly, his gaze heated, hungry, full of so much love.

"Like this?" I ask, sliding my legs apart.

"Just like that," he rasps out and with a gentle dip of his head, he crawls towards me, his eyes never leaving mine. When his knees press against my inner thighs, he drops back onto his haunches, his hands cupping my knees, his thumbs gently massaging circles against my skin.

My breath hitches, the warmth of his hands, and the softness of his touch making me melt. With slow, deliberate movements, his palms slide higher, his fingers tracing gentle circles over my inner thighs. Then, ever so gently, when he reaches the apex of my thighs, he presses the pad of his thumb against my clit through the lace of my underwear.

"Dalton," I gasp, feeling my body come to life beneath his touch.

"Too much?"

"Not enough. Don't stop."

"I've got you, my love," he replies.

My love.

As he continues to stroke me, softly caressing my clit over the material of my knickers, the slight friction only adds to the intensity, and I feel myself becoming wetter with every swirl of his thumb. My hips rock, my body yearning for him as much as my heart swells from his sweet words, from his love.

He doesn't move my knickers aside. He simply rubs me, drawing out the most delicious pleasure, until I'm whimpering and moaning. My fingers grip the duvet cover, holding on as my back arches and this coiled tightness begins to build deep inside.

"Dalton, please," I whimper, my voice trembling as the pleasure intensifies.

Sliding his hands beneath the elastic of my knickers, he pulls them down over my hips as I lift my arse and raise my legs so he can pull them free. Dropping them onto the bed beside me, he adjusts his body between my legs, then lowers his mouth to my pussy. The feeling of his warm breath against my wet folds makes me shudder, and when his tongue darts out and he licks me, I can't help but moan his name.

With each swipe of his tongue, I grow more and more aroused, my fingers tangling with his hair as he eats me out. He's not hurried, he takes it slow, licking gently, over and over again until all I can do is succumb to him, to this pleasure, to him loving me. Gently he sucks on my clit, the tip of his tongue grazing the hardened nub, and I arch my back feeling that beautiful, white-hot heat swarming in my lower belly.

"I've missed this. I've missed us together like this," he murmurs against my skin, his voice muffled yet raw.

"I've missed this too," I reply, gasping as he presses the flat of his tongue against my slit and licks me in one firm stroke.

"Fuck, your pussy is so wet for me..."

He licks me again.

"You taste so fucking good..."

He circles my clit with his tongue, over and over and over until my mouth drops open and starlight glitters behind my closed eyes.

"Dalton," I whimper, needing more, wanting it all.

Coasting his hand over my stomach and between my thighs, he slides a finger inside of me, gently, slowly, with utmost care. My pussy tightens around it, my internal muscles squeezing as I moan..

"Fuck, yes... You like that, huh?" he rumbles, flicking his tongue fast across my clit, pumping me gently with his finger..

"Yes. So much. Oh... Oh... Ahh... Dalton, please," I cry, my words almost unintelligible, the wet, slippery noises only turning me on more.

"I've got you," he mutters, alternating between sucking and licking my clit to running his tongue between my folds, keeping up the steady rhythm with his finger.

My legs begin to tremble, overcome with the sensation as he

worships me, and then, as he twists his hand between my legs, and crooks his finger, pressing against that spot deep inside, he sends me over the edge.

"Dalton!" I cry, my entire body convulsing as an orgasm barrels out of nowhere. My toes curl, my fingers tighten in his hair as I come, and in that moment of pure bliss all the broken parts of me begin to stitch back together. All the unhappiness turns into joy, into this huge, beaming warmth that ripples outwards from my core, settling into every inch of my body, my heart, my soul.

As the pleasure subsides, my muscles turn liquid and I sink into the mattress, breathless, spent. I look at Dalton as he pushes up on his hands, a smile quirking up his lips, his mouth and chin glistening with my arousal.

"Better?" he murmurs against my skin, gliding his lips higher before pressing a kiss ever so gently against the tiny pink scars left behind from my surgery.

"Much," I reply, stroking his hair.

"Do they hurt?" he asks me.

"No," I reply.

"I'm so sorry," he whispers, resting his cheek gently against my stomach. "I'm so sorry for what you've lost."

"What we've both lost," I whisper, stroking his hair as he nuzzles against my stomach, pressing hot kisses against my skin.

"I wish I could make everything better," he says, lifting up slightly, his elbows pressing into the mattress as his warm hands rest against my stomach as though he's trying to heal me with his touch.

"You can," I say, cupping his cheek, running the pad of my thumb over his bottom lip.

"How?"

"By loving me. By making love to me," I say.

"Isn't it too soon?" he asks, the tip of his tongue tentatively licking my thumb.

"It's been a month since my operation, Dalton. I'm okay. You won't hurt me. For now, just be gentle."

"I can be gentle," he replies, kissing my stomach. "But if it hurts, you tell me, and I'll stop."

"I will," I agree as he pushes upright.

Kneeling between my legs, he edges his boxers over his erection, pushing them down his thighs before removing them. I reach between my legs, coating my fingers in my wetness, then smother the crown of his cock, loving how soft his skin is, how hard he is for me, how he groans.

"Daisy," he murmurs, his hips thrusting into my palm as I gently grip him.

"I'm aching for you, Dalton. Please just make love to me," I beg as our gazes clash, this rush of love blooming inside of me. I imagine it growing with every passing second, spreading out to every single part of my body, seeping from my skin, feathering outwards and grazing against him until we're both encased in this blissful bubble of love.

"Always. There will never be anyone else for me, only you, always you. I will make love to you for the rest of my life. I'm so fucking lucky to have you. Why did I waste all those years?" he asks, his voice cracking as I release him and he lays his body over mine, his cock sliding against my slit.

"None of that matters now, *husband*," I reply, smiling softly up at him.

"Fuck, I've missed you calling me that," he says, and I pull him towards me so I can kiss him tenderly, impressing everything that I feel inside against his lips.

Our tongues tease and explore, and as we kiss he rubs his length up and down my seam until I'm panting for him, my clit throbbing, needing to be filled.

"Ready?" he murmurs, searching my gaze for any uncertainty,

his hair flopping forward, tickling my brow, the deep blue of his irises scolding my skin.

"Yes, Dalton. Make love to me," I whisper as he reaches between us, grasping his cock and guiding it to my opening.

Slowly he slips an inch inside of me, and I widen my legs, pushing up against him, urging him deeper.

"You feel... Fuck, it's bliss, Daisy. You're all that I didn't know I needed. You're mine," he adds as our breaths mingle and his eyelids stutter shut, a moan releasing from his lips.

"Deeper, Dalton," I urge against his lips, stroking my hands down his spine, palming his arse.

Inch by delicious inch he sinks into me, stretching me wide, fitting me perfectly until he's seated to the hilt.

"My love," he groans, holding still, my nipples gently chafing against the lace of my bra as our chests meet.

Then with slow, deliberate movements he begins to move his hips, pulling out only a little, before sinking back inside of me once again, his gaze never leaving mine as our bodies move together, rocking into each other. I can feel the love and tenderness he has for me in every gentle thrust, every gasping breath, every delicate kiss, and soft caress.

Everything falls away, until there's just us.

There is no pain.

There is no fear or anguish.

There is no heartache. Just love.

"*This* is what it feels like to be loved," I tell him. "Right here and now, us joined together. *This*."

"Yes," he croons, rocking into me. "I feel it."

Every stroke is filled with gentle passion, every brush of his lips against mine a tender gesture of his love, and as the minutes pass I'm enveloped in him, in the beauty of us. All the hurt I've felt these past few weeks fades away.

We don't rush to come, instead we move together slowly,

strengthening the connection between us, stitching together the wounds these past few weeks have inflicted until, eventually, I feel my orgasm building once more, my inner walls clenching around his cock.

"Dalton," I gasp, my fingers digging into his arse, urging him on as he continues to slide into me with a perfect, agonising rhythm.

"Come for me, wife," he breathes, his lips feathering across my jaw, his expression set, determined. "Let me feel you shatter around me. Give yourself to me as I give myself to you, whole-heartedly, until death do us part."

"I already have," I reply and our words of devotion are like a match to gasoline, igniting a spark within me that quickly blazes into an inferno. My eyes roll back in my head as my orgasm crashes over me, my body convulsing around him, every muscle tensing and relaxing in waves of pleasure.

Dalton's body shudders against mine as he releases shortly afterwards, his cock pulsing, coating my insides with his cum. "Daisy, you're my everything. You're my home, my sanctuary, my sweetest joy," he says, palming my face.

"And you're my forever, Dalton. Nothing and no one can take that away," I whisper, repeating what I'd said to him on our honeymoon

"Nothing and no one," he agrees.

CHAPTER THIRTY-SIX

"Ready?" I ask Daisy as she applies a soft pink gloss to her lips the following day. We've spent most of the morning in bed, enjoying each other's company, talking about our future, making tentative plans, and readying ourselves for the fallout.

She places the tube back in her makeup bag and turns to face me, her bright blue t-shirt with unicorns printed across the front clashing perfectly with her lime trousers, and rainbow trainers. "Do you think Carl will like my outfit, I wore it especially for him," she replies with a naughty grin.

"I'm sure he'll absolutely love it," I joke, holding my hand out to her.

Sliding her palm against mine she stands, and I tug her into my arms, pressing a kiss against the top of her head.

"He's going to hate it," she giggles, her laughter so fucking beautiful to hear.

As she looks up at me I capture her face in my palms, overcome with a rush of love that for a moment all I can do is stare at her, my beautiful, precious wife. "It's good to see you smiling again," I say, pressing a soft kiss against her lips, tasting the sweetness of her gloss.

"I've got a lot of things to smile about," she replies. "I have you. We have each other, and maybe when the timing's right, we'll have a family of our own."

"It may take some time before we can afford IVF treatment," I warn her, wincing a little at that. "But I'll work my arse off to make sure I can get that for you because you're *going to be* a mother one day. I want that for you so much. I want that for us."

She nods, smiling. "I'll work too, we'll do this together, and it will be all the sweeter for it. This is a partnership, Dalton. It's you and me, okay?"

"Yeah, it is, isn't it?" I agree.

"So, how do you feel about living in the flat above the gym whilst we get ourselves sorted?" Daisy asks, her brows pinching together with a frown. "I know it's not quite what you're used to, but Drix texted me earlier offering it to us."

"He already mentioned that to me last night," I say, swiping my finger between her brow. "And just so you know, wherever you are that's my home. I'd live in a tent pitched in the ruins if I have to, so long as you're by my side."

"I wonder if that old witch would have predicted that the heir to the Gunn fortune would be a man happy to slum it," she muses, tugging on my hair and pressing a kiss against my cheek.

"Who knows," I chuckle, nuzzling my face against her neck. "All I care about is making a home with you, wherever that may be."

"That's very good to know."

"And Sterling has already begun the process of transferring the five million to my account. He's arranging a viewing of his current art pieces to some interested buyers in a gallery in London at the end of next week, so we're covered where the debt's concerned," I add.

"I'd love to see his paintings. Do you think he might let us go too?" Daisy replies.

"I'm sure he would," I say. "I'll give him a call."

Daisy's hands glide up my back, as she hugs me. "I guess this is it then, shall we get it over and done with?" she asks.

I nod. "Yeah, let's do this."

WE ENTER my father's office a few minutes later, our hands tightly intertwined as we brace ourselves to face him. The scent of cigar smoke and polished leather lingers in the air, the familiar sound of a ticking clock on the mantelpiece echoing throughout the room, like an ironic countdown of sorts.

My father sits behind his grand mahogany desk, wearing his usual sharp, tailored suit, giving off a picture of authority and excessive wealth. As we step inside, he looks up from his desk, a dark expression on his face.

"Yes?" he questions, easing himself back in his chair as he eyes us both.

"There's something we'd like to discuss with you," I say, guiding Daisy to the seat opposite my father. She sits, and I stand beside her, resting my hand on her shoulder, giving it a reassuring squeeze, her presence grounding me.

"Father," I begin, my voice steady as I meet his gaze. "There's something important that we need to discuss with you."

"Is that so?" he questions, his tone clipped as he glances between us both.

"As you know, Daisy was rushed to hospital a month ago," I begin.

"I'm well aware," my father replies, crossing his arms over his chest.

"And—"

"I'm also very aware of *why* she was in hospital," he adds, his lip pulling up in a sneer. "So, as a matter of fact, it's quite fortuitous that you're here now."

"You know?" Daisy questions, her voice steady despite the tremble of her hands.

"You really think that you could keep something like that from me?" He shakes his head with a scoff.

"Who told you?" I ask, my fingers gripping Daisy's shoulder.

"I may be old, but I'm not an old fool. In fact, I pride myself on being very observant. The dinner we had recently, and your reaction to Florence's pregnancy was enlightening to say the least," my father says pointedly to Daisy, before settling his narrowed gaze on me. "Not to mention your rather aggressive request to run the hotel in Paris. So, I did some digging of my own, and this morning received the news from an unscrupulous nurse at the hospital who was very eager to tell me everything I needed to know after offering her quite a substantial amount of money in exchange for that information.."

"You conniving bastard!" I snap.

"With that in mind, I'd like to speak to Dalton, *alone*," he says directly to Daisy.

"Whatever you need to say, you can say it to the both of us," I retort tightly.

"Very well," he replies, before opening the top drawer of his desk and pulling out the contract we both signed.

He presses his finger against it, sliding it across the desk. I stare at it, hating everything it represents—the man I was, the obligations expected of us both, the sheer lack of any care or compassion for myself, let alone Daisy.

"Do I need to remind you what you both agreed to in this contract?"

"We're fully aware of what's enclosed, and your point is?" I ask.

"This contract was drawn up to protect us all," Carl continues, looking pointedly at me.

"No, that contract was drawn up by a selfish man who doesn't give a fuck about protecting anyone but himself. Cut the shit, and say what's really on your mind."

Carl slides his gaze from me to Daisy. "You lied."

"I lied?" she repeats, looking up at me in confusion, before turning her attention back to Carl. "About what exactly?"

"About your ability to conceive a child of course!" Carl says, his voice laced with ice. "And before you try to lie to me, don't."

"Daisy did no such fucking thing, you bastard." I say, gripping her shoulder.

"Well?" Carl snaps, ignoring me and demanding answers of his own.

"I never lied about anything," Daisy replies, her voice trembling with repressed anger as she tries to remain calm in the face of his hostility. "When I signed the contract I believed I could have a child. I had no idea this would happen."

"You don't have to explain yourself to him, Daisy," I say, sliding my hand across her shoulder to cup the back of her neck, stroking my thumb against the base of her skull in an attempt to soothe her.

"Yes, you do," my father insists.

"Christ, what kind of man are you?" I ask, anger bubbling inside of me like a kettle on the boil. "She's been through enough. Don't make her relive that again."

Daisy presses her eyes shut briefly before blowing out a steadying breath. "It's okay, Dalton," she says, trying to reassure me before continuing. "I went into this with every intention of having Dalton's child, and I was devastated when I found out the news. I wasn't being deceitful, I had no idea about my medical condition, and yet, despite everything that's happened, something wonderful has come out of this. I love Dalton with everything I am, and he loves me. Surely that has to count for something?"

"You do realise this changes things significantly?" Carl asks coldly.

"Do you not even give a shit about what Daisy has been through? She miscarried our baby. She had an ovary removed for fuck's sake. She's been through hell. Where's your sympathy?" I seeth.

"In answer to your earlier question, I'm the kind of man who has his son's best interests at heart," he retorts. "And sympathy does nothing to solve this rather disappointing issue, wouldn't you agree?"

"Don't give me that bullshit!" I spit, vibrating with anger now. "If you had my best interests at heart you'd be trying to salvage our relationship by making amends for your shitty fucking behaviour, but instead you shove that fucking contract under our noses. I'm not your fucking business associate. I'm your son, and Daisy is *my wife*."

"In an *arranged* marriage," he reminds us both with a sneer. "One you both signed up for, and one that had certain stipulations," he adds, tapping the contract as he glares at Daisy. "Marry my son, give me a grandchild, and Drix's debt would be cleared. But it seems you're incapable of fulfilling your end of the deal."

"Truthfully, I don't know," Daisy replies stoically. "There's the possibility of IVF. It might work, it might not."

"IVF?" Carl spits with a shake of his head. "No."

"No?" I question. My voice is low, controlled, as my hand drops from the back of Daisy's neck, and my fingers curl into fists. I'm one fucking step away from beating the shit out of him. Daisy notices and reaches for my hand, she brings it to her lips, kissing it.

"Don't, Dalton. It's not worth it."

"I'm not throwing good money after bad," Carl continues, giving Daisy a dismissive look.

"Good money after bad?! I suggest you fucking apologise you piece of shit, or this day might just end up being your worst," I growl, giving him a warning, even though it's more than he fucking deserves.

Daisy sighs. "Carl, we both came here this morning knowing how you would react, but a part of me had hoped that maybe you'd love your son enough to support us. I know you dislike me, I can live with that, but I don't understand how you could want anything other than happiness for Dalton."

"Happiness has fuck all to do with this!" he snaps, face reddening with anger.

"My dad would be so disappointed in you. If he were alive—"

"He's not, but *I am*," my father cuts in and Daisy visibly jerks as though he's slapped her.

"Enough!" I shout. "That's enough. You've said your peace, and now we're going to say ours."

"No, I'm done listening to you. This is how this whole fucking shit show is going to play out," my father continues, steamrollering the conversation like he always does. "You will divorce Daisy, releasing you from this marriage, and you will find someone else to impregnate."

I knew this was coming, but the effect of his words is no less of a punch to the gut. Daisy's eyes fill with tears, but she holds her chin up refusing to let him get the better of her, of us.

"Absolutely not!" I growl, shaking my head vehemently. "I'm not divorcing Daisy. I *love* her."

"It's not up for discussion," my father replies coldly. "You have an obligation to your family name and legacy."

"I don't give a fuck about our family name or legacy," I snap back. "I care about Daisy and what we have together."

"This is business, and business comes before pleasure," he counters.

"This is not fucking business, and you sure as fuck don't get to dictate my personal life or tell me who I can or cannot love!" I argue back.

"I think you'll find that I can and will. The debt owed to me remains unpaid, but as a gesture of goodwill, I will release both Drix and Daisy from the debt so long as you divorce her. If not, Drix will return to his duties effective immediately!" he shouts, spittle flying from his mouth as he slams his fist on the table, causing Daisy to jump in her seat.

"A gesture of goodwill?!" I bark out a laugh. "You're asking me to divorce the woman I love and call that a gesture of goodwill? Fuck you."

"Releasing them both from this debt is a pretty good deal, don't you think?" he counters. "Just do as I say, and this will all be over."

"FUCK YOU AND YOUR DEMANDS!" I roar, and in two strides I've got my father by the lapels of his jacket and am lifting him roughly out of his seat.

"Ah, there he is, I did wonder when you'd finally grow a backbone," he taunts, calm yet smug.

"You're nothing but a piece of shit!" I grind out, shaking him, seeing fucking red.

"You think you can intimidate me? I raised you, boy. I know every move you make before you even think of it."

"Oh really? You think you know me that well, so what's my next move?"

"You will come to your fucking senses. You will release me, say your goodbyes to Daisy and divorce her, then you will remarry and give me a fucking grandchild. Then and only then will you inherit your billions as planned."

"No!" I spit back defiantly.

"Dalton, let him go," Daisy says standing.

I flick my gaze to Daisy, shaking my head. "He's just insulted you, insulted our relationship. I'm going to fucking murder him, not let him go!"

My father throws his head back in a maniacal cackle, the sound echoing off the walls as he taunts me with pure malice.

I lose it.

In a blur of motion, my fist connects with my father's nose, a satisfying crack resounding through the air as blood sprays from the impact. A mixture of fury and pain twists my father's features as he stumbles backwards.

"You fucking shit!" he growls, reaching up to touch his nose as he stares at me, his jaw clenching and unclenching as he rocks on his feet and grasps the back of his chair to keep himself steady.

"I won't be controlled by you a second fucking longer," I say, my voice thick with anger. "This is over."

"The hell it is!" he counters, reaching for the contract and waving it in front of my face as blood drips from his nose. "This contract and a debt of eight-point-five fucking million states otherwise."

I snatch it from him, then rip the contract in half, throwing it on the table. "It's over. You'll have all your money by the end of the month. In fact, I can give you five million now as an act of *goodwill*," I retort, smirking as his face pales.

"You don't have that kind of money."

"It will be in your account in a few hours. The rest will follow. Daisy and I are done with you," I say, rounding the table and taking Daisy's hand in mine. "You okay?"

"I'm more than okay," she replies, rising onto her tiptoes as she kisses me. "I'm so proud of you."

"If you walk out of that door, you will no longer be my son. I will cut you off. You will live a life of a fucking pauper!" my father warns.

I let out a bitter laugh. "I was never your son. I was only ever your property. That ends today. Daisy and I will make our own way, and we will show you that love is far greater than any amount of wealth. So go ahead, cut me off. It's a debt I'd gladly pay to be free of you!"

"You'll come running back, and when you do, don't expect anything from me!" he shouts back.

Gripping Daisy's hand, we walk over to the door, opening it. I throw one last look over my shoulder and say, "Goodbye, *Carl*. I hope you enjoy spending the rest of your days alone, and when you realise you've lost everything worth living for, because believe me that day will come, don't expect any sympathy from me."

With that, Daisy and I walk out of his office, leaving behind not only my inheritance, but also the toxic relationship that has plagued me for years. I feel a rush of freedom, of empowerment, knowing that we are now in control of our future, and feeling all the more richer for it.

CHAPTER THIRTY-SEVEN

"Sterling, these are utterly beautiful," I exclaim, my gaze coasting over the exquisite artwork that adorns the walls of the art gallery in London.

There are fourteen paintings in total, each of them as stunning as the last. Swirls of bright pinks, greens, blues and yellows, turquoise, red and oranges, all shaping Harlow's features into a beautiful mosaic of emotions. The brushstrokes capture her essence in the curve of her smile, the depth of her eyes, and the tilt of her head as she throws her head back and sings. It's clear that each painting is an intense labour of love, a silent confession of his feelings for her.

Sterling smiles modestly. "Thank you. Though I'm honestly glad to see the back of them," he says, his smile faltering as we both stare at the huge ten by ten foot canvas hanging on the wall in front of us, each colourful brushstroke a testament to the emotions he's hidden from the woman he loves.

"Why?" I ask.

"Because they're a reminder of the one thing I cannot have," he says quietly, swiping a hand through his hair.

"Is Harlow coming tonight?"

"No, I didn't invite her."

"Why on earth not?"

"Honestly, because I'm not sure how she'd react to the fact that her face is on every single one of these canvases," he adds with a lopsided smile that doesn't quite reach his eyes, a smile that carries the weight of his feelings.

"I'm sorry it's been so difficult for you," I say, pressing my fingers against his arm.

"It is what it is," he shrugs. "How are things going anyway? I hear Carl needed his nose reset after Dalton punched him."

He smiles, and I grin. "It was no more than he deserved."

"Oh, I know. That man has had it coming for a long time."

"He has, and things are great between Dalton and me. We've unpacked the last of our belongings at the flat and are settling in," I reply, glancing over at Dalton who's chatting with Lia and Drix, feeling a sense of contentment settle in my chest. "We're finally finding our rhythm and are creating a home together, and that's partly down to you. I'm so grateful for what you've done for us."

"You're welcome, Daisy. Dalton and Drix have been good friends to me over the years. I wanted to help."

"We will pay you back. I promise," I say.

"As and when you can, there's no rush. Besides, if I sell each of these canvases for the asking price I'll make more than enough to cover the rest of the debt and set myself up for the future."

"Wow, that's a lot of money," I say. "I'm so proud of you, you deserve this success."

"I appreciate that, Daisy," he murmurs, his gaze drawn back to the painting in front of him.

I follow his gaze, my eyes falling on Harlow's face. It's my favourite of the fourteen, the one depicting her in a moment of pure joy, her image caught within a snapshot of time. But despite her happy expression, there's something else hidden within the brushstrokes, a longing, a heartbreaking yearning. It makes my heart ache for him, for the love he holds inside and cannot express to the woman he clearly loves.

"You know, I never thought Dalton would settle down. You're good for him, Daisy. I'm glad you've found happiness," he says after a moment, his words laced with sincerity.

"Me too," I reply. "And, Sterling..."

"Yes?"

"If I've learnt anything these past couple of months it's that love can blossom in the most unconventional ways. Remember that, okay?"

He nods. "I'll try."

As the night draws on, and more people arrive, I find myself musing over the past few months, caught up in the memories and emotions that have brought me to this very moment.

It's been a long road, one that has challenged us both in so many ways, but despite the ups and downs I can't help but feel grateful for where we are now. My future as a mother might be uncertain, Dalton and I may have more hurdles to overcome, but for now I feel a sense of peace wash over me. I'm no longer that terrified little girl my parents tried so hard to destroy, or that woman so many people have discounted or dismissed. I'm happy, content. I'm worshipped and adored. I'm blissfully and unequivocally in love.

With Dalton beside me, our fingers entwined, I watch Sterling interact with the guests, his eyes lighting up with passion as he discusses his art, his talent undeniable, and it makes me long to fulfil my own dreams.

"What are you thinking?" Dalton asks me as Lia and Drix wander off with Ben to greet some mutual friends.

"I know it's a long shot, but do you think that Matilda would be interested in seeing some of my designs?" I ask. "I mean, I know that she probably has a raft of her own..."

"Your designs are incredible, Daisy, there's no harm in asking," he says, drawing me into his side and wrapping his arm around my waist.

"I'd still be happy to work at Drix's gym alongside Clementine on reception, it's fun, but..."

"But it's not what fuels your fire?" he asks knowingly.

"No it doesn't," I admit. "Don't get me wrong, I'm super grateful to Drix for giving me a job, but I want more. I already have the love of my life, and whilst we gather funds to start IVF treatment, I'd like to pursue my passions, at least on the side. Is that selfish?"

"Absolutely not," he replies, shaking his head. "I'll support you in every way I can. The world will be a much brighter place with people wearing your beautiful designs."

I smile up at him, my arm wrapping around his waist. "Thank you. If she's not interested, then at least I've tried, right?"

"Exactly," he agrees. "But even if she says no, that doesn't mean you stop chasing your dreams. I believe in you, Daisy."

"Thank you," I murmur, pressing a kiss against his lips, before pulling back. "How is your job hunting going?"

He puffs out a breath. "Well, considering my father owns most of the businesses in town, I've not even got an interview, let alone a job offer. However..." he grins, eyes sparkling.

"What? Tell me."

"Ben is going away for a month in April, he wants me to take over managing Bandits Bar for him."

"He does? Where's he going?"

"Los Angeles with Princetown Bandits. They're currently in talks with a couple of record labels."

"Wow, on all counts," I exclaim.

"And even better, if they get a deal, Ben will need someone to take over running the bar whilst he manages them full-time. So it could be a long-term position. Plus he's been wanting to expand

Bandits Bar into a franchise and he's asked me to take the lead on the project," Dalton says, his eyes lighting up with enthusiasm.

"I'm so happy for you, Dalton. This could be an amazing opportunity for you," I exclaim, hugging him.

"For us both," he replies, dropping a kiss to my head. "Thank you, Daisy."

"For what?"

"For..." He pauses, a broad smile lighting up his handsome face. "For *everything*. For the first time in my life I'm truly happy, and that's down to you. I love you so damn much."

"I love you too," I reply, leaning into his embrace.

And in this moment, surrounded by the hum of voices and the soft glow of lights illuminating the room, I'm consumed by an over-powering rush of gratitude. Our path to love may have been unconventional. It might've been born from two individuals who once loathed each other, who signed a binding contract months ago. But now those inked signatures have been obliterated with genuine vows of devotion, they've been replaced with heartfelt promises, the contract torn to shreds by our commitment to love one another, to put each other first.

Always.

EPILOGUE

Fourteen months later

MY STOMACH FLUTTERS with a mixture of excitement and nerves as I step out onto the catwalk, the soft glow of the runway lights catching the gemstones sewn into the bodice of my dress, the very same dress I wore to my wedding to Dalton exactly fourteen months ago to the day.

Beaming, I stride down the catwalk, whilst behind me the models sway gracefully, their steps synchronised to the beat of the music that fills the room, each one wearing one of my designs from my collection aptly titled *Rainbow*.

Each colourful dress represents a different emotion that I have felt over the past fourteen months. The vibrant red symbolises the passion and love I feel for Dalton, the serene blue embodies the peace I have found within myself and our relationship, the emerald green the growth we've both made together as a couple and individually, the sunny yellow signifies the happiness and joy that fills my heart, the soft pink those moments of bliss where

Dalton and I have made love for hours on end. Every colour of the rainbow is represented, each dress designed and made with love.

Standing proudly at the end of the catwalk, I look back at the long line of models shimmering in the colourful array of floor length gowns, each with floating chiffon skirts and jewel-encrusted bodices. This moment is a dream come true. From the first sketch on paper to this unveiling of my collection, it has been a whirlwind journey, much like my relationship with the man I love.

Among the sea of faces, I spot Dalton, his gaze unwavering as he watches me with pride, his beaming smile matching the rainbow coloured silk shirt that he insisted on wearing. I grin, motioning for him to join me. Climbing up onto the catwalk, he takes my hand in his, pressing a kiss against my temple as he slides his hand into mine.

"Ready?" he asks me, and I nod.

Raising my hand, I wait for the audience to become silent, and as the music quietens, I take the microphone from the emcee.

"Firstly I'd like to thank you all for being here today. Designing has been a passion of mine for many years, and I am overwhelmed with gratitude to Matilda for believing in my designs and allowing me the freedom to bring to life this story of colour," I say, my heart swelling with emotion as I smile at her. She dips her head, deep lines forming around her eyes as she smiles. "But most of all, I want to thank my husband, Dalton, for being my rock, my inspiration, and my love. Without your steadfast support none of this would be possible."

The crowd erupts into cheers and applause, and I feel tears prickling at the corner of my eyes. Dalton squeezes my hand encouraging me to continue.

"This collection is more than just fabric and thread. It's a reflection of the journey Dalton and I have been on together, and the unwavering love that we share. Each dress tells a story, not just of colour, but of passion, growth, happiness and love."

"Here, here!" Drix shouts from the crowd, grinning up at me.

"And this dress that I'm wearing, some of you might recognise. It was the dress I wore to our wedding, a dress that I designed and Matilda brought to life all those months ago, gifted to me by Dalton in an act of generosity, understanding and kindness. It's woven together with many of the colours that you see here on this catwalk, and it is a representation of everything I hold dear, but more importantly," I pause, my throat constricting with emotion, my eyes brimming with tears. "It represents both the beginning of our love story and the start of a new chapter in our lives. Because, you see, this collection has been named Rainbow not just because of my love for colour, but also because after many gruelling months of IVF treatment I am now four months pregnant."

The crowd erupts in joyful applause, wrapping us both up in happiness as Dalton pulls me into his arms and kisses me deeply. Eventually we pull apart, breathless, happy, and with a final deep breath, I lock eyes with Dalton, grasp his hand and rest it on my gently rounded belly. "Here's to love in all its shades and hues. Here's to us, and here's to our miracle rainbow baby..."

THE END.

**Read on for an excerpt from *The Painter and His Poet*
#3 Princetown Heirs series**

THE PAINTER AND HIS POET #3
PRINCETOWN HEIRS

Read on for an excerpt from **The Painter and His Poet**

PROLOGUE
STERLING

Closing my eyes and pressing my fingertips to the bridge of my nose, I try in vain to stop the kaleidoscope of colours from forming in my mind. There are shades of cobalt blue, radiant sunlight yellow, soft hazy pink, spring meadow green, and deep blood red blending together to create a masterpiece that I have yet to bring to life with my paintbrush. Each hue shimmers and shifts behind my closed eyelids, tempting me to run from this goddamn hotel and back to my studio so that I can capture the image on canvas and relieve myself of the fucking torture.

And it's all because of her, Harlow Richards, whose voice is as enchanting as an angel's and as seductive as the Devil's.

Despite drinking five shots of whisky, I still can't shake the insatiable desire to create art that was inspired by Harlow's performance at my father's wedding.

Fuck.

She's the woman I had a one night stand with several months ago. The woman who gave me a false name after I heard her sing at a dive bar in New York, who spent hours tangled up in my arms afterwards as we talked and fucked. The woman who I've been trying to find ever since.

The shock of seeing her again hit me like a ton of bricks as she walked down the aisle, and if that wasn't enough, she was also singing. Her voice, so fucking alluring, had triggered my synesthesia and caused a riot of colourful emotions to explode within me.

Emotions I've been battling ever since.

As I sit here with my three friends, Ben, Drix and Dalton, in the bar of the five-star hotel my father was married in last night, I can't help but wonder what I did in a former life to deserve the pain of this one. Then again, I'm not the only one in agony. The bottle of whisky we've consumed between us only seems to deepen the shadows of our thoughts, making it even more difficult to come to terms with the fucked-up reality we've found ourselves in.

"What a fucking night," I mutter, swiping my hand through my hair as I catch Dalton's own weary gaze.

Drix shifts in his seat beside him, turning his attention to Ben who's lost to his own thoughts. "I'm assuming you've had just as little sleep as the rest of us," he says pointedly.

Ben glances up at him, his lack of words, and harrowed gaze, conveying a multitude of emotions we can all relate to.

"Yeah, that would be none then," I say, blowing out a sharp exhale of breath.

We're four heirs to our family's riches. Four men who've been rocked to the core by the women who have entered our lives and felled us just like the giant oaks surrounding my father's estate.

There's Benedict Pike, my best friend, whose brilliant mind is consumed by a forbidden love for a married woman who once shattered his own heart into million jagged pieces. A woman whose bastard husband is willing to accept two million pounds in an indecent proposal so that Ben can spend a month alone with her.

Opposite him sits Drix, adopted son to the late Hubert Hammer, who was forced into the role of enforcer for our families in order to pay off a debt putting his new relationship, to a single mum fleeing domestic abuse, in jeopardy.

Sitting beside him is Dalton, womaniser and self-confessed playboy, who has been manipulated into an arranged marriage with the one woman off-limits to him—Drix's younger sister—all in order to fulfil his duties as son and heir to the Gunn's immense wealth.

And then there's me, Sterling Blade, a secluded artist, and a perpetual source of disappointment for my overbearing father who wants nothing more than for me to take over his businesses and turn my back on the only thing that has ever made me happy.

This morning I had every intention of leaving town and never looking back. My relationship with my father has always been strained, but how can I leave now knowing that the woman I've been searching for will be moving into our estate?

A woman I want but can't have.

I should leave. I should put the past behind me and never look back.

And yet I won't.

Because everyone knows that an artist needs a muse, and ever since that fateful night, that person for me is Harlow Richards.

My goddamn *stepsister*.

READ HARLOW **and Sterling's romance in The Painter and His Poet**

ABOUT THE AUTHOR

Bea Paige lives a very secretive life in London... She likes red wine and Haribo sweets (preferably together) and loves to write about love and all the different facets of such a powerful emotion. When she's not writing about love and passion, you'll find her reading about it and ugly crying.

Bea is always writing, and new ideas seem to appear at the most unlikely time, like in the shower or when driving her car.

She has lots more books planned, so be sure to subscribe to her newsletter: www.beapaige.co.uk

Books set in the brand new world of Princetown

#1 The Thug And His Doll

#2 The Rogue And His Flower

#3 The Painter and His Poet

#4 TTAHJ

Books set in the same universe as the Academy of Stardom series - by recommended reading order:

The Brothers Freed Series

#1 Avalanche of Desire

#2 Storm of Seduction

#3 Dawn of Love

#4 Brothers Freed Boxset

Academy of Misfits

#1 Delinquent

#2 Reject

#3 Family

Contemporary Standalone

Beyond the Horizon

Finding Their Muse

#1 Steps

#2 Strokes

#3 Strings

#4 Symphony

#5 Finding Their Muse boxset

Academy of Stardom

#1 Freestyle

#2 Lyrical

#3 Breakers

#4 Finale

#5 Encore

Their Obsession Duet

#1 The Dancer and The Masks

#2 The Masks and The Dancer

Grim & Beast's Duet

1 Tales You Win

#2 Heads You Lose

The Deana-Dhe Duet

#1 Debts and Diamonds

#2 Curses and Cures

Short Story

Force of Gravity

(available FREE via my website if you signed up to my newsletter)

For all up to date book releases please visit

www.beapaige.co.uk